THE BET

Doug Stewart

An Even Money Book
Los Angeles

Even Money Press
Los Angeles
Copyright © 2016 by Doug Stewart
All rights reserved.
evenmoney.press
First edition. October 2016.
Reprinted April 2018.

ISBN 978-0-9962204-4-6
ISBN 0996220445

Cover photograph: Hollywood Park, Los Angeles, California.
Author's photo.

There have been many times when I have bet twenty thousand dollars and at other times I hesitated about betting one hundred dollars, although the figures might show that the two horses were equally probable winners. "It all depends," and upon that little sentence hangs a world of worry and work in a maelstrom of excited humanity, the betting ring.

--Pittsburgh Phil

THE BET

The most lucrative bet I ever cashed was keyed on Red Warrior. It was the fourth race at Santa Anita, a minor stakes race run on the dirt at six furlongs, a chaotic race in which the Superfecta paid $10,472.80. If you check *The Daily Racing Form* you'll see that the racing surface that day was listed as sloppy, a description that hardly captures what the track was really like. It had been wet and rainy for days, that day being no different, just one more in the middle of what turned out to be a record-setting rainy season. They'd done all they could at Santa Anita to make the racing surface safe but the track was still a mess, just about as bad as a track can get in southern California. The summary for Red Warrior's race that day reads: "Red Warrior wide early, angled in and settled a bit off the pace, swerved out leaving the turn, came out again in upper stretch and rallied under some left handed urging while lugging in a bit to prove best." He had, in other words, dropped back at the start then ran wide, and though closing on the lead was still no better than fifth at the top of the stretch. He did, however, run strongly in the stretch with a bit of encouragement from the whip, though tiring, wandering a bit as he did, drifting in from his normal racing lane towards the rail. It was an erratic trip at best, but still, he won, which was a huge surprise (he hasn't won since). There were eleven horses in that field and only one went off at higher odds than Red Warrior.

But I didn't win that bet because of something I found in Red Warrior's past performances. It was because I'd anticipated that the dynamic characteristics typical of races run under normal circumstances weren't going to appear that day, not given the extreme off-track conditions. When horses are asked to do something like that, something that's novel, something that feels awkward or uncomfortable, most will fail to run their race. "Their race" is the key here since most horses typically have only one way to successfully run a race, a combination of running style and energy expenditure that is their signature. Even the greatest horses are captives of their signature style, typically failing when unable to follow their preferred pattern, as I saw Cigar succumb to a blistering pace duel at Del Mar one summer. So I didn't need to pore over Red Warrior's past races to know what to do, it was enough just to know that his chances of winning were suddenly far greater than normal. That's why, contrary to what other bettors thought of him, I knew that on this particular day, a day when any horse could be the worst horse in the field, he might as well be the best horse in the field, which is exactly what I bet on.

What that rainy day offered was the hope that the normal—and hence barely profitable—patterns of horse racing were temporarily not in play. There would still be the favorites, of course, but they would be the product of bettors and handicappers just as captive as the horses they were betting on to stubborn patterns of behavior ill-suited to coping with novel circumstances. So the crowd failed to see that a thick fog of uncertainty hung over the track that day. Or if they did they failed to make the connection that here was a day when nothing could be taken for granted. But then that which is taken for granted relieves us of such a huge burden, essentially so, since it forms such a large part of our lives, so it's understandably hard to set that aside even for one race. But if there is one thing a bet can be counted on to do, it's to make explicit the taken-for-granted, and painfully so if it's a losing bet. Then the inadequacies of our taken-for-granted are starkly revealed. Red Warrior did that for a lot of people. Far too infrequently are we able to say that normal counts for nothing, but it's a joy when we can, especially so when we've predicted it. All in all, it was the rarest of days for me.

The Bet

PART ONE

Don't mistake getting lucky for
knowing what to do.

The Bet

1

"Believe me, she has no idea what she's talking about. I still can't believe they gave her tenure."

I turned around. It was Lee. "And I came this close," I said, holding my thumb and index finger close together.

"So I noticed. But then you must have sensed my disapproval."

"No, it's the $24.95, and it's Habermas."

"Still not interested, huh?"

"Frankly, I'm surprised anyone ever was."

"Well, you're the one who almost bought it."

"I know. Sometimes I'm even a surprise to myself."

"Then it's lucky I came along when I did."

"I'll tell you what else surprises me," I said, resting my hand on her arm. "You."

"Seeing me, you mean?"

"That, and how nice you look. Not that there's any reason why you shouldn't," I said, suddenly floundering.

"Yes, well I'm a bit surprised by how you look, too," she said, making a show of studying me, head to toe.

"Remember, I said nice."

"Oh, I haven't forgotten."

This was Friday afternoon. The end of another week of missed opportunities and misjudged probabilities. Another dismal week in what had become an epic run of dismal weeks, not that I hadn't tried to break the pattern, I had, repeatedly, but so far nothing had worked. But still, all it would take was one simple little thing occurring at just the right moment. And the day had begun so well. I'd made a few decisions. Lingered under the pepper trees by the driveway to savor the lucid winter light. Found a really good place to park over on Ocean Avenue. Stood at the fence gazing out at the Pacific pondering its indifferent, incomprehensible solitude. Walked over to Wilshire to buy an herbal iced tea and vegan scone that I ate while sitting on a bench before making my way over to Midnight Special. That bookstore and I have a history, or at least we used to since it's no longer in business. But when it was you entered through a number of large tables displaying new books—ones mostly political or polemical—before reaching the rows of tall bookshelves at the back, each more or less subject specific. There, my preferred destination was the one that was all philosophy, both sides, and these were real philosophy books, hardcore academic press titles, with none of that bizarre mishmash of philosophical, religious, inspirational, and New Age stuff found elsewhere. We were talking about an MIT Press book, one of many they used to publish on, or by, Habermas, this one being a collection of essays I'd never seen before, which was a bit of a surprise since I'm familiar with the literature. I have to say, it was hard not to smile when looking at the table of contents. Philosophers toiling away on topics I'd left behind in graduate school. But why shouldn't they be? The pace of change in philosophy is glacial, at best. Yes, just another reminder of why I was happy with my decision.

It's a funny thing, but in looking back on this I can see that if I'd been paying attention I would have seen those subtle warnings that something important was about to happen. That subtle foreshadowing of what was about to occur. I might even have noticed that fate was, for once, actually tipping its hand. No. Again, I was blindsided, startled, and surprised, which is just how it's been for weeks.

So that's how it was, standing there arguing with myself over whether or not to buy that stupid book. That's when I suddenly realized someone was standing behind me. Actually, what I realized was that I'd been monitoring their presence for some time. Not consciously, of course, but still, I knew. So taking a step or two to my right—and I was tempted, but I rarely buy books anymore—I leaned forward and returned Habermas to his proper place on the shelf, even taking a moment to tidy up, turning my book face-out, full-cover like it was my store. That's when I heard a woman's laugh. A nice laugh, too, like she was really amused, though clearly at my expense. How fitting that I should turn around like that, with that embarrassed smile on my face and hardly a thought in my head, and run smack into that familiar gaze.

Sandals, tight black slacks, pale green sweater, and a jean jacket with the collar turned up. Long hair gathered at the back with a silver clasp, sunglasses perched precariously on the top of her head, large beige leather bag slung over her left shoulder. Still trim, athletic, bright skin, freckles scattered across her nose and cheeks, greenish-brown eyes, finely shaped nose, high forehead, lovely proportioned hands and feet. I knew her instantly. Of course she looked older, but no less preternaturally alert, assertive, smart, or beautiful. I was stunned, I won't even try to deny it, and not just by the details but by her actually being there, just standing there right in front of me present in all her vivid particularity. But that gaze of hers . . . that I kept coming back to. The knowing way she looked at me. Well, that brought it all back with a thunderous crash. That I still loved most of all.

Chuckling to herself as if she might be enjoying a private joke, she finally broke the silence, starting all over again from a different place.

"Well, Nick," she said, taking a step forward and cocking her head to one side to better see what I might have to say, "This is such a pleasant surprise. How are you?"

"Okay, I guess. You know, health good, happy, lucky, or at least I was until recently."

"Lucky?" she asked, her eyes widening with surprise.

"Ah, I thought that might pique your curiosity."

"What piques my curiosity is that you'd actually keep track of such a thing."

"Why not? Tracking something like that can be pretty useful."

"Then I hope you're tracking what's happening right now."

"Meaning luck's the cause of our running into each other like this?"

"You're saying it's not? I come walking in here, for some reason thinking of you, something I rarely do these days, and then oh my God, there he is. Really? After all these years of *not* seeing you, this is how I finally *do*?"

"Were you really thinking about me?"

"Yeah, well don't look so startled because it was nothing very profound. You know, is he still out here somewhere in California? Did he ever manage to get a real job? Which trailer park do you suppose he lives in? Then I innocently walk in here looking for something to read and practically stumble over you. But I wasn't even surprised. It was like I was expecting you to be here. So then I walk over here to surprise you, practically breathing down you neck, and you don't never even bother to turn around. I know her book isn't that good."

"I knew you were there."

"No way."

"I knew someone was there, some bookstore lurker."

"Uh-huh. I suppose that's why you looked so shocked when you finally turned around."

"Only because it was you. So," I said, pausing to smile at her. "How are *you*?"

"Tenured, married, and starving."

"Starving?"

"I skipped breakfast. I was hoping you'd take me some place nice for lunch."

"And the other two?"

"Let's just stick with lunch."

"So," I asked once we were out on the mall, "how is it that we find you walking around Santa Monica this lovely morning?"

"I'm here for a conference."

"Here, where?"

"UCLA."

"And the conference?"

"*Critical Social Theory: Contemporary Prospects.*"

"Seriously?"

She put her hand on my arm as she laughed. "Yes, I know, but I was invited to give a paper and I thought, well, L.A., this time of year," and she paused to look at the clear blue sky, the tall palms, the throngs of people in t-shirts. "So I got in late last night and slept in. Today's open, so I thought I'd come down here and walk around on the mall. Get a little lunch. Do a little recreational shopping."

"And so here you are."

"Yes," she said, staring at me. "Here I am."

"But?"

"But what?"

"You look like there's something bothering you."

"It's not really bothering me, but there is something I'd like to hear you say."

"Like I've ever known what that would be."

"Oh, please."

"Sorry. So what is it?"

"That you come here all the time. That this isn't the first time you've been here in months."

"Well, I do come here all the time."

"But?" she asked, hands on hips.

"But I can't remember the last time I was here on a Friday morning."

"Of course," she said, shaking her head.

"Sorry. I guess this is just one of those little surprises that make life interesting."

When we came to the end of the mall I led her over to Ocean

Boulevard and Il Fornaio.

"I know," I said, seeing her hesitation. "But this is the best I can do if we'd like someplace quiet."

"Just as long as I can get a glass of wine."

It was nearly empty, so we chose a nice sunny table by the front windows. After the waiter dropped off the menus we argued about wine, finally agreeing to split a half-bottle of Dolcetto d'Alba. As she talked the light from the windows fell across her lovely face. How I wished I knew what she was thinking.

2

It was after the waiter brought the wine and we'd each had a sip that she said: "I'm still amazed by how we ran into each other like this. Today. This morning." She began ticking them off on her fingers. "In Santa Monica. In the bookstore. In the philosophy section." She shook her head. "What're the odds?"

"Of all that happening?"

"Yes, and in that exact order."

"Probably not as steep as you think. The frequency of rare or unusual events is a lot greater than people commonly believe."

"That hasn't been my experience, but then you and the unusual probably share a different sort of relationship."

"We certainly share one that's more ironic."

"You're not saying you expected to run into me like that?"

"No, though it does have a certain predictability when viewed from a slightly different perspective."

"How slight?"

"Not that slight, actually. It's just that things seem to be more likely to occur if they're ironic."

"Ironic for who? You? Me? Everyone?"

"Me."

"So your irony takes precedence over everyone else's?"

"All I'm saying is that how I'll react to an event seems to skew its probability of actually occurring."

"So our meeting like this was your doing? Is that what you're saying?"

"Well, it was certainly ironic."

"Yes, but not just for you."

"All the more reason then for why we might expect it to happen."

"And this is how you've been living you life? Calculating probabilities based on how ironic it would be for you if something happened?"

"If I had the time, but since I don't I just stumble along like everyone else."

"Like right now."

"You know what," I said, hoping to change the subject. "I forgot to ask if you came alone."

"Yes. Charles stayed in Philadelphia. What about you?"

"Alone to the bookstore?"

"You know what I mean."

"Yes, but I'd much rather talk about you."

"Uh-huh. And working?"

"What a strange question."

"What a strange answer."

"Perhaps I just took the day off."

"Yes," she laughed, "but from what? Playing the horses?"

"So what did you think of those postcards?" I'd sent her a few after we'd parted ways, always of racetracks.

"The ones that kept showing up in my mailbox with no name or return address? I was sorry when they stopped. I thought, well either he's finally forgotten me, or he's gone into a more legitimate line of work."

"Yes, well legitimate or not, I'm still at it."

"And?"

"You're not pouting, are you?" She clearly was.

"Maybe."

"Well, don't, because I'd hardly forgotten you, or at least not all of you."

"Nick," she said, brightening perceptibly, "are you trying to tease an old married lady?"

"Old?"

"But still married."

"I know. Charles. He's on your website."

"My website?" She was grinning at me.

"What's wrong with that?"

"Nothing. I was just wondering how you came to be looking at that."

"Oh? Like you've never Googled my name to see what might pop up."

"Googled!" Now she was laughing. Clearly, the idea had never occurred to her. "Oh, my God," she said, staring at me. "Don't tell me you have one of those dreary little narcissistic blogs?"

"Of course not, but you might have at least checked."

"And Facebook? Are you going to friend me?"

"I'm not on Facebook."

"Poor Nick, all alone in the middle of the night hunched over his computer Googling people."

"And you've really never wondered?"

"Never."

"Late at night, tossing and turning, unsatisfied and all alone on your side of the bed, even then I never crossed your mind?"

"Nope."

"No wonder you were so startled to see me. For all you knew I could have been dead."

"Don't be ridiculous. As for startled, if only I had been. And just what was it I was supposed to discover if I had? That you're a gambler? Like I didn't know that already."

"Yes, well your life didn't look all that exciting to me, either."

"I'm sure it didn't, but that doesn't mean I'm not happy."

"Doesn't mean you are."

She sat her wine glass on the table before she spoke. "That's what you'd like to hear, isn't it? Well, sorry. For the most part it's all worked out rather well. Pretty much like I always thought it might. Though I will admit that Charles isn't as entertaining as you were."

"Were?"

"Are, then."

"So," I asked, smiling at her, "any other comparisons where I come out on top?"

"Not really," she said, smiling back.

When the waiter returned we ordered. Capellini al Pomodoro for me, a Caesar salad for her

"Tell me more about being lucky," she said, nibbling on a breadstick.

"I was just kidding, though chance events do occasionally work in my favor."

"So you're not really lucky."

"Not like I'm tall. It's just assessing probabilities. Weighing risk versus reward."

"And what is it when you lose?"

"Nothing, that's just how it goes when you deal in probabilities, sooner or later everything gets a chance to happen."

"Like us, today."

"Exactly."

"And gambling? Because so far you haven't mentioned it."

"Should I?"

"Isn't that common usage for what you do?"

"Common usage has never described what I do."

"So people aren't going to the racetrack every day doing this thing you won't name?"

"They'd better be, since I take their money home with me every day."

"Ah. So they *are* gamblers."

"I'm only worried about what I do. About trying to make things a little less random. A little more open to rational assessment. The way you talk—gambling, gamblers—way too pejorative, way too many unfortunate connotations. Ones I'd rather avoid."

"Such as?"

"The colorful gambler, the wise guys, the bigger than life winners, the cigar-smoking caricatures, the Damon Runyon argot, the inevitably ruinous fate of the gambler, the compulsive, addictive behavior, the gambler out of control, down to his last bet, letting it all ride on luck or fate."

"None of that's true?"

"Only if people make it true."

"I see," she said, looking amused. "It's the analytical part that interests you."

"For the most part."

"But you are still betting money, aren't you? So what difference does it make how you got there."

"None at all, if all I did was walk up to the window and make a random bet. But since my objective is to minimize the intrusion of chance and randomness in what I do—"

"Minimize the risk-taking?"

"I try.

"What's it called when you run out of money at the track?"

"Tapped out."

"Have you?"

"You think that makes me a gambler?"

"It might."

"So it's just the bet? That's enough?"

"Why not? You take a gamble, you're participating in what's commonly referred to as gambling."

"People can't be wrong about what's commonly referred to?"

"Not when it comes to something like that."

"Then I guess my world's a bit more resistant to how we talk about it than yours."

"So tell me about your world."

"Those people you call gamblers? What I see is their frequent use of gambling as a means of fulfilling needs or satisfying desires that are largely extraneous to gambling. For them, it's not about winning a bet. It's not even about the money."

"Sick bastards."

"That's where all those pathological connotations come from, the ones animating your cultural stereotypes. Worse, all that pathology can't help but seep into their psyches."

"What about yours?"

"Me? I don't see why it should, since all I'm interested in is knowing what happens next. And that remains true even if the measure of that is how much I win."

"I'm surprised to hear you can make do with so little."

"Knowing is little?"

"If all it results in is a bet."

"Maybe you don't understand what a bet is."

Leaning back, she smiled at me before she spoke. "My poor, austere gambler," she said.

3

"This might interest you," I said as we ate.

"What's that?"

"It's something I discovered at the track."

"Discovered, like an explorer?"

"In a sense. It's about our world. Our rational world, that is if you still believe we inhabit one."

"Does today count?"

I laughed. "Yeah, today might be an exception, but overall, most of the time, right?"

"With reservations."

"Yes, but even then, what we at first found troublesome eventually does come to fit within the normal flow of our lives. Not that we didn't need to shift things around a bit to make room; broaden our assumptions to accommodate it."

"But?"

"But—and this is what I discovered—there are events that stubbornly insist upon retaining a certain nagging, residual irrationally."

"No rational explanation at all?"

"Not even a probabilistic one, and of course this lack of rationality makes them highly disruptive. Erupting into our lives seemingly from out of nowhere, calling into question all sorts of commonplace beliefs and assumptions. The truth is, sometimes it seems like winning and losing just happen."

"How very postmodern of you," she said with a big grin. "The Enlightenment finally comes to grief, foundering on the jagged rocks of unreason in the backstretch."

"Yes, and there I am doing fieldwork. Waiting for one more illustration of reason's limitations. Seriously, you'd be amazed by what I've seen."

"So," she said, summing it up for me, "we have this rational world, one we all share, if not create, which is where we find our brave handicapper grappling with the irrational."

"We all grapple, it's just that we're obliged to do so more often, and in a more focused manner."

"Because everything rides on your being able to understand."

"Yes, and in that we really have no choice."

"Sounds more like a question of faith. That even though it makes no sense to our brave horseplayer, surely it must to someone."

"It would be very hard to carry on if we didn't believe that."

"Do you?"

"Not really. But that's just my point. That there are those times when it's just not possible to say why it was that one thing happened rather than another."

"But something had to happen. I certainly hope you don't find that puzzling."

"Uh . . . not usually. I mean, yeah, that's a perfectly natural expectation. But that doesn't change the fact that there are times when there's no more explaining left to do. When we've exhausted all our resources and there's still no compelling reason for why this and not that."

"It's hardly news that science and reason have their limits, but there are those certainties that aren't subject to reason or explanation—like the certainties of our existence. The necessities we find in how we live. The hinges upon which our lives swing. You sound like you're obsessed with trying to find an explanation for everything. So, yes, I agree, at some point explaining comes to an end, but that doesn't change the fact that you're still here. So what do you do?"

"Take a look at the next race?"

Smiling, she said, "Yes, and I can see that I still can't explain you. Yes, you appear to be serious, but I'm never really sure you're not just teasing me. Of course, now I'm remembering how I used to like that about you. I suppose I still do, actually, though it's always been frustrating. I can also see that you still have no idea how to do philosophy. That hasn't changed, either."

"Why this and not that? That wasn't good stuff?"

"Oh, no," she said, taking her napkin and dabbing at her right eye as she laughed. "It was wonderfully pre-Socratic. Oracular. For a moment there I thought I even smelled burning hecatombs."

"I'd burn them every day if I thought it would help."

"I thought you said you were doing well?"

"I am."

"And happy?"

"With?"

"Your life."

"Why not?"

"Why not!" She leaned back to stare at me. "What's that supposed to mean?"

"It means my life is just fine."

"So nothing to complain about, other than a few losing bets?"

"Nothing," I said, smiling at her. "What about you?"

"Nothing here, either."

"So why are you smiling?"

"Because we're a couple of liars."

"Are we? You're married. I have a few nice companions."

"And that's enough?"

"It seems to be."

"Uh-huh."

"So what were you lying about?"

"That I've never missed you."

"You know," I said, trying to make a joke of it, "I've always wondered why I can't find a woman who'll say that before she leaves."

"I believe I did, though it didn't stop me."

"You certainly were determined."

"I certainly was."

"This isn't regret I'm hearing, is it? About all those wasted years with a dull academic when you could have been having fun with me out at the track?"

"The track? You've got to be kidding. And he's hardly dull."

"*Derrida and the Pedagogical Imperative*? I could hardly put it down."

She laughed. "I know. He just needed a better title."

"He needed a lot more than that."

"Now Nick, be nice, don't pick on poor Charles. Maybe if you'd actually read it."

"I actually tried."

"The reviewers liked it."

"How exciting, reading book reviews to each other."

"Better than sharing a losing bet."

"Lee, did you see that review on that new Levinas book?"

"I've never read a book on Levinas."

"Still don't care for French philosophers?"

"He wasn't French."

"They certainly adopted him."

"Did you know Charles and I spent a year in France? You probably don't since it's not on my web site. We took our sabbaticals together, though it was chiefly for Charles's benefit."

"How'd it go?"

"Fine. We met some interesting people, though not many who shared my interests. Jacques Bouveresse?"

I nodded.

"Charles gave a series of lectures at Paris X-Nanterre that were well received, though he sulked a bit when he discovered how dated some of his work had become."

"Too much Derrida and not enough Jean-Luc Nancy or Badiou?"

"You really do keep up with this stuff, don't you?"

"I know a few names. So would I be right in assuming that Charles doesn't share your passion for all things Habermas?"

"And if he doesn't? We're like any professional couple, he's got his career and I've got mine. We hardly need to be collaborators to appreciate each other's work."

"Well, like you said, it's about what you expected, though one might have thought you'd have expected more."

"Nick . . . "

"Sorry. Have you ever told him about us?"

"What's to tell?"

"Quite a bit, as I recall."

"Charles, you'll never guess who I ran into out in Santa Monica. Nick. Oh? I never told you about him? He was a boy I knew in graduate school. Hasn't changed a bit."

"A boy?"

"We were very young," she said with a grin. "Or at least I was."

"Seriously, you've never told him?"

"No. Why should I?"

"I have no idea, but if he doesn't know about me then I can't help but wonder what else he doesn't know about."

"He knows enough. Anyway, you've always had way more curiosity than most people."

"About you I did. There wasn't anything about you I didn't want to know."

"Yes, believe me, I haven't forgotten. You know," she said, looking at me a little more seriously. "It's not always best to know so much, and there are those things I'll never tell, things I'll never share with anyone."

"Unless you want to."

"Unless I want to, though I never will."

4

"What are you working on these days? You don't mind talking about that, do you?"

"No, but you're just going to say I've been going round in circles."

"Have you?"

"Well, I still think Habermas is the most important contemporary social theorist."

"But?"

"But lately I've been considering other options."

"You? I'm amazed."

"It is a shock, isn't it?"

"Just a bit."

"So for some time now I've had this nagging feeling that perhaps we ought to set aside this project of a critical social theory, or at least my belief that it involves something universal and non-contingent."

"Please, not back to immanent critique?"

"You remembered." She looked so pleased with me. "Well, I certainly hope that's not where I'm headed. You know, I used to agree with Habermas on all this, but now . . . well, it's difficult. I guess I do and I don't."

"That's bad? Embracing a contradiction? It actually sounds rather responsible, almost adult-like. You do realize that sooner or later every true believer has to grow up?"

"I'm not a true believer."

"You were in graduate school."

"What graduate student isn't? Or at least they are if they ever hope to have a career. Of course," she said, grinning at me, "there were those exceptions."

"I was a true non-believer. Glad to hear you've finally joined our little club."

"I'm not saying I no longer believe, just that my faith has gotten a bit more subtle, a bit more nuanced."

"For example?"

"Remember how I used to argue that speaking, or acts of communicating, were dependent upon a communicative form of reason?"

"For their very possibility? Yes, I remember, though what I remember most is *Habermas says this* and *Habermas says that*, ad nauseam."

"How the universal characteristics of this communicative reason play a crucial role in our ability to create, learn, and sustain normativity and meaning? Not to mention reach discursive consensus and agreement?"

"I haven't forgotten."

"So now I find myself a little less enthusiastic about that than I used to be."

"Really, just *a little* after all this time?"

"Which has me wondering if Wittgenstein wasn't right."

"Wittgenstein?" I laughed. Really laughed.

"I know," she said, looking embarrassed. "Where'd that come from?"

"Uh . . . someplace kind of scary?"

"You know, that these actions rest upon nothing more than a conglomeration of learned rules, techniques, and practices. Learned and transmitted by our doing and participating, by socialization. So there are no universal, somehow necessary conditions of possibility. We have, we engage or act within, contingent practices, and even if these practices function or make sense only within particular forms of life, these forms of life are, themselves—no matter how natural they may seem to us—just as contingent. That we're unable to imagine how we'd live if not within them means nothing. Even though we find it absurd or impossible to imagine them being other than as we find them." She looked at me and sighed. "The consequences of this point of view are rather hard for me to accept."

"I'm sure they are."

"So you do understand?"

"Of course I do."

"That there are no underlying, universal forms of reason to deduce or discover, here, or anywhere else. No quasi-transcendental conditions for the possibility of this or that human action, ability, or practice, to tease out and codify. That whatever certainty there is, and it's an odd form of certainty at best—if it's one at all—is found in our practical engagement with the world." She looked at me and smiled. "I seem to have gone over to the dark side."

"You can't be happy with a contingent form of necessity?"

"Well, I suppose I don't really have any choice in the matter, do I? So, yes, I live my life on the basis of contingent necessity, but no, I'm not all that happy about it. But I don't mean to suggest I'm unhappy. That's not what I mean at all because I'm usually quite happy. It's just that I find it leaves me feeling a bit hungry, philosophically speaking. If that makes any sense."

"Absolutely, though I'm amazed to hear you admit to this split between how you live your life and your philosophy."

"Is that what I'm doing?"

"Aren't you saying you can't live your philosophy? Isn't that what you've just been telling me? Me, of all people."

"Oh? And just how authentic is your life, mister gambler?"

"All I'm saying is that I'm surprised to hear you admit to such a thing. To me, I mean. That's certainly not something you would have done in the past."

"No, but maybe that's because I've finally managed to gain a clearer understanding of what's life and what's philosophy. Believe it or not, they're actually quite different."

Smiling at her, I said, "And you were worried I'd think you'd just been going round in circles."

"Well, it probably still is just one big circle."

"Nothing wrong with that. What about your conference?"

"Is it going round in circles?"

"Yes," I laughed, "little bitty ones. No. Just give me some sense of what it's going to be like."

"For you? Boring."

"Yes, that part I think I already knew."

"Well, let's see. I expect I'll hear a few vague assertions of a decidedly quasi-transcendental nature, endless references to empire, globalization, and emergent postcolonial realities, perhaps even a defiant call or two for new dynamic forms of praxis." She paused to smile at me. "That's the one that really used to annoy me, though now I just find it charming that anyone still cares. And then the usual theoretical hunting and pecking for new, more fertile grounds for immanent critique."

"So this is typical . . . "

"For this sort of thing? Afraid so."

"Well, I suppose everyone needs a hobby."

"Oh?" she said, staring at me. "And what's wrong with having a hobby? They're certainly more enjoyable than jobs. All that long-term passion for what one's doing. You're not saying there's anything wrong with that, are you?"

"No, but—"

"But what?"

"I just thought that by now things might be getting a bit dull."

"Things? Like my job and career? Is that what you mean? Or are you referring to my marriage and my husband?"

"No, just wondering if there aren't a few wispy little gray clouds seeping in under the door."

She paused to look at me. "You just can't say it, can you?"

"That I've missed you too? Because I can say it."

"Anytime soon?" she laughed.

"I've missed you too."

"Thank you."

"Though I'm surprised to see by how much."

"I'm not."

"You're not? Then why did I just bother telling you?"

"Perhaps you were telling yourself."

"Wonderful. So now we both know what you knew."

"Are you sure?"

"Uh, if that smile's any indication, probably not. You know, we'd better watch out here or I just might do something foolish."

"Well, don't let me stop you," she said with a big grin on her face.

5

Upon leaving the restaurant she accepted my offer of a ride back to her hotel, but the walk back to the car was very quiet, as if we no longer knew what to say to each other.

At the car, I unlocked her door and held it open, but she hesitated. "Oh, my God!" she said. "I can't believe you still have him." She swept her hand gently across the roof. "He looks fantastic." Then looking at me: "Is he finally paid off?"

"You're not really going to bring that up again, are you?"

"I just thought it was foolish for you to spend so much money."

"You can't still disapprove?"

"Not at all. I'm very happy to see my two boys again."

"Is that so?" I said, playfully taking her in my arms.

"Uh-huh," she replied, holding me tight when I tried to pull back.

"Well—"

She shook her head. "You'd think a man your age would know what to do."

"I was getting there."

"You know," she said, once I'd kissed her, "you could probably get me to do just about anything if you let me drive."

"Really? Then you'd better watch out because I might drive a pretty hard bargain."

Stepping back, she held out her hand. "I hope you do," she said.

I watched her unlock the driver's side door, then get in and lean over to unlock mine. "Look familiar?" I asked as I sat down, turning to watch her pull the seatbelt over to snap it shut.

"It even smells familiar."

"Do you know how to get back to your hotel?"

"Why? Are we in a hurry?"

"No, I just wondered if you knew where you were going."

"I thought you liked to just drive around? You certainly used to."

"No, that's fine. But," I said as she pulled away from the curb, "just for the record, and this is for the official record, not your self-serving, revisionist one. The day I bought this? You weren't particularly cooperative."

"Can you blame me? You and your bullshit story about how you thought I might like a break. Then you got all vague and mysterious when I tried to ask you a few questions. I only gave in so you'd stop pestering me. Actually," she said, turning to look at me, "now that I think about it, I was very cooperative."

"I just thought you might like to get out. Drive down to Denver. Go to Cherry Creek. Hit The Tattered Cover. I even offered to buy you lunch. But you said you'd rather stay at your place reading Habermas all day."

"Because I knew you weren't telling me the truth."

"Part of it was the truth."

"Not the part about wanting to buy a new car, which had absolutely nothing to do with me."

She'd sat her book down to stare at me. "You have a car," she'd said. "I even like your car."

"I like it too, when it's running."

"So now you don't like Italian cars?"

"No, but it's a Fiat. What I'd like is something a little more reliable."

"Such as?"

"Well . . . "

"You're afraid to tell me, aren't you?"

"Only because I know what you're going to say."

"Then you might as well."

"A Porsche?"

"That's reliable? I was expecting you to say you wanted Honda or a Toyota."

"They're certainly more reliable than Fiats."

"Wow, what a recommendation." At that point she'd taken the book from her lap to lay it on the arm of her chair. "Shall I look in the paper for you? Find you a reliable car you can actually afford?"

"I'm not buying a new one."

"And what's with this sudden passion for Porsches? Have you even driven one? Because you've certainly never mentioned it."

"What's that got to do with it?"

"Oh, I don't know. Just seems like a lot of money to spend on something you've never driven. How do you even know you want one?"

"How do we ever know?"

"Amazing. I would never have taken you for the Porsche type."

"There's a type?"

"Dentists."

"Just what type did you take me for?"

"Pick-up truck with a gun rack."

"Thanks so much." Then I'd stared at her. Pleadingly, I'd thought. "Seriously, Lee, I really wish you'd come. I meant it about lunch."

"What an incentive."

"Well?" I'd asked.

"What color?"

"Guard's Red, if I can get it."

We bought it out at Vern Hagestad's on West Colfax. It was three years old, had a little over 22,000 miles on the odometer, and looked and smelled just like new. Yes, it was ridiculously expensive, but she never mentioned that again, nor did she try to hide her enthusiasm. She even read aloud sections of the owner's manual for me on the drive downtown.

When we got to Cherry Creek we had a hard time finding a place to park, or at least one that felt safe for my new car, but we did finally manage to find one at the back of a small parking garage on East 2nd Street just across the street from where the original Tattered Cover used to be. Then, as promised, after the bookstore I took her to lunch at a deli I liked over on Milwaukee. It was on the way back to the car that I remarked that since we were already so close to DU anyway, why not show me where she used to live. It was a dangerous suggestion. Any mention of what she'd done in Denver never failed to annoy her. But for some reason this time she relented—if I let her drive.

I watched her settle herself in the drivers' seat. It was like a tea ceremony the way she did it. Slowly pulling the seatbelt over, starting the engine, tentatively moving through the gears with the clutch in, checking the mirrors, pulling her seat forward a bit, slowly backing out, revving the engine twice before easing the clutch and driving us out to the street.

She took us down University as far as East Iliff, turning there and then again several blocks later at South Filmore. It was partway down that block where we came to a halt in front of a comfortable looking house across the street from Observatory Park. I watched her, looking for any indication of what she was thinking, but there was nothing. I then asked if she'd had many roommates. I didn't dare phrase it any more directly than that. "Nick," she said, turning to look at me. "It wasn't that important." So that was it. She put the car in gear and soon we were back out on University headed home.

Only when we were on the Valley Highway did she turn to look at me. "Pretty quiet over there," she said. "You're not worried about your car, are you?"

"No. Just wondering when I might get to drive again."

"Not today," she said with a laugh.

6

She rented a small two-bedroom house on Spruce just west of 20th Street. It sat down at the end of a long narrow gravel driveway behind a much larger, older home. It was very quiet and peaceful back there. We usually made love in the late afternoon, lying in the bright sunlight filtering through the thin golden colored sheets she'd put up over her bedroom windows. She always ended up on top, rocking back and forth as she gazed down at me in her typical cat-like manner. I'd see her thick dark hair framing her face and neck, her greenish brown eyes and beautiful pale nipples. Afterwards, we'd go out for dinner. When we came home I'd get to be on top. She'd close her eyes and sigh as she held me tightly in her arms, her legs wrapped over the backs of mine. At some point she'd press her hand firmly in the middle of my back holding me very still, with me one moment and gone the next as another wave carried her away. Towards the end she'd take her hand from my back and follow my excitement, groaning and pushing her hips against mine, taking me in as far as she could as I became harder and harder. I often found myself watching the alternating play of pleasure and attention on her face, the spark of awareness in her eyes glowing brighter and brighter like an ember as she smiled at me and held me close. But it was so much more than sex.

Our first significant conversation occurred during the break in one of our Tuesday evening Merleau-Ponty seminars. This was upstairs in Hellems, an older building with wide hallways, high ceilings, and terrazzo floors, all very reminiscent of those large inner-city high schools built during the Depression.

When the seminar broke I stayed in my seat reviewing my notes, then stood and walked out into the hallway. It was quiet, dimly lit, empty, and cavernous. Down the hallway I saw her leaning back against the wall smoking a cigarette. Then for no particular reason, or at least for none I can still recall, I decided to walk over to speak to her. Maybe it was the casual way she leaned back against the wall with her left leg tucked up, the sole of her boot resting flat against the wall. Or maybe it was nothing more than how her arm hung down with the cigarette dangling from her fingers. There's no question but that she had an attractive personal style. Truthfully, though, I really have no idea why I did it.

She turned to watch as I walked towards her. She wore tight jeans and a dark green sweater over a black turtleneck. Her hair was swept back and gathered at the neck. Closer, I saw there were tiny turquoise pins in her ear lobes. I also noticed how her eyes grew bright with amusement when she realized I really meant to speak to her.

"I thought you didn't care for French philosophy," I said.

"Where did you hear that?"

"You mean that's just gossip?"

"I'm certainly not a member of your Merleau-Ponty cult, if that's what you mean."

"Cult? If that's how you feel, why are you here?"

I watched her take a drag on her cigarette, then blow the smoke up over my head. I waited. Was she really not going to say anything? Well, apparently not, which was something I soon got used to, that she often didn't; that she often just watched. So that was my first taste of what I soon grew to be very fond of: being the focus of all that disconcertingly direct, calm, and thoughtful attention.

"Actually," she finally said, cocking her head to one side in anticipation of my response, "I find it much more interesting to speculate about why you're here."

"Over here talking to you? Or in this class?"

"Exactly."

"Well," I stammered, "if we're talking about this class, then I suppose it's because I'm interested in phenomenology, or at least I'm interested in Merleau-Ponty. You know," I said, looking at her expectantly. "Lived experience, the lifeworld, embodied consciousness, intersubjectivity?"

"Really? Then perhaps you'd care to explain to me how it is that the subject constitutes this intersubjectivity."

"In our cult?"

"Yes," she said, grinning at me. "In your cult."

"Well, first off, I think your question applies more to the cult of Husserl. Merleau-Ponty sees intersubjectivity as part of lived experience. Something we always already find ourselves in. In the lifeworld."

"Yes, so I've heard, but then how does your cult explain the creation of this lifeworld, and how it's sustained."

"It being a cult, I believe that's a secret."

"It must be, since no one seems to be able to tell me. What about learned, or changed? Any thoughts there?"

"Why pick on me?" I asked, holding my hands out to show my innocence. "I'm just some poor, harmless graduate student sitting there taking notes."

"Then perhaps you should be more careful which cults you choose."

"Or who I talk too."

"You do know the philosophy of consciousness is dead?"

"Really? I sure wish someone had told me." I had no idea what she was talking about.

"I just did."

"I know. I meant beforehand. So I wouldn't feel so foolish."

"Well, don't wallow in it," she said with a grin. "Anyway, I'm sure you're no more foolish than any of the rest of them."

"You know, this is really amazing. I mean, all I did was walk over here to ask a simple question, and now it's cult and the philosophy of consciousness is dead. Whatever that means."

"And let's not forget foolish."

"And foolish."

"So?" she said, watching me as she took a long drag on her cigarette.

"Why am I over here talking to you? Well, I saw you over here by yourself and . . . I don't know. I was surprised, so I came over. I didn't even think about it."

"Yes, well I was a bit surprised, myself. So impulsive! You don't do this sort of thing all the time, do you?

"Not after today."

"Too far outside your comfort zone?"

"I can be spontaneous. If that's what you're implying."

"Well, I was wondering," she said, a look of perfect innocence on her face.

"Well, don't."

"Yes?"

"Uh . . . don't give up on me yet," I said, smiling at her. "I'll think of something."

"Good. I'm looking forward to it." Then she dropped her cigarette on the floor, stepped on it, and glanced down the hallway towards the seminar room. "Time to go," she said.

Looking back on it now this is what I most remember: that I was wondering if I'd ever be able to get enough of that alert, thoughtful attention. As it turned out, the answer was no.

7

Had she merely been teasing? Over the next few weeks that question was uppermost in my mind as we never seemed to recapture that spark. This was true even when I managed to sit next to her in the seminar. Or maybe it was because it was impossible to get her alone. She'd joined up with a loud, bantering group of students who hung out before class and afterwards left for drinks. I was invited, of course, everyone was, but I'd long since lost my enthusiasm for the graduate student lifestyle. Then in late February came an evening of unseasonably warm weather. A mild chinook had blown all day, sweeping down across town from the high peaks to the west, warming and drying as it spread out across the plains. During the break I went outside to enjoy it. The bare branches clattering together, dancing in the wind over my head, the stars shimmering like fiery sparks in the gusting wind, rivulets of water seeping from mounds of dirty snow, dark wet tracks across the flagstone, lights twinkling across campus, the scent of evaporating moisture on the wind.

"It's beautiful."

I turned. She was standing a few feet behind me smoking a cigarette. "A lot of people hate the wind," I said, watching as she clenched the cigarette between her teeth to free her hands to gather her hair back, making a ponytail with a scrunchie. I wondered if she'd come outside to find me. Maybe it was just an accident.

"How do you feel about Merleau-Ponty now?" I asked, trying to get her to say something.

"About the same as before, though he's more interesting than I'd given him credit for." She dropped her right arm, flicking her cigarette. "The later stuff, I mean." We were working with the *Phenomenology of Perception*. I had no idea what his later stuff was like. "You don't participate much anymore, do you?" She nodded in the direction of Hellems.

"Not really. I just find it all sort of—"

"Pointless?"

"I suppose, but you seem to enjoy it."

"Sometimes." She was watching me. "I hope you're not going to quit."

"I'm thinking about it."

"But why quit now?"

"Because I probably should have left a long time ago."

"To do what?"

"When I find out I'll let you know."

"Yes, do that. You can send me a postcard."

"I should. You'll probably need it. Something to brighten your day as you trudge ever onward across the barren wastelands of academe."

"Yes, a cold snowy day, another day of boredom and misery, but wait, what's this in my mailbox? A postcard from Barcelona?"

"It could happen like that."

"So, travel, that's what you'll do?" she asked, stepping in front of me to see my face more clearly. Once again giving me a glimpse of that special look she got on her face when she really wanted to understand something. Frankly, it was spellbinding being so close to her, caught in her gaze like that.

"I don't know, maybe, other than a few things I'd like to try."

"Such as?"

"Oh . . . things," I said, smiling at her.

"Will you be staying in Boulder to do these things?" she asked, now amused.

"More likely Los Angeles."

"Los Angeles?"

"I spent a year out there before graduate school."

"Doing what?"

"Oh, hanging out, working some. In a bookstore," I added, heading off her next question. "It was run by a bunch of UCLA students. Fashionable radicals, I believe we'd call them. But just part-time, which was fine because that left my afternoons free."

"Don't tell me you're one of those people who needs a nap every day?"

"What's wrong with naps?"

"Nothing, if you don't mind wasting your time."

"Maybe I just stayed up too late."

"Yes, I can just imagine."

"I meant reading."

"Like what?"

"Lacan?"

"I'm sure. What were you really doing?"

"Like I said, it was a radical bookstore run by a bunch of students. So I came in at eight and left around noon."

"To do what?"

"Oh, lots of things. Driving around to the wholesalers filling book orders. Helping them manage their inventory. They had a lot of managerial issues," I said with a smile. "Mostly because they tried to run it as a collective."

"Seriously?"

"Totally. They all liked to talk about what needed to be done, but none of them were very good at actually doing it. That's where I came in, and they weren't really all that radical, either, most just wanted to go to law school."

"But then you came back to Boulder. How come?"

"I like Boulder. I have friends here. I wanted to study philosophy."

"And now that's changed."

"The philosophy part has. I just don't see the point. But it's not just me, not if you really think about it."

"In what sense?"

"In the sense that it doesn't really make any sense." I nodded towards Hellems. "All those students, all those programs, all that hard work and effort, and for what? A mere handful of jobs that never seem to be someplace you'd actually want to live, and that's assuming they're even genuine tenure track positions in good departments, which they seldom are. And even then you're going to spend the bulk of your time teaching."

"Well, we've got to keep these big departments up and running somehow, don't we? And what's wrong with teaching? That's just what we have to do to justify our existence in the university. But it's funny you should bring this up because I've been thinking about getting out of here myself, though not for the same reasons as you. The truth is, I only came here by accident."

"By accident?"

"After graduation, I wasn't sure what I wanted to do. Then I came out here for a visit. This was down in Denver. Well, I liked it, which was a bit of a surprise, so then I thought, why not, so I went back home and packed-up. It seemed like the right decision at the time, even though I'd already been accepted in several other programs."

"But not now?"

"Not really."

"So you're looking elsewhere?"

"That's the plan."

"How soon does this happen?"

"Too many questions," she said, grinning at me.

"Sorry."

I saw her glance over her shoulder towards Hellems, a clear sign the time to return had arrived. And just like that the moment was swept away forever in the gusting wind.

8

I had a number of jobs when I was in graduate school. One was working for a Boulder wholesaler that supplied books and magazines to convenience stores, grocery stores, drugstores, hotels, bookshops, and truck stops around the north Denver metropolitan area. They had a number of different sales routes. I was fortunate to have one of the two in Boulder. It was a good job. I enjoyed being out on my own all day.

The job had a set routine. Mondays and Wednesdays, deliver new magazines. Tuesdays and Fridays, straighten up the racks and update inventories. Thursdays, distribute new paperbacks and comic books. At times, the workload got pretty heavy, which meant I often found myself working late or Saturdays, and then there were those holidays I skipped. But the worst days were those Wednesdays when the new issues of *Playboy* and *Penthouse* came out. Then my Ford Econoline van would be stacked to the ceiling with heavy bundles, twenty copies per. It made for a long, exhausting day. Worse, I always managed to cut my hand on the metal bands the printers used to strap the bundles together. Not surprisingly, my best customers were the convenience stores near campus, in particular, the old run-down Cornucopia on Arapahoe. There I'd be, my hand truck stacked high with heavy bundles as I struggled across the uneven gravel parking lot—potholes, ridges of ice and snow in the winter—but then one Wednesday afternoon in March someone kindly held the door open for me.

"Thanks," I said, not yet seeing who it was, then, "What are you doing here?" when I realized it was Lee.

"Buying some cigarettes on my way home. Over on Spruce," she said, gesturing with a gloved hand.

I was having a hard time with my bundles. To keep them balanced I was tilting the hand truck back more and more, then just as it seemed they'd tumble to the floor she pushed them back in line with her boot, leaving a muddy footprint.

"Stick around," I said, maneuvering the hand truck over to the magazine rack. "This won't take long."

"I didn't know you had a job," she said, walking over to join me.

"An important one, too." I was stacking the bundles on the floor. "See?" I clipped the strap on one and removed the paper wrappers.

"*Penthouse?*"

"Want to lend a hand?"

"No thanks," she said, playfully punching my arm.

"Well, don't run off."

"Will you give me a ride home?"

"Yeah. Just stick around."

Five minutes later we walked out to the van. "I need to write this up," I told her as we got in. "Then run it back inside for a signature."

"You don't work full-time, do you?"

"Usually." I paused to look up at her.

"Sorry. Go ahead."

When I came back she was smoking.

"All set?" she asked.

"Yes. Where to?"

"Spruce, over by 21st. I'll show you when we get there."

"Have long have you been living over there?"

"Two years, this August. I should have moved up here sooner, but I had a hard time finding a decent place in my price range."

When we got there she had me pull into a long gravel driveway. "That's my little house down there." She was pointing to the end of the drive.

"You rent the whole thing?"

"It's not as big as it looks." She turned to look at me. "Would you like to see?"

"I'd love to, but not right now. I've still got a long day ahead of me." Looking surprised, she sat up in her seat to stare at me. Obviously, it had never crossed her mind I might decline. "Why don't I come back later, after work?" I said, suddenly desperate to hang on to the moment. "Say around six?"

"Well . . ."

"We can get some dinner."

She opened her door and hopped down to the ground, then turned to look back at me. "All right," she said.

9

When I pulled up she was standing on the sidewalk waiting for me in the dim twilight.

"I hope you haven't been here long," I said as she got in.

"Just long enough for a cigarette." She took one more drag, then rolled her window down a few inches to flick the butt out into the street. "Get all your porn delivered?" she asked.

"You make it sound like I should feel guilty."

"Do you?"

"Just filling a need, ma'am."

"How long have you been filling it?"

"Two years." I turned to look at her. "Why the disapproval? But then you might feel differently if you'd ever had to work." Few students in the program did, or certainly none as much as me.

"I've had jobs."

"Where you had to get up early every morning?"

"Sometimes."

"And drive some place where they paid you for sitting around all day doing stuff?"

"It was volunteer work."

"That's what you call a job?"

"You know, class resentment like this is going to make for a very long evening."

"Just out slumming with us scruffy blue-collar types, huh?"

"Well," she said, shaking her head, "I can't say my friends didn't warn me. Stick with those private universities, they said. State schools are such a mess. Marginal students. Massively in debt with foolish student loans."

"But you didn't listen."

"No, but I should have."

"At least I'm not massively in debt. Paid my own way." I looked at her. "You have heard of that?"

Rolling her eyes, she said, "And I suppose that means I'm supposed to buy dinner?"

"No, we'll split the cost—for now. Labor isn't comfortable with capital footing the whole bill, though the day inexorably approaches."

"Yes, and then you and your comrades will no doubt move into the big house on the hill and stupidly rip out all the cooper plumbing for a quick profit."

"Well, who knows, they just might. I expect to be more interested in appropriating their women."

"You? That's sure going to work out well."

"All right, their cars, then. They're more fun anyway."

"Except you've always been saddled with those clapped-out high-mileage beaters. Where it's just one test drive after another while they wait around for a real buyer."

"We are still talking about cars?"

"Whatever we're talking about you wouldn't have the faintest idea what to do if by some miracle you suddenly found yourself behind the wheel of something sleek and new."

"Uh . . ."

"Yes, I know" she said, smiling sweetly. "You angry blue-collar types always flounder when confronted by a woman who's smarter than you. Not that you've had much experience with that sort of thing. But then like any man here you are desperately hunting around for a rejoinder."

"I don't dare say a word, do I?"

"Only if you're very brave."

I took her to Tico's, not the best food in town, but because I used to work there it still felt comfortable. In fact, we sat in the sunroom facing Walnut at my favorite table and our waitress was a friend of mine, as was the bartender, a guy I'd known since high school. I asked for a gin and tonic, Lee had a martini.

When the waitress left Lee turned to me. "Isn't she Linda's friend? I think we met at Linda's party."

"You probably did."

"Why weren't you in that class?"

"The Wittgenstein seminar?"

"Not fashionable enough for you?"

"He certainly used to be."

"Only now it's Merleau-Ponty?"

"It's never going to be Merleau-Ponty. Anyway, I find all that analytic versus continental stuff pretty tedious."

"I don't."

"You know," I said, smiling at her, "I used to work here."

"Changing the subject?"

"God, I hope so."

"Doing what?"

"I was a cook."

"How was it?"

"Just fine, until I developed insomnia, which finally got so bad I had to quit."

"So you really didn't like working here?"

"No, I did. The owner's a nice guy, and it wasn't the job it was the hours, five in the afternoon until two in the morning. By the time I got home I couldn't get to sleep."

"That was what, two-thirty, three?"

"A little later than that."

"Oh?"

"More like four or five." I shrugged. "What can I say? Things just always seemed to come up."

She smiled at me. "You were drinking."

"Right over there," I said, laughing as I nodded towards the bar.

"So it wasn't the job so much as it was sitting around drinking until dawn."

"That might have played some small part in it."

"Maybe if you hadn't slept alone."

"Slept alone?"

"Well? Like you do now?"

"I don't see what that's got to do with it."

"It's got everything to do with it. At the very least, you wouldn't have been sitting over there drinking. Not unless you just didn't want to go home."

"It was the sunrise that bothered me, not the empty bed, and in the summer that comes pretty early around here."

"I'm just saying—"

"What about you? Care to talk about that?"

The olive in her martini was impaled on a tiny green plastic sword. As I watched, she took that sword and put it in her mouth, closing her lips around the olive so that just the end of the sword was visible. Then slowly, using just her fingertips, she pulled it out, leaving the olive behind. Chewing, she stared at me. "I've never had insomnia," she said.

10

Later, when we came back out onto Walnut, the air felt much colder and smelled of snow. There was already a dusting of dry powder at our feet that billowed up in a sparkling cloud as we walked. At the car I brushed it from windshield with my gloved hand, then held her door open. I looked down Walnut towards Broadway. Empty. No cars. No pedestrians. Just us. But the flakes grew larger and wetter as we drove around. The snow starting to accumulate in the streets, on tree branches, streetlights, signs, and parked cars, the angular lines of the city softening under the mounting snow, the night sky taking on a diffuse magical glow.

I tried to get her to open up, to tell me a little bit more about herself, but she deftly sidestepped my questions with ones of her own. What was it like growing up Colorado? How had it changed? So I told her my stories, carefully watching for any signs of flagging interest, but she seemed happy enough snuggled down in her seat smoking, occasionally laughing, encouraging me to tell her more with her steady stream of questions.

"So how long have you been in the program?"

"Six years."

"Six!" She studied me. "Just how old are you?"

"Well, there was that year I took off before graduate school, and the six I've been here. And then the five it took to get my B.A."

"Well, looks like I've finally gone out with an older man."

"Yes, and you have no idea how lucky you are."

"Uh-huh. So, six year? I guess what I'm wondering is how

48

you've managed to fill the time."

"Like I said, I like it here, that's part of it, and then graduate student life can be pretty good. I mean it's not life like in the real world, is it? So that's been fun. But six years is, as you suggest, a long time. But then it always takes me a long time to make up my mind."

"Clearly. So now you suddenly find yourself worried about what to do with the rest of your life."

"Something like that."

"Finally old enough to see you actually have one to live. One you may even need to think about. Or is that not it?"

"Have you ever noticed how it's often best to answer an uncomfortable question with another? But then you never answer any, so I suppose you haven't."

"For example?"

"Like what brought you here to CU."

"I already told you. When I graduated from Brown I wasn't sure what I wanted to do, so I came out here to visit friends. Then I got into the program and moved up here."

"By friends you mean what, some guy?"

"Guy?" She grinned at me. "So now I suppose you think we're going to have one of *those* conversations."

"We might."

"We might not. Anyway, I don't seem to recall hearing any of your stories about all those friends you've no doubt had over your surprisingly long life."

I smiled, watching the snowflakes swirling and bobbing in the headlights. "Well, it's true," I said, turning to look at her. "I do like women, and as amazing as this may seem to you, sometimes they even like me back."

"At least as a friend," she said, turning sideways in her seat to watch me.

"Friend? That sounds dangerously close to what a woman tells a guy she's about to dump."

"We *are* close."

"You do realize we never want to be just friends?"

"Some of you do."

"If that's what they said they were lying."

"Would you?"

"Lie to get what I want? Perhaps, if I wanted to be your friend."

"But since you don't I can believe you? Because I am starting to."

"Would you like an example?"

"I'd love one."

"There's this guy I know. Good looking. Nice. You'd like him, though I'd never introduce him to a heartbreaker like you, but it's a fact that women do like him."

"But only as a friend?"

"Exactly."

"You really think I'd hurt his feelings?"

"And enjoy it. But in his case I don't think you really could because there's not much left to hurt. At least not where women are concerned."

"It works both ways, you know. I'm sure he's done his share."

"Not this guy. So what was his reward for being this nice guy? This good friend? Endless agony, that's what. Truly more than you could ever imagine, and all at the hands of his female friends."

"I'm still waiting to feel the sympathy."

"You will. We were talking one time, or he was, I was just listening.

"Being sympathetic."

"Very. This was after his divorce. He was trying to date again, but the women he knew were all just so eager to tell him what a good friend he was. Some couldn't even wait until that first date was over. Just blurting it out."

"Maybe that's how his ex-wife felt."

"Oh? Well, you tell me. He gets home from class one afternoon and she's sitting there in their living room waiting for him. She'd even left work early just to make sure she was there in time to make her big announcement."

"She was dumping him?"

"She was moving out."

"What did he say?"

"What could he say? It was so totally out of the blue."

"At least from his perspective."

"Well, that's sort of the perspective he was saddled with, wasn't it?"

"But he did ask her?"

"Of course he did. She said it wasn't because she'd met another man, discovered she was a lesbian or anything like that, which would have at least made some sort of sense."

"What did she say?"

"She was leaving him because he was boring."

"Well, someone had to tell him."

I looked at her and smiled. "You women really are too kind."

"We have to be to put up with our male friends."

"Does that mean it's time for me to take you home?"

"Why? Friends like us still have a lot to talk about."

"Yes, friends like us might even want to share."

"I'd love to, but I just don't have anything even remotely interesting to tell you. So far, it's been a rather dull life."

"Okay. So let's see if this works. I'll dredge up a painful memory or two about some old girlfriend, then you tell me something about your friends in Denver."

"Well . . . "

"Why not?"

"All right. But only tentatively."

"I'll run with that."

"So," she said, settling back in her seat, "tell me something about your first girlfriend."

"Which sort of first are you referring to?"

"Well, if you can't even remember who she was . . ."

"I can certainly remember the first woman I slept with, if

that's what you're fishing around for, though calling her a woman might be a bit of stretch since we were both still in grade school."

"Yeah, I can see why you might be a bit reluctant to talk about that."

"I know, but there it is. So this was in a tent in her parent's backyard. A pup tent. That's where we spent the night. I still think of her whenever I smell canvas."

"The whole night?"

"Yes, a beautiful, endless night, a night of sweet cool air, romance, and the tang of canvas. In the morning she woke me by tugging on my ear."

"Just your ear?"

"Though she did like to pick up spiders and chase me around."

"Spiders bother you?"

"Always. Anyway, she lived next door, but we moved away and then her family moved to Santa Barbara. Then she got married and lived in Reno."

"When was the last time you saw her?"

"When I was twelve, though I did have a drink with a woman who'd gone to high school with her."

"Did you ask her about your little friend?"

"I did when I heard she was from Santa Barbara."

"Where was this?"

"Breckinridge. I was having a drink in a ski lodge when she sat down next to me."

"Why weren't you skiing?"

"Because I'd sprained my ankle. So I was devoting the rest of my day to recuperation."

She grinned at me. "Does this count as another one of your stories?"

"No, unfortunately all we shared was a drink."

"Just checking. But I do like your camping story, and I'm hardly surprised by that spider thing. But I don't think your story really honors the spirit of our agreement."

"All right. So, when you were a teenager, did you have a horse?"

"Are you changing the subject, or is this just a clumsy segue to another story?"

"An artful segue."

"Then, no, I never had a horse, though I occasionally rode one at school."

"Seriously? What sort of school did you go to?"

"A prep school," she said, making it plain just how unhappy she was to be sharing that little scrap of personal information.

"Did you play lacrosse? That's all I know about prep schools, that the girls all play a lot of lacrosse."

"Not this girl."

"Sorry. My first serious girlfriend was into horses. I know that's not uncommon, and lots of teenage girls in the West are really into it. So I just happened to be the guy who came along as she was shifting her attention to boys. That's why I asked about horses. I thought you might have had a similar experience."

She shook her head.

"So her parents were divorced, and during the summer her mother spent most of the day out at Boulder Reservoir."

"What was she doing out there?"

"Well, there's a beach and an area for swimming, but yeah, what was she doing out there?"

"Probably the same thing her daughter was doing."

"But she seemed so old. Like my mother."

"Too old for a man?"

"Wasn't she?"

"Boy, were you naïve."

"I know, but then at that age I found a lot of adult behavior pretty incomprehensible. Didn't you?"

"No."

"Really?"

"Not a bit. So what happened?"

"They lived on several acres out in the countryside a few miles from town. So when the mother left for the day the daughter would call and I'd be on my way."

"And this was your first sexual experience?"

"Wow, no foreplay for you, just straight to the point, which is a shame since there might be all sorts of important stuff going on here worth knowing about."

"Sorry, but you get sidetracked so easily I wasn't sure we'd ever get to the point, and for teenage boys sex is always the point."

"Is that so?"

"Without question."

"Then all I'm going to say is that she was my first love and that I was very fond of her. In fact, I still think she was wonderful, even though she eventually dumped me for a guy who was the lead singer in a rock band."

"She dumped you for a musician? How pathetic."

"An older guy, too. Naturally."

"Poor Nick. But I do find it charming how you refuse to share any of those sensitive details. Sort of undercuts the pathos of your story, however. How you selflessly helped this young woman make that difficult transition from horses to musicians." Then putting her hand on my arm as if to offer comfort: "Were you really hurt when she dumped you?"

"In a silly teenage sort of way, but I knew it was just practice for those more serious heartaches to come."

"Now I really do feel bad. Poor innocent little boy getting his first taste of just how awful we women can be."

"Trust me, I was never that innocent, and she was always very nice to me."

"But?"

"But nothing."

"Then why are smiling like that?"

"Because I was just thinking about something I'd forgotten. How we used to run into each other at rock concerts. I'd be there with my buddies. She'd be there with her little pack."

"This was after your break-up?"

"Uh-huh. So I always made a point of standing next to her where her boyfriend could see us while he was performing."

"Well, I must say, I'm truly flattered by your willingness to share such painful memories with me. The little girl who tormented you with spiders and the groupie."

"What about cheerleaders? How do you feel about them?"

"Seriously?"

"I'd never joke about cheerleaders."

"I'm not sure. I guess I've never given them much thought." She paused. I could feel her watching me. "Can I tell you something?"

"Sure," I said, glancing her way.

"Not many men would be this foolish. You know, telling a woman they hardly know about their involvement with cheerleaders."

"Cheerleader," I said, holding up one finger.

"Whatever. It makes you seem creepy."

"So what you're really saying is that I'm never going to hear anything about those friends in Denver, let alone anything else, which is too bad because I was just about to tell you about Heartbreak Hotel."

"Like the song?"

"Better."

"This was a real place?"

"Very, for me and any number of people."

"How'd it get its name?"

"By earning it."

"You mean you earned it," she said, a big smile spreading across her face.

"I helped."

"So your name and your heartbreak?"

"I moved out years ago, which is all I'm saying."

"You'll tell me someday."

11

I suggested the Boulderado when she said she'd like a beer before I took her home. Parking was no problem, no one else seemed to be out, but that meant we had to make our own trail from the car through the snow and up the steps to the big front doors. Then from the lobby I led her downstairs to the Catacombs, not at all surprised to find it nearly empty. Wanting as much privacy as possible, we settled for one of the tables in the small room at the back. It was delightfully cozy sitting back there all by ourselves in the dim light while outside the snow continued to mount up.

"You seem pretty familiar with this place," she said as she draped her coat over a chair.

"I should be. This was one of the few bars we could get into when we were underage."

"I can't believe you did that."

"Oh, come on, you must have done a few irresponsible things when you were a kid." It was just so obvious she hadn't.

"Not really, which makes me wonder how someone like you ends up a graduate student studying philosophy."

"Seriously? They practically begged me to enter their stupid program."

"Begged?"

"Don't let my silly stories mislead you, by the time I got to college I was more than ready to be a serious student. Unlike all you neurotic over-achievers who lost it the moment you got out from under mommy and daddy's thumbs."

"That was hardly my problem, and I've always been an

excellent student. Though I did have friends who struggled a bit."

"Speaking of struggled, I think it was sometime during my junior year it finally hit me.

"What?"

"They were all gone."

"From CU?"

"Yes, and probably from everywhere. But how had that happened? Suddenly, like overnight? Or gradually, finally reaching a point where I couldn't help but notice?"

"Notice they were gone?"

"Gone. Vanished. Slipped away in the night. Disappeared without a trace."

"Maybe they just flunked out."

"Or dropped out."

"Lost interest."

"Got arrested. Got drafted."

"Ran out of money. Got pregnant."

"Ran off to San Francisco or New York. But at least I knew one thing for sure, they were no longer there."

"How'd that make you feel?"

"I found it liberating."

"What about the draft? That must have had something to do with your being there?"

"Not a bit."

"Were you?"

"Drafted? You think they'd have me?"

She smiled at me. "Only if they didn't know what they were doing."

"Well, fortunately it never came to that because I flunked my draft physical."

"Flunked?" she said, leaning back to stare at me.

"Too skinny."

"How much do you have to weigh to kill people?"

"See? It's surprising, isn't it? I'd already filed as a

conscientious objector, but that was hopeless, so I'd pretty much given up."

"But then you got lucky."

"Lucky?" I took a sip of beer as I leaned back in my chair. "Remember the lottery? When we were each assigned a number for our birthday? Well, mine was really low, which was very *un*lucky as far as I was concerned. Of course, that meant I got called up right away, which is how I found myself sitting with a busload of guys on our way down to Denver for our physicals."

"Which is where they said you were too skinny."

"That's right. Turns out, they had strict guidelines. Who knew?"

"How much were you supposed to weigh?"

"The minimum for my height was one hundred and forty-one pounds, which was great because I only weighted one hundred and twenty-eight."

"That must have made you happy."

"Actually, it didn't, or at least not at first. I mean I'd always been skinny, but too skinny? I'd never felt too skinny. Then one of the doctors asked if I'd recently lost a lot of weight. No, just skinny. Then he warned me, saying they could call me back at anytime. Go right ahead, I told him, it won't make any difference."

"Did he believe you?"

"He didn't say he did, but he did smile, and they never did call me back. So then I turned around to leave and the next few guys in line were shaking their heads like they thought I truly was lucky."

"Well, you sort of were, weren't you?"

"It's not luck when what happens to you is fair, which is certainly how it seemed to me."

Later, she opened up a bit, becoming a little more forthcoming about her career plans and her frustrations with the department. As I'd already guessed, her ambitions were sizeable.

"So this is what's driving you elsewhere?" She'd been complaining about how hard it was to form a committee. "But Wittgenstein, with this department? It shouldn't be all that hard."

"If that's what you're interested in."

"You're not?"

"Hardly. I've been trying to work up something using Habermas. Unfortunately, I seem to be the only one who has any interest in it."

"Sorry. I don't know why I thought it was Wittgenstein."

"They're not incompatible. Habermas even has some interesting things to say about Wittgenstein in the context of grounding a critical social theory." She paused to look at me. "Do you read German?"

"Sort of."

"Then you should take a look at Habermas's *Theorie des kommunikativen Handelns.* Karl-Otto Apel, too. It's about using the social nature of language as the normative basis for a critical theory of society. Grounding it in the communicative act of speaking."

"I don't suppose any of this ties in with Merleau-Ponty?"

"Not really. Like I've said, you'll never find this social dimension if you start with the subject, but you will if you start with language. Human actions. Practices like speaking, like speech acts."

I smiled at her. "I see. This wouldn't happen to be more of that *the philosophy of consciousness is dead* stuff, would it?"

"You know," she said, staring at me, "you're much better at this than you let on."

"Possibly, but then again I'm not obsessed with it."

"Like me?"

"It certainly gives you something to talk about."

Leaning back, she frowned at me. "Am I boring you?"

"Not at all. I like hearing about Habermas. It gives me a much clearer understanding of the problems you've been having with your committee. Too bad you're in such a rush to get out of here. I was thinking you might be able to tutor me."

"In what?"

"Habermas? Or maybe you could give me a reading list and I'd tutor myself."

"Even if I did you'd never stick with it."

"Maybe with a little encouragement . . ."

"That's the last thing you're going to get from me," she said, giving me one of her better looks. "Not that there's much I could teach you even if I tried."

"I think that all depends on what the teacher has in mind."

"Believe me," she said, eyes wide open, "*this* teacher has nothing in mind. But why put the burden all on the teacher's shoulders? What about the student's willingness?"

"Who's unwilling?"

"Well," she said, looking around the room like she was hunting for something. "I suppose I might be able to find some use for you. Though I really have no idea what that might be."

"I do."

"Yes, but will we still be friends?"

12

When we came back upstairs and walked out through the lobby doors to the terrace I was struck by how much the snowstorm had intensified. As we'd been downstairs chatting it had quietly blossomed into one of those big, smothering snowstorms Boulder often gets in the spring. Ones that typically dump down heavy wet snow over the Front Range for hours on end as warmer moisture laden air is pushed up from the southeast and pinned against the Rockies. Already there were at least eight inches on the ground. There would be many more by morning.

The snow squeaked underfoot as we walked across the terrace. Pausing at the edge, I was struck by how still the air was, a little warmer, too, the sky now very bright, so bright it was possible to track each fat flake as it slowly drifted down out of the darkness, marking its slow progress until it disappeared in the heaps of freshly fallen snow at our feet. I looked towards the courthouse. Stoplights wore tall caps of snow as they cycled through for empty streets. It was shockingly quiet. The normal sounds of the city muffled by the heavy wet snow. I took a deep breath, savoring the wonderfully tangy scent of cold air and snow.

"Isn't it amazing how the snowstorm delimits this space?" I said, sweeping an arm out in front of us. "Like this is just for us."

"Yes," she said, reaching up to brush some snow from my hair.

Laughing, I shook off the rest, then looked up and tried to dodge the snowflakes as they came spinning towards us. There was one particularly fat one. I noted its path as it came in our direction. Followed its steady progress as it spun and spiraled down out of the sky. Then, just as it reached us, I stepped back and caught it neatly on my tongue. "Let me try," she said, grinning at me as she leaned her head back and shuffled to the side, just managing to do the same. I thought she looked like a child, making a point of sticking her tongue out to show me before it melted. Then she surprised me, stepping in front of me to slip her hands under my coat and wrap her arms tightly about my waist. I laughed, wanting to say something, but she grinned and tightened her grip, pulling me very close, making me laugh even more as I was forced to exhale. Wondering what she was up to, I leaned back to see her face. What I saw were raised eyebrows and calm amusement as she waited to see what I might do, and of course I didn't do much of anything, or at least not at first, not until she'd playfully rolled her eyes and gently pinched my back. Playful behavior she keep up even after we'd kissed, shifting her body until she could bump her hips against mine, running ice-cold hands up and down my back under my sweater in an oddly contradictory form of arousal, which is how we were standing when we were forced to step aside as another couple came out of the hotel.

Later, she knelt beside me on her bed as she attempted to remove her black wool sweater. I watched her work it up over her head, but there it became entangled in the purple turtleneck she wore underneath. "Nick! Help!" she said, laughing at herself as she held her arms up helplessly over her head. Getting up on my knees, I gently worked the turtleneck up over her chin, her nose, and then her forehead. Then smiling at me, she shook the hair from her face and pulled first one arm free and then the other before flipping everything onto the floor next to her bed. "Thanks," she said, dropping her arms down over my shoulders.

I ran my hands slowly up and down her back. "You're so quiet," I said when she didn't speak. "What is it?"

She looked at me and smiled, then placed her hands on my chest and gently forced me to lie back on her bed, swinging her right leg over my hips to straddle me. When I tried to pull her down on top of me she resisted. Then without looking at me she took my right hand and placed it on her left breast. Her nipple felt hard as I rolled it back and forth between my fingers. I tried to take it all in. The tousled hair, the flat plane of her stomach, the deep shadows under her breasts, the sculpted definition of her body, how she was staring at the soft light coming through the curtains over her bed. I wondered what she was thinking.

Finally, she let me pull her down and I stroked her back with my hand. Cool and taut, I traced its muscular curvature all the way down to the soft silky hairs at the base of her spine. When I took her nipple in my mouth it was like sucking on a pebble. Then she leaned forward and I slid my hands inside her pants, down and around her hips until my fingers were resting on the flat of her stomach. Sighing, she rose up so I could loosen her belt and undo the buttons at the front of her jeans. Then she tugged them down over her hips to her knees and took my hand. I'd never felt a woman more aroused.

Later that night I had a moment of infinite peace and certitude as I lay bathed in the beautiful soft light pouring in her bedroom windows. I felt safe and warm in her bed knowing that outside the snow was relentlessly piling up. At the quietest time of night on the quietest possible night I heard nothing but the gentle sound of her breathing. Nothing that happened later added to or changed in any way what I knew in that moment.

13

"Of all the names they might have chosen, why Nick?" She was talking about my parents. "You don't even look like a Nick."

"Oh? And what's a Nick supposed to look like?"

We were having dinner at Fred's, sitting in a booth at the back from where I could see the kitchen. I always ordered a grilled cheese sandwich. She almost always had the Caesar salad.

"Greek. Masculine, with dark curly hair and soulful dark brown eyes."

"And lots of hair on his back."

"Hairy backs are sexy."

I laughed. "Then I must be a terrible disappointment."

"No, because you're not a real Nick. You're just my watered down, suburban Nick."

"Suburban!"

"Sort of a Nick-lite."

"What about Lee?"

"I know, it doesn't fit, does it?" She had a bite of her salad as she thought about it. "Let's pick new ones. I've never felt like a Lee, and you're certainly no Nick."

"Yes, but unlike you I like my name. But I do agree with you that Lee doesn't suit you. How about Dixie?"

"Or Dixie Lee. Like a southern girl."

"We'll be Nick and Dixie."

"No, Nick and Mona." She smiled at me. "The fun couple."

"Sorry, but you're no Mona."

"I could be."

"I don't know how. Mona's are Greek, with thick curly dark

hair and soulful brown eyes. They also have lots of hair on their upper lips." I gently ran the tip of my index finger across her upper lip. "Plus, any couple named Nick and Mona would have lots of kids. Do you want to have lots of kids?"

"I would if I were married to a real Nick."

"Yes, and only a real Nick would be brave enough to go in there and get the job done."

"Really?" She reached over to shove my shoulder. "I had no idea you've been so terrified. My, but you've certainly been very brave."

"Which is why," I said, patting my chest, "my name is Nick. The man with the courage to go where few men dare."

"Yes, spoken just like a man. So proud of himself for getting it in there like that was some great accomplishment."

"Actually, I view it more like a dangerous adventure."

"You mean more like a dangerous *mis*adventure."

"A trip up the Amazon into unexplored territory. Headhunters, Amazons, poison darts, thick, impenetrable foliage, those awful wasting diseases people get in the tropics."

"You know," she said, staring over my head, "it's a puzzle why I ever thought I might want a man. Any man. Maybe I never did. I certainly don't right now."

"You certainly won't get any arguments from me. I've never understood what you women see in us. I think we're disgusting. But I suppose we should blame it on your biological natures. At some point you just get overwhelmed and then there's nothing to do but go along for the ride."

"You know how that ride looks to me, like an incredibly boring trip down a bumpy road full of potholes in a construction zone. All the way out to the edge of town where the pavement ends. I see a lot of abandoned cars out there."

"Well, if that's how you really feel about it we can always pull over on the shoulder and stop. Seriously," I said when she sighed and looked away from me. "I certainly don't want to make you do anything against your will."

"You couldn't even if you tried," she said, turning to stare at me.

"So the problem is . . ."

"The problem is that at some point this ride's going to end."

"Just one more abandoned car?"

"Be serious, Nick."

"I am. This is a joyride in a stolen car. I know that. And when I run it out of gas it's all over."

Groaning, she hung her head, staring blankly at the table.

Laughing, I picked up my beer. But I knew what she meant. Right from the start she'd been painfully clear about her intentions, though so far none of that had made much of an impression on how I felt about her.

"Lee? Hello, this is Nick, can you hear me?"

"Unfortunately," she said, sitting up straight to look at me.

"Don't worry." I pushed her wine glass towards her. "I've been tracking the mileage. We've still a lot of gas left in the tank."

"And when it really is empty?"

"Then I'll just hotwire another one."

"Not like this one you won't."

I watched her pick at her food, no doubt thinking about something she'd never share. How odd our conversations always became whenever I tried to get her to talk about her feelings. At first, I'd chalked it up to her natural reluctance to speak about herself, or to her stubbornness, the latter a quality she had in abundance, but later I realized it was simply that she didn't have many such feelings to report. Rather astonishing, really. Not that the details of her life weren't important to her, they were, just that she wasn't obsessed with how she felt about them. And though I often complained about it, that lack of expressiveness, she could be incredibly refreshing to be around. Think about it. To never be burdened by an endless stream of dreary narcissistic reportage about how it felt to be her. I loved that about her. It was like standing in a sunny clearing in the middle of the deep dark woods.

I watched her look up to survey the room, noting how she observed the people sitting at the other tables. Of course, when she realized I was watching her she made a face.

Smiling, I leaned back to watch the cooks in the kitchen trying to keep up. Then our waitress came around to see how we were doing. She mentioned dessert. We told her we were fine, that she might as well bring the check.

"What were you just thinking about?" I asked, knowing the chances were slim she'd tell me.

"About hypnosis, actually. Wondering how it works."

"I'm not so sure it really does," I said, sitting up to lean over the table. "But why were you thinking about that?" She shrugged her shoulders, looking over my head at something across the restaurant. "You think you've been hypnotized? Is that it? Because if you have I don't see how you'd ever really know."

"Ah, you see," she said, dropping her gaze to look at me. "Now I've got you interested."

I laughed and leaned back against the seat. "Well, it is a puzzle."

"What I was wondering is whether it doesn't suggest something odd about our neurophysiology or neuropsychology. How and why we've evolved as we have, brain-wise."

"Because we can be hypnotized?"

"Yes. Why should we even be hypnotizable? What possible purpose could it serve?"

"Or ever served."

"Exactly. Pick any level of analysis you like. Species. Organism. Social being. And then I thought, well, maybe it's the unintentional side effect of something else we're capable of doing that is important. Although I have no idea what that might be."

"It's a design flaw, in other words."

"Or a sign of underutilized neural architecture."

"But maybe it's even odder than that. What if it's not a side effect at all, but some malicious little feature of our mental life meant to function like a trick. A fail-safe means for gaining access to our wills when all else fails. A neurological backdoor we're unable to secure."

"Oh, I like that," she said, grinning at me. "Like some functional relic of the brain that once served a useful purpose, but a purpose now unknown, perhaps even sinister. One that leaves us vulnerable."

I smiled at her. "Yes. Sort of makes you wonder who'd ever need such access."

"Me? Is that what you're implying, because I hardly need a secret neurological backdoor to gain control of you."

"Well, I'm sure I wouldn't know if you had, which is actually quite scary."

"Exactly," she said, patting my hand. "So there's no reason for you to be worried about it."

"What on earth made you think of this?"

This was how it so often was with her. Not being privy to her deliberations, not knowing what went on off-stage, her remarks often seemed to suddenly appear as if by magic out of thin air. It was like having dinner with an idiot savant.

"Thinking about all those areas in our lives where we live as if hypnotized. Then one thing led to another . . . "

"As it so often does with you. But maybe it would be better if you just tried to focus on this nice, quiet little dinner."

"I'm such a total bore. It's a wonder you can stand me."

"Bore?" I asked, staring blankly.

Not responding at first, she watched me as she sipped her wine. And then it was: "Nick?"

"Yes."

"You're certainly looking very relaxed. Are you feeling relaxed?"

"Yes."

"That's right, it feels good to be relaxed, doesn't it?"

I nodded.

"Now, I want you to listen very carefully to what I'm about to tell you. Do you understand?"

"Yes."

"That's so good, because later this evening a lovely young woman will come to you and ask you to do things for her."

"Do things."

"That's right, and you will feel so good when you do. So relaxed."

"I'm relaxed."

"Yes, I know you are, but you'll be even more relaxed when you do as she says. And so very happy."

I stared at her, nodding my head.

"That's right," she said, nodding her head along with me. "It makes you feel good to think about, doesn't it?"

"I feel good."

"And you will feel even better when you do as she says."

"I feel good."

"I know, but later will be even better." She stopped to watch me. "Nick, I'm sensing a bit of resistance. Why don't you just lean back and try to relax. Just listen to what I'm saying."

I leaned back to stare at her.

"That's right," she said, watching me. "So this lovely young woman will tell you what to do, *later*, which is when you'll feel especially good. Much more so than you do right now."

"What will she tell me to do?"

"Let's not worry about that. All you need to know is that you'll desperately want to please her, and that doing so will make you feel so very good."

"I feel good."

She stared at me. "The way you're acting . . . you haven't been hypnotized already, have you?"

"Is this the sort of thing you were wondering about?"

"I feel good," she said in an empty tone of voice, staring at the tabletop.

14

It was early summer when I drove Lee up to the Gold Hill Inn for dinner. It's a lovely drive up Four Mile Canyon, the highway faithfully following the twists and turns of the narrow valley before forsaking it for a series of tight switchbacks. And once you're in Gold Hill itself it's then possible to continue on to the Peak to Peak Highway, drop precipitously down Lickskillet Gully to Lefthand Canyon, or head back to Boulder by way of Sunshine Canyon. At one time the area was laced together by a network of narrow gauge railway lines (The Switzerland Trail), now abandoned roadbeds of soft decomposed granite cutting gently through pine forests and clearings when not hugging narrow ledges high above deep canyons. The rail lines were built to serve the mines in the area, linking together the many small mining towns like Gold Hill that were once scattered throughout that part of Boulder County. By the war most were all but abandoned, killed off by the Depression. Only later did they slowly revive, the early live-free-or-die types giving way to bohemians and hippies who were later bought out by affluent newcomers whose big homes obliterated much of the charm—the story of the West.

"They hear Frankfurt School and immediately assume he's just another Marxist philosopher." We were in the car. She was gesturing angrily with her cigarette as she spoke about Habermas.

"Isn't he?"

"Only by derivation, and much less so than Marcuse or Adorno, and way, way less than Lukács or those French pseudo-Marxists. You know," she said, staring at me, "I gave this committee thing a shot. I really did. But it's hopeless. They're not the least bit interested in what I'm doing."

"What about Podolor?"

"Yeah, well you'll love this," she said, stabbing the air with her cigarette. "He said I should take a look at Derrida."

"So? Everyone else is."

"Have you?"

"I read *Of Grammatology*."

"And?"

"It's fine. It's just not what I'm interested in. Husserl crossed with Heidegger crossed with Saussure crossed with Nietzsche."

"Which is why I don't care for French philosophy. Always recycling dead Germans."

"Yes, so you've told me any number of times."

She never did get that committee formed. I guess the faculty really weren't interested, which is somewhat ironic since in just a few years that sort of thing was all over the journals. But being a philosopher in an institutional setting—which is the only setting in which one can be a philosopher—means being employed to perform certain socially defined actions within the context of a particular social practice. This is a social competency, one philosophers need to master just as much as they need to master the history of their discipline. Implicit, though rarely stated, is their concomitant willingness to become a particular sort of person. As a self-imposed identification with something one is not this knows no bottom. But being a professional philosopher is no different from being a practitioner of any socially defined discipline or profession. Unfortunately, Lee wasn't very good at that sort of thing, or at least not when I knew her.

I pulled over to stop at the top of the ridge. I'd been there before: a lovely spot with a spectacular view that exudes a strong sense of place I never fail to respond to. I was hoping it might help to coax her out of this latest funk. How nice it would be to have a peaceful dinner with no philosophy.

To the north, hidden from view, several rivers run east down steep canyons all the way out to the plains. The canyons themselves are cut into what was once a high plateau, now no more than a series of parallel flat-topped ridges receding into the distance. And looming over them all, the Continental Divide, an unbroken series of bright snowy peaks stretching from the south to the north in a sweeping arc. So I told Lee my story about a similar summer evening when I'd sat there with friends in that very spot watching awestruck as a huge thunderstorm boiled up high overhead into the stratosphere, finally resolving itself into that classic anvil shape as its top was sheared away by the jet stream.

"It was very humid, almost balmy, like a sticky summer evening back East. While over there," I was pointing to the southeast, "these long trains of dark, heavy looking wet clouds just kept coming and coming. Feeding all that moisture and energy into the bottom of the storm cell."

"I love storms like that."

"Then you would have really loved this one. You could feel the energy in the air. It was amazing. Spectacular lightening. Darting back and forth across the sky, cloud to cloud, hitting those ridges over there, but never any thunder, or at least none we heard over here. Same with the rain."

"Too far away."

"Dead quiet, too, not even a breeze, it was eerie as hell. And no shadows, which really made it strange."

"No shadows?"

"All that indirect light from the clouds. It just washed them all away." The cell was massive. It's top towered over us. Like dazzlingly white cauliflower in the late evening sun. While underneath, banks of clouds glowed with every conceivable shade of orange, pink, and purple. The overall effect was a world tinted a soft golden-orange.

"How long did you sit here?"

"Until it got dark. It's still the most intense thunderstorm I've ever seen up here, and that includes the summer I worked up at

Silver Plume."

"And no rain over here. I'm surprised."

"So were we. But they got plenty over there." I was pointing to the north. "A cloudburst, then that massive flash flood I was telling you about. The Big Thompson? Where they found those bodies all the way out on the plains?"

"But how does that happen? Couldn't they see the storm coming?"

"Not when it's miles upstream. The first they knew of it was when the water began to rise. After that, it was just a question of luck whether or not they reached higher ground before that wall of water came roaring down the canyon. Of course, over here we had no idea any of that was happening, but it wasn't a huge surprise to read about it the next morning in the *Denver Post*. We knew we were witnessing something extraordinary."

She put her hand on my shoulder and smiled at me. "Are you really sure you want to leave this all behind some day, because you really do seem to love it." "

"You mean *is there life after Boulder?*" I asked, quoting a common joke around town.

It was true that many people did wonder, and the choices were stark. Stay, and never find the job you desired or deserved. Stay, and never have enough money to buy a house. Stay, and push marriage and family back into your thirties. Always just hanging around as the years slipped away. As for me, leaving when I did was the right choice, one that freed me in so many ways, not the least of which was from having to witness the ugly lurching spasms of growth that devoured the Front Range. Something I would have found too dramatic, too comprehensive and unsettling to bear under any circumstances. This point was driven home for me during my last visit. When I suddenly realized I'd never be back. I saw it everywhere. Boulder was now a place unknown to me. No longer *my* place, but merely a place I'd once believed was—this wasn't change, this was erasure.

"College towns are like that," she said. "At a certain age we bond with where we are and then it feels as if we can never leave. For us, being there has become our natural state, which means it feels unnatural to be anywhere else. So much so, we can't even conceive of it. So we end up telling ourselves a bunch of lies to make our staying seem reasonable. But you," she said, pointing at me, "you really should move on. Being here so long has made you insufferably sentimental."

"Nostalgic. There's a big difference."

"Not the way you talk."

"You know, this used to be such a pleasant place before you obnoxious outsiders started showing up."

"Well, I can hardly speak for them, now, can I? But I certainly know why I'm here. It was all these amazing stories I'd been hearing about these hordes of sentimental graduate students who'd do just about anything for a little kind attention. Wow, was that ever the truth! I mean, really, just look at you. You look like you're about to cry."

"Just trying to maintain my dignity, which is all any man has."

"You don't even have that."

Perfect. An insult. Perhaps we'd have a nice evening after all.

We had a ten-minute wait for our table so we sat outside on the porch. What a delightful evening, warm for that altitude, the air heavily scented with the smell of resinous pines after a hot, sunny day. To entertain her while we waited I told her a story about some friends who used to make banzai runs up the canyon for shooters at the Inn just before closing, roaring up the canyon in a '55 Bel Air with a Vette engine and lots of speed parts, sitting on folding chairs because the car's interior had been stripped, everyone hanging on for dear life as the car careened up the canyon.

"You know," she said, "I often find myself wondering if it's really possible that we both grew up in the same country at the same time."

"Because you didn't know any guys like me while you were growing up? Because I'm sure they were around if you'd been paying attention."

"Yes, and my father would have slammed the door in your face if you'd come sniffing around. Sniff, sniff, sniff," she said, wrinkling her nose. "Following his nose from one woman to the next like some old dog."

"That doesn't mean you wouldn't have snuck out for a little fun."

"Not for that kind of fun."

"Have I ever told you about the girls we knew from that Catholic boarding school that used to be in Boulder?"

"No, and I don't suppose there's anything I can say that will stop you, either."

"I was just going to say that they were more than willing to sneak out, and those were nuns."

"What a recommendation."

Once we were seated the waiter came around with the menus and we kept him there until we'd each ordered a glass of wine.

"What looks good?" I asked as she studied the menu.

"Elk? Is that any good?"

"I don't care if it is, I'm not ordering any."

"No?"

"Have you ever heard an elk bellowing out in the woods in the fall? I just couldn't do it."

"What's he bellowing about?"

"It's rutting season. He's letting all the little girl elks know he's ready."

"Is that how you handle it?"

"Wait a few months and you'll find out."

"What about trout? You don't know anything about their mating practices, do you?"

"Nothing at all."

"Then I'll have the trout." She took a sip of her Sancerre.

"What about you?"

"Pasta."

"No meat?"

"Not tonight."

"But you would eat trout, wouldn't you, if you didn't want pasta?"

"I'm not so sure. I've known some pretty nice trout. It would be hard to eat one."

She laughed and leaned back in her chair. "You're so considerate. Not eating your friends."

"None of us should."

"Nick, before I forget, I've been meaning to ask if there's some special reason you brought me here, not that I don't like it, but I have been wondering."

"Not really, I just like taking you places you're unlikely to find on your own, and I've always liked it up here, so I was pretty sure you would too. Actually, Gold Hill was quite the place back in the Sixties. Things have really calmed down since then."

"You know, it's a funny thing about you," she said, watching me, "but sometimes I get this feeling that there are certain things you're not telling me. Maybe even things you won't tell me."

"Oh?"

"Not about other women. I know I could worm that out of you if I really wanted to. But sometimes, like just now, the way you tell me something makes me wonder if you're not stepping rather carefully."

"Stepping carefully? No, I just don't want to bore you with too much information."

She smiled at me. "Man, are you slippery."

"So why not just ask me what you'd like to know."

"All right. So, about Gold Hill, there was something in the way you just spoke that suggested you were doing a bit of editing, and not just because you thought I'd be bored."

"It was nothing significant. I was just thinking about some friends of mine who used to live up here."

"Where do they live now?"

"In New Mexico. In one of those communes down there. When I can, I like to get down there for a visit."

"Some of your old Naropa buddies?"

"What old Naropa buddies?"

"The ones you've never told me about."

"What about all those things you've never told me? I have a theory about that, by the way, if you'd care to hear it."

"You have a theory about everything," she said, shaking her head.

"So that's a no?"

"That's correct."

"So just keep hammering away and sooner or later I'll slip up and tell you something lurid? Is that about where we're at?"

"How lurid?"

"Gosh, I don't know. How about psychedelics and tantric sex down at the old commune."

"Okay," she said, steepling her fingers under her chin to stare at me. "Now I'm certain there's something you're very cleverly not telling me."

"So ask me again sometime when you're ready to tell me something important about yourself."

After dinner it was a short walk back up the hill to the car. I held her in my arms as I leaned back against the fender. Overhead, the Milky Way was huge and bright, the air so thin and clear the stars barely twinkled.

"I should bring you up here to see the Perseids. At this altitude it's incredible."

"I've never seen a meteor."

"Everyone's seen a meteor."

"Not me. I've always lived in the city where it's too bright."

"That is just so pathetic."

"I've missed out on everything, haven't I?"

15

We took Sunshine Canyon back, for much of the way treated to fleeting glimpses of bright city lights between the dark jagged silhouettes of the pines.

"Teaching's a big part of it," I said. "If that's what you really want to do."

"You keep saying that, but I'll manage."

"Yes, what a satisfying way to spend a few decades."

"Unlike you, still floundering around Boulder selling used cars."

"Used cars? Whatever happened to becoming a cult leader?"

"I was just trying to think of another use for your endless patter."

"Does that mean you want me to be quiet?"

"No, you can talk."

When we came to a switchback I pulled over and stopped. I watched her light a cigarette, then drop her arm out the window, the cigarette's glowing end bobbing up and down as she flicked it between her fingers.

"I know what you're doing," she said, turning to stare at me.

"What? I just thought you might like to talk."

"Talk? Why bother? You never take anything I say seriously anyway, even when it concerns you." I watched her turn away from me to stare out her window. This is how it will end, I thought, in silence. "You know," she said, not looking at me. "If you really wanted me you'd do something about it."

"Become an academic, you mean?"

"You could."

"My goodness, what a disappointment I must be. Unwilling to become the boring clone you so desperately need to impress mommy and daddy."

"You wouldn't have to be boring clone all the time," she said, turning to me with the start of a grin on her face.

"No? Have you ever taken a good look at the guys in our program?"

"I'd rather not."

"Well, those are the idiots you'll be picking from."

She took one more drag on her cigarette before grinding it out in the ashtray. "Nick," she said, smiling at me, "why can't we just leave each other alone?"

"Yes, it was the best sex I ever had, but in the end he never really cared for Habermas so I just moved on."

"You don't care for Habermas," she laughed. "At least that part's true."

16

Friday evenings were often spent at Tom's Tavern. There, we, or friends, would snag a booth and we'd down a few beers, maybe even eat a cheeseburger if we stayed long enough. Tom's, for me, epitomized any number of things about Boulder in those days, as, for that matter, did the arrival of the mall on Pearl Street, which unfortunately changed everything. Then Boulder, like the mall, became a scene, a place to be, and the changes that accompanied that shift in identity weren't always for the better, especially if your income was unable to keep up with escalating rents and housing costs. The way I saw it, Boulder was transformed from an oddly eccentric western college town into just another generic upscale yuppie enclave. VW Microbuses became BMWs. Hipster mountain towns started hosting wine tastings. A bar named Tom's Tavern became, well, Tom's Tavern.

"Based on the infantile stories you two love to tell, it sounds like aimlessly driving around was all you two ever did in high school." This was Lee, explaining with infinite patience to my good friend Jeff the foolish ways of our youth.

"But that's when the most amazing things occur. When you set out just to drive around," he said.

She lit her cigarette, waving it in our direction before sliding the pack across the table to Jeff. He claimed to have quit, but whenever Lee was around he quickly fell back on old ways.

"Go ahead," she said, looking at us. "I know you're both dying to tell me more of your idiotic stories,"

"Not me," Jeff said. "I'd rather get something to eat. How about you, Lee? The usual?"

"My goodness," she said, looking meaningfully in my direction. "A considerate man."

"It doesn't mean he's going to buy you your dinner."

"No," she said, turning to him with a smile. "I imagine they usually offer to feed him."

"Well, yes, they often do invite me home for dinner."

"Don't expect Nick to understand, he's always eaten out."

"I've been invited home for dinner."

"When?"

"Not by you, thank God, since all you can cook is toast."

"Which is why we're here tonight," Jeff said as he stood. "Now, if you two will excuse me, I'm going to go speak to our nice waitress about getting us some dinner."

We watched him walk to the end of the bar where our waitresses stood waiting for a drink order. As we watched they struck up a conversation. Soon she put her hand on his shoulder.

"Does he know her?"

"I doubt it. That's just how women are around him."

"Jealous?"

"Not really, since some of my more memorable girlfriends were best friends of his girlfriends."

"Well he certainly seems to know what he's doing," she said, watching him gesture and say something that made our waitress laugh.

"Sure, for something like that, but not for a long-term relationship."

"Never had one, you mean?"

"No, mostly just lots of short, intense ones."

"Because he's living in a state of perpetual sexual distraction."

"What?"

"There's always someone new and alluring."

"That's not my theory."

"Oh?"

"No. This all stems from his first relationship."

"Because it was his first?"

"Because it seemed most serious."

"Really? Because I thought you were going to say it was the only one that lasted for more than a few weeks."

"I see. So it's duration that's the proper measure for the depth or significance of a relationship?"

"Is there something about the quantitative approach that troubles you?"

"Not necessarily, though in his case I think it's got more to do with something that remains unresolved."

"Still? How long ago are we talking about?"

"High school."

"A significant relationship in high school? That's delusional."

"Like that would make it any less significant."

"Yes, but he's had way more than enough time to sort it all out by now."

"Oh? So I guess that means you don't want to hear about it."

"Like you'd ever be able to *not* tell me."

"I'm able."

"Uh-huh." She watched me sip my beer, then twirl my bottle across the tabletop several times admiring the trail of wet semi-circles in its wake. "Need to go outside for some air," she asked, watching me pluck the menu from behind the napkin dispenser and lay it out flat on the table in front of me.

"It is a bit stuffy in here," I said, turning it over to read the back.

Laughing, she leaned against me and put her arm under mine. "I have to say, it makes me very proud to see you being this brave."

"And resolute."

"Absolutely, and such suffering. But perhaps you should just go ahead and tell me."

"But not because I have to."

"Of course not. So this girlfriend, what was she like?"

"Smart. Pretty. Preferred him, of course, but it all worked out just fine because her pal, who was just as smart and pretty, preferred me."

"But then she broke up with you and you've never gotten over it."

"I got over it."

"So she did!"

"Yes, but it wasn't a break-up, it was more like things just sort of wound down."

"And of course you still have no idea why."

"I thought we were talking about Jeff?"

"So you really don't know. Poor baby," she said, leaning over to kiss my cheek. "I'll have to remind you of this later when you're feeling stronger."

"Are you through?"

"Sorry. So she broke up with Jeff and . . ."

"This was after we got out of high school. She was still in high school. We're a year older. Actually, we were roommates in college."

"All right."

"So we were in our dorm room and Jeff was reading a letter. I thought he looked upset so I asked him what was wrong. He said she'd written him a letter. Apparently, she'd hooked up with some guy we knew in her class."

She turned to watch Jeff at the bar. "What did he do?"

"What could he do?"

"But there's something else, isn't there?"

"No, that's about it."

"I don't mean about Jeff, about you," she said, putting her hand on mine.

"It's nothing. I was just thinking about that summer after my first year at college."

"And?"

"Just something that happened."

"Are you going to tell me? Because we already know you will."

"It's not important. I was just remembering how unhappy

people can be. So I was back home for the summer and this girl I knew who was still in high school came by to see me. This was in the evening. So I went outside and then we took a little drive."

"Oh dear."

"Relax, it wasn't like that."

"Then you must have changed."

"Not that much."

Smiling, she carefully placed her cigarette in the ashtray, then put her hand under my arm to snuggle up against me. "Just teasing. So far as I can tell you haven't changed a bit. Thank God."

"So we drove out to this place we knew."

"You'd taken her there before?"

"Once or twice."

"And?"

"And so we talked."

"Talked? Why didn't make love to her? That's what she wanted you to do."

"No, she just needed someone to talk to. How she had one more year of high school. How much she hated it. Bored, lonely, unsure of what she wanted to do."

"But it still crossed your mind."

"It annoys me when I act like everyone else."

"I know it does, but Jeff would have."

"Yes, but Jeff and I are different. And like I said, nothing like that happened. We were friends. We talked like that all the time."

"Which is why she could tell you things she'd never be able to tell someone like Jeff. Plus, she knew you'd understand what she was feeling."

"My, what a wonderfully sensitive guy."

"But you are, that's why women like to talk to you."

"Right, confide in me, sleep with guys like Jeff."

"Yes, but we're never going to marry them."

"That just makes me feel so much better."

"Why? Talking's not so bad," she said with a grin.

"For who?"

"So that's really all there was to it? Just another sad little girl crying on Nick's shoulder."

"Pretty much."

"Whatever became of her?"

"Married and living out in the suburbs somewhere?"

"Well, I'm not so sure about yours, but that story about Jeff is rather unfortunate. Although," she said, glancing his way, "he's always seemed happy to me."

"Does that mean you do, or you don't, agree with me?"

"About?"

"That he's still suffering the effects of an old emotional snag."

"Snag?"

"Like I am for you."

"I'd hardly call you a snag, though it's true that at times you complicate my life."

"Well, that's easy enough to fix," I said, standing as if I meant to leave.

"Oh?" she said, grinning up at me. "I dare you."

"So you can hook up with Jeff? Because he'd certainly never complicate a woman's life."

"If I do I'll break his heart. Is that what you want to see happen to your old pal?"

"You'd do that?"

"I'd make it my top priority," she said, pointedly looking in his direction.

I looked as well. Yes, she probably could.

"My goodness," she said, staring up at me. "What's our hero to do?"

"You never take anything I say seriously, do you?"

"Of course I do," she said, grabbing my arm. "Now sit down and stop scaring me."

"And I really complicate your life?"

"It's not your fault. I never should have let myself get this involved with you."

"Sorry I'm so adorable."

"I'm not."

"Food's on its way."

I looked up. It was Jeff sitting down.

"Who's your friend?" I asked.

"I have no idea, but she sure is friendly."

"Nick claims this is how women are around you."

He looked at the waitress again. "They do seem to want to be friends."

"She seemed pretty insistent on it," Lee said.

He looked at Lee and smiled. "What's he been telling you?"

"Enough to know he has no idea what women really want."

"He seems to be doing all right."

"Don't mistake getting lucky for knowing what to do."

Yes, that right there might have been the truest thing ever said of me.

17

"What was going on with you last night?" It was the next morning. We were sitting in my sunny kitchen eating the English muffins I'd toasted. "All that business about your life's getting complicated? I was just wondering because you seem a bit down this morning."

"Do I?"

"Just a bit."

"I suppose it's because I made it sound like such a dreadful cliché. *You complicate my life.*"

"It is sort of a cliché."

"I know, which makes me wonder if my whole life hasn't been one. Like it's just some role I've assumed. A ready-made role."

"A standardized version of you? Like anyone would be foolish enough to pick that."

"I'm not so sure we do pick them."

"But if you know it's a role then to some extent you're aware of being a player, and being aware of that changes everything. After that, you're no longer just blindly doing anything. You've even given yourself a little breathing room within which to make some choices."

"Then why does it still feel more like a performance than living a life?"

"Yes, but it's *your* performance."

"I suppose."

"Man, are you all bleak and hopeless this morning."

"Well, yeah. People blindly living their lives, re-enacting stale performances, unaware of the choices they've already made just by living them?"

"But maybe that's wrong. Maybe these are just ordinary people living within the given confines of their available opportunities. Just trying to make do with whatever skills and abilities they posses. And that's really living, not just some role or performance."

"And not even ironically, like us," she said, grinning at me.

"Exactly. So where's the deception? This is just how it is to live a life, everything all messy and chaotic, random, irrational and unenlightened. We might even be tempted to say such lives are unique."

"Really? Each one?"

"Would you rule that out?"

"Probably."

"Too much philosophy," I said, shaking my head. "That's where all this alienation comes from. You've lost yourself in a conceptual haze."

"It's the intellectual's disease."

"Yes, well I prefer things a bit closer to the ground. More concrete. Where the world stubbornly insists on not being me. Resisting me. Not giving a damn about me. It's just life, Lee. You know, the one you're actually living? Something you'd see if bothered to take a look."

"I'm surprised. You rarely bother to be this critical with me anymore."

"Because you're too stubborn to argue with."

"But it's really Habermas, isn't it?"

"Not unless you've only been giving me the good stuff."

"I have been sort of protecting you."

"Then please don't ever let me see the bad stuff, because he's apparently unable to talk about anything without ending up someplace far more complicated and obscure than where he began, especially where it concerns human life."

"He's German. You know, overly systematic? But then you don't care for most contemporary philosophy, anyway."

"Because it's all just conceptual poetics.'

She stared at me. "What does that mean?"

"Like literature, just pitched at a conceptual level. Like poetics because it possesses, or aims at, a certain form of beauty."

"But not truth?"

"Whatever truth it may once have had has been peeled away by the sciences, which is why no one knows what to do with what's left."

"Thus no longer of much importance?"

"Except aesthetically."

She stood and walked to the refrigerator for a bottle of Calistoga. As I waited she twisted the cap off and had a sip. "You do realize you're still doing philosophy even as you question its importance," she said, handing it to me.

"Perhaps, but that hardly makes it an important activity."

"It certainly makes it an unavoidable one, or at least it does for you."

"No, it's avoidable," I said, smiling at her.

I watched her reach for her purse to get a cigarette, crossing her right leg over her left once it was lit, cupping her left elbow in her right hand as the cigarette dangled from her fingers. Bare feet, dark shiny hair slung over her right shoulder, left ear exposed, she looked very tan in her pale yellow t-shirt, her nakedness underneath quite apparent. Was it possible anything could be lovelier? Certainly there'd never be anything I wanted more.

"Are you all right?" She'd noticed my expression, and when I didn't respond she stood and came around to stand behind my chair, cradling my head against her breasts.

"I notice the world, Nick. You don't need to be worried."

"Did you also notice the ash you just dropped on my head?"

"Oops." She laughed as she brushed it off.

I saw her put her cigarette in the ashtray on the counter and then I felt her kiss the top of my head. Reaching under her t-shirt, I moved my hand up her smooth inner thigh. Chuckling, she shifted her leg to accommodate me. Then I stood and turned her so that her butt rested on the edge of the table.

"Nick—"

"Quiet."

I dropped my sweatpants down around my ankles and leaned forward to pull her t-shirt up over her hips. As I did she pulled my head down and kissed me, her mouth wide open. Slowly, she leaned back on the table as I entered her, lying very still as I thrust hard, over and over until I came. Then she wrapped her legs around my lower back and held me. Smiling when she felt me getting hard, taking my hair in her hands and kissing me, thrusting her tongue in my mouth when I began again. Finally, she lay back with her head resting on the table, eyes closed, mouth open, tiny beads of perspiration on her upper lip, each breath in sync with our motion. Suddenly, she opened her eyes to stare at me. Was I supposed to stop? I wasn't sure what she meant. But she pulled me to her, reaching up to put her right hand on my back, pushing me into harder, quicker thrusts.

"Oh, Nick," she gasped, "you have no idea what you're doing to me."

I froze. Staying very still as I felt contraction after contraction. Some short, some deep and intense. Then groaning, she wrapped her arms tightly around my back to whisper in my ear, "Come in me now."

Later, we sat facing one each other in the tub. The water, as she preferred, was very hot.

"You're going to be sore."

"You were huge."

"You didn't seem to mind."

"Umm," she said, sighing as she stretched her right leg out next to me in the tub.

"Do you remember what you said?"

"Why? Are you going to embarrass me?"

"I hope so."

"Can I first have a cigarette? Yes, I know I smoke too much.

I also know how much you hate to see me to smoke in the tub. But I could really use one right now."

I got her purse and handed it to her, then watched her pull out a Bic lighter and a pack of cigarettes. It took forever for her to shake one free and get it lit. It's such a dodge. It's a wonder we don't all smoke.

"All set?" I asked.

"Not really."

"Oh?" I raised my eyebrows.

"Lust? Was that it? Because if it was that means I can't be held accountable for anything I might have said."

"What you said was that I had no idea what I was doing to you."

"Why would I say that? You seemed to know exactly what you were doing to me."

I reached under the water and gave her big toe a tug. "You seemed to know as well. But that's not what you meant."

"You know," she said, frowning at me. "You really are a huge temptation for me."

"That works both ways."

"Doesn't that make you angry?"

"Sometimes."

"Like down in the kitchen?" she said, motioning with her cigarette.

"A bit."

I watched her slump over to stare at the water, the cigarette dangling precariously from the corner of her mouth. Yes, she was stubborn and insistent when it came to getting her way, but what about me? Why couldn't I just acquiesce? Just go along for the ride? More importantly, why did our behavior even need to be like this? Was there was some reason why we couldn't just choose our mood? No? Well then why not just pick the one she wanted? Was there some reason why I shouldn't try to ensure her happiness? No? I looked. I waited. No objection raised its hand.

I sat up straight, inhaled sharply and took stock. Here's what I saw: two piles of clothes and a little puddle of water on the linoleum floor, walls a pleasant yellow, small blue rug on the floor in front of the washbasin, dappled sunlight filling the room, a slice of green from the lawn next door visible through a half-open window. Yes, I could smell freshly cut grass, hear the distant hum of traffic, a car driving by, a nearby motorcycle, water gurgling in the drain, the refrigerator humming downstairs in the kitchen. I looked at Lee, the water lapping at her breasts, one brown knee up out of the water like an island, the toes of her right foot tucked up behind my back next to the smooth edge of the tub, her dark hair hanging down over her shoulders in wet strands. I saw her greenish eyes, wet eyebrows and eyelashes, the small freckles on her nose and cheeks, the texture of her skin, her vitality and how alive she was, so healthy, so complex, so vivid, particular, and discrete. In some sense it was as if I'd never seen her before—or perhaps anything. Such a feast, such sensuousness, such a feeling of carnality in just looking, in just being there, being aware, in just being aware of being there. I watched her smoke, lost in thought though clearly thinking about something of importance. To me? To us? I didn't ask. Perhaps I never would. When she glanced up to look at me I could actually see her pupils focus as she became intrigued by my change in mood.

"So here's the deal," I said. "From now on no more complications. We'll just keep it light like I know you'd prefer. But in return you've got to agree to more sex on tabletops."

I watched as she sat up straight in the tub, as the water ran down around her breasts and into her lap, as she took a long drag on her cigarette and languidly blew a cloud of smoke upwards towards the ceiling. "You see," she said, pointing her cigarette at me, "I was wrong about you. You do know what you're doing to me."

18

It was August when Lee flew back east to see her family, or at least that's what she told me she was doing. The run-up to her trip was very odd, topped off by her insistence that she'd take the shuttle to the airport. She even turned me down when I offered to pick her up upon her return. The whole thing made me very uneasy. So that's how it began, and it was a full two weeks before I saw her again, Saturday night, very late, when I pulled into my driveway and there she was sitting in the shadows on my front porch in one of my old-fashioned metal lawn chairs, legs up, hugging her knees to her chest, bare feet resting on the chair's wide seat. Surprised, I sat there for some time with the engine off watching her through the windshield. There was just something about the way she sat, that, and her sudden reappearance on my front porch in the middle of the night, that gave me pause. Like, look out, this is going to be a stormy night.

I opened the car door and stood. I could smell her cigarette, the engine as well, faintly popping as it cooled. I glanced down the street. As usual, bats were darting in and out of the bright cone of light under the streetlight at the bottom of the hill, while off to the northeast, faint flashes of lightening, the lingering traces of the thunderstorm that had rolled through town earlier in the evening now many miles away across the plains.

I pulled the other metal chair over next to hers and sat and she leaned over to kiss me, then I waited for her to say something, but of course she didn't. To fill the time I listened to the sound of cars coming up Ninth, surprised to find I could hear them long before I saw their headlights bobbing up the hill. Finally, I just turned to watch: calm, no jiggling foot, no tapping finger, just quietly sitting there smoking. I wondered if she'd been upset to find me not at home. Just waiting, sitting there like that. When I reached over to stroke her hair she held my hand.

Then she stood. This was quite sudden, without a word. At first I thought she was leaving, that she was going to walk home, but then she began unbuttoning my jeans. "Not here," I said, trying to stop her, but she just pushed on my chest until I settled back in my chair. Reaching into my pants, she took my penis first in her hand and then her mouth, using her tongue to stroke up and down, then her lips, then deeper as she moved her tongue from side to side. At one point she lifted her head to look at me, holding my penis in her hand as if to show me what she'd done. Then she unzipped her cut-offs and let them and her panties drop to her ankles, stepping out of them to slowly lower herself, straddling me in the chair. Almost immediately, I felt her rippling with excitement, then she groaned, leaning her head on my shoulder as her body shook. It felt as if she might snap me in two as she rhythmically clenched and jerked her body back and forth. "Come on," I said, once she'd relaxed, lifting her off so I could pull on my jeans, gather up her clothing, and unlock the front door. Gently, I pushed her inside. The curtains were up. The room danced with patches of bright light filtered through the gently swaying trees. I could see her clearly, standing there in the middle of the room. She looked lost. "Let's go upstairs," I said, taking her hand. Before she got in my bed she held her arms up over her head for me to remove her t-shirt. How beautiful she was lying naked on my bed, the alternating bands of light and shadow playing across her body.

I took my clothes off to lie beside her. "You missed me," I said.

Smiling, pulling me over on top of her, holding me in her arms, staring into my face, she corrected me. "I missed how you smell."

"Oh, you missed more than that," I said as I began to enter

her.

She stopped me. "Really," she said, playfully sniffing my neck before nibbling at my ear. "You have the most amazingly attractive scent. I'm beginning to think it's addictive."

She sighed and took my penis in her hand, rolling her hips back a bit to make it easier. I watched her eyes as she took me in, as she playfully contracted around me. Not once, not even for a moment, did I see her gaze drift away or her total attention to the moment waver. I don't think she even blinked. It was intensely erotic.

19

By now the sun was a rosy-red glow in the east and we were still awake.

"Let's get out of here," I said.

"Now?"

"Why not? Summer mornings like this are magical. We can sleep later."

She sat up to look out the open widow. "But it's still dark outside, and I'm not so sure I'm through with you."

"You're through, now go get ready."

She wasn't prompt. The sun was already peaking over the horizon by the time I finally got her outside. But the dawn was beautiful: the world vivid in the low-angle light, the shadows deep and dark.

We followed Ninth to Canyon and then over to Broadway, driving slowly, neither of us speaking, unwilling to intrude on the pleasurable solitude of our quiet world. It was while we were waiting to turn right at Broadway that we finally saw another vehicle, a delivery truck that turned east onto Canyon. We could hear it going up through the gears, the sound growing fainter and fainter until it was gone.

We angled off at Thirteenth to drive through the Hill, stopping for a red light at College. It was still very early. There was no one around. When the light changed I glanced up at the Flatirons. They were crimson in the sunrise.

At Baseline we turned right again. Soon we were ascending Flagstaff Mountain, pulling over every now and then to gaze down upon the city.

Closer to the top, I swung out and stopped on the gravel shoulder in the middle of a large switchback. I told her we needed to get out; that I wanted to show her something. Taking her hand, I led her up a faint trail beneath the pines that abruptly emerged into bright sunlight at the edge of a cluster of large boulders. "Up there," I said, pointing, and we clambered up the nearest to sit. There spread out before us was a vast panorama: the city looking like a toy world, everything impossibly small but clearly recognizable, while over there, stretching off as far as the eastern horizon, the high plains.

I watched her fumbling in her bag for a cigarette. "That's your first of the day, isn't it? Are you trying to quit?"

"It's awful."

"I'm sure. But that's big news. Anything else like that you'd care to share?"

"I knew you'd crack," she said, grinning at me.

"I didn't crack."

"Please. You can't stand it when I don't tell you things. But then that makes perfect sense for someone like you. Someone who can hardly stop himself from telling me everything."

"I only ask because you seemed to have something on your mind last night. No, not that," I said, when she reached over to pat my leg.

Looking at me, she squinted into the bright sun. "Aren't you tired?"

"Too tired to talk?"

"Too tired for anything."

"But I thought you said I was addictive."

"No, I said your pheromones were."

"How reassuring. Women like me because of how I smell."

"And because you're a good listener. It's a strange thing," she said, leaning back on her elbows to stare at the sky, "how few men really are."

"Too bad, they're missing out on a lot of great sex."

I leaned back beside her. I felt the coarse texture of the rock, the cool breeze blowing across my face, delicious in the bright sunlight, heavy with the turpentine-like scent of the surrounding pines. I've always liked that spot. I was in high school when I first brought someone there. It hadn't changed much, though what was down below certainly had. I turned to look at her. She was staring off to the east, shading her eyes with her right hand. As always, I wondered what she was thinking.

Neither of us had much to say as we drove back down the mountain. Then back in town I stayed on Baseline until I could turn in at Chautauqua Park, driving halfway around the large circular lawn to park by the dining hall, a large wooden building dating to the 1890s, one both utilitarian and sparse in function and design, in those days functioning mostly as a dining hall for the people who rented the nearby cabins, so it was a bit of a surprise to walk in through the screen doors and find it as busy as it was.

We shuffled through the serving line. I picked scrambled eggs, hash browns, and toast, while Lee chose fruit, and a bagel with cream cheese. We walked around with our trays looking for a place to sit, picking an empty table by the front windows. Conversation was pointless, the big cavernous hall was far too noisy. When she finished she leaned back in her chair sipping her coffee. She'd never been there before. I could see she liked it. When I was ready we walked to a long table and placed our cups, silverware, and plates, in gray plastic tubs. Out through the screen doors, back on the porch, we watched the sprinklers jetting out long arcs of water over the lawn, the air suffused with the delightful odor of wet grass. On the walk back to the car I held her hand.

"Time for naps?" I asked once we were settled in the car.

"Almost. Just let me sit here for a few minutes."

She rolled her window down to rest her arm on the sill. For several minutes she sat like that looking at the park, then she yawned and sat up, stretching her arms out and turning to smile at me.

"It's such a relief to be back."

"Ready to talk?"

"There's not much to tell. As usual, I had a boring time."

"Yes, but last night you seemed upset about something, especially when I first got home. I was just wondering if something happened. You have to admit your behavior was a little strange."

"It was?" She was pretending like she had no idea what I was talking about.

"Just a bit."

"I was just sad."

"About what?"

"That this will be my last semester at CU."

"Oh."

"Nick, please," she said, seeing the stunned look on my face. "You knew this was coming. We've certainly talked about it often enough."

"Ad nauseam."

"So don't lose your sense of humor now," she said, putting her hand on my shoulder. "Not when we need it the most."

And there it was. The burden for maintaining her happiness had been shifted to my shoulders. Not that she was intentionally being manipulative, but she was clearly begging me to do her one last favor. To do for her what she was incapable of doing for herself. Of course I knew I would.

"Sense of humor, huh? Well, I suppose we could always start off with a bit of ridicule."

"Ridicule?"

"Relax," I said, smiling at her. "You know I want to hear all about it. Go on," I said when she hesitated.

"So I flew out and stayed with my family for a few days, then I flew down to Duke to see if I could really make it work."

"Duke? Wow. And?"

"I could."

"What about your Habermas obsession?"

"They liked it. They even offered me some money."

"That must have been flattering."

"Is that so bad?"

"Not at all. So this was your plan right from the start, wasn't it?"

"Not right from the start."

"Just wondering, since you never bothered to share any of this with me."

"I am now."

"But why one more semester here?"

"Nick, I . . ." she stammered, looking absolutely stricken.

"Well," I said, watching her, "I certainly hope you know what you're doing."

"I'd better, since I'm doing it."

"Okay," I said, patting her hand. "I'm sure it will all work out just fine. Plus, this gives you one last chance to store away a few more fond memories. I certainly hope you're paying attention."

"I'm storing them away right now."

"Because the day will come when you're going to need them."

"Oh?" She was grinning at me.

"You know, something pleasant to hang on to once your life's become all barren and empty?"

"Barren and empty? How dreadful. But that's really what you foresee for me?"

"That's certainly how it looks from here."

"I hope you're not referring to a job and tenure, because that will hardly seem all barren and empty."

"Actually, I was thinking more along the lines of an everyday sort of all barren and empty."

Almost laughing, she said, "Well, Nick, I must say, that was very impressive. That took what, three, four, minutes? And now here we are all back to normal. Thank you. I feel much better now."

"You're welcome."

"Seriously, I wasn't sure how you'd take it."

"I hope all that wild sex last night wasn't just to soften me up."

"Soften?"

"I meant soften the blow, and don't say it."

"No, that was authentic. Lust. Unbridled desire. That sort of thing."

"And affection? Love?"

"Yes, even some of that."

She ran her hands through her hair, pushing it back from her face as we drove back around the huge lawn to rejoin Baseline.

"So what did you do while I was gone?" she asked.

"Oh, the usual."

"The usual?" She turned to look at me, her eyes suddenly much more alert. "You know, I can always tell when you're not telling me something."

"I know you think you can."

"Am I wrong?"

"I can live with your unconfirmed hunches."

"They won't be unconfirmed for long if I can get one of your pals to tell me."

"Have you ever done that?"

"No, because you've never been that hard to understand, which is why this attempt to appear mysterious is silly."

"Is it really? Then perhaps you'd care to tell what it was I was doing while you were away."

"No, too close to guessing, which, if you had any sense, you wouldn't want me doing."

"Right. A bluff, just like I thought. But," I said, turning to smile at her, "you're right about guessing. Probably best to avoid that."

"So?"

"I took a quick trip. Just a long weekend, actually."

"To?"

"I was down in New Mexico."

"New Mexico?" she said, sitting back sharply in her seat.

"Camping," I said, patting her knee. "My friends down there? I've told you about them. What a nice place they have up in the mountains? So when I can, I like to get down there for a visit. Do a little camping on their land."

She sat very still. I knew what she wanted to know. What I didn't know was whether she'd give in to her desire to ask. But in the end she didn't, just smiling as she turned to look out her window.

20

It was the second weekend of the fall semester and Lee was dragging me to a party at the house of one of the department's current star graduate students. I didn't want to go, I'd never even met the guy, though I certainly knew the type. You know, the ones who somehow manage to garner more than their fair share of faculty attention and departmental monies. But maybe he deserved it. I was hardly in a position to say otherwise, having by then perfected a state of sublime indifference to all things departmental. Of course, not everyone felt that way.

We parked on Sixth just around the corner from where he shared a duplex with another graduate student I didn't know, but then I insisted on taking the long way around the block. "Only if you quit stalling," she said, tugging my hand, but of course I balked again when we arrived, groaning at the sight of all those people milling around on the lawn and up on the front porch. "Almost there," she said, putting her hand in the middle of my back to give me a shove.

I said hello to the few people I knew as we made our way across the lawn to the porch. I'd brought two six-packs, so once we were inside I made straight for the two large coolers on the flagstone hearth in front of the fireplace. It was while I was bending over dropping the cans into the icy water that a man came up behind me. "You brought Coors?" I twisted around to see. He was tall, with glasses and thick black hair, sort of handsome, actually, but in a soft, plump sort of way, not so much that he was overweight, just kind of pale and unformed looking. I thought he looked very East Coast, very preppy in his chinos and light blue golf shirt, his loafers, no socks, but for all I knew he could have been from Chicago or Seattle. He was holding a bottle of Anchor Steam in his hand.

"I always make a point to bring something I know I'll like," I said, dropping the last of the cans in the water.

"Not a bad idea," he said, nodding his head. He held out his hand. "We haven't met. I'm Mark. This is my place."

I straightened up and wiped my hand on my pants and shook his hand. "No, we haven't. I'm Nick."

He smiled. "I know who you are. You're Lee's man of mystery."

"Well," I said, chuckling. "I suppose that's one way of putting it."

"I see you two have finally met," Lee said, joining us by the fireplace.

I reached into the cooler for a Coors. "Yes, finally," I said, handing it to her.

"I was just telling Nick how all I know about him is that he's your man of mystery."

Laughing, she put her hand on my shoulder. "You must mean it's a mystery why I hang around with him, because there's nothing very mysterious about Nick."

"Oh, I doubt that. Everyone's mysterious in some way."

"Frankly," I said. "I'd like to think I'm mysterious all the way down. Stubbornly remaining non-identical with anything you might happen to say about me."

Stopping with her beer raised halfway to her lips, Lee stared at me. "You're non-identical?"

"Even with that."

"So . . . unknowable?"

"Irreconcilable."

"Ah," Mark said, "now the mystery really deepens."

"Or ends," I said as I popped my beer.

"I can't believe it, you're still in the program?"

"Hey," I said, turning around, "how're you doing?" I paused

to look at Lee. "You two know each other, don't you?"

"Hello, Pam," Lee said, nodding curtly.

"Lee," Pam replied, leaving even more frost in the air.

"Want a beer?" I asked.

She looked at what I was drinking and smiled. "Sure," she said.

Raising his eyebrows, smiling at me, Mark said, "I'm with you. You are mysterious."

"Nick?" Pam said. "What's mysterious about him?" She seemed greatly amused.

"Yes," Lee said, watching her very carefully. "Though it's been suggested that the real mystery is why any woman would want to waste her time with him."

"No reason to take a survey," I said, suddenly feeling nervous.

"I certainly wouldn't," she said, smiling at me as she said it. "Too skinny."

Yes, I'd forgotten how she used to tease me about that, about being thin, but I didn't dare laugh. But Lee couldn't possibly know. We'd been very discrete, and it had been a long time ago. I looked at her. No, this was just another example of her competitiveness. But I sure remembered Pam. What a delightful partner, loudly erotic, so full of fun. There wasn't anything she wasn't up for in bed.

"So . . . Mark," Pam said, smiling wickedly in our direction as she put her hand under his arm. "Let's see this nice apartment."

"Okay," he said, looking quite surprised.

"Well, he's certainly not too skinny," Lee said as we watched them make their way to the kitchen.

"Doesn't matter, he's not her type."

"Oh?" She turned to me with a tight smile. "But then you'd know all about that, wouldn't you?"

"Only what I've heard."

"Which part did she find too skinny?"

"Uh . . ."

"Uh?" she said, grinning at me. "Surely, you can do better

than that."

"Not at the moment."

"Get back to you later?"

"There's certainly no rush."

Rolling her eyes, she took my hand to lead me out through the screen door to the front porch. "You're such an idiot," she said, pulling me down so she could kiss my cheek.

"You really don't think I'm mysterious?"

"You certainly have your secrets," she said, glancing back towards the house. "But you're not mysterious."

"I'm disappointed."

"You know what he really meant by that, don't you?"

"Mark?"

"That the boys in the program can't understand why I spend so much time with you and none with them."

"Yes, why is that?"

"Beats me."

"Seriously?"

"I just like how it feels, being with you."

"That's rather vague."

"Intentionally so."

"Just what sort of philosopher are you?"

"The sort who knows when not to speak."

"Right, unlike me. I get it. So . . . " I said, taking a moment to look around us before turning back to her. "I am still allowed to speak?"

"Occasionally."

"Then I'd like to get out of here for a while."

"I'd rather stay."

"Why? You're not going to miss anything." I wanted to take a walk, enjoy the evening. Dusk, the rapidly cooling air, anyone who bothered to notice knew fall was just a day or two away.

21

An irrigation ditch winds its way through that neighborhood, and wherever it meets a street there's a small concrete bridge with a wide balustrade. The one nearby was old and weathered, its once square corners and sharp edges now rounded and crumbly, but it made for a wonderful place for us to sit with our feet dangling above the swiftly flowing clear water. Next to the ditch, defining the space with their waxy green leaves, grew several large cottonwoods, their old bark thick and gnarly. There was that wonderful odor in the air, the bright smell of water in dry high attitude air mixed with the spicy balsam of the cottonwoods and the dusty scent of dried grasses. Off through the trees to the southwest the Flatirons were already deep in evening's dusk. To me it felt like a very special place.

Lee sat her beer on the balustrade to light a cigarette. Khaki shorts, loose fitting Brown t-shirt; she looked very tan in the evening light. I watched her use her free hand to pull the scrunchie from her hair, letting it cascade down around her face.

"I like your hair like that."

"I was thinking of cutting it."

"I hope you don't. I'm not that into cute."

"It would take a lot more than short hair to make me cute. But I'm surprised to hear you say that. Pam's hair is very short, but maybe you've just grown out of it."

"Out of cute? I have. I now prefer my women somber. No laughs."

"Except at you."

"Yes," I laughed. "I guess that never changes."

She put her cigarette in her mouth and pulled a leg up to her chest. "You know what really bothers people."

"About?"

"About you."

"Is this because of Mark?"

"It's not just Mark."

"Then no, I have no idea what really bothers people. I'm not so sure I even care."

"It's how aloof you seem, which they take to be condescending."

"Just because I'm not interested anymore?"

"That, and because you think they're all idiots."

"Well . . . " I really didn't know what to say.

I watched her finish her cigarette, then flick the butt in the ditch where it was quickly swept away by the rapidly flowing water.

"See how cold it is," I suggested.

Slipping her sandals off, she leaned forward, carefully placing one foot in the gap in the balustrade while gingerly dipping the toes of the other in the water. "It's freezing," she said, rapidly pulling her foot back.

"Because it's snowmelt. You should try tubing in it sometime."

"Freeze your little boy parts?"

"I'm not sure they've ever regained their former size."

"Well," she said, patting my arm. "I've certainly done all I can."

It was such a beautiful evening. The sweet cool air, the deep pervading quiet, I felt like I often had when I was a child. Outside playing all day and now this beautiful summer evening, so intoxicated with it that when my parents called out for me to come inside I pretended not to hear.

"What did you think of Mark?"

"You know," I said, putting my arm over her shoulder, "you never cease to amaze me. How you can think about something so mundane, so utterly banal, so lacking in significance, while sitting here in the midst of all this."

"Sorry," she said, leaning against me as we watched a car drive slowly past, its tires crunching up a gravel driveway, doors slamming, lights coming on in the house.

"You've always been like this, haven't you?" she said, turning to look at me. "So attentive to everything."

I looked down the street to where several streetlights winked at us through the trees. "I certainly was by the time I was a teenager. Like this one beautiful night in March—"

"Out in the countryside drinking beer, driving around listening to the radio?"

"Sorry." I laughed. "You must have heard all my stories by now."

"No, but they do tend to share certain thematic elements. A car. You and your pals aimlessly driving around."

"Drinking."

"Drinking. Followed by a series of amusing anecdotes featuring the antics of drunken, teenage boys. Capped off, of course, by this really *unusual and most amazing event.*"

"I wish you hadn't told me that, because what I was about to tell you does have all those elements. Now it's going to sound hopelessly clichéd, though what's unusual and amazing is how well I remember thinking how much I wanted to remember it."

"Which you apparently have."

"Also how it felt to be standing there in the middle of that open landscape staring up at the moon, the wind swirling around me—"

"Was this before, during, or after you were drunk?"

"During. There were a bunch of us out there, several carloads, in fact, but not by design, we all just happened to be there at the same time. Though that seems rather improbable given how hard it was to find this place. Of course, now it's just another subdivision, but at the time it was still this vast open space surrounding an old lake. That's where we were parked, next to the big earthen dam that backed it up."

"Is it still there?"

"The lake? No. The farmers used it to store the water they brought in from the foothills. Lots of big irrigation ditches out there, or there were. Much bigger than this one," and I gestured to the water flowing beneath us. "Deep, twenty feet across. They were still there when I was a kid. Curving around out there in the countryside. You could tell where they were by the cottonwoods. But those all died when the developers cut off the water."

"So the lake was dry."

"By then it was, but the dam was still there. Thirty feet high or more at midpoint."

"Unusual and amazing?"

"Right. So there was this really big chinook—"

"As there often is."

"In my stories?"

"If it's at night, and you're drunk, then, yeah, the wind is often blowing."

"Okay, but this time it was really blowing."

"Fine with me. It's your story."

"Which meant it wasn't all that cold. But I was still wearing my heavy winter coat, and when I stood up on top of the dam it billowed out behind me like a sail. I thought it was going to pull me off. So I gathered it up and pressed it against my chest. That's when I finally got a chance to have a good look around. It was just so exhilarating, standing there in the middle of that immense landscape . . . under that infinite sky . . . in that spot . . . on that night."

"Not that being drunk had anything to do with it."

"Does that really lessen it any? Since that's how it was for me."

"I suppose not."

"Everything was so clear in the bright moonlight. The dam, the dry lakebed, the people who were there, the high thin clouds racing across the face of the moon, the dark shapes of the mountains to the west. Like I said, it was a significant moment not only for that feeling of being so rooted in a specific time and place, but for my desire to take note of that, or my desire to take note of noting that."

"What does that mean, you felt rooted? And please don't tell me you had to be there."

"Well, language does have its limits."

"Yes, but that doesn't have to mean unknowable."

"No, I think it means unmediated."

"An unmediated experience? No language? No concepts? That sort of thing?"

"That sort of thing."

"The sort of experience one has to live to understand?"

"The *sort* of experience? Like that isn't what life really is."

"Like right now," she said. "As we're sitting here. This is what you're having? Some sort of unmediated experience?"

"Possibly. If I were paying attention to the world around us."

"For instance."

"Well, how about the cottonwoods, can you smell them?"

"Hmm, I think so."

"How the night feels on your skin?"

"Too poetic, but I do feel the cool evening air."

"The water gurgling under the bridge?"

"Hear it, you mean? I do now."

"The leaves rattling in the breeze?"

"Yes."

"The reflections of the streetlights off that car's windshield?"

"I'm noticing."

"What about the grainy texture of the concrete, and how cool it is?"

"Yes," she said, sweeping her hand across the bridge. "It almost feels damp."

"So, did any of that present a problem for you?"

"None at all."

"I only ask because it certainly seems to for a lot of philosophers."

"It does?"

"Things that are hidden or unknowable, mere appearance or representation, in need of disclosure? Yet here it is, the world, right here, right now. So why are you waiting for something else?"

"I'm not," she said, grinning at me. "I'm totally here in this world with you right now."

"No separation between yourself and this world?"

"None, and believe me I've looked."

"No chasms you can point to that need bridging?"

"No bridging needed here."

"What I notice is how hard it is to pull myself away from this natural existence long enough to give these notions even a semblance of sense. The irony, of course, is that we don't need to think about this to live; that such thinking just gets in the way. But we couldn't possibly think about this or anything else if we weren't first living it."

Sliding over next to me, she put her left arm around my shoulders. "Would you like to know what I think? You're an artist."

"Not a philosopher?"

"Not the way you disrespect the primacy of the conceptual."

"The unmediated?"

"A myth."

"I guess that takes care of that."

"Oh? Like we're not rooted in intersubjectivity? Swimming in a sea of socially constructed concepts, meanings, and normativity? Always already active participants in forms of life or lifeworlds?"

"Yes, language, history, culture. Got it. But what if we strip that away, all that sedimented meaning and intentionality, and just look at what's left."

"But is there anything left?"

"Seriously? *Everything* is left. The lives we live, our world. Wow, what a surprise, they've been here all along. So now we can see our engagement for what it really is. See that we're as much a part of this world as anything else. See that our sense of estrangement is due to the intervention of language and conceptual understanding, wrenching us away from this natural engagement."

"Well—"

"And this is what you want to offer up as the real, this pathological sense of estrangement and irreconcilable difference? Is this really the best we can hope for?"

"I'll tell you what I'm hoping for, less poetics and more clarity. Perhaps something less inspired and more conceptual."

"More mediated?"

"Works for me."

"So what did you think of Mark?" she asked, once we were headed back.

"What is it with you two?"

"I was just wondering how he struck you."

"No you weren't. You're just annoyed because he's getting all the attention, which I really don't understand since you'll be gone in a few months."

"I know, what makes me think it will be any different elsewhere."

"It won't."

"Then maybe I need to find something else to do. Like you."

"Like what?"

"I don't know. There must be something."

"Not for you," I said, reaching over and putting my hand on her shoulder.

"But it just seems so pointless," she said, sighing rather hopelessly. "Isn't that your official position?"

"No, my official position is I enjoy philosophy but I have zero interest in teaching it. Your official position, or at least it would be if you stopped being so resentful, is that you do."

"Do you know what he's working on?"

"Lee," I said, stopping to stare at her. "Have you even been listening?"

"Semantic externalism." She was looking at me as if it were impossible to understand why anyone would do such a thing. I, of course, refused to say anything more until we were back.

22

We found it brightly lit, with more people on the lawn than before and several clusters of people scattered about inside, the one in the kitchen being the largest and most boisterous. That's where Lee headed.

What I heard was a lot of derisive talk about one of the lesser lights among the faculty, a guy with so little juice he apparently lacked even one fawning student acolyte. Not surprisingly, that meant he was fair game, not that it mattered to me, but it was interesting to see how the fear of being repeated had gone on holiday, not that being repeated is always such a bad thing, a few well-placed compliments about the faculty can do one a surprising amount of good.

Yes, I suppose my view is a bit jaundiced, but taken en masse few philosophers are truly creative, which means most are camp followers or exegetes. The sad truth is that they haven't arrived at where they now find themselves due to the force of the better argument, as Habermas so quaintly puts it, but in response to the fashions of their age. What little philosophical fluidity they once may have possessed has ebbed away as their interests crystallized in graduate school around some one person, idea, problem, time period, school, trend, topic, or belief. But that's all right, it's hard not to believe, not to follow, not to join in and belong, harder still to be critical all the way down. After all, we all have to stand somewhere, though that somewhere is almost always a place we can't articulate. We just say here I am and leave it at that. As for me, I'd decided just to listen, which in this case was proving to be quite boring.

Desperate to fill the moment, I began a careful examination of the kitchen. Initially, my eyes were drawn to the colorful postcards on the refrigerator. All shiny and bright, held there by magnets, most depicted European destinations, hardly a surprise, European travel being a traditional part of standard issue graduate student identity. But there were two outliers, both of skiers cutting down steep slopes of powder snow, one in Taos, the other Crested Butte. Who was the skier? Looking at Mark I found it hard to believe, but I've always welcomed the suggestion that someone might be more than they appear to be.

Sighing, I looked at the clock over the sink—so bored, so feeling sorry for myself—then towards the door out to the back deck. Pam was staring at me. You know how that is? Out in a public place but at the same time lost in your own little world? Preoccupied by something and then you suddenly realize someone's been watching you? It's that other point of view, their point of view, the one you can so easily imagine, that jerks you back to the here and now. Disconcerted, a bit embarrassed, and of course she'd seen all that, which was why she was smirking at me. Then she pointedly glanced at Lee, raising her eyebrows as if to ask if what she'd heard was true, which, when I shrugged, was immediately followed by a perfect pantomime of incredulous disbelief. Oh yeah, that playfulness was so typical of her, and it awoke in me many pleasant memories, not to mention a little bit of that old affection. So that's how we stood, stealing quick but meaningful glances at one another as the inane conversation swirled around us. And then, finally, a lull in the conversation, which she took as her cue to begin edging her way around the circle of students towards the open doorway at my back. Anticipating her, I stepped forward to give her what little room I could, and as she squeezed past I felt her hands on my shoulders as her breasts brushed slowly across my back. It was the surprise as much as anything that made it so erotic, and, yes, she certainly had my attention, which is why I found myself turning to watch as she crossed the living room to the coolers and bent down to fish out a Diet Coke. Sipping, she turned to grin at me. She knew I'd be watching.

I turned to Lee. "I could use another beer. How about you?"

"No thanks." She was focused on the conversation.

"Are you as bored with this as I am?" Pam asked when I joined her.

"More," I said, reaching for a Coors.

"Well, she certainly doesn't look bored." She was looking over my shoulder towards the kitchen. I glanced back at Lee. No, she didn't. "You know, you two are quite the topic of conversation these days, but until tonight I've had my doubts. Lee's always seemed so cold and remote, but I guess she's got more enthusiasm than I've given her credit for."

"Be nice."

Sipping her Coke, she carefully turned her body so that only I could see her face. Gone was that playfulness of just a moment ago, replaced by a look that was both open and frank. Then she stepped closer, just touching my leg with her hip. She didn't speak, but then she didn't need to, it being about as direct a communicative moment as there could possibly be between a woman and a man.

Pam was very attractive. This in a way Lee was not. A little taller, more feminine in her mannerisms, her figure a bit more womanly. An extrovert with a pretty face and a fair freckled complexion who cut her thick reddish blond hair short and was rarely without an amused look in her gray eyes. She was a most comfortable person to spend the night with.

I could see her amusement at the effect her closeness was having on me, and it's true that I was at least momentarily swamped by any number of intensely erotic memories—bodily memories—of how it was to make love to her, to enter her, to taste her skin, to hear her groan and sigh. Startled by their vividness, I actually recoiled in a mild state of panic, taking a step backwards as if that might break their spell. "Skinny," she said, giving me an affectionate pat on the arm as she moved past me to the front door, holding it open to look back knowing I'd be watching.

"Resisting temptation?" Lee whispered when I rejoined the circle.

"You weren't supposed to notice," I whispered back.

In my absence the conversation had drifted around to Jim, a nice guy I'd known for some time, one of the remaining few who'd been in the program back in my early days. He was defending in a few weeks, something to do with Aristotle and the philosophy of biology, hardly a fashionable topic at any time but he was the scholarly type, the one among us most likely to launch a successful career. I found their subtle denigration amusing considering how many of them would gladly have taken his help in preparing for their comps.

"How long has it been?" a woman I didn't know asked, clearly implying it had been too long, and because she seemed to be looking at me, I said, "Let's see, he was already here when I got here, and that's been what, six years now? Though he had a few detours along the way, like getting married, having a daughter, learning Greek. But he's in great shape," I said, smiling at them. "He may even get a real job." Of course, to that no one had anything to say.

"*Six years*?" someone else asked. "When do you think you'll finish?"

"What? You think that's taking too long?" I said with a laugh. "But you're probably right, which is why I've decided to wrap things up with an MA and be on my way."

I could see them looking at one another, silently putting themselves in my place, trying to imagine what that would be like while vigorously rejecting the notion—quite naively, I thought— that such a time might ever come for them.

"And then what will you do?" It was Mark asking.

"Whatever I want, I guess. Once I figure out what that is."

"Well," Lee said, "if we're going to be talking about getting out of here then I suppose I might as well jump in."

"Oh?" Mark asked.

"Yes. Next semester I'm off to work with Randy Holden at Duke."

Silence. I could have told her it would be an empty gesture. They didn't care. Not really. Or at least not in the sense she was hoping for. The only ones who ever do, the only ones who ever remember, are the ones who leave.

"Lee, that's fantastic," Mark said, politely breaking the silence. Then he looked at me. "So, Nick, what do you think of North Carolina?"

"Not a damn thing."

23

We'd been to see *The Hidden Fortress* at the University Theatre, now we were walking across campus, momentarily pausing to admire the stark silhouettes of the bare trees in the bright moonlight. A network of shallow concrete-lined irrigation ditches crisscrosses that part of campus. Often full of fallen leaves at that time of year, Lee now stood in one kicking up a swirling cloud that soon enveloped her.

"Seriously? Waste a lovely night like this on a party?" I'd been trying to talk her out of going to the Halloween party at my friend Gary's.

"It was your idea," she said, laughing as she stood in the swirling cloud.

"I know."

She brushed the leaves off as she walked up to me. "Do you think the princess marries the old general?"

"I think she wanted to."

"I would."

"She'll be an awfully young widow."

"That's okay. She'll just get another one."

"Another general?"

"It's feudal Japan. They were hardly in short supply."

"You like that idea, don't you? Of multiple husbands."

"Do I?"

"You should, since it's going to take you at least three to get it right."

"Women like her needed a husband, I don't."

"For anything?"

"I can't think of anything a husband can do for me that any man can't."

"You know, it's funny you should say that because that's just how we feel about it. For what we want, who needs a wife. Thus freed from the burdens of matrimony they both got what they wanted and went home alone."

"But where's my snuggle? I get cold at night."

"Tell you what, you learn to cook and you'll get all the snuggles you want."

"Yes, and thank God for electric blankets. Besides, you're the one who'd make an excellent cook."

"Please, if you can cook as good as you—"

"No," she said, jerking my arm to spin me around. "We'd hire a cook."

"Or just continue doing what we do now. Eat out every night."

"Not if we were married. Married people live in the suburbs. Out there it's take-out pizza or McDonalds, which is why it makes far more sense for you to learn to cook."

"Is that what you want? Get married and live out in the suburbs. I'm just wondering, because you seem to have a plan for everything."

"You're just worried it might be you," she said, grinning at me.

"Hardly. Then there's the issue of children. The cute little soccer mom."

"What's with all these questions?" she asked, stopping to stare at me. "And what about you? If there was ever a man who was meant to be married—"

"He wouldn't be me."

"He most certainly would be, and multiple times."

"Just like the princess."

"Uh-huh," she said, taking my arm to lead me up the sidewalk.

24

We paused on the corner in front of The Sink to watch the costumed students trekking down to Pearl Street for the annual Halloween free-for-all.

"We could always go down to the mall instead," I suggested, still looking for a way out.

"Have you ever done that?"

"Dressed-up like an ass? I'd rather just soap a few windows."

"I used to love trick-or-treating when I was a kid, but it was hard because of where we lived. The houses were too far apart," she said, noting my puzzlement. "So my mother drove us into town."

"To the blue-collar neighborhoods?"

"Mostly."

"They did let working-class kids into your part of town?"

"Only to cut the grass."

"That's not how I grew up."

"No one had a lawn to mow over at the trailer park?"

"That's right, make fun, but it was pretty nice for a doublewide. It even had a little sliver of lawn, or it did until we started to drive."

"My, I had no idea you had such authentic working-class roots. Did you have a mullet?"

"A mullet! Hardly. When I was a teenager working-class kids still sported that Fifties look, sort of rockabilly, especially the hoods. Now those guys were scary."

"So were guys with mullets."

"Only if you let one drive. Stoners?" I said when she stared at me. "But hoods were different. You really had to be on your toes when those guys were around. I was at one of their parties once—"

"In high school?"

"In high school, and one of them cornered me. Wasted, belligerent because I was there."

"Why were you there?"

"Because one of the girls who threw the party invited me. Actually, I think it was her house."

"One of your little pals?"

"Not really, I just thought she and her friends were interesting."

"Other than just being women, you mean?"

"They were certainly different from any of the other girls I knew.

"Because of who they hung out with?"

"And eventually married."

"Okay, so I can see why you were there, I mean that's just so blindingly obvious, but what I don't understand is why someone like her would invite someone like you."

"But why shouldn't she?" I smiled at her. "It's this stepping over the line business that's got you so agitated, isn't it? All those secretive, forbidden class barriers you worry about."

"Did you?"

"Ah, I see. Well, you can relax because nothing much ever came of it. Really," I said when she looked disbelieving. "A little teasing around at school. Sneaking out to sit with her in her car while she smoked. It was all pretty innocent."

"Yes, well, as I've learned, your definition of innocent is remarkably unlike anyone else's."

"Like I care what they think."

"Yes, and no doubt you and your little friend weren't bothered much by any of that either, sitting out there in her car innocently doing whatever it was you two were doing."

"It's nothing I wouldn't innocently do for you."

"Don't I know it."

"So he had me up against the wall, all set to kick my ass, when she noticed and came over to distract him long enough for me to slip away."

"So you left?"

"And miss a great party?"

"Come on." She'd heard enough. Taking my arm, she turned me around on the sidewalk and began marching me up Pennsylvania towards Gary's. Along the way we saw glowing jack-o-lanterns, which were everywhere, as were the students, some in costume, all in motion. The night pulsed with the anticipation of things about to happen.

25

The front door was wide open, the little house bursting at the seams with students. Initially, Lee had shown little interest in going, but when she heard that Gary and I used to work together at Tico's there was no stopping her. "Come on, you can do it," she said, tugging on my arm as we stepped around a green plastic tub full of ice chilling a large keg. "Boy, I really hate to see that," I said, nodding at the sorry remains of the smashed jack-o-lantern by the front door. "Move," she said, giving me a hard shove in the middle of my back.

We entered a room hazy with smoke, awash in a sea of white noise, a mix of loud music, shrieks of laughter, and incomprehensible scraps of conversation. But where was Gary? Honestly, I didn't recognize a soul, but then they were all probably in the sciences like Gary and his girlfriend, Helen. Then I heard his voice in the kitchen. "This way," I said to Lee, taking her hand.

He was standing next to the refrigerator talking in a very loud voice to three people I didn't know. Helen was there as well, standing behind him with her arms wrapped around his waist.

"Nick, you came!" he said. "We'd just about given up."

"Yes," Helen said, looking very drunk as she disengaged from Gary to give me a big hug.

I turned to Lee, pulling her into the space in front of me. "Gary, Helen, this is Lee."

Gary took her hand and smiled. "Glad you could make it. Would you like a drink?"

"Do you have any Diet Coke?"

He opened the refrigerator and turned to look at me. "Nothing for me, thanks." I pointed to the front of the house. "Who smashed the pumpkin?"

"Someone smashed my pumpkin?" Helen asked.

"Not a pretty sight."

"Probably one of the engineers," she said disgustedly.

"Next year," Gary said, smiling at her. "No engineers."

"Next year, no party."

"Where's your bathroom?" Lee asked.

Helen pointed. "Down there."

"There?" She was looking uncertainly at the crowded hallway.

"Come on," Helen said, taking her hand.

"I can't believe you invited all these people," I said, watching them disappear into the crowd.

"I'm not so sure I did. But I hope you two can stick around."

"We can, but not for long." I looked around us at the crowd. "Really, Gary, I don't think I recognize anyone."

"I know. And Helen really hates having her life disrupted like this."

"So why do it?"

"Oh? And when has this sort of thing ever bothered you?"

"Never, though now I'm wondering how I ever managed."

He grinned at me. "Guess who I ran into while I was down at Liquor Mart picking up the keg?"

"I have no idea."

"Janice."

"Not the legendary Janice?"

He smiled, nodding his head. "Do you think I should've invited her?"

"No, and I hope you haven't told Helen about her."

"Well . . . "

"You have?"

"I bet you've told Lee a few things you regret."

"Nothing like Janice."

"Yes," he said, smiling at me. "But then that's you, isn't it?

126

Mister no regrets."

"Excuse me," a woman said as she tried to step between us to open the refrigerator.

"Charlotte! Sorry," Gary said, stepping back to open the refrigerator for her.

"Thank you."

He pointed to me. "This is Nick. He's in philosophy. I have no idea why he's here."

"Hello, Nick," she said, shaking my hand. She was very attractive. Very poised.

"He's right, why am I here? There's no one here to talk to but drunk scientists."

"I don't drink," she said, looking at me teasingly.

"Then you must really be at the wrong party."

"Probably." Then assuming a more serious look, she said, "I took a philosophy class once."

"Oh?"

"I hated it."

"It happens. I hated the science classes I had to take when I was an undergraduate."

"Then I guess we don't have much to talk about."

"Yeah, too bad."

"Charlotte's in astrophysics. She's one of Helen's friends."

"Actually," I said, smiling at her, "I liked astronomy. Especially cosmology."

"Actually," she said, "I thought the pre-Socratics were sort of interesting."

"They still are."

She smiled. She was totally charming. Then she found a ginger ale and shut the door.

"Nice to met you, Nick. I'm sorry we didn't have anything to say to each other."

"Me too."

I watched her walk into the living room. "You think the guys ever leave her alone?"

"I seriously doubt it. But if you're interested, ask Helen."

"That's okay."

He looked at me and smiled. "You can't be tired of Lee already?"

"I'm not."

"I wouldn't think so. But then you never mentioned how attractive she is."

"Gary, the world's full of attractive women."

"Like Charlotte?"

"Like Charlotte. It's the intelligent ones who're interesting."

"Which would be Lee?"

"Oh, yeah," I said, raising my eyebrows.

"So why don't you look happier?"

"I'm happy."

"Not much."

"Well, maybe that's because this is her last semester."

"And then what? She's just out of here?"

I shrugged. "She does what she wants."

"Sounds to me like you need to rethink this fascination with intelligent women."

"Find someone like Janice, you mean?"

"She's looking pretty good."

"Did she invite you over for old time's sake?"

"I'm not making that mistake again."

"Look out," I said. "Here they come."

Lee was amused. When she reached us she put her arm around my waist.

"Down there somewhere? Right?" I pointed to the people jamming the hallway.

"Right past that guy with the joint," she said with a laugh.

I looked. Yes, a large man smoking a joint. "Who is that?" I asked, turning to Gary.

He leaned forward to see, then shrugged.

"Pharmacy," Helen said.

When I returned I heard Gary say, "You should ask him about

it," and Lee reply, "Thanks. I will."

"Time to go?" I asked.

26

Outside, Lee turned to look back at the house. "Anything wrong?" I asked.

"I was just wondering if there's anyone in there with even the slightest bit of critical self-awareness."

"As scientists, or as people?"

"Both."

"They're just drunk."

"And arrogant."

"No, just not saddled with all the self-doubts and obsessions that plague philosophers. And they actually do stuff. You know? Which is a wonderful way to build up one's self-confidence."

"Only to become more obtuse."

"They should pay more attention to philosophers? Is that what's bugging you?"

"Nobody pays attention to philosophers."

"Yes, and whose fault is that? And that's not even true. There are any number of people in the humanities these days paying attention to philosophers."

"To *French* philosophers."

"Ah, here we go again, poor old Derrida is about to take another beating."

"You know how you feel about Heidegger? Well, that's just how I feel about Derrida."

"Don't be so sure you know how I feel about Heidegger. After all, there was that one brief moment during the return of the repressed."

She laughed. "The what?"

"When the epigones finally had to face up to that pesky little Nazi interlude, if it's possible to speak of something like that as an interlude. When it seemed like he'd finally fallen from favor. That at last the faddish cult was dead."

"I remember."

"What I remember is thinking this might just be my moment. That soon I too might think things in a Heideggarian manner. Learning from *the philosopher*. Taking that hike up the mountain to his hut."

"Though you never did."

"No, like the cooling morning mists over Todtnauberg, the moment soon dissipated. And we might as well blame your guy Derrida for that as anyone. Leading the apologists in a successful counter-offensive. Heidegger faddishly back in style like at no time since the 1930s."

"So let me see if I've got this straight. What you're really telling me is that you decide what, or who, to study based on its popularity."

"Why would I want to do what everyone else does? That just means I've failed to make a choice. Merely submitting to whatever obscure causality is at work among my peers."

"Which is bad because . . . "

"Because when I do or think the same as everyone else you can bet those actions aren't my own. All I've done is succumb to the efficacy of causal powers, not the suasion of reasons."

"But you never succumb to anything."

"Suasion?"

"Even that."

"So I look around, what do I see?"

"I'm not so sure I want to know."

"Huge phalanxes of philosophy students marching in lockstep, and that's not because they all just happened to make the same decision at the same time. There's a cause for that sort of aggregate behavior. But for me it's a work-around. I see what others do and decide not to, and that's not because I'm stubborn, or not *just* because I'm stubborn, but because I want to remain non-identical. There's enough of that going around already without voluntarily submitting to any more."

"Nick, this is just so bizarre. I don't see how you or anyone else could even have a life based on this way of deciding what to do."

"It's more about what not to do, actually."

"You're not kidding, are you?"

"It's not something I've mapped out as a life strategy, but yeah, for the most part I'm not."

"But won't the most likely result be that you never do anything? Because any action you're likely to perform is always going to be part of some larger whole? Which means you'll always decide not to do it. So I have to wonder when you think you'll be in a position to do anything other than just say no."

"I can at least do what few people do."

"The fewer people the less likely it's the result of hidden causal factors?" She laughed at me. "That's your notion of freedom? Did it ever occur to you that people act alike on the basis of similar reasons? Reasons that stand alone, uncaused by any factor other than other reasons?"

"That's not how causality works. I see that people are behaving in similar or identical ways in similar or identical circumstances. They're even offering up the same explanations for their behavior. Now, it's hardly a stretch to conclude that this is the expression of some hidden causal factor. I see that a number of men are now sporting goatees. Is this just a coincidence that there are now so many? Can one really explain something like that by saying they all just happened to decide to grow them at the same time?"

"Like I said, they act more or less alike on the basis of similar reasons. Now, I'll grant you that they might not be able to sort that all out, but they're still reasons."

"If they don't know the reasons for their actions then they were causes. Reasons are the choices we make. If you don't know why you made one you didn't. Then it was caused, not chosen."

I watched her light a cigarette. "I don't know why I can't work this out," she said as she exhaled. "But once you get going like this I'm never really sure just how seriously I'm supposed to take you. Is he just playing with these ideas? Does he even know the difference?"

"Of course I know."

"Then you must be playing with me. Well, guess what, that makes your actions totally predictable, which, by your logic, makes you the least free person I know. And don't waste your time trying to articulate the reasons for why you do what you do because there aren't any. With you it's self-delusion and deeply entrenched causes all the way down."

"Wow. All the way?"

"Are you really sure you never took that hike up the mountain?"

"Heidegger said this sort of thing?"

"No one said this sort of thing, ever, and for good reason."

"All the more reason I should."

"I've got an idea. When we get back to your place let's see if there isn't something you *are* willing to do."

"Like sex?"

"But surely that falls under your embargo of commonly done activities."

"I don't know. I guess that all depends on how many men you're having sex with."

"Just one, unfortunately, and the wrong one at that."

"And the reason for that is?"

"I'm not sure, but there's certainly no *cause* to."

At Marine Street she paused to drop her cigarette on the ground, then crushed it under her boot. "Gary told me to ask you about someone named Lenny."

"How did that come up?"

"We were talking about Los Angeles and what you did before graduate school."

"Gary doesn't know what I did before graduate school."

"Well, he seems to know about Lenny, whoever he is."

"That's because he met Lenny when he came through here a few years ago."

"So, who is he?"

"Lenny? Mostly, he's an old Marxist."

"Is there any other kind?"

"We met in Los Angeles. We worked together just like Gary and I did. At that bookstore I told you about?"

She nodded. "So what was Gary was driving at?"

"I have no idea, unless he wanted me to tell what else Lenny did other than work in that bookstore."

"Protest marches?"

"No, I think you could safely say that by the time I knew him Lenny was just another disillusioned ex-radical who'd spent too much time up at Berkeley."

"He wasn't going to UCLA, was he?"

"Lenny?" I laughed.

"You're not going to tell me, are you?"

"Sure I am. What would you like to know?"

"So shifty."

"No, you're just not asking the right questions."

"Oh really?" Pulling me close, she put her arms under my jacket to hug my waist, holding me very still. "Nick, what was it you and Lenny did in L.A. you don't want me to know about?"

"There. You see? I knew you could do it."

"Nick!"

"This all started when Lenny lost interest in school, back when he was up at Berkeley, so he started going out to Golden Gate."

"Horse racing?"

"Uh-huh. Just sort of drifted back to old habits. Like what he'd done as a kid growing up back East."

"And then one day he took you."

"Exactly."

As a teenager he'd been part of a bell ringer team with his older cousin Harvey, Lenny being the spotter, Harvey the takeoff man. Of course, by the time I knew him bell ringing was a thing of the past, killed off when the tracks eliminated those few golden moments between the opening of the starting gate and the closing of the tote machines.

"So what Gary wanted me to know was that you spent the bulk of your time in Los Angeles playing the horses."

"He thinks it's a character flaw."

"Is it?"

"I don't think so, but it is interesting."

"Is that what you meant when you said you might move back?"

"I knew I shouldn't have told you."

"Yes, God forbid you'd ever do anything normal."

"Sorry. I certainly don't seem to."

"That's all right," she said, giving me a little kiss. "I gave up on trying to domesticate you a long time ago."

"Did you know there's an official Heidegger hike? Up through the hills above town to his hut? From what I've read it's quite the tourist attraction." This was Lee telling me this while I fumbled around in the dark on my front porch looking for my keys.

"Seriously?"

"Sort of the philosophical equivalent of a pilgrimage to a sacred shrine."

"Wonderful. One more thing I've missed out on."

"Well, like you said, timing's everything."

Then I found my keys and got the door open, flicking on the lights and tossing my coat over a chair as I made my way to the kitchen. "Are you hungry?" I asked, opening the refrigerator. "Because I've got some left-over pizza in here."

Joining me at the refrigerator, she took a Perrier from the shelf and lifted the lid to see.

"What do you think?"

"Maybe just one."

"One?" I was laughing because she'd just taken the biggest piece.

It was amusing, watching her try to get the long triangular end in her mouth. But it was often like that with her, like I was secretly observing the actions of some rare or exotic cat. One more or less unaware of my presence as it focused on the task at hand. Then she smiled at me, making a silly face as she tried to chew the large bite. "Are you sure?" she mumbled, pointing to the box.

"Not after you took the biggest one."

As I ate she leaned forward to watch, her right elbow on the table, her chin cupped in the palm of her hand. "What? You're going to ruin my appetite staring at me like that."

"Mmm," she said, almost purring.

"Okay, what is it? I can see you've got something important you want to tell me."

"No I don't, I'm just observing. But then you always get so worried, like you've got something to hide."

"Maybe I was born with a guilty conscience."

"If so, you've certainly overcome it."

"You know what this makes me feel like, some poor little gerbil staring out through the bars of his cage at a great big cat. We both know something's coming I'm not going to like."

"Gerbil? How about the little boy who stubbornly refuses to do what his parents and teachers want him to. Never choosing to do or be anything popular. Always struggling to escape becoming what he hasn't chosen to be. Not that there isn't some sense to that, that resistance, though I certainly don't believe popularity necessarily entails blind causality. But what I haven't heard you explain is why that's of any importance. So, okay, you won't go along, that part I get, but *why* won't you go along? That's the part that's puzzled me."

"Until now, you mean."

"Shall I tell you?"

I shrugged. "Doesn't matter to me one way or another."

"You see! You're incapable of agreeing. It doesn't even matter what I say. You're just so fearful it might make you into some *thing* over which you have no control. But the truth is even more amazing than that because you don't want to be *any* thing."

"Any thing?" I said with a laugh. "Maybe you just don't realize how hard it is being nothing."

"It does seem to take up most of your time."

"So maybe I should devote all that time and effort to something more practical. Trying to gain control of you, for instance."

"Me? Don't waste your time. In your life I function strictly as a cause."

"I can still say no."

"Like we can't we find a cause for that as well," she said, her eyes bright with amusement.

27

"Did you really soap windows?" It was late. I'd been asleep. Now she was ready to climb back in bed, for some reason ready to chat at 2:30 in the morning.

Rolling over, I looked at her in the dim light. She stood at the edge of the bed, the covers gathered up in a tight bunch in her left hand, hair hanging down around her shoulders, wearing that sloppy t- shirt she liked when she stayed at my place. For the thousandth time I thought about how unselfconscious she was with her natural, unaffected style. If anything, it just made her that much more appealing. But this was so typical of her, picking up a conversation like that right where we'd left it several hours earlier.

"I thought you said you found my tales of misspent youth boring?"

"No, foolish, which is one of the things I like about you." She pulled the blanket back and eased into bed. When she draped her leg over mine her feet were ice cold. "I hope I'm not keeping you up," she said as she snuggled my neck. "But it's your own fault, keeping me awake all night thinking about soaping windows."

"Thought you'd wake me up and we'd go do a few?"

"I might have a few candidates."

"You'd never risk it. Getting into trouble isn't your style. Better to stay here in this warm bed where you're safe from the law. Don't forget, I was a teenager when I soaped those windows. At worst, it would have been a slap on the wrist, but we're a little older now."

"Do hard time?"

"I certainly would, you'd probably get parole or end up marrying the district attorney."

She raised her head to look at me. "Were you ever caught?"

"Lee, it's the middle of the night. Ask me in the morning."

"But you can't just leave me hanging. I'll never get back to sleep."

"Okay, but just the abridged version."

"But not too abridged."

"So . . . this was probably in ninth grade. It was certainly before any of us could drive. We'd been out walking around town all evening. It was cold, too. Much colder than it was tonight, but not freezing, more like crisp, with that fall smell in the air."

"Like tonight."

"Not so much, which is probably why tonight didn't feel all that much like Halloween."

"It didn't feel all that much like Halloween because you're past that slap on the wrist stage."

"I also seem to remember throwing eggs against the side of someone's house, though that seems rather improbable."

"Not to me."

"Not that I doubt my own memories, it's just that I can't come up with any plausible explanation *now* for why I might have done something like that *then*."

"In which case most of our memories are in real jeopardy."

"I also remember there were a lot of us out that night and we kept running into each other. We'd hang out a while, then split off and go our separate ways."

"Aggregate behavior?"

"I suppose, though that was long before I had any real understanding of its significance, and what little I did have was mostly intuitive. I did instinctively avoid it, I know that, but I couldn't have told you why."

"How about why you liked soaping windows?"

"Innate? Though now that I think about it, soaping screens was more satisfying."

"I hope this isn't some of that non-conforming behavior you're so eager to protect."

"I know. I really should feel awful about this."

"Too bad you don't."

"That's not true. There's a bit of remorse in there."

"Where?"

"Somewhere. I'm even feeling a little guilty."

"Guilty enough to drive over there in the morning and apologize?"

"You know, we really should. Maybe when I have a little more time. Though it's unlikely they're still around."

"Now isn't that always the way?" she said, patting my shoulder. "Just when you finally manage to get a guilty conscience it turns out to be too much bother."

I took a look at the clock and yawned. "So . . . had enough for tonight?"

"Enough what? This shameful display of feigned remorse?"

"I'm remorseful about some of it."

"No you're not. You love telling me this stuff."

"But I know I should be. That's got to count for something."

"I don't know what."

"But at the time it just seemed so innocent. Hardly worthy of remorse."

"That just makes no sense at all. So . . . soaping windows?"

"Heading home, we passed an elementary school, all dark except for two brightly lit classrooms in the middle. Well, what the hell? So we started soaping the windows down at one end and worked our way in from there, not stopping until we reached the first of the two classrooms."

"Was anyone in there?"

"The janitor; sweeping the floor with one of those big push brooms. But his back was turned so he didn't see us."

"Like that would've stopped you."

"No, but we were certainly very quiet about it. All these nice big swirls."

"You know, I'm listening for the remorse, but so far I'm not hearing it."

"Just wait. So it was kind of frustrating, expecting him to turn around, but he just kept going back and forth with his broom. Then one of us, and I really don't remember who, tapped on the window with his bar of soap. Okay. Now we had his attention, although he still didn't turn around."

"What did he do?"

"He just sort of went rigid, like we'd really startled him."

"No. You mean he hadn't been expecting you guys to drop by?"

"Not like he probably did the next year. But then he did turn around, looking very confused, like he just couldn't believe what he was seeing. Then all hell broke loose."

She raised her head to look at me. "Are you laughing?"

"Sorry, but I wish you could have seen the look on his face. It was amazing. Like he'd lost his mind: eyes popping out, face beet red. I was transfixed. I'd never seen anyone that angry. Then we realized he was yelling at us. Really yelling. We could hear him through the glass."

"What was he saying?"

"Well . . . " I smiled at her. "Who can say? He seemed a bit incoherent."

"Probably because he wasn't speaking English."

"It really was just the strangest moment, like I was watching something that had nothing to do with me. Though that didn't last for very long because he suddenly flung his broom down and sprinted from the room. It all happened so quickly, we just stood there staring at each other, dumbfounded."

"But you must have realized he was coming after you?"

"It took a moment."

"And you still don't feel sorry for him?"

"No, I do, but at the time I was too busy running away."

"He didn't catch any of you, did he?"

"No, but he came close. So we finally came to our senses and took off across the lawn towards the street. That's when he came crashing out the front doors. Flinging those big heavy metal doors back against the railings with a bang, which is when I turned to look back, just as we reached the sidewalk."

"So he really was close."

"Maybe thirty feet. I have to say, he looked totally crazy, yelling and cursing, charging up the sidewalk right behind us. But you know what's really stupid about all this? We could barely stop laughing long enough to outrun him. It just seemed too funny to fully commit to the notion that we ought to be afraid. Then after thirty or forty yards he just gave up, though he never stopped yelling. I'll never forget it. How we could hear him yelling as we ran up the hill. How it grew fainter and fainter until he stopped, or we just couldn't hear him any longer."

"You sound like that pleases you."

"It was satisfying."

"And then you went home and slept the untroubled sleep of the innocent."

"Lee, tell me the truth, am I a bad person?"

"Well," she said, stretching her body out next to mine, "at times you certainly have been, but not always. Maybe we should just hope it all balances out. Though this innocence thing with you is fascinating."

"Can we be fascinated in the morning? Because I really would like to get back to sleep."

28

"You've got a postcard here from Australia." She'd seen the mailman working the other side of the street and had gone out to get the mail.

"I don't know anyone in Australia."

"Well, it seems you do," she said, sitting on the couch. "Lenny?" she asked, reading the back of the postcard.

"Let me see." There on the front was a photograph of horses and jockeys in bright silks—it was a turf course—and in large red letters across the top: *The Melbourne Cup*, and yes, right there on the back under some text was Lenny's signature.

"His handwriting is terrible. Can you read what he says?"

"He says he's there for the Melbourne Cup and that he likes it there, which I take to mean the racing. He also says it's so easy he just might stay."

"Easy money?"

"Presumably, though nothing's ever truly easy for Lenny, which means this could be big news."

"That's he's finally a winner? Doesn't sound all that significant to me."

"It would if you knew Lenny. He's always pissed off about something. One day it's the trainers. They're all cheats. The next, it's the jockeys intentionally stiffing his mounts. But every day he's angry at that mysterious cabal of insiders who secretly control everything."

"Lefties are always paranoid."

"Well . . . "

"You're not saying any of that's really true?"

"No, but strange things do happen, not that you can tell Lenny that, he's too busy looking for secret clues and cryptic signs, for portents, or anything else that might help him divine their intent."

"Amazing."

"Not really. Not when you consider he's built his whole life around never being a chump."

"How about never being a loser?"

"Same difference. So to avoid being a chump he's got to convince himself that this conspiracy really exists, which just fuels his paranoia."

"It's not his fault he loses, in other words."

"Exactly, which, as a belief, is quite a distraction if you're trying to win a bet. But that's Lenny, the perpetual combatant in a never-ending, all-consuming, guerrilla war against unseen enemies."

"Unless he's finally won his war in Australia."

"He does sound happy."

"Are those numbers?" She was pointing to a scrawl across the bottom written in a minuscule hand to fit the space. "Because that looks like six thousand with a dollar sign."

"He won six thousand dollars?"

"But is that Australian or American?"

"I have no idea, whichever is worth more, I hope. But whichever one it is that's a lot of money for someone like Lenny to win. Maybe he really will be staying."

"Because he's finally a winner?"

"That's no small thing, believe me. In the six months we went to the track together I never saw him win more than a few hundred dollars at any one time, and that only happened once or twice."

"What about you?"

"Me? I was just there for fun."

"So you lost."

"I lost my share, but by the end I was actually up a couple

hundred dollars. What's the postmark on that, by the way?"

"November 8th."

"So when do you suppose they run the Melbourne Cup?"

"In the spring? Spring in Australia, I mean."

"Most likely. So eleven days to get here. And he probably waited a few days to mail it. So that makes it what? Late October? Early November?"

"Presumably." She held the card up to look at it. "Will I get a card like this from you someday?"

"From Australia? I very much doubt it."

"The loser down under?"

"Why do you ask?"

"Because I know how anxious you are to get out of here."

"As are you."

"Yes, but I know what I want to do."

I put my hand on her shoulder and she tucked her legs up and snuggled against me. "Well, unlike you," I said, resting my chin in her hair. "I've never felt the need for a detailed plan to get me from here to there. And unlike Lenny, I trust life. I even enjoy it. I certainly don't believe in unseen forces secretly controlling everything."

"If there are they've certainly overlooked you."

"Think how frustrated they'd be if they hadn't."

"You are frustrating."

"Sorry. I wish there was something I could do to help."

"If only you understood how it's for your own good."

"Not likely."

"You're such a malcontent. Do you suppose you'll ever be truly happy?"

"What about you?"

"Absolutely."

"Then so will I."

"I wonder."

"Well, I certainly intend to try, which is all any of us can do. Even you. Or do you disagree?"

"No, I don't disagree."

"Strikes me, the problem only arises because what we intend is so rarely what happens, which is why it's never a good idea to place all our trust solely in the choices we've made."

"Maybe so, but making choices is still better than not making them."

"Well, time will tell, won't it? But you know what I'd like to do right now? Finish off that Riesling from the other night and take a big nap."

"It is getting awfully close to nap time," she said, yawning.

"Would you like some?"

She looked at the clock. "At 11:30?"

"That bothers you?"

"Okay," she said, sitting up straight. "But just a sip."

"You know, it's a funny thing," I said as I walked into the kitchen, "how I'm only a malcontent when I refuse to do what you want me to. As a personal characteristic it can't run very deep if it can come and go like that."

"No, it's deep. Like bedrock."

"Then what am I when I'm not your malcontent? A conformist? Is that the opposite of a malcontent? Because I'm certainly no conformist." I opened the refrigerator and took out the half-full bottle, pulled the cork and got a glass from the cupboard. "Well?" I asked, walking back into the living room.

"I don't know. Well-behaved? Obedient? Neither of which describes you at any time."

I poured some wine into the glass and handed it to her. "Whoa! I thought you said you only wanted a sip?"

"Just trying to show you what being obedient looks like, in case you've never actually seen it."

"I've seen it, it's just that I'm highly resistant to you authoritarian types."

"Which is what you've been reading about."

"Yes, you and the F-scale."

"I still can't get over this newfound fascination with Adorno."

"It is odd, isn't it?"

"Very. Even odder is someone actually reading *The Authoritarian Personality.*"

"Well, read might be a slight misnomer, but I do have a certain familiarity with it."

"What a scholar."

"Oh? I bet I've come as close as anyone to actually having read the thing."

"Yes, and now here you are the world's preeminent authority on the F-scale."

"Yes, and I also have the proud distinction of possessing the lowest F-scale score ever measured."

"But is that good or bad?"

"It's beyond good or bad."

"Oh, really?"

"A one," I said, holding up one finger. "You can't get a lower score. Not unless you just refuse to answer the questions or go off and live the life of a solitary hermit who refuses to speak to anyone. Of course, someone scoring a one came as a huge shock. The testing company was so worried they flew me out to Chicago for an intensive battery of follow-up tests and in-depth interviews. Actually, I think they were terrified something was wrong with their diagnostic instrument. So when I got there they had me wait in an adjacent room. I could hear them arguing. Something about instrument failure and the role of the superego." I paused to tap her on the shoulder so she would look at me. "This is how serious they were, they insisted I test for the G-scale measure. The G-scale! Can you believe it, that one's so acute they hardly dare to use it. They even have to call in stand-by emergency medical personal just in case, which was a good thing because at one point during the verbal segment one of their examiners fainted. No warning at all, just blam, down she went. But then if anyone was going to faint I thought she'd be the one, the way she'd been staring at me, I think she meant to skew me."

"As I understand it," she said, shaking her head as if she heard a ringing in her ears, "F stands for fascistic, right? Isn't that what you've been telling me? That it's meant to measure the potential fascistic, or anti-democratic, predispositions of certain types of personality structures?"

"A one," I said, again holding up my index finger.

"Yes, a one, how wonderful for you, but—"

"It is wonderful, because it is, as you say, a quantitative measure of authoritarian tendencies."

"Tendencies Adorno believed ran rampant in Americans, with the possible exception of you, of course."

"I'm running rampant in the other direction."

"So what does G stand for?"

"Well, they were pretty secretive when it came to G."

"Really? So they went to all that trouble to measure you but never told you what it was they were measuring?"

"I don't know. Getting along?" I shrugged. "You know how it is with social scientists, maybe even they didn't know."

"Did you also get the lowest score ever for that measure as well?"

"I was never told my score, though there was a lot of talk about statistical outliers. Also the suggestion that I might have been the least cooperative person they'd ever measured."

"Not the most foolish?"

"I don't think it measured that."

"Too bad. Well, you know what?" she said, taking my hand. "I'm really getting very sleepy. Probably close to a ten on the N-scale."

"Nap?"

"Come on."

Upstairs, she flopped on my bed, unbuttoning her jeans and raising her legs for me to pull them off over her white cotton socks. I helped with her sweater, too, before she slid under the covers to lie there watching me with silent, feline-like curiosity.

I sat the wine glass on the dresser. "You drank all the wine."

"Wasn't that the idea?"

"You might have left me a little."

"You can always go downstairs for more."

"And watch you drink it?" I pushed her hip. "Slide over."

She watched me undress, but when I laid down beside her she turned her back. "Oh really?" I said, kissing her neck and pulling her snug against my body.

"Not quite what you had in mind, is it?" she said, making a show of yawning.

"I resent that, the suggestion that I'm some sort of schemer."

"Oh? Getting me full of wine and into your bed in the middle of the afternoon? Well, it worked, except now all I want to do is sleep."

"So don't let me stop you," I said, slowly moving my hand down between her legs, gently wiggling my fingers until she laughed and rolled over.

Smiling, she moved her hand down my chest to touch me, but as she did I rolled over on my stomach. "Fine, do that," she said, pulling her hand out from under me. "But I want you to remember this moment because the day will come when the memory of this will torment you. You and Lenny, two middle-aged losers each with a ton of regrets, just killing time somewhere at a racetrack with nothing to look forward to."

"Yes, and I'll probably be telling him more of my amusing stories about the much younger women I know."

"There won't be any amusing stories if this is how you're going to behave. Look at you," she said, shaking her head. "Here you go to all this trouble, getting a beautiful young woman—"

"Like yourself?"

"Like myself, into your bed in the middle of the afternoon, all cozy and interested, and you want to nap?"

"Have you noticed how much sex we've been having lately?" I asked, rolling over to kiss her.

"Hard not to," she said, smiling a sleepy smile as she reached to hold me.

"Do you think maybe we're trying to store it up?"

"If we are then it's going to be a long winter," she said, running her fingers up and down my penis.

29

Her final day in town was barely a week before Christmas. I'd been dreading it for months but when it finally arrived I was amazed by the sense of relief I felt.

We were away to DIA fairly early, which left us ample time for one last chat as we waited for her plane to board. She told me she'd give me a call once she was settled. She suggested I plan a visit. I smiled, agreeing I should. I told her how surprised I was that she'd let me drive her to the airport. Then I teased her about appearing so anxious to leave. For that she apologized, assuring me that she just wanted to get started at Duke as soon as possible. I nodded, saying I was sure that was it, but as we spoke I couldn't help but be acutely aware of just how carefully she was treading. I suppose she was worried she'd say something to upset me, something that might jeopardize her safe escape. At first I was fine with that, yes, let's do get you out of here without any dramatics, but in the end this one last effort to manage me just felt absurd. Worse, it made me wonder if it hadn't all been absurd. What, if anything, had our life together actually meant? Perhaps it had meant nothing at all. Now here it was just fading away in a haze of inane small talk and self-serving lies. So I asked her: "Lee, once you're living in North Carolina, all settled in, how do you think you'll look back on all this?"

"Nick, please."

"I know, but in a few minutes you'll be gone, as will this one last opportunity to say something meaningful. Who knows, we may never even see each other again."

"That's ridiculous, and I know what you're doing. You're just trying to see if I'll say I'm going to miss you."

"Will you?"

"Yes, in more ways than you'll ever understand. Now, please," she said, staring at me, "don't spoil the moment".

"Seriously? Spoil *this* moment?"

She shook her head. "Fine, here comes the melodrama."

"Better than tragedy."

"So is farce."

"Farce is just melodrama we can laugh at."

"That we *have* to laugh at, you mean."

"Yes, because the joke's on us."

"And in this case?"

"It's just that I'm worried we'll never be able to duplicate what we've had with anyone else."

"I'm not so sure I'd want to," she said with a little laugh.

"Really? Don't you have this awful fear we're unique?"

"Nick—"

"I know, and I'm not saying we've made a mistake, though it makes me uncomfortable to pretend it couldn't be."

"I'm not pretending anything, I just don't see any sense in talking about it."

"I do."

"Of course, you always do."

"I guess what I fear most is that at some point in the future I'll find today's behavior rather astonishing. Did we really believe there was more yet to come? Or why were we so willing to let things just slip through our fingers? My life . . . your life . . . anyone's life . . . flows from a very limited set of unique possibilities. When one's gone it's really gone. I mean it's never going to come back around again, which means our chances for getting it right even once are pretty slim."

"Do you really believe we'll never see each other again?"

"I certainly think it's possible."

"Won't that be sad," she said, snuggling up against me as she put her arm under mine. "We'll talk on the phone, write a few letters, but after a while, less and less. I'll still think of you, of course, but eventually, not as often. Then it will finally come . . . nothing. No longer in touch. No longer aware of each other's lives. Yes, we'll still have our memories, but they'll be of a life that's now empty. I'll wonder at how strange it is to live like that."

Yes, finally, here was the woman I loved. It was a stunning moment. How she spoke to me. I've never forgotten it. Then it was time for her to board her plane. We joined a long line of waiting passengers, and as we waited I put my arm over her shoulders. Then it was her turn. "I know," I said when she turned to stare at me. "I don't know what to say to you either." Smiling at me, she reached for her bag and slung it over her shoulder. One last time she looked at me in that appraising manner, the one I loved so much, before turning to walk up the corridor and disappear. She never did turn to look back.

I hung around to watch them pull her plane back from the gate, then followed its slow progress across the tarmac and up to the far end where it hesitated before thundering down the runway to abruptly angle up in a steep climb.

She was gone. What a strange mood I was in as I walked back to my car. A saudade-like tangled up mix of emptiness, serenity, tranquility, melancholy, regret, nostalgia, anticipation, and loss.

It was a beautiful winter day. Cool and dry, comfortable in the bright sun, the air smelling of oranges, that oddly tangy scent I always associate with Denver winters, while far to the west the jagged teeth of the foothills stood out in stark relief against the snowy white shimmer of the Continental Divide. How cozy and warm my car felt when I sat down; how stale was the smell of her cigarettes. I rolled my window down, letting the cool breeze wash over my face, savoring the moment, in no hurry to get back to Boulder. Later, I started the engine and began backing out. Then I stopped. Opening the door, I looked at the asphalt pavement beneath the car: damp, a narrow white stripe just visible beneath a complex swirl of sand and grit. Reaching for the ashtray, I pulled it from the dash and held it out at arm's length over the pavement, shaking it until it was empty. This time when I looked the asphalt was covered with cigarette butts and ash.

Once out on the highway, I just drove. Other than not wanting to go home I had no idea where I was headed. Eventually, I found myself miles out on east Colfax headed towards downtown. There were Christmas decorations everywhere, looking colorless in the midday sun.

Some years ago I had friends who lived near the intersection of Pennsylvania and Colfax. The apartment they rented was on the ground floor of a large house just across the alley from the Immaculate Conception Cathedral. Sitting on one of the corners of that intersection was a McDonald's, one of those really old ones with red and white tiles, lots of glass windows, and two curving arches. It was roughly thirty-five years later that something familiar caught my eye. I was in the Fraenkel Galley in San Francisco, there to see an exhibit of photographs by Robert Adams, in this instance ones he'd taken in and around the Denver metropolitan area in the early 1970s. Typical of his early work, they're black and white photographs of bleak looking housing developments and the wanton destruction of the Front Range landscape. Of these he once said: "Whatever power there is in the urban pictures is bound to the closeness with which they skirt banality. For a shot to be any good—suggestive of more than just what it is—it has to come perilously near being bad, just a view of stuff." And then down at the end of one of the rows of photos I found an anomaly, a simple shot of a McDonald's restaurant, one that clearly didn't fit with the others, even its placement on the wall suggested its odd-man-out nonconformity. But it's still a great photograph. In some respects it's even a perfect photograph.

He's out with his wife driving around Denver taking photographs. As they drive down Colfax they see a McDonald's. Are you hungry? How about a couple of Cokes and some fries? They pull in and park. That's when he feels it, the rightness of that spot, and it's that rightness which prompts him to take what is, for him, an unusual photograph, unusual in the sense that it's pretty, or just pretty (it's suggestive of nothing but itself). I think of it as a pure photograph. An unmediated response to a place and a moment he just happened upon and was wise enough to capture. And of course I thought I recognized it. It's a summer afternoon. There's just been a brief shower. It's left the parking lot a black sheen with white stripes. We see people hurrying in and out. But what really convinced me was the feeling it evoked. The feeling of how it is *to be* in that spot. That he got just right. There's the sound of heavy traffic and the busy intersection at our back. The air is bursting with the smell of wet asphalt in the hot sun. We step back and stand in the cooling shade of the elms along Pennsylvania. We feel the solidity of the pavement under our feet as we aim the camera. Somatic. Bodily. I know all this. This is that spot.

They kept a price list in a clear plastic sleeve at the reception desk. When I matched the photograph's number with the number on the list I found it was entitled *Colfax Avenue* and cost several thousand dollars. That's where I pulled in and sat drinking a coke and eating some fries on my way home from the airport.

Later that day, late in the afternoon as I came down into Boulder from Rocky Flats, the foothills were jagged pieces of torn paper against a bright golden purple sunset. Long thin gray lenticular clouds sat up on the Divide. A chinook was on the way. No, she wasn't there when I got home. The pain of that made everything feel different. I couldn't wait until it was my turn to leave.

After New Year's I had a chat with my advisor and with his help quickly cobbled together a committee. I wrote about the possibility of an interpretive and critical social science, a tip of the hat to Lee for that. Then it was all over, which left me more with a feeling of finality than of having actually accomplished anything significant. But at least the time passed quickly, working and writing, spending the weekends with Pam. I felt bad about leaving her behind when I moved to L.A. over Memorial Day weekend.

PART TWO

. . . to be a loser is at least to be something, and being
something in this life is what it's all about.

The Bet

30

The first thing you notice about contemporary racetracks is how empty they are. How forlorn they feel, especially the older ones, which were obviously built for better times when the big race days drew throngs of eager bettors. Well, those throngs of eager bettors don't come around any more. Worse, the few who do only make matters worse by clumping together in a relatively small handful of areas scattered about these cavernous facilities. This near fatal decline in on-track attendance is mostly due to the availability of off-track and online betting and to the fact that hardcore gamblers can now take their gambling pleasures elsewhere. In one sense, the loss of these hardcore gamblers hasn't been all that bad since they never loved horse racing anyway, but in another it's been very unfortunate since they also took their money with them. This has made life much more difficult for the real horseplayers. It's a lot easier to get a good price on a horse when the betting pools are awash in foolish money. So the impact of the smart players on prices has become more pronounced, which only serves to drive down prices even more. The fear, of course, is that they will get too low. So low that it will no longer be possible to make a reasonable profit. So winning has become much more competitive, and what was already a hard game has just gotten harder. Nevertheless, there's still plenty of money to be made at the track, and it often surprises me to see who's making it.

I was in the grandstand at Del Mar, this was the old grandstand, that wonderful relic from the 1930s that Bing Crosby and his pals built to give themselves something to do when they came down to stay at their vacation homes in Rancho Santa Fe. I never bought a seat that summer, being much too busy running back and forth from the paddock to the grandstand, convinced that an understanding of a horse's appearance, its body language and behavior, was the key to picking winners. Something I no longer worry about, by the way, though it was a useful stage to work through.

To get a good view of the post parade and finish line I'm standing with a large group of bettors milling around in the grandstand's main aisle. I glance up from my program as the horses come out for the post parade, carefully watching as they parade up the track to my left and then back past the grandstand again on their way out to the backstretch to warm up. What I hope to see is my horse up on her toes, prancing along, neck bowed, body language loudly proclaiming she feels good today. It's when I take a quick look down at my program that I see him, the frail looking old man standing directly in front of me. He is very short. If I wanted to I could easily reach out and pat the top of his head. Somewhere in his eighties, he has the pale translucent skin, sparse white hair, and stooped posture of the elderly. I can see that he's oblivious to his surroundings, totally focused on whatever it is he's doing. Yes, but what is he doing? It's then I realize he's counting money—lots of money. It's in his left hand, a fat wad of one hundred dollar bills, bills he's slowly, methodically, peeling off, one at a time. I surprise myself when I realize I've been silently counting along. One, two, three . . . as he just keeps peeling them off. I look up to see if anyone else has noticed this amazing sight. Fifty guys standing there shoulder to shoulder, any one of whom could easily look down and see what I'm seeing, but no one is looking at anything but the horses. Then we reach a count of fifty: five thousand dollars, all in one hundred dollar bills. I watch him fold them over, again making a big fat wad that he somehow manages to stuff in his left front pants pocket. Of course, by now I'm laughing because there seems to be no end to the ironies I'll be forced to endure at the track. Then, as if to prove my point, he reaches down into his right front pants pocket and pulls out another big fat wad. Again, I watch him peel off fifty one hundred dollar bills. Again, he carefully folds them over and slowly stuffs them back in his pocket. Am I in an altered state? That's sure what it feels like. As if the whole of existence is filled with a here and now that is nothing but this old man and me. I see an old suit shiny with wear, a dull white shirt, and a faded tie. There's nothing else. Then it's over. He turns to walk past me, carefully picking his way through the knot of people to disappear up the ramp into the grandstand where the betting windows are. I find myself following. I no longer care about the horses. I look for him. There he is. He's in line at one of the large transaction windows. Suddenly I feel as if I'm in a huge soap bubble that's just burst. Pop, I'm back in real time standing in the grandstand. No big deal, just a little old man who can't weigh more than 120 pounds walking around with ten thousand dollars in his pockets.

I don't care for luck and I refuse to use it as an excuse or an explanation. That's cheating. It means I've overlooked something or been lazy. That's my official position, anyway, since who knows how I might feel if I ever had any. So when I handicap a race I do all I can to keep the unexpected at bay. I might view this differently, say be more spontaneous in my handicapping, if I were ever in tune with the oddities that constantly crop up during the running of a race. But for me things only go well when I'm able to account for most of what's likely, or unlikely, to occur. Yes, I know I'm ignoring the profits to be gleaned from correctly anticipating when events are about to radically deviate from the norm. But what choice do I have? Such events will always be beyond the normal range of my predictive powers, which stands in stark contrast to guys I know who find the track an endless banquet of winning bets made on long shots, informed hunches, or just a feeling they had about a particular horse or race. I do envy how they nonchalantly stand around waiting to cash. Well, not for me. No shortcuts. No expectations of beneficial spur of the moment decisions. No luck.

An early glimpse of this came one sleepy mid-week afternoon at Hollywood Park. In those days I rarely had much betting money so there were often long stretches during the day when I felt free to wander enjoyably about the paddock and grandstand. That's how I found myself down towards the end of the grandstand near one of the entrances to the Turf Club, and not wanting to pay the few dollars it cost to crossover I decided to stay where I was to watch the next race. Waiting, I leaned against the railing above the top row of seats to survey the handful of people in my vicinity. One was a man about my age standing at one of the large transaction windows with an attractive looking younger woman. There wasn't much more to it than that, I just noted his presence before turning to watch the gate attendants loading the horses into the starting gate. It was just before the race began that I glanced over my shoulder. Now he was leaning on the counter chatting with the teller. Then I heard the bell and turned to watch the horses sweep past into the clubhouse turn, watching as they began to sort themselves out on the backstretch. Taking another quick peek over my shoulder, I was surprised to see that neither of them seemed to be paying any attention to the race. But then maybe he hadn't made a bet. I tried to concentrate on the horses as they entered the far turn, but something kept nagging at me. Then I realized what I'd seen. He was filling out a form. Well, the only form one ever fills out at the track, and this typically at one of the large transaction windows, is an IRS W2-G. I'd never even been close to a *signer*, not in those days, that was just something to aspire to, but there he was filling one out before the race was even over. For the rest of the race I keep turning to see if they would ever pay any attention to what was happening out on the track. No, only as the horses reached the finish line did they bother to look up. Smiling, the teller nodding his head, they then resumed their conversation. I didn't know it then, but that was never going to be my style.

Betting at the track is like other forms of investing—the stock market, commercial real estate, venture capitalism—it takes money to make money. Yes, the typical bettor may occasionally hit a hefty winner with a small bet, but the serious money is most often won by making large bets in the exotic pools: pick threes, fours, and sixes, exactas, trifectas, and superfectas. Played well, these are expensive bets to make, which is why it's foolish to play them half-heartedly, otherwise stick with win, place, and show. But it's very tempting, since there's little fun and rarely any significant profit to be found in grinding it out day after day with low priced winners. It's this which drives the serious bettors to seek more value for their betting dollars, and since doing so isn't cheap, such well-funded professionals gain a huge edge over less well-funded players.

For a new horseplayer the way the big players bet, not to mention the amounts they bet, is a revelation. For example, while still more or less a neophyte I took a trip to Florida, which is how I found myself at Gulfstream one afternoon standing in line at one of the autototes, voucher in hand waiting to bet a few dollars on a race. The line was long but in no hurry. In that lull that falls over the track after people have cashed their tickets from the previous race but before the betting picks up for the next. Finally I was second in line, waiting as I took one last look at *The Daily Racing Form*, but the guy in front of me seemed to be taking much longer than normal. Wondering why, I took a peek over his shoulder, mostly expecting to see he'd screwed up. No. The first thing I noticed, right up there in the upper right hand corner of the computer screen, was the balance on his voucher. It was, at that point, just over twelve thousand dollars. I say at that point because it was rapidly declining as he played $50 trifecta part-wheels, $200 exactas, $100 multiple pick-three tickets, even hundreds to win, all ratcheting that total down like an odometer spinning wildly backwards. I have no idea how much he'd already bet, but in the brief time I watched he ran that total down several thousand dollars. Then he turned, clutching the small wad of tickets in his hand that represented the bets he'd just made, though what was most intriguing to me was the one slip that represented the remaining balance in his account. I wondered what would happen if he dropped that one little slip of paper. There was nothing to stop someone from running it through the machines or taking it to a teller and cashing-out. Amazing nonchalance.

I vividly remember the first bet I ever made: the daily double at Hollywood Park. I won the first leg with ease, betting on three different horses, but I'd singled in the second, a six furlong sprint for twelve thousand dollar claimers. I was nervous about it, but Bill Spawr trained the horse and its jockey was Laffit Pincay, a fairly lethal combination in those days. I didn't expect to see my horse on the lead, even with my rudimentary handicapping skills I knew he'd prefer mid-pack, but I did hope to see him emerge at the top of the stretch to take the lead. Unfortunately, that's not what happened, but he was an up-close and slowly gaining second, and twenty yards from the finish he and the lead horse were neck and neck doing that head-bob thing where one will win and the other lose depending upon whose head is going down instead of up at the wire. I should add that even though I was tightly focused on the race I was still very aware of the screaming and yelling of the crowd around me, and it did seem to be taking forever for the two horses to reach the finish line, but then racetrack time, as I would soon learn, is often like that. So it was then, just as they reached the wire, that my horse seemed to lunge forward, which proved to be just enough for it to win by a nose. My horse! I was thrilled, though it was bedlam under the grandstand; so many angry faces. "Pincay, you son of a bitch!" "Motherfuckin' Pincay!" I was stunned. I couldn't figure it out. Then I noticed that not everyone was yelling. That a few even seemed serene, with smiles on their faces that made them look somewhat foolish or simple-minded. It was, I suddenly realized, the very smile that was on my face.

What *I* saw as the two horses hit the wire was Pincay lose his balance in the stirrups and fall forward onto the neck of his horse, which had the fortuitous effect of forcing its head down at just the right moment. I thought he'd been lucky to hang on, luckier still to win, but perhaps not. There was a man standing behind me muttering to himself, and when the results became official he tore up his tickets and threw them angrily to the ground at his feet. "Never, ever, bet against that fuckin' Pincay when he's on a long shot," he said. I pocketed over eighty bucks when I cashed that six dollar ticket. I remember standing there counting my money, thinking how easy this game was, fantasizing about all the money I was going to win, which is just one more reason why I hate beginner's luck.

You may not think so, but handicapping constitutes a discipline, and like any discipline it comes with its own complicated history, traditions, and literature, not to mention differing methods, schools of thought, styles, and strategies, all of which have their own fanatical adherents. Also like any discipline, it has its share of towering figures, who, if not necessarily tormented geniuses, are often brilliant, iconoclastic, and hugely eccentric. Ask the cognoscenti and you'll find votes for the likes of Andy Beyer, Len Ragozin, Mark Cramer, or Steve Crist, just to name the most well known, though for me it will always be Howard Sartin.

The Sartin Methodology, as it is called, is a variant of pace handicapping, which I won't explain here other than to say it's all about how the pace characteristics of the horses in today's race match up with one another. Jockey, trainer, track bias, class level, these are "other" factors, secondary when it comes to understanding what a horse will or will not do today vis-à-vis his or her fellow entrants. Sartin added to this view of handicapping a number of mathematical measures for charting the pace characteristics of a horse's performance, and these became increasingly esoteric as his earlier insights were taken up by mainstream handicappers, this in large part due to the impact of his most literate and influential acolyte, Tom Brohammer.

I used to drive up to Las Vegas to stay at the San Remo Hotel, a then frayed-around-the-edges déclassé dump (now the Hooters Casino Hotel), for Sartin's conferences, led by Sartin, Brohammer, and Jimmy "The Hat" Bradshaw. This was the old Las Vegas, not too long after the major casinos finally began letting the Sartin crew into their sports books. I know, ancient history, but prior to the arrival of the pari-mutuel pools all bets were made against the house and not only did the house not have to take your action they didn't even have to let you in the front door. The Mirage was there by then, sleek and new, but many of the older casinos still remained, yet to be felled like some old growth forest. There's absolutely no sentimentality in Las Vegas, then or now, though there was, and I know this sounds absurd, a sense of propriety or proportion that can't be found in today's Vegas. I'm greatly amused by the people who hold up Las Vegas as an example of excess since the excesses they refer to are so mundane—drinking, gambling, a little recreational prostitution—and trivial in comparison to the wretched excesses of today's highly marketed "Las Vegas experience."

The conferences were always a mix of learning how best to make use of Sartin's latest computer program, refreshers on the few handicapping fundamentals he was willing to tolerate, and inspirational lectures from the man himself. In Sartin's view, becoming a successful, that is to say, profitable, horseplayer, wasn't that difficult. (He despised the connotations of the word *play* when it came to handicapping and betting, by the way.) What was difficult was mastering all the psychological impediments we place in our path to that success. In this he was like any practicing psychologist (which he was), having little sympathy for those who refuse to make an effort to help themselves, or, in this particular case, refuse to become winners using his methodology.

I was always amazed by how hard it seemed for so many

people. The Sartin Methodology just isn't that difficult to understand, though as I've already noted he was well aware of the difficulties most people faced in consistently putting it into practice. The sad truth is that most bettors will fail serially, often ultimately, and often in the gaudiest and most perverse manner imaginable. Just ask your typical bettor about this and they will soon reveal a deep cache of woulda—coulda—shoulda stories that would break your heart if they took place in any other area of life. Knowing exactly what they ought to do, for some inexplicable reason they went ahead and did otherwise. Knowing it was a ridiculous risk, they went right ahead and took it. Knowing it couldn't possibly succeed, they attempted it anyway. Knowing it flew in the face of everything they'd learned to be true or at least probable, they still felt that just this once it would turn out differently. Clearly understanding all the various alternatives, they again picked the wrong one, and again for the very same wrong reasons. A pitiful litany of tales in which the protagonist should have known better, could have done otherwise, but for some obscure reason just went ahead and did it anyway. It's always the same refrain: if only . . . if only . . . if only. And it's not like they can't learn because they can, it's just that they can not not do what they do. At some point it's as if their better nature just falls away as they lose control over what is a mildly self-destructive behavioral pattern. But it would be a serious mistake to characterize these people as compulsive gamblers, that's not at all what's going on here, far better to think of them as compulsive losers. What an odd thing that is.

Sartin would tell the tale of how he, a practicing psychologist, became involved in handicapping and betting. It began with a therapy he devised for a group of truck drivers who'd been convicted on misdemeanor or felony charges springing, or so it was maintained, from their gambling. So in lieu of jail time each was offered the option of participating in some form of therapeutic intervention into what legal and psychological authorities had judged to be a pathological disease—their compulsive gambling. But what Sartin came to conclude was that his truckers had been misdiagnosed. Not only were they not compulsive or pathological gamblers, their difficulties actually stemmed from something far simpler—they were losers. In that at least they were lucky because treatments predicated upon the view that gambling is a mental disorder or form of addictive behavior have abysmally low cure rates. It was in this sense that he used to maintain that there's nothing wrong with gambling that winning won't cure. His more radical claim was that even those who have been legitimately diagnosed as compulsive or pathological gamblers suddenly seem far less problematic in our culture when they're winning. Well, is he wrong?

So Sartin set out to cure his truck drivers of their losing by making them winners, and it was in betting on horse races that he found a type of gambling that offered them a reasonable chance of success. The catch, however, was that this success was predicated upon their adherence to his strict rules for handicapping and betting. And though the rules were often byzantine, hedged, and in need of artful interpretation, from a therapeutic point of it couldn't have been simpler: just follow the rules and you'll be a winner.

In the early days his truckers rarely won much money, but win they did, and over time their betting began to show a stable and predictable profit. From a therapeutic point of view it looked like a success: not only did they now know how to win, they also knew how to continue to win, which meant they no longer had to suffer the stigma of being losers. But, and here was the most interesting part for me, Sartin soon found that some of his patients simply refused to embrace their new found winner's identity. Was it possible they had too much tied up in being losers to throw it all away over something like winning? In fact, some did shift their losing over to other areas of their lives where it was more sustainable, which led me to wonder if it might not have been kinder to leave their losing alone, confined as it was just to gambling and not spread about like that, though I suspect in most cases it already was. It was in this context that I once heard him say that no matter how inexplicable it may appear to others, people do what they do because it gets them what they truly desire—even if that's losing. I would put it this way: to be a loser is at least to be something, and being something in this life is what it's all about.

So from this the methodology grew, but Sartin never left behind his practitioner's point of view, and for good reason. I can attest to the fact that normal bettors, or normal losers, reacted to their successes by speaking of themselves within the psychological discourse of personal growth and self-help. Never, and I mean never, did I hear them speak of themselves or what they'd accomplished within the discourse of the gambler or horseplayer. Making money was fine, but it was the fact that they'd mastered themselves, perhaps even taken on a new identity or found a bit of self-worth in their accomplishments, that got them excited. I think the conclusion Sartin drew from this, or perhaps it was his working hypothesis all along, was that the act of winning was more about attitude than the mechanics of his methodology. Whatever, people like me who weren't losers picked up the mechanics and moved on.

So I'd sit at the back of the conference room at the San Remo and watch the show. The way it went, when Sartin ran down he'd turn it over to Brohammer, who, with the air of the patient and loyal man that he is, would bring it all together, smoothing any troubled waters. Bradshaw was another story. He's a short, wiry little dude in a big cowboy hat with the twang of Oklahoma in his voice. To me, he's always looked like a guy who could rob a bank, and I'm sure the way he looked and spoke led many to underestimate his considerable skills as a horseplayer. Unfortunate, too, was the fact that at these seminars his native and unpolished shrewdness stood in a very unflattering light next to Brohammer's urbane scholasticism. But then, after endless questions and pleas for clarification, the meetings would finally adjourn, giving everyone the chance to make a foray up the Strip to pillage the sports books, putting theory into practice in an immediate and unambiguous fashion hard to come by in other walks of life. The conferees would listen and wonder: "Does this shit really work?" Well, they would know the answer to that question in just a few minutes.

31

I was in Las Vegas with an exceptional woman, there to attend the second of the *Horseplayer's Expos*. All the big names in handicapping were there to give presentations or to serve on panels with topics like playing the pick six, early speed, trainer patterns, and so on. Because the woman I was with was not attending the conference we parted ways at registration table, but I later ran into her in one of the sessions. She laughed, telling me that a well-known trip-handicapper had talked her into registering and that she was having the time of her life. She was, by the way, the best natural horseplayer I've ever known. To win she rarely needed to do more than note the probable pace, which horses would lead, press, or close, and then study them in the paddock and post parade. She also displayed an admirable mix of quick certitude with no second-guessing that was both a personal and professional trait. Then once her mind was made up off she went to make her bets while I remained lost in my agonizing analyses. And when she did win, which was often, it was rarely less then my grind-it-out small change. But she took it all in stride, winning or losing, never succumbing to bravado or tormenting self-doubt.

Only once did I see her down, and that was the day a big one got away. She watched the post parade, took a look at *The Daily Racing Form* and then her wad of bills. She was short. She wouldn't be able to cover all the trifecta combinations she wanted to play. She never asked to borrow money, I certainly wouldn't have dared to offer her any, but I did suggest she pay a visit to one the of the many ATM machines in the concourse. I know she considered it, but then, like the person she is, one not afflicted with racetrack superstitions, she decided just to play what she could afford. I urged her to reconsider. I knew what would happen to me if I did something like that, one of Bradshaw's *ugly horses* would somehow sneak in there and spoil it. Then I saw the shocked look on her face when that's just what happened, that damn horse somehow getting in there for show and sending her trifecta up in smoke. It paid quite a lot, too. Well, I just left her alone, and she hardly spoke until after the next race. But it wasn't the money—believe me, she's got plenty—rather it was that wholly unexpected confrontation with a particularly perverse strain of fate. That gratuitous slap in the face she was forced to endure on that lovely sunny afternoon. No, of course she didn't deserve it, that's what she objected to, but then none of us ever does.

But I've seen far worse. One of the worst, or so I surmise, not being privy to any of the details, happened one stunningly gorgeous summer evening in Encinitas, California. I'd spent the day at Del Mar with a group of friends. Now, after the races, two women and I were having dinner at Piret's, an excellent French-style bistro that used to be in a small shopping center along Highway One. That summer everyone knew Andy Beyer was in town forgoing his usual summer at Saratoga to play the races at racing's West Coast equivalent. Well, what I'd heard was that so far things had not gone well, something I found far too easy to believe given Del Mar's legendary difficulty. As for me, I was just hoping to get out alive, by then reduced to chasing a few big scores to tide me over until racing moved back up north to Hollywood Park and Santa Anita. But Beyer is famous for the big score, for not being one to shy away from making those really big bets it takes to hit a home run. So when I say I'd heard that things had not gone well I think it's safe to say that the monetary side of that would have stunned most of us into numb silence, if not also a pointless, blind rage. Far worse, or at least it certainly would have been for someone like me, was the collateral damage that would have entailed for my belief that I was a smart horseplayer. I can tell you from personal experience, it takes a long time to recover from that sort of pummeling.

We came in, were seated, and then one of my friends said to me, "Isn't that Andy Beyer?" I turned. "That's him," I said. He was sitting a few tables away with a woman and another couple. We ordered some wine, looked at the menus, and then my two friends began to laugh. "What?" I asked. "It's Beyer," they said. "When we tell you to, turn around and look." A few minutes later they did. It was his left eyebrow, that's what I noticed first, how it twitched. But then I realized it wasn't just his left eyebrow that twitched, it was the whole left side of his face. One moment he seemed just fine, nothing out of the ordinary, but the next, and this without any warning change in his manner or speech, all hell broke loose. He seemed quite calm, they all did, sitting there conversing, the most normal looking scene imaginable, yet all the while the left side of his face was periodically and unpredictably erupting in a flurry of tics, twitches, and squints. "Now *that's* losing!" I said, turning to my friends. It wasn't too long after that I heard he'd retreated back East to where he better understood what was going on. Many years later I heard him joke that those bitter days had tempted him to write another book: *Del Mar on $1500 a Day*. No, I didn't feel sorry for him, that's just how it goes in his profession. But I will qualify that by saying it takes years of losing—an odd sort of on-the-job-training—to get to the point where one can play through a losing streak of more than trivial duration. The winning isn't hard to take, but the losing can suck the life out of you. One needs to stay in shape.

32

The natural, whose name is Barbara, invited me to accompany her to Boston where she was to attend an oncology conference. I wanted to go, but that meant missing a week at Del Mar, so we struck a bargain, we'd visit Saratoga on the way. After all, one week more or less wasn't going to make that much difference, and I do love Saratoga. So we flew into Albany and Barb rented a car I drove.

Saratoga was muggy, the air thick with humidity, but it made for a wonderfully soporific, sleepy New England summer afternoon. We found our motel, got checked in, and drove over to the track. Not there for any serious betting, we felt free to take our time strolling about the old grandstand, then out to the cooling shade under the trees in the paddock, and whether it was that slow pace, the weather, or my lack of concern for the handicapping, it made for a very relaxing day. It's nice to have a day like that. One that reminds us of why we love horse racing. But of course Barb eventually found a horse in the paddock she liked, so after *riders up* we trailed the crowd back to the grandstand to watch the horses on the backstretch. Or at least we tried to, since even with binoculars the air was too opaque to see very much. Nevertheless, Barb was soon convinced that what she'd seen was correct. Well, why not? I certainly trusted her judgment and I certainly liked the odds (11-1), so just for fun I gave her fifty dollars to bet to win. When she returned she was all smiles.

"What's so amusing?"

"While I was waiting in line I got into this conversation with the two guys in front of me. They were arguing about exacta and trifecta combinations, so I warned them not to overlook my horse."

"What did they say?"

"Plenty, but not to me." Then she laughed. "So I said you'll be sorry."

"Could you see what they bet?"

"They showed me. One did use him on the bottom in a couple of exactas, but the other guy ignored him completely. Exactas, trifectas . . . nothing."

"You're certainly sure of yourself today."

"Aren't you?" she said, handing me my betting slip.

"That all depends on what you bet." I held out my hand. "Let's see." Okay, one hundred dollars to win, exactas of varying amounts keyed to her horse. So far so good. Less good, several clearly impossible trifectas and one of those crazy ten cent superfecta stabs-in-the-dark.

"What's wrong?" she asked when I shook my head.

"Nothing—for you. But you always do this to me. Make the kinds of bets that tempt the gods to enter into my affairs and muck things up with ironic outcomes."

"So don't bet with me."

"No, for some reason I actually feel protected when I do. Maybe it's because all those ironic mishaps that plague me rarely happen to you. It's like if I can just keep my head down and maintain my anonymity I'll be able to slip unnoticed into the winner's circle in your wake. There once again to be awestruck by how the gods favor you."

"I thought you were awestruck by how smart I am?"

"And that."

Her horse, the eventual winner in an eleven horse field, went off at 9-1. The favorite was second and the exacta paid $58. As we waited in line to cash our tickets I noticed her watching the lines at the large transaction windows. No, they weren't there, but if they had been I'm sure she would have walked over to show them her winning tickets. Not that she wanted to brag, but she'd certainly enjoy pointing out how her picks had been smarter than theirs. How foolish they'd been to presume they couldn't be wrong and she right. How foolish to reject such a notion out-of-hand. Rather ironic, too, since if they'd known her even in the slightest they would have rushed to the windows to follow her advice. But my take on this is slightly different from what she might have said. The strength with which we hold an opinion is no inoculation against being wrong, and offers no sanctuary whatsoever from the impersonal nature of probability, which is perhaps the hardest lesson there is to learn at the track—or anywhere.

After the races we drove over to a small restaurant I like on a shady tree-lined street not far from the backstretch. It's where many of the owners, trainers, and backstretch workers eat. After we were seated we were surprised to find ourselves one table over from Shug McGaughey and another gentleman. All I knew about McGaughey was his training prowess, but it wasn't long before we both knew he was angry. He's a small man, slightly overweight, clothes too tight, with an Irishman's red face, though he speaks out of the side of his mouth in a drawl. He was complaining to his dinner companion that Phipps wanted him to stop drinking. Phipps, we both assumed, being the Phipps who's his biggest owner. Hearing all that bitter, angry talk, so full of denial, made us both very uncomfortable, so much so that we ate in silence, downing our beers and eating our food as quickly as we could. But it wasn't just that it made us feel uncomfortable, it was how it evoked in us an unwanted empathetic response. I mean, who needs that?

We spent the night in a modest motel near downtown. Our room was clean and air conditioned, but the décor was old and tired, with knotty pine paneling and ancient bathroom fixtures. I slept fitfully, repeatedly awakened by buzzing mosquitoes. In the morning we walked down the length of the building to the office where they were serving complimentary coffee and pastries. We both had a cup of coffee and I bought a *New York Times*. Back in our room Barb packed while I sat in a chair by the window reading the paper. Later, when we left, we walked past a number of middle-aged men in Bermuda's and T-shirts sitting in lawn chairs outside their rooms studying *The Daily Racing Form*. We decided it must be some sort of Saratoga ritual.

We had a nice brunch in a coffee shop downtown, and though we both would have loved to stay Barb's conference began bright and early the next morning so we really did need to hurry. The drive was uneventful, down to the Mass Pike and then straight east to Boston, arriving in town just in time for the Friday afternoon rush hour.

Totally exhausted, by the time we finally got up to our hotel room all we could manage was to flop on the bed. It took all my strength just to turn on the television, though that worked out well as there was a Red Sox game on. Uninterested, Barb just stared at the ceiling, but it wasn't long before she sat up, groaned, and staggered over to the desk by the window to fetch the hotel guide.

"See anything you like?" I asked, as she leafed through the room service menu.

"Baked scrod. I love to get baked scrod when I'm in Boston."

"Let me see." She handed me the menu. "Four cheese pizza. That should work, with a salad and a Coors."

Once she'd used the phone to order she walked over and stood looking out the window. "Have you decided what you're going to do tomorrow?"

"I still think I'll drive up to Rockingham."

"Add another racetrack to your list?"

"I've never even been to New Hampshire."

"My ex-husband and I drove up Mount Washington once while we were staying here."

"When was that?"

"Oh, eleven, twelve years ago. I can't believe it's been that long."

"And twelve years before that where were you?"

"Twelve years before that I was in junior high," she said, coming over to sit on the bed. "Now that really does seem impossible."

"I know. The way time insists on ending up in the past is very troubling."

"What about you? Where were you twenty-four years ago?"

"I certainly wasn't in junior high."

"College?"

"Just trying to stay out of the army."

"But in college?"

"Uh-huh. Suddenly there were millions of us interested in a college education. It was quite the growth industry."

"But I thought you liked college?"

"I did."

"So what were you like back then, when you were in college?"

"Like I am now."

"No different?"

"Not really."

She smiled at me. "Always so elusive."

"What's elusive about a bunch of blank pages? Anyway, you're the one with an ex-husband and all that personal history."

"You're so full of it," she said, leaning back on the bed next to me to watch the game.

Too bad they weren't running over at Suffolk Downs in East Boston. I have a real fondness for that track. But Rockingham wasn't that far, so it was off to New Hampshire the next morning in the rental car. But there was one stop I wanted to make on the way. A bookstore I like up by Harvard Square specializing in academic press titles, though by the time I found a place to park and got over there I barely had enough time to take a look at the philosophy section, let alone anything else. Nevertheless, not only did I find a new book on critical theory, it contained an essay Lee had written on the colonization of the lifeworld.

Having skipped breakfast in my rush to get on the road, I decided to stop by Au Bon Pain on the way back to the car for an iced tea and a croissant. It was crowded, so when I got my order I took my tray outside and sat at a table next to the busy intersection. There I read a bit of her essay. It reminded me of the things we used to talk about back in Boulder, though I have to say that I didn't recognize her voice in what she'd written.

Wanting to save the rest for later, I laid the book on the table and leaned back in my chair to watch the people walking by. It was oddly pleasant to think of her in the midst of all that commotion, though thinking of her was something I rarely did in those days. But even when I did, as I did that morning, the memories were comfortably remote. After all, I'd done more than enough in my life to accumulate a healthy buffer between then and now. And Barb? Well, what can I say? She was every bit as intelligent and driven as Lee, no question about that, though her actions didn't reveal it quite as vividly. Equally successful, a prosperous oncologist from La Jolla, decent, charming, attractive, a woman in the midst of her post-divorce transition period between husbands—she was certainly the most interesting woman I'd known since Lee. We were having a nice time while she decided what to do about men in her life.

33

How did we meet?

It was Saturday afternoon at Santa Anita. I was leaning on the railing by the paddock watching the grooms walking their nervous horses around the ring as jockeys, trainers, and owners huddled together in tight little clusters discussing their chances. Then I heard someone call my name. It was Wendy, standing with a group of people talking to Bobby Frankel and Eddie Delahoussaye. She was motioning for me to come over and join them, but I just shook my head. Then she laughed, turning so no one could see, and pointed to a well-dressed guy in her party, rubbing her fingers together like—*that's right, he's the one with the money.* I smiled, nodding my head because he really did look like an owner. Then it was *riders up* and the horses and everyone else slowly filed out. As they did she came walking over with Barb.

"Nick, why didn't you come over? Does Frankel know you?"

"We've never met."

"I wanted to know what you think of our horse."

"He's okay."

"Oh?" She looked at me suspiciously. "Sounds like there's something you're not telling me."

I laughed. "No, he's fine. A legitimate favorite."

"But?"

"But nothing, except he looks like that to everyone. What's he going to pay? $2.40? At that price it's not even worth the effort to see about getting a better price in an exacta or trifecta."

"See?" She looked meaningfully at Barb. "What did I tell you?"

"Oh, and what was that?"

"That you think like a monk."

"A monk!" I stared at Wendy. "What's that supposed to mean?"

"It means you're so pious about your betting. Sitting here day after day never once succumbing to temptation. Just waiting for a bet to come along worthy of your consideration."

"The patience of a saint? Is that what you mean, because as you well know I'm not."

By then Barb was grinning, enjoying our little game, and yes she was attractive, I'd finally noticed, with that lean lanky look of a runner, light brown hair stylishly cut, strikingly intelligent face, well dressed, sort of elegant. Then the moment arrived. The one I've noticed before: the moment of sexual selection. I have no idea why it's so commonly overlooked. Even in a pressing moment it's not that hard to spot. Ingrained, unbidden, deeply preconscious, there to be felt, or at least its effects are, as we suddenly feel more alive. Yes, I know it's probably nothing more than the other side of freshly minted neurotransmitters flooding select areas of the brain, but you know what, that's not the side we live on. Over here what I experienced was one very simple thought: hey, this is an interesting woman.

"Nick, I'm so impolite," Wendy said. "Let me introduce you two. Nick," and she looked at me, "this is Barbara. Barb is staying with me this weekend. I've finally manage to coax her up from San Diego for a weekend at the track."

"Nice to meet you," I said, taking her hand in mine. "What do you think of things so far?"

"It's certainly not like going to a Padres game."

"Is that what you were expecting?"

"I'm not sure what I was expecting, but I do like it."

"You should," Wendy said. "With all the money you won in the last race."

"I'm glad someone did," I said.

"Tell Nick what you bet."

"Oh—"

"Go ahead," I told her.

"Wendy told me what to say, so I told the teller I wanted three five dollar trifectas with the two on top, then for place, and then for show, with the four, the six, the nine, and the ten."

"That's some bet for a beginner."

"Isn't it?" Wendy said, looking knowingly at me.

"What made you key the two horse? The odds?" It had gone off at 8-1.

"I didn't even notice the odds. I just thought he looked like the obvious winner."

"Looked?"

"Didn't he?" she asked, looking at the two of us.

"Uh, not to me." I smiled at her. "Are you sure you're just a beginner?"

"I swear."

"Well, good for you. Now keep this up and we'll all get rich." No kidding. She must have cleared over $1200 on her $240 bet. God, how I loath beginner's luck.

"My goodness, *so* jealous," Wendy said, laughing at me. "Looks like the saint just spotted a sinner."

"So," I said, trying to ignore Wendy, "you had your winner. What made you pick those other horses?"

"The same thing. What I saw in the paddock and post parade."

She borrowed my binoculars," Wendy said.

"It wasn't that hard to see which ones felt like running today."

"Well—"

"You really didn't think so?" She'd noted our disbelief.

"I have no idea, since I guess I wasn't looking. Now I'm wondering if I ever have."

"Maybe you'd better start," Wendy said.

"So," I asked, smiling at Barb, "who do you like in this race?"

"Oh, my God!" Wendy exclaimed. "I don't believe it. Come on, Nick, you're sitting with us up in my box."

So I did, and Barb and I were together a lot over the next several years whenever she could find the time for us in her busy life. I never knew a woman who liked my world better, or one who could have excelled in it more.

34

When I got back to our room that evening Barb was napping, but when I laid down beside her on the bed she rolled over to smile at me.

"How'd it go?"

"Have you ever driven in Boston?"

"Not much. I know people always talk about Boston drivers."

"I'm amazed there isn't gridlock."

"After Los Angeles you should be used to that sort of thing."

"Yeah, well just try driving across Cambridge and Somerville some time. I got all turned around over by Tufts trying to find a way through all the traffic. Tight little streets, ugly looking triple-deckers, I didn't think I'd ever find I-93."

She was sitting up now looking down at me. "So what was Rockingham like?"

"Interesting. Nothing fancy, but in better shape than some I've seen. Got a nice table in the Turf Club, which was air-conditioned, thank God. Little TV so I could watch Del Mar and Saratoga. Not too crowded. It was nice."

"I don't like to sit inside."

"Today you would have. It was like up at Saratoga, but I stayed nice and cool. A few iced teas, a grilled chicken sandwich. I could get used to it."

"How'd the betting go?"

"You tell me," I said, handing her my wallet. "You should see how slow the horses are. I wasn't sure some of them were going to make it to the finish line. Then I got a little annoyed at the jockeys because they clearly weren't trying very hard once they saw they weren't going to win. But then it struck me how it's all about the horses. They have to run them, but there's no point in forcing them to do more than they're ready for. It's not Saratoga, just a third tier track like Portland Meadows. It's just what they have to do to protect them while they cycle back into competitive form. Though I have no idea how you're supposed to know when that is. It's certainly not a style of racing I've had much experience with, which is why I didn't have much confidence in my betting."

"But you did bet?"

"A few exactas, a couple of win bets. The big one was the exacta in the fifth, a maiden claimer. By then I'd started to like one of the trainers. You know how I am. So he had this nice filly with one previous start. To me, she looked pretty good, especially when she got up to 8-1."

"I'm surprised you didn't talk yourself out of it. You usually do."

"I flirted with it. I thought, well, the crowd can't be that wrong, can they? After all, it's their track, what do I know? But then I thought, why not? If that dumb jockey just lets her run her race, at the very least she's good enough for second in this field. So solely on the basis of that I wheeled her on the bottom with the whole field."

"You, the whole field? I'm amazed."

"I know, what a crazy bet."

"It's worse than crazy, it's completely out of character."

"Right. I know, but I just couldn't sort it out, so I thought I might as well, then just sit back and wait to see what happens. Then it did."

"Maybe you should make crazy bets like that more often, since you've got $423 in your wallet."

"Really? That much? It's that exacta. I had it twice."

"You did have a good day."

"I suppose so, since I started out with $170."

I thought about my two hundred and fifty dollars. Barb earned more than that in just a few minutes. In fact, the difference in our incomes was breathtaking. But she deserved it. You couldn't help but admire how she stuck to her grueling schedule, getting up early to run before driving over to the hospital to see her patients or perform surgery, returning again late in the afternoon after dealing with her lab and all its attendant administrative responsibilities. I didn't see how anyone could possess more discipline or self-control. Where did I fit in all this? Usually I didn't, not unless I was with her, like for this trip, or when she'd made a special effort. That was her biggest problem, being too busy to worry about having much of a personal life. Rarely having the time for those casual moments most couples build their lives around. But I'm making it sound worse than it was, like that didn't work for me. I'll gladly admit that the two summers I spent with her down in La Jolla playing Del Mar were the two most peaceful summers of my life.

"How about your day?" I asked.

Yawning, she stretched her arms up over her head. Pfizer was emblazoned across the back of her t-shirt—I didn't have to guess where that had come from—and she'd pulled her hair back in a ponytail.

"I guess the highlight of my day were the researchers I met from Lahey Clinic."

"Oh?" I watched her tuck the covers up around her legs to ward off the chill from the air conditioner.

"Stem cells."

I nodded. I knew of her interest in stem cells.

"I've been invited out there tomorrow morning for a visit, but I'll need to be back by two. I was hoping you'd be able to drive me, then maybe we could get a lunch somewhere on the way back. That should still leave most of your afternoon free."

"I'd love to. What about dinner tonight?"

Groaning, she flopped down on her back beside me.

"What does that mean? Room service again?" Like many busy people she loved room service.

"Have I mentioned how glad I am you came along?" she asked, gently brushing the hair from my forehead.

"Several times." I smiled and pulled her ponytail out from under her head. "Now, what is it you're hesitant to tell me?"

"Oh, just that I somehow managed to commit us to dinner tonight. It won't be that bad. We just go downstairs. Laura will be there. You like her."

"How many?"

"Four, I think."

"I don't suppose there's anyway I can whine my way out of it?"

"Not this time," she said, sitting up to dangle her ponytail in my face.

Putting my hands under her t-shirt, I slowly ran them up and down her muscular back before cupping her soft warm breasts. Smiling at me, she sat up to pull her T-shirt off, then leaned over so I could kiss each nipple, gently nibbling, running my front teeth over them as they became erect. She chuckled when I slide my hand inside her sweatpants; rolling over on her back to pull them off. She's interesting. As a doctor I knew she harbored few, if any, illusions about our bodies. I suppose most doctors don't. I mean, honestly, how could they? Still, you'd think that lack of sentimentality might wreak havoc with their sexuality. Not Barb's. For her it just meant she was ready when she was ready. No melodrama. No second-guessing. You want to have sex? Fine, works for me. Let's go. It was rare that I didn't find her directness and spirit of cooperation admirable.

"Are you sure we have the time?" I asked, honestly trying to be considerate.

Laughing, she said, "Isn't this just a quickie?" Then as I sat up to take my clothes off, she asked, "What's that book over by the television?"

187

I turned to look. "A philosophy book I bought this morning up at Harvard Square."

"You still miss philosophy, don't you?"

"I enjoy keeping up with it, but I don't miss it."

"Do you ever see any of your old friends from graduate school?"

"Do you?" I asked as I slid under the covers.

"Of course, but I stayed in my profession, while you went off and became a horseplayer. I don't suppose you meet too many philosophers out at the track."

"None that are professionals."

She pulled me towards her. "So, any pals in there?" She was nodding towards the book.

"Why do you ask?" I replied, trying to sound as casual about it as possible.

Smiling, she held my head in her hands, staring into my eyes as if she were trying to read something shrouded in smoke.

"What's this? More of your famous bedside manner?"

Still smiling, she drew me down to kiss me, then moved her hips under mine, but in the middle of my fumbling around she placed a hand on my back to stop me.

"What?" I asked, rising up on my elbows to see.

"Do you know where she is?"

"She?" I stammered.

Watching me flounder, she laughed. Then, "Come on, big boy," as she playfully slapped my ass. "You've got ten minutes."

I found I was very aroused. She noticed, too. It was embarrassing. Afterwards, I lay in her arms as she stroked my hair. She was humming a song I knew but couldn't identify. Suddenly, she stopped.

"Now what's wrong?"

She sighed and stroked my hair again. "I bet she misses you."

"I doubt it."

35

Dinner that evening went about as expected. Doctors just can't stop talking shop, but they're such polished purveyors of reassuring interpersonal chitchat that there was never a moment when I didn't feel like I was included. Horseplayers don't often feel that way around professional people, though my feeling of inclusion may have had more to do with the excellent job I was doing ensuring that their friend was happy and able to carry on with her work. Looking at her sitting next to me, cheeks flushed, eyes sparkling, engaged in animated conversation, there couldn't have been much doubt about that. Yes, as if reading my mind Laura turned and smiled, raising her eyebrows as if to say we haven't seen her this happy in a long time.

One of the doctors, Jack, a man Barb knew from their intern days together in Los Angeles, had been to a Red Sox game, and when he asked if I'd gone Barb laughed and asked me to tell him what I'd done instead.

"Working," I said. "No ballgames for me today."

"Is that so?" he replied, smiling, unlike most people apparently not bothered by being the butt of a joke.

"Uh-huh," I said, glancing at Barb. "Had to drive up to New Hampshire to check on some volatile short-term investments. Long day, but worth it."

"Investments?" Laura broke in.

"That's why I had to be there in person. Assessing their potential."

"Yes," Jack said, "I believe I've heard about your investments. How did it go?"

"Well enough that he should buy us all a drink," Barb teased.

"You know," he said, "I've been thinking about doing a little investing myself. Maybe I should give you a call when we get back to Los Angeles"

"That's a wonderful idea," Barb said. "You could both use a playmate."

"Sure, give me a call. Who knows, you might even turn out to be as good an investor as Barb."

We had a nice dinner, and as is so typical of medical professionals, we wrapped-up early.

36

The next morning we were up early to get in a run before driving out to Lahey. It wasn't much of one: over to the Commons, Beacon, downhill to State Street and Faneuil Hall, back up Tremont and Boylston to the Ritz-Carleton. Then after showers and room service I called for the car. This time I-93 didn't seem that bad, or maybe I was just getting used to Boston drivers.

Lahey's size surprised us. We actually had to ask a security guard how to get to the oncology wing. Then once we'd found it I stayed with Barb until I had some sense of how much time she'd need, at which point I told her I'd meet her back downstairs in the lobby at eleven.

With a lot of time to kill, I rode the elevator back down to the ground floor and walked over to the cafeteria. Dirty, it smelled like a cheap breakfast anywhere and the instant iced tea I bought was dreadful, but there was a copy of the *Globe* sitting on a table by the windows so I sat down. I was surprised to see so many doctors and nurses, many in their blue and green scrubs, many with trays full of the foods they no doubt warned their patients against.

Forty-five minutes latter, back outside, it took me a few minutes to find our rental car in the Clinic's vast parking lot. Then once I had I held the door open to cool the car's interior, only then getting in to put the key in the ignition to lower all the windows. The breeze was soothing, but it was already a muggy, uncomfortable day.

I stared out the window. Now what? I reached around for my bag and sat it on the seat beside me, then pulled my book out and turned to Lee's essay. No. I tried, but I was too sleepy to read. So yawning, I got out of the car and stood, stretching my arms up over my head, taking several deep breaths. The sky was thickening with ragged, puffy clouds, clouds that later in the afternoon produced a brief but violent thunderstorm.

I strolled down my row. The place was jammed. Everywhere I looked cars sat doubled-parked, blinkers on, which is when it struck me just how factory-like Lahey was. Okay, I'm sure they received excellent care, but that wasn't really the issue. Rather how, given those endless streams of patients pouring in and out, anyone ever got recognized or treated as the singular, unique lives they were. The hard truth is it doesn't really matter, not from the standpoint of medical practice. One just has to accept being nothing but a data point in a larger and wholly indifferent statistical sample. Accept that one's fate gets played out in terms of probabilities in an indifferent bureaucratic environment. Still, trying to be fair about it, when faced with an endless number of people to treat and care for, medical practice on such a vast scale has to depend upon the routinized procedures the health care industry has devised to get the job done. But what a dismal, alienating thought. I felt distinctly uncomfortable. The colonization of the lifeworld and the reification of social relations, that was Lee's contribution to the collection of essays I was reading. How ironic.

It was just before eleven when I walked back inside and stood in the lobby by the front doors. What a sight, that vast expanse filled with people, most of whom seemed to be doing nothing but waiting. In lines, on chairs and couches, pacing back and forth, the quintessential modern experience, especially in the bowels of a large service provider like Lahey. But who were they? Well, some were clearly visitors. Just as obvious were those who were nervously waiting to be checked-in. As for the rest, like those who sat in wheelchairs staring at nothing, well, it was hard to sort them all out. Then I saw Barb. I had to smile as I watched her walking towards me. I mean I could really see it, that as crazy as this world seemed to me this really was her world, the place where she felt most at home.

When she reached me I got a little kiss on the cheek, then I watched her turn to look back at the chaotic scene in the lobby. I gave her a few moments and then took her arm. "Come on," I said. "That's enough medicine for today."

"You should see the successes they're having," she said once we were outside.

"Why don't you tell me about it later. You look worn out."

In the car she leaned over to turn on the air conditioning, fiddling with the vents on her side to get it just right. "I am tired," she admitted, smiling at me. "Maybe we should just play today."

I nodded my head. "Totally a bad influence."

37

We had a nice day. On the way back to town we ate lunch at Kelly's, which was just as good as I'd remembered, then after the rain showers we went for a walk. Barb looked great in her sloppy Stanford t-shirt, her hair pulled back in a loose ponytail. We stopped in all the used bookstores. She looked at handbags in the shops up and down Newbury and Boylston. We had gelato. I spent a long time in Tower Records looking at Link Wray CDs and 60s garage band compilations. All this in the midst of a sea of students and tourists, honking cars, cars sitting empty, double-parked in the middle of the street, the sun shining around the remnants of the thunderstorm, the air chilly, the sidewalks and streets glistening from the rain.

As we walked Barb talked about what she wanted to do when we got home, about pursuing new directions for her clinic, about how much she wished she had more time for research. I smiled, nodding my head, making a few comments, knowing this was just her way of relaxing, of regrouping before the next big push. When she finally stopped she held my hand.

We were standing on the sidewalk window-shopping in front of a store with very expensive looking women's clothing when she turned to me.

"Are we in love?"

"Why not?"

"But what kind of love do you suppose that is?"

I took her in my arms and smiled. "Does it really matter? We're doing all right."

"I know, I guess I was just wishing we could be madly in love."

"Like in the movies?"

She laughed. "Not that foolish. Though maybe just a little."

"Well, don't worry about it. We've both known for some that this was never going to be enough for you. Not in the long run."

"Nick—"

"It's okay. I completely understand. I've more or less resigned myself to being a pleasurable interlude."

"You're definitely pleasurable," she said, putting her arms around my waist.

38

Although there was still one more week to go at Del Mar when we got home, I just couldn't seem to muster much enthusiasm. I watched the replays that night at Barb's and scanned the results on my computer to see how things had played, but for the most part it just felt too much like going back to work. I guess all the subtle magic of that day at Saratoga had finally worn off. But I'm not complaining. I was staying at Barb's where things couldn't have been more pleasant. Mornings, we took a brief run up the beach to Scripps pier, then ate breakfast sitting outside on her small brick patio. Later, once she'd left to chase her busy day, I was free to do my handicapping. Then around noon I'd drive up the hill past UCSD and through Torrey Pines. If I was lucky I might see the pelicans skimming the waves where the Coast Highway spanned Los Peñasquitos lagoon.

39

Jack finally called and we agreed to meet out at Santa Anita the following Saturday. I teased him, telling him to be sure to bring a lot of money, then gave him detailed instructions on where to park and how to find the box I share with several other handicappers.

He showed up early, of course, well before the first race, and I introduced him to the gang, a convivial bunch, or at least they are until the races begin, after which they're prone to long periods of stony silence. Still, speaking or not, most horseplayers have a special affection for doctors, one that springs from the medical profession's willingness to bring much needed capital to the more expensive, and often much more lucrative, types of wagers. Not that I needed any of that friendly capital myself, but some of my colleagues often did.

He had a lot of questions for me during our walking tour. Down to the paddock to watch a group of horses being schooled. Out to the apron in front of the grandstand to look at the winner's circle, the track, and the tote board. Back upstairs to see the Turf Club, where to place his bets, get something to eat, and where the ATM machines were located. All of this while offering a running commentary on the social and economic importance of what we were seeing, in particular, the profitable difference to be found between how the crowd viewed things and how we viewed them. It was while I was pointing out some of the finer points of *The Daily Racing Form's* cryptic presentation of information that Tommy showed up.

"Tommy," I said, introducing them, "this is Jack Danton. He's here to see what all the fuss is about."

Smiling, Tommy came down the row to shake Jack's hand. "I hope we're not getting you in trouble with your wife," he said, "but welcome to the club if we are."

"Jack's a doctor. He's one of the Barb's friends."

"Really?" Tommy said, beaming at him.

The social world at the racetrack isn't all that complicated, what with its crowds of casual bettors and racing fans, its pros, its numerous track employees and administrative staff, its trainers and their the employees, jockeys and their agents, owners and their guests, its media people, and, well, that's about it. But most important are those singular individuals whose social roles set the tone. These are the trendsetters, the opinion makers, the leaders. Those whose actions keep this social world in balance as they offer up sound judgment, wisdom, praise, and, when necessary, blame. Such was Tommy, one of the indispensables. But there was more to Tommy than that, for unlike the rest Tommy possessed something truly wondrous, rare, and sublime, something that was even transcendent: winners.

To share a box with Tommy was like sitting at the Don's table, like being the trusted aide to a powerful Senator, like being an up-and-coming junior partner at a fashionable hedge fund. They came to our box all day, suppliants seeking an audience, patiently waiting for Tommy to give them what they needed most, or most desired. He'd beckon and they'd enter, often deferential and obsequious, and then, after a brief conference, and rarely was it ever more than that, the tip would be given and they'd quickly depart. I'd see them scurrying off to the betting windows, later nodding to Tommy as they walked past knowing they owed him.

Who were they? Well, contrary to what one might expect, they were not all hapless losers. Actually, most were just casual fans with lots of betting money or successful people from other walks of life there not just for advice but the opportunity to buy into the big exotic bets Tommy was always running. Then there were the pros stopping by for a consultation. There to see if there might not be something they'd overlooked, always with lots of professional courtesy and respect. Yes, endlessly entertaining, and frequently profitable.

The boys in our box were happy. The payout after the eighth for the pick-three was big. Jack was happy too, entranced by this new world, while I was pleased by how well he fit in. Deferential to Tommy—I didn't need to explain hierarchy to a surgeon— soon he was included in Tommy's little discussions, the two of them huddling together as Tommy showed him something in *The Daily Racing Form*, listening as Tommy pointed out something about the odds or explained why a particular jockey-trainer combination was so deadly in this race. It was a solid start in the education of a horseplayer.

But there was something else Jack did, or, more accurately, didn't do, that cemented his welcome. Not once did he ask for a tip or utter that phrase most hated by horseplayers: *Who do you like?* Most importantly, he didn't act like a loser or give off that pathetic loser's vibe. How horseplayers do hate that, going to almost any lengths to avoid contact with it. And not just because losers tend to be annoying or a distraction, or because they're so often from the very dregs at the track, but because losing is so often experienced as something both highly personal and threateningly inexplicable. So much so, that most pros will instinctively seek to avoid contact with it in any of its forms. Well, who's to say whether or not contamination by contact is impossible? That such a fear is irrational or foolish? What if one really can acquire losing like one acquires a cold? If so, then quarantine isn't such a bad strategy. As we shy away from the unclean and the damned to avoid spiritual contamination, so too the unlucky and the loser. Why pick up a disease for which there's no cure?

Before the ninth Tommy asked Jack how it was going.

"I'm down a little, though I wouldn't be if I'd paid more attention to what you guys have been telling me."

"But that's one of the great things about the track, taking a stand all by yourself. Of course," Tommy smiled, "you have to win to really enjoy it."

"Oh, I'm enjoying it. In fact, it hardly seems fair that you all get to come out here every day and have this much fun."

"Well," I said, "no one's stopping anyone from coming out here, though there are certainly those who'd like to try."

"At times," Tommy said.

"We hear it all the time. Gambling, betting on horse races, is immoral, personally destructive, socially unacceptable, not part of a productive economy, a pathetic holdover from a bygone era, a marginal pastime at best, hopelessly old school, too chaotic and disorganized to deserve a place at the table in our more rational, regulated, contemporary world. We've never been given more than grudging permission anyway, and they've never stopped trying to make things as difficult for us as possible. Exorbitant take-outs. Punitive tax laws." I stared at Tommy. "I guess it's still fun."

"It is for me, and why are you complaining? Jack's a doctor. I'm sure he faces far worse problems with taxes and regulations than we do. Let's not discourage him. Who knows, we may need a doctor someday."

"Then we'd better make sure he doesn't go home empty-handed."

"Jack," Tommy said, motioning for him to join him "Let's see what we can find for you in this next race."

40

For a while Jack was a frequent weekend guest, he even gained enough self-confidence to make his own small contributions to our discussions. And yes, he did prove willing to put up the big bucks so often needed to get those more lucrative bets over the top. I was a little worried by that, but I knew he had the money and I could hardly say he didn't know what he was doing.

On one of those weekends Barb and I were standing by the paddock in a small patch of shade. It was hot. I was drinking some iced tea and she a bottle of mineral water.

"I'm almost afraid to ask, but how much did you bet in that race?"

"Too much," she said. "I had the winner, but I lost it all chasing the trifecta."

"I hope you and Jack aren't getting carried away."

"Did you know he's still alive in the pick six?"

"Only because he bought into one of Tommy's bets."

"Yes, but he's still going to be bragging when he walks out of here with all that money."

I had my doubts. Even if they'd gone deep in the nightcap—a hopelessly contentious maiden claimer—which they undoubtedly had, if the low priced favorite won the next race it wasn't going to make any difference. Their pick-six payout was going to be a major disappointment.

"Well, good for them." I said.

"You're never jealous, are you?"

"I try not to be, just like I try not to get too cocky when I win. All that emotionalism just gets in the way of good decision making."

"I've seen you unhappy at the track."

"Not because I lost."

"That's sure how it looked."

"No, because existence had once again revealed itself not only to be capricious, but personal in its insults. It's an ontological thing with me," I added, laughing at how pompous that sounded.

"More of that perverse irony you're always worrying about?"

"Yes, why do these oddly repetitive mishaps continue to occur? Well, the only answer I've ever been able to come up with is because they're happening to me."

She nodded. "Which is what you discovered here at the track."

"Which makes it sound trivial, I know, but without that triviality I'd probably never have spotted it."

"Spotted how the joke's always on you?"

"Apparently so, and one that's not always all that amusing. Prior to that I was just like everyone else. Just stumbling along through life believing the world's indifferent to my fate. But then I was confronted by a bit of evidence that seemed to suggest otherwise."

"Oh?"

"Oh yeah. What I found, or what I discovered, is that the world at times evidently does take an interest in me, though that interest is never less than ironic, and often downright malevolent. But it's not just me. Look at all those gamblers with their pathological superstitions and ritualized forms of behavior. All those devastating self-doubts."

"Yes, but that certainly doesn't describe how you are."

No, thank God, but I still can't shake this feeling that what happens often seems to have no explanation other than it's the most ironic thing that could possibly happen—"

"To you?"

"Only to me."

"So, is this perverse strain of irony in evidence today?" she asked, looking quite amused.

"Not so far," I said, looking around just to make sure. "I'm even tempted to say it's been a pretty good day. No pick-six, of course, but otherwise, very few complaints."

"Let's just hope none of this perversity rubes off on Jack," she said, smiling at me. "Because he really needs to find something else to do besides work."

"I just hope you won't come to regret it. But the guys like him, and not just because he's another doctor with deep pockets."

"I never told you, but his partner died last year. He was sick for a long time. Of course, he never talks about it. But I had a hunch he'd like it here. It's a good distraction."

"Yeah, well he's certainly distracted. So how long have you two been friends?"

"Fifteen years, give or take. He was one of my ex-husband's friends. We all interned together. He was best man at our wedding."

"You and your ex-husband, you keep in touch?"

"Yes, but not so much now that Marty's moved to Chicago. That surprises you?" she said, laughing when she saw the look on my face. "Maybe if you'd ever been married. But there must be a few semi-permanent relationships in your past."

"Semi-permanent?"

"Well, what do we call them? They're certainly not marriages, and you're too old to call it dating. But then you never mention women, so I'm just guessing." She took a step back to look at me. "You're very discrete, aren't you?"

"You better hope so."

"Why? I've got nothing to hide. Unlike you."

"I'm not hiding anything."

"You know, when I meet a guy your age who's never been married it's usually not all that hard to see why, but in your case it took some figuring."

"Oh?"

"Like how much you like women. I mean that's just so obvious, which is probably why we're all so comfortable around you. You're hardly the sort of man a woman's going to kick out of the house. But then why are you still single?"

"Because it just never worked out."

"Is that what you think?"

"Shouldn't I?"

"It's because you're one of those guys with a woman in his past."

"A woman? Don't you mean women?"

"No, I mean *the woman*."

"Come on, that's just silly. As for semi-permanent, there've been a few. At least I think there have. How long did they have to last to meet your criteria?"

"I have no idea. I'm more interested in how they ended."

"For the most part they ended just fine."

"Most? Which didn't?"

"It was nothing. I'm not even sure it counts as semi-permanent."

"But it could have ended better?"

"It wasn't like there was some big fight or anything. And no, we haven't stayed in touch. But she hardly qualifies as *the woman*, as you so melodramatically put it. She was just one among many. I rarely even think of her."

She smiled. I could see that she didn't believe a word I'd said. Yes, how is it, I wondered, that I somehow always manage to get involved with women who are smarter than me. I knew she'd tell me if I asked.

41

Back at our box everyone was eagerly anticipating the final two legs of the pick six. Still alive to three horses in the eighth—two modestly priced long shots and the solid favorite—they were, as I'd surmised, worried that the favorite would win and ruin their chances for a big score. Then it really wouldn't matter how deeply they'd gone in the ninth. But a few winning tickets of a lessor amount and a bunch of consolations would still be better than nothing.

"Where's Jack?" Barb asked.

"Over there," I pointed. "By the stairs." He was talking on his cell phone, and when he saw Barb he motioned for her to join him. I watched them huddle together as Jack spoke, then growing concerned, I walked over to join them.

"One of Jack's patients isn't doing very well," she said.

I listened. Jack was worried.

"What do you think?" Barb asked when he finished.

He rubbed his face before looking at her. "I'm sure Fred's right, and there's been some bleeding. I need to get over there." He sighed and looked around at the crowd. "He was doing so well. I was just over there last night and we were joking about getting him up today." He put the phone in his pocket and looked at me. "Tell Tommy I'm sorry, but I had to run." I nodded, then he leaned over and gave Barb a little kiss on the cheek, patting my shoulder as he walked past us to go downstairs.

"He seems pretty upset."

She nodded.

"Do you know what happened?"

"Complications. They look for it, but it still happens."

On the way back to our seats I glanced at the tote board. The favorite's odds had sunk even lower, now holding at 6-5. Not much doubt about it now, if it won no way that pick six was going to be a life-changing event even if the guys did manage to bring home a longshot in the nightcap.

Once we were settled I took another look at the *Form*. No, I still didn't see anything in the eighth that looked profitable. "See anything?" I asked. She was using her binoculars to watch the horses warming up out on the backstretch.

"Barbed Wire?"

I checked his odds. They were 15-1. Then I took a quick look at his past performances. "Well," I said, "I do love the price, but he's not going to win."

"How about in the money?"

"Uh . . . never won at this distance," I said, looking at the *Form*. "In fact, he's rarely won at any distance. However, there are some intriguing seconds and thirds. He's a closer. Once in a while he does get up there, but he always seems to hang."

"What's he going to do today?"

It's an amazing thing about horses, how they have preferences or patterns of behavior that predispose them to do things over and over again in the same way, and not unlike people, they will, if not disrupted by too many distractions or unusual circumstances. That's why a fair amount of handicapping comes down to discerning what each horse in a particular race most wants to do, all things being equal, which of course they rarely are. However, on those rare occasions when they are, and even more rarely when your fellow bettors fail to see that they are, well then, that's when it's time to open your wallet.

When I didn't say anything she lowered her binoculars to look at me. "Well?"

"If you really think he looks good—"

"Which I do."

"Then given this field, he might very well get up there for third or even second, but no way anyone beats the favorite." I paused to grin at her. "Might make for a pretty good trifecta, especially if he's overlooked."

"That's just what I was thinking."

"Even better, if you can come up with another longshot. Get them both in there, well . . . that could be quite nice."

"Let me take another look," she said, turning to watch. Then: "The nine. Who's that?"

"Abram's horse. Shadowman. Valenzuela is riding." I looked at the tote. "18-1." I waited. "So what do you think?"

"First tell me how he looks to you."

Looking at the *Racing Form*, I said, "It's been two years since he's done anything noteworthy, but his recent form does show some improvement. He likes to be on the lead. That's a plus with Valenzuela riding, but still, no way he hangs on to win this thing, as for second or third, maybe, if he's having a really good day. Is that how he looks to you?"

"I like him," she said, lowering her binoculars to look at me. She had such a knack for this sort of thing, finding those horses everyone else overlooked, those that were most profitable.

"I think I feel a bet coming on," I said, watching her stand and look at the tote board.

"Any last minute advice?"

"Just stay with the favorite on top, then wheel your two guys, plus the three and the eleven. I don't see anyone else, unless you want to play the superfecta."

"Are you betting with me?"

I got my wallet out and counted out three hundred and twenty dollars. "Single the favorite on top and do a part-wheel with the rest of our happy little family. Twenty bucks."

She looked surprised. "I thought you liked to structure your trifectas a little more carefully."

"Not this time."

Once she'd disappeared into the crowd Tommy leaned over. "What was that all about?"

"You know how she gets. Now it's Barbed Wire and Shadowman."

"Not to win, I hope."

"No, she's taking a stab at the trifecta."

He looked at the *Form*, then sorted through some printouts. "I just don't see it," he said, clearly uncomfortable. "But then that's what I always say when she lands a big one." Groaning, he looked at the tote board. "Shadowman," he said under his breath. It was bettor's agony, or at least that's what I call it, when one gets caught up in a painful moment of indecision. Not wanting to waste money, yet afraid to miss out or be damaged by something one's now aware of. Yes, I'm sure he would have been happier if hadn't known, but now that he did the agony was unavoidable.

"Left them out?"

"No, I've got Barbed Wire, but only for fourth, but I tossed Shadowman completely. You know, when she gets like this . . . and now," he shrugged and looked to the heavens. "I guess I better go make sure I can still get something out of this."

"Bet the super?"

"That I did," he said, rolling his eyes.

I watched him step up to the concourse where he paused to nervously light a cigarette. He was trying to quit but the superfecta when done properly is a costly bet to make. Worse for Tommy, much of that money wouldn't be his. Now he had to make sure he was covered if Barb was right about Shadowman. It really is an awful feeling.

A few minutes later I saw them, Barb and Tommy, slowly walking back, deep in conversation. As they reached the box he said, "So, Jack had to leave? Too bad, he's going to miss out on all the fun." Then he patted her on the back. "If you're right I'll really owe you."

"Me too," I said.

42

Of course she was right. Barbed Wire came up for second, hanging in the stretch just like I'd predicted, and Shadowman miraculously held on for third, carefully nursed most of the way around on the lead by Valenzuela. The favorite, Genocide, won easily by six lengths, the second and third favorites finished out of the money close at Shadowman's heels. The trifecta paid $287 dollars for a $1 bet and the superfecta paid $3,892. Tommy was so relieved he hardly spoke, just looking at Barb to wink.

"Time for paperwork?" I asked.

Smiling, she held out a handful of betting slips. She'd made my bet twenty separate times. The IRS would not be involved today.

"And you?" I asked.

Laughing, she held up another clutch of slips, which, when I counted them, numbered twenty-one. She was, as I've said, very competitive.

"Too bad Jack isn't here so you could brag."

"Oh, he'll hear about it."

I put *The Daily Racing* Form down, yawning as I stretched my arms up over my head.

"Do you want to leave?" she asked.

"No, for Jack's sake I'd like to stick around and see what happens. I don't know why I'm so sleepy," I said as I yawned again. "I guess the old handicapper's had too much excitement today."

"It has been a good day," she said, sighing contentedly. She slouched down with her head resting on the back of her seat.

She'd threaded her ponytail through the back of her Padres cap and now it hung down almost to the concrete.

"Nick, have you brought a lot of women here?"

"A few. Why?"

"I was wondering if they ever made you as much money as I just did, and if they did how you thanked them."

"No one has ever made me as much money as you have. As for thanking you, what did you have in mind? Ten percent, like Tommy?"

"No," she said, sitting up straight in her chair to look at me. "But I would like to know if you ever brought her here."

"Her, being *the woman*?"

She nodded.

"No, so far as I know she's never even set foot in a racetrack. And that was all a long time ago. Long before I started doing this sort of thing for real."

"Good."

We settled back to watch the last race. I was too tired to get very excited, but I was pleased when the favorite didn't win. The horse that did, Slinky, went off at 9-1, the bettor's fourth choice, and, as I'd predicted, there were many winning tickets, each worth a little under $3,500. Tommy's informal little syndicate had four. They probably had a number of consolation tickets as well, which paid $126 for five winners. Not a grand amount, but Jack would be happy and I could see that Tommy took it in stride. He'd made a modest profit, tomorrow he'd be back to try again, full of his customary optimism and bonhomie.

We watched him slowly gather up his papers and *Form* and pack them in his small briefcase. When he stood to leave he walked over to where we sat and held up a betting slip.

"Who gets this?"

Barb held out her hand. "Jack's going to be pretty excited."

"It should have been more, but . . ." he shrugged and looked at me.

"He won't mind," I said.

He paused before starting up the steps to the concourse, looking first at the track and then at the nearly empty grandstand. When he turned to us he smiled, we nodded, and then he was gone.

I leaned back to watch the track crew harrow the racing surface. Around us a few people scurried among the seats scooping up discarded betting slips and stuffing them in trash bags while others remained in their seats chatting, though most were already gone or slowly walking through the grandstand towards the exits. It's a melancholy time at the track. The excitement, the anticipation of early afternoon, is now long gone, replaced by a melancholy resignation, an acceptance of what has just occurred. Well, what other attitude could you take? You were there. Did you not see it with your own eyes? Have your own chance to understand the mysteries? Each day is like that, a pilgrimage to the sacred grove. What will be revealed today?

Barb put her hand on my knee. When I looked at her she was smiling. "Come on," she ordered, standing up, "let's go get our money."

I followed her under the grandstand. It was now just a big empty space, a few bettors wandering through, the tellers closing up, lots of paper litter on the floor. She went up to one of the tellers and fed him the betting slips, one at a time. When he counted out the last of her money she scooped it up off the counter and turned to me. "He's still going to be insufferable," she said.

43

There never was a third La Jolla summer, though I could have postponed the end of our relationship indefinitely if I'd been willing to move down there, but sooner or later it was still going to end. So as late spring ran into early summer the subject of our phone conversations revolved more and more around the commitments her busy schedule imposed and less and less around those few times she could still find for us. She was apologetic, of course, guilty for how infrequent our times together had become, but because she was unable to state the obvious I finally had to explain it to her.

"Don't misunderstand, I do appreciate the offer, but I don't think I should come down this year."

"But you'll miss out on all the fun. Jack will be down a couple of times with his new partner. Have you two met?"

I laughed. "Oh yeah. You should have seen it when Jack brought him around."

"What happened?"

"An awkward moment, then everyone got embarrassed because they'd shown their surprise. But all that vanished pretty quickly when they heard he was a cardiologist and part owner of a couple racehorses. Now they love the guy."

"A couple? You do know who's training them?"

"Sure. Some of the guys have know Canani for years."

"What do you think?"

"I think it won't be long before Jack's sitting up in the Turf Club."

"No," she laughed. "About their horses."

"All I know is that they have a promising two year filly named Marianne. What I hope is that they're having a lot of fun spending all that money. I certainly wouldn't be."

"You're really sure you won't come down? Not even for a short visit?"

I hesitated. It was very hard to walk away from another peaceful summer in La Jolla. "Probably not, not that it hasn't been fun staying with you, but we really do need to get on with our lives. That's not something that's going to happen if I'm always hanging around."

"Nick, are you breaking up with me? Because this conversation makes me feel like I'm a teenager again."

"I hated being a teenager."

"Wasn't it awful? And I did break up with a guy in high school. Very melodramatic."

"Believe me, if we were teenagers you'd be far too hot to break up with, but since we've somehow managed to reach adulthood, well, presumably we know what's best."

"Really? Because I'm not feeling all that mature right now."

"Absolutely, though I would like my class ring back."

"Lost it," she laughed, all the tension evaporating. "Sorry. But seriously, nothing at all this summer?"

"I doubt it. I've been kicking around this idea of seeing how much money I can lose playing a different circuit."

"Where?"

"Back East."

"This isn't just because of me?"

"Not at all."

"Nick, I want you to be serious for a moment. Will you?"

"I'll try."

"How upset are you, really? And no teasing, because I know this is all my fault."

"No it's not."

"Yes it is. You're just too nice to say so."

"Listen, first off, I'm not that nice, and secondly, if I am upset it's only because of how people always seem destined to wander off in different directions. So, yes, over time things change, but it's no one's fault. That's just what having a life is like."

"You know, when my ex-husband and I had our last big fight he said it's all your fault, you bitch, or something like that. Sure you don't want to get one in while you've still got the chance?"

"Did he really say that?"

"Pretty much."

"What did you say?"

"I said I wasn't a bitch when you married me."

"But doesn't that seem to suggest you were?"

"And now?"

"Now I pronounce you cured."

44

So there I was, it was almost Memorial Day and not only was there suddenly no Barb, there didn't seem to be much desire for finishing out Hollywood Park or gearing up for Del Mar. Emotionally and professionally, I was at low ebb.

The following Monday I left early, headed north, stopping for an early lunch at Paradise Cove and then a pit stop at a Starbucks in downtown Santa Barbara. Being close to Ojai, I thought about driving over to see some old New Mexico friends, but decided against it to save time. I spent the night in San Luis Obispo and had dinner at a Mexican place downtown the students seemed to like. Tuesday, I drove over to Morro Bay, then loafed along, stopping several times to hike down the access trails to the beach, just wandering over the sand and rocks enjoying the cool air pouring inland off the Pacific. I spent that night in Cambria at a motel near Moonstone Beach that was full of tourists who'd been to San Simeon, something I've never been able to make myself do. Up early the next morning, I was on the road by seven, stopping for an early lunch at Nepenthe, which was really just an excuse to sit with a beer and stare at the ocean, then it was on to Carmel where I turned to head out east through Carmel Valley. I was going up to Tassajara for a few days. I hadn't been in several years. Actually, I hadn't been since I'd met Barb. I parked in the lot by the turn-off and waited for the shuttle; it's a rough road up the mountain. Turned out, I was the only passenger. On the way up the driver told me about the rockslide they'd had that winter, how it had closed the road for two weeks. When I checked in they put me in a single yurt, which was fine, if a little cold at night. I skipped the dining hall that evening and stayed in, eating the sandwich I'd bought at Nepenthe. The brown rice could wait until tomorrow. In the morning I was up very early. I had the hot springs all to myself as everyone else either slept in or meditated, or at least I did at first.

"Nick!"

I opened my eyes. Someone was looming over me in the bright sunlight. Using my hand, I shaded my eyes. "Gail?" It didn't seem possible.

"It hasn't been that long, has it?" she laughed.

"It's the light. I can barely see you."

"Is this better?" she asked, moving towards me.

"Much."

"When did you get in?"

"Yesterday afternoon."

"Really?" She poked my arm with her sandal. "I sure didn't see you."

"No one did. I was hiding in my yurt."

"When was the last time? Was that when you came down to stay with Toni and Peter?"

"And you were there with Michael."

"Still am."

I leaned back, sinking deeper into the hot water. "Michael's here?"

"He leads one of the meditation sessions for the tourists."

"He's not going to be very happy to see me."

"I am."

"Now Gail, behave yourself."

"Oh, Nick, you're always so judgmental."

"Judgmental? That's what's wrong with you Zen types, no ethics."

"Please, ethics are for people who don't know what to do. I always do."

"Very true, except for that nagging question of whether it's what you *ought* to do."

"Or," and she raised her eyebrows, "what I ought *not* to do?"

"Yes, maybe you should try to explain that to Michael some time."

"You explain it. He loves to argue with you."

"Gail, I'm just here to relax. Okay? I'm way too old for this sort of nonsense."

"You are?" She pushed her sunglasses up to peer down into the water. "That's not what Toni said, when she and Peter were in San Francisco last winter. Now, what did she say? Something about a grad student from the University of Maryland and a teepee?"

"Michigan, and she was a post-doc in psychology. And I always stay in the teepee."

"Toni said it was the funniest thing she'd ever seen. You stumbling around as you tried to keep up with her on her hikes."

"Didn't I just say I was too old?" I shook my head. "And I wasn't stumbling around. It's the altitude. I'm not used to that anymore."

"Toni said she was tempted to intervene, but you looked so earnest she just couldn't."

"She did intervene! She took her down to town for the day so I could get a nap."

"I hope you're not here just to nap. How long are you staying?"

"One more night."

"Then it's back to L.A.?"

"No, San Francisco, maybe Sonoma, I haven't decided yet."

"You know Gretchen lives in Ojai now."

"I heard that."

"And?"

"And so does everyone else."

"Don't get cranky. I just wondered if you knew."

"Yes, and like I told you the last time you brought this up, there's nothing there. There never was. So give it a rest."

"I guess there's just no going back with you, is there?"

"No, there isn't," I said, sitting up in the water to stare at her. "Because going back never fails to be a fucking disaster. So I'm in no mood for any of your pointless nostalgia. Especially when it annoyed me so much the first time."

"You still see Toni and Peter."

"That's different. They've moved on. Some of us have, you know."

"Which just means they're what you call normal."

"Your words."

"And we're not, living up here for four months every summer."

"I think it's normal for Michael, I have no idea what you're doing here."

"Why do old lovers always have to get so nasty?"

"Do they?"

"Oh? So now you're saying we're not?" She sounded honestly surprised. "Then how would you describe us?"

"I have no idea, but to say we were lovers suggests there was at least some sort of minimal commitment."

"Or attachment?"

"Briefly, while it lasted, but after a couple of weeks it faded like the summer."

"And that's it?"

"No," I said, reaching over to tap her toes with my wet hand, "it's still a fond memory, what little I *can* remember." I looked up at her and smiled. "I really have no idea why we always fight like this."

"Because we can!" she said with a hearty laugh. "I can't tell you how much fun it is to know a man I can fight with. It's much more difficult than finding someone to love or have sex with, which in your case is two out of three."

"At best," I said, not even wanting to try and figure out which two she was counting.

"How about sliding over and letting me sit next to you," she teased.

"No thanks. I like it here. I rather not get tossed out for fooling around in the hot springs. I know how you folks feel about tourists."

"Even we aren't allowed to fool around in the hot springs anymore."

"My, times have changed. Is it possible you really are developing a little ethical sensibility?"

"Hardly," she said, snorting with amusement. "It's just part of the effort to avoid getting any more bad press. Mustn't embarrass any of our rich benefactors."

"So they don't know you're up here harassing the tourists all summer?"

"I haven't harassed anyone in ages," she said, grinning at me. "I'm only here to keep Michael from getting lonely."

"Michael? That would be a first. What you really mean is neither of you trusts the other to be alone in the midst of so much temptation."

"That never made much difference in the past."

"Yes, and it's always the sex thing that ruins a good communal situation, isn't it?"

"How should I know," she said, giving me an innocent smile that was actually rather charming, all things considered.

"Yes," I smiled, "how should you know?" She was shameless. Her behavior had blown the whole thing wide open and still no remorse. Michael wasn't any better.

"Well, I've got to run," she abruptly announced, for some reason suddenly in a hurry. "But I'm sure I'll see you later. We've still got a lot to talk about."

I looked up, startled, and she was grinning. "We do? Are you sure you remember who I am?"

"I remember."

Once she was gone I slid down in the water and closed my eyes. For the rest of the day I avoided the meditation sessions and ate my meals quickly. I never did see Michael, and Gail, thankfully, kept her distance. My hunch was that Michael had strongly suggested she stay away from me.

45

Early that evening I took a hike up through the oaks and coastal scrub to a mountaintop with a view. Unfortunately, I couldn't see the Pacific, the marine layer was too thick, but I knew it was out there somewhere, its immensity lost in the clouds. Simple relaxation, that's all I was looking for, though I was still captive to the unresolved, like the empty hollowed-out feeling I got whenever I thought about Barb or the summer to come.

I leaned back on the grasses. The thick gray marine layer filled the sky right down to the tops of the peaks around me. So what did I want? Winning? That's the answer most handicappers would give, if not also a world not only rational and predictable but stable and forgiving, perhaps even overwhelmingly lucky, a mythical handicapper's paradise where handicapping amounted to nothing more than identifying the one among several abstract possibilities most likely to be realized when the race was run. Yes, but the real world didn't work like that. There, handicappers were forced to make do, picking from among a sea of such possibilities. Yes, well no one can do better than that, and even doing that is hard.

I'm at the track and I'm worried about a horse. One I'd like to rule out as a legitimate contender if not for something that urges caution. Rarely explicit, an uneasy feeling, a soft voice whispering in my ear; I feel compelled to take another look. Concerned, I look for an explanation, for some rational grounds for my unease. Yes, there's this horse, and in her last few races she's looked terrible, though in the past she's always done well on the turf here at Keeneland. Or it's true, for some reason this jockey appears to be the only one who knows what to do with her. But what about a situation like this. Here we have a horse that rarely wins, just three times out of twenty-five lifetime starts. More troubling, no current form and she doesn't appear to be training well. Then in looking back through her past performances I notice that her last win was exactly two years ago in this same stakes with this same jockey and trainer. Am I really willing to bet this happens again? What will I say if it does? That she did so for no reason other than that odd things like this occur? And they do. We've all seen them often enough at the track. But what about the other horses in this race, have their histories now suddenly become irrelevant as the way is cleared for this one very odd and ironic thing to occur? What kind of world is it that saves such an honored place for such perverse irony? Sorry, I can't make that bet. In fact, I won't, even though I see perversely ironic things like this happen all the time.

But why won't I? Well, just what is the relationship between the outcome of a race and myself? There's what I know about a race beforehand and how it actually turns out, which is the arc within which I handicap. There is how I feel about the results and the money won or lost. It seems absurd to suggest there could be anything more. Don't we want to insist that the outcome of a race bears no significant relationship to me at all? I may be in some sort of relationship to the prices that were paid in that I bet in the pool along with everyone else, but to the outcome itself? To which horse won? To which horses lost? Which jockey? Which trainer? Could the world really work like that?

But just suppose it does. What then could handicappers do about it? I know what most would try to do, drain the fear away by staying on point. Yes, perversely ironic things do occur, and yes their occurrence certainly does make one wonder, but in the end none of this really matters because just as in real life all we need to do is stay the course. That is, if we're any good, and if our play is consistent, then over the long haul our actions will show a profit. The law of averages works reassuringly in our favor. The setbacks, the inexplicable, capricious, and cruel things that dog us will eventually average out. So we have a plan, and though it's certainly not God's plan it does have some metaphysical clout in the form of the reassuring regularity of probable outcomes. Given a long enough period of time and a large enough number of races a form of statistical regularity will emerge that we can count on. So even if not today, in the long run we will be winners. No fear.

Yes, but sometimes things are impossible to get right at any point. When any choice will be the wrong choice, any bet the wrong bet. In such situations it's impossible to get ahead of myself. Even changing my mind won't help. I get this crazy idea: I'll wait until the last possible moment and then suddenly do just what I had not intended to do. But isn't this now what I *had* intended to do? It gets worse. That which I first thought of but did not choose? The fact that I did not now somehow makes it far more likely to occur than if I had. It's always going to be too late in a world that awaits my actions to take on concrete characteristics. Ones that are, of course, just the ones I was afraid of but did not bet on.

I laughed and sat up. Although I couldn't see it, the sun was setting, casting a golden hue over everything in the cooling air. Why did I even bother with this stuff? But I'm semi-legendary for the way perverse irony clings to me, especially when I'm deep in the trough of a losing steak. I actually have friends who will listen attentively to my analytical analysis of a race, then rush off to bet on just what I hadn't predicted. For them, this is as close to a sure thing as they'll ever encounter, while for me it's next to pointless to even bet because whatever I bet will never happen. It's always already never going to happen, even though what will happen is clearly related to, if not dependent upon, what I do.

It's hard to gauge to what extent such perverse irony pervades our lives outside the track, though I think the evidence suggests it's fairly pervasive. But there's no question that it's much easier to spot at the track where life's many complications get winnowed down to just a few key acts, the reasons for those acts, and their unintended, but feared, consequences. Of course, accounting for something when you make a bet is hardly the same as dealing with that something, or at least it's an anodyne way of dealing with that something in that nothing's changed.

I stood, stretching my arms up over my head. The aroma of dry grass was delicious. Around me the fog poured like heavy smoke over the ridge into the valley below. I was thinking about the guy I saw at Belmont who used a crystal dangling on the end of a chain to make his picks, holding it over his program as he waited for it to signify by its motion or stillness that here was the winner. I knew that would never work for me. Action, inaction, decision, guessing, it never changes the outcome, which is always different from what I've bet if hardly ever different from what I've feared.

I zipped up my sweatshirt and began trotting down the trail. I needed to get back before it got too dark down in the woods. Yes, but maybe life isn't really like that. Perhaps it's only like that at the track. I shoved my hands deeper into the pockets of my sweatshirt, bouncing down the trail, darting in and out of the wispy tendrils of fog sweeping the mountainside. I'm just worn out, tired, spinning out racetrack superstitions across my life where they don't belong. After all, doesn't it all finally just come down to estimating the likelihood of one thing's occurring rather than another? It's such a simple goal. Why shouldn't pursuing it be a simple life? That's all I wanted. So where was it? Lost in a momentary panic, I stopped running and looked back up the trail. Nothing near was very clear and not much at all beyond thirty or forty feet. Feeling the cold mist in my face, I pulled the hood up over my head and turned my back to the wind. I looked down the trail to the valley below. I couldn't see it. I turned full-circle. No, all I saw was me standing on a steep hillside in the middle of a deeply rutted trail as the fog scurried around me impatient to reach the valley somewhere down there in the dark.

46

The next morning I decided to take the early shuttle down the mountain. The sooner I was out of there the better. But as I was packing there was a knock on the door. I knew who it would be.

"Hello, Gail."

"You don't seem very surprised."

"I thought you might drop by." I held the door open so she could slip in.

"You're leaving?" she asked when she saw my bag.

"I said two nights."

"Have you had breakfast?"

"Just got back."

"That's where I'm headed. I thought you might like to join me."

"No Michael?"

"He's meditating," she said, plopping down on my bed.

I watched her yawn. "You're bored up here, aren't you? Why don't you ride the shuttle down the mountain and go over to Carmel or PG. Get away from here for a few hours."

"Is that an offer?" she asked, grinning up at me.

I shook my head. "Why are you still with that guy?"

"I don't know. We always seem to patch things up and then I forget why I was ready to leave. And where would I go if I did?"

I put the rest of my cloths and books in my bag and zipped it shut. "I have no idea. Maybe for you that is happiness. That, and boredom."

"Maybe." Standing, she put her hands on my shoulders, then when I didn't try to stop her snuggled up against me to hold me tight.

"Gail," I said, resting my hands on her hips. "This isn't what you really want. Like I said, you're just bored. Now don't distract me or I'll miss my ride."

Taking my hand in response, she placed it on her breast. I felt the firmness under her cotton t-shirt. "Gail, that's not fair," I said, dropping my hand to my side. Wetting her lips with her tongue, she pulled me close and kissed me, then leaned back to see my reaction. When she saw how hesitant I was to stop her she laughed and tugged at my belt. Suddenly I no longer cared why she shouldn't. I heard her sigh of approval as I slid my hand into her running shorts; when I pulled them down and let them drop to the floor. In a rush now, she unzipped my pants and took my penis in her hand as I ran my fingers over her. Then slowly, she maneuvered me over to the bed where she lay back, cocking one leg to the side as she grinned up at me. I pulled my pants down. It didn't take long. She groaned once or twice with my rising pleasure and then it was over.

"Sorry that was so quick," I said, stroking her hair, "but you caught me off guard. But then you always do." It was always like that with her, not wanting to fuck her right up until fucking her was suddenly the most important thing in the world.

"You're always quick the first time. The second, you're much sweeter."

She raised her arms over her head and stretched, thrusting her breasts up as she arched her back. Well, whatever else she was she was undeniably lovely. I leaned down and kissed her, then held her in my arms, momentarily lost in her wonderfully sensuous nature. The second time was, as she'd predicted, much nicer.

Riding the shuttle, I wondered how long it was going to be before she told Michael. Sooner or later she'd catch him coming back from a walk with a nice young tourist. Then she'd want to hurt him. Yes, I should have known better. Yes, I'd given in far too easily. But then I'd forgotten how desirable she could be, and somehow she always found a way to remind me of that. I shook my head, thinking of her and what a hell of a summer we'd once had.

47

The plan was to drive up Highway One to Santa Cruz, then over the mountains to Los Gatos on 17, getting up the peninsula to San Mateo in time to catch the last few races at Bay Meadows. But all that changed when I got off the freeway at Santa Cruz looking for a place to eat.

Downtown, I was surprised that nothing looked familiar. I'd been there before when I'd driven up from L.A. to visit Lenny. Yes, but that was years ago, and now the old downtown I remembered was gone. It was the Loma Prieta quake. I'd forgotten about that. Not that the new buildings weren't nice, just that I'd wanted to remember and now I wouldn't get the chance. That's why I ended up down at the pier where things seemed more familiar. So I drove all the way out to the end and had a nice lunch at Stagnaro's, sitting upstairs at a small table from where I could watch the surfers across the small harbor at Steamer's.

48

The first time I'd been in Santa Cruz the air was humid and hazy, a balmy winter day thick with mist and the pungent odor of sea and brine that one could smell all over town. I'd driven out along West Cliff Drive to watch an enormous winter swell breaking in massive waves less than a hundred yards off shore, the waves carrying right on up to the rocks under the cliff to crash in thunderous spouts of spray and roiling white water. I'd parked my car and gotten out to lean against a fence, watching in utter fascination as the enormous waves emerged abruptly out of the haze. Their faces were steep and high. Not surprisingly, only a handful of surfers were out there. I'd wondered how that felt, getting hammered like that, pinned to the rocky bottom as tons of water broke over your head. Back at the car, the windshield was coated with a thick gummy film from the spray. I'd squirted the windshield and run the wipers, then sat with the window down, my arm resting on the sill, watching the procession of cars and people down at the beach to see the huge winter surf. There was something about the balmy feel of the air that day—such a contrast to what that winter light suggested the weather ought to be, the odd sensation of warm mist in winter, the plants greening, looking like spring in January, not to mention my utter lack of concern for winter, for all the cold and inconvenience it brought elsewhere—which reminded me of the delightful surprise of that first winter in the Southwest after I'd moved from Colorado.

I was there to see Lenny, at that time living up the coast a few miles north of town in an old run-down campground fifty yards from the beach. Scaroni Road. I should swing by later and take a look just for old times' sake. It was a small sandy area just up from the beach in a shallow valley along a creek that came down from the hills on the other side of Highway One. From Lenny's van it was just a few yards across a field of weeds to the path that led to the beach. We could actually see the waves breaking from his van.

It was a wonderfully run-down live-free-or-die private beach that allowed for paid admission in the summer as well as for a few semi-permanent guests whose campers and beat-up RVs dotted the campground. I have no idea who owned it, but the caretaker was one of Lenny's old Berkeley comrades. A guy who'd washed up there one day like a weathered piece of driftwood and had somehow managed to turn his stay there into some form of employment. Lenny was there because he was broke and because he was hiding from his demons. Hunkered down waiting for a sign that it was safe to return to the track, safe to once again trust himself to know what to do and when. I stayed with him for about a week, sleeping out there just above the beach in my sleeping bag under a big coyote bush whose pale yellow flowers smelled like buttered popcorn when the sun hit them. It was an amazing place: the ocean, the proximity of the hills and redwoods across the highway, the benchlands above us covered with fields of artichokes and Brussels sprouts.

Our days were structured. In the morning, first thing, it was coffee, then a run up the beach and back. Midmornings, we drove into town and hung out on Pacific Avenue, then had lunch. Evenings, we smoked a little dope and strolled down the beach to watch the surfers.

In town, Lenny seemed to know everyone. We were constantly stopping so he could chat. That's when I realized how Santa Cruz seemed to exist in a bubble, as if it had been set aside for posterity by a Cultural Conservancy whose mission was the preservation of strange and rare cultural formations. Here it was always going to be 1969. A fixed point in time jealously protected by the hippies who'd taken control of the town back in the 1960s and 1970s. This was their sanctuary, a moment in American cultural history frozen as if in a snapshot. That was their intent, anyway, though I can't say that the relics I saw walking around town were as well preserved. But Lenny certainly seemed to know everyone, friends and acquaintances from his former lives in Berkeley, the Haight, Marin, Venice, Laurel Canyon, and God knows where else. I found it all vastly entertaining.

Friday evening, we drove up into the Santa Cruz Mountains, up Route 9 through Felton and Ben Lomond to Brookdale and the Brookdale Lodge. The place was packed, it was like stepping back into the Summer of Love: tie-die, a light show, old hippie bands, that night the remnants of Big Brother and the Holding Company and some of the guys from Quicksilver. Amazing. We ended up spending the night on the floor of what originally must have been someone's little weekend mountain retreat, now the cozy home of old radicals who'd fled the madness of the late '60s and early '70s for life in Boulder Creek. The drive home in the morning was long and lovely as Lenny guided us through Big Basin and the redwoods to Bonny Doon, dropping down the steep grade to the beach and Highway One.

It was the next morning that Lenny announced he was going to make stew for dinner, which necessitated a run into town so Lenny could buy several bags of groceries at The Staff of Life, a natural foods store that felt like an adventure in time travel. Once we were back he got out a small propane tank and burner, then fumbled around in an envelope looking for what he said was a recipe, holding it up with a big smile when he finally found it. Curious, I picked up the envelope. Yes, numerous little slips of paper, each a carefully written recipe. When I asked who'd written them, since none were in his scribbled hand, he laughed and said they were recipes old girlfriends had written down for him. When I asked him whose recipe we were having for dinner tonight he said it was his favorite, meticulously written down for him by Sharon. I knew Sharon! Now that was a surprise.

As he cooked I teased him about the contrast between the longevity of the dish and the brief life of the relationship that had spawned it. He laughed, admitting he'd never really thought about it like that, but he did collect recipes and women, both activities intertwined in a way that seemed to him both natural and unremarkable. And I have to say that the stew that night was pretty damn good, and it was oddly charming to sit there in one of his beat-up old plastic lawn chairs eating Sharon's stew, remembering her from many years ago, the interesting young woman who must have liked to cook. I thought, well, if in nothing else, at least her memory still lingers in his cooking, a memory that was probably just as savory.

The next morning as we sat sipping our coffee Lenny finally began to talk about what had happened to him at the track. He told me he'd moved on in his handicapping to what I'd call trip handicapping, although that's not quite what it was and certainly not how it functioned in Lenny's calculations. He called them his stumblers. He was patient. They didn't come along every day, but when one did he carefully tracked its progress, waiting for its luck to change. These were horses that had been the unlucky victims of circumstance. What handicappers might more commonly describe as victims of a bad trip: the jockey lost his whip in the stretch, the horse reared in the starting gate at the break, got pinned inside on the rail or fanned wide at the top of the stretch, shuffled back when it clipped heels with another horse or was up against a track bias that put it at great disadvantage. There's no end to misfortunes like these at the track, and it only takes one to ruin a handicapper's day. The obvious reason for taking note of these events—a time honored handicapper's strategy that Lenny seemed unaware of—is that such horses will now appear to the crowd, and hopefully even to the sharper bettors, as much worse than they truly are. Given a new set of circumstances and better luck, such a horse might even be worth a second, possibly even a third look in its next few races.

Ultimately, what this all boils down to is looking for a race in which a misunderstood horse fools the crowd to our advantage. Looking for a race where the odds, or price, is out of line with a horse's true chances of winning. The pro is always looking for an inefficient market. Picking stocks, picking horses, it's all the same. Of course, I'm stating this using mainstream handicapping concepts Lenny rarely used. For Lenny it wasn't about price or probability, it was about waiting out fate and chance and believing that at some point things just had to even out for this unfortunate horse. That at some point the universe just had to cycle back into a more harmonious balance, and when it did he would be there waiting for it, anticipating it, even betting on it.

I listened and thought he sees only what he is, a stumbler, a man who views his life as largely beyond his control, full of bad luck and happenstance, which is what he was doing living out there in his van at Red, White and Blue Beach, waiting for the blessings of balance and just proportionality to once again descend upon him.

When I asked him if he thought he'd get back in the game he sighed and stared down the little valley to the beach.

When I asked him how he'd know when it was time he just shrugged his shoulders.

49

I sighed and rolled up the window, then started the car and drove back down the pier to West Cliff. Eventually, Lenny did get back to the races, moving to a cramped apartment in Berkeley to play Golden Gate, but he never sunk so low as to need a job, becoming a teller at one of the betting windows like some of his pals. But then he'd never intended to participate in the capitalist economy anyway.

I never made it up to San Mateo. Instead, I drove all the way up Highway One and came into San Francisco the back way through Pacifica. I stayed for a couple of nights in a cheap motel out by the Presidio. I didn't do much. Some Italian restaurants in North Beach, the DeYoung, Amoeba in the Haight, Moe's over in Berkeley, and dinner at Greens the night before I left for home.

50

As I've already mentioned, I was in the middle of an epic losing streak when Lee showed up. It began out at Santa Anita a few days after Christmas. I was downstairs by the paddock taking a break before the seventh race, absolutely nothing on my mind, just contentedly enjoying the flow, when I got blindsided.

"Jesus Christ! When did they let you out?"

"Who do you like, bro?"

"Scully." At first that's all I could say. Then we shook hands as he rocked me back and forth, that big hand on my shoulder.

"How're you doing, Nick?"

"Not as good as you." Tailored slacks? Expensive loafers? I was stunned. "So what happened to the pins?" I touched my lip. "And the shaved head?" I stepped back to look at him more carefully. "Is that a silk shirt?"

Laughing, he shook his head, amused by my surprise, but when he offered no explanation for his startling transformation I began to feel a bit of that old dread in the pit of my stomach. The one I used to feel when he came around pestering me for a quick score. Finally, I just said it. "I don't want to know anything about it. Okay?"

"Nick, it's fine."

"Really?"

He nodded. "I've got a web company that sells stuff." He smiled at the shocked look on my face. "Legal stuff."

"My, you have changed," I said, for the first time really smiling. I wanted to believe him.

"How about you? Still scratching around out here trying to make a living?"

"I do all right, as you well know." I stared at him, trying to remember. "How long has it been?"

"A long time."

I was trying to calculate how long. Ten years? Close to that, anyway. It didn't seem possible. "How long were you in?"

"I got out in six."

"So for once you were a good boy."

"For once," he said, looking slightly embarrassed.

We'd met down in Huntington Beach. I knew a woman—a much younger woman—who'd coerced me into taking her to a punk club down there. It wasn't at all my sort of place, but she was into it and I liked her. It turned out to be loud, chaotic, angry, and exuberantly nihilistic. Nietzsche would have called it Dionysian. The bands were Agent Orange and Black Flag. Scully dated, if that was the word for it, her little sister. That's how we met.

"So where have you been hiding yourself since you got out?"

"Mostly over in Phoenix."

"You don't miss L.A.?"

"I miss the winning," he said with a laugh.

"Is that what brought you here today? You need a winner?"

"No," he said, suddenly looking a bit evasive. "You remember Hank? We're here today with some dudes he knows."

I raised my eyebrows and waited for more, but yeah, I remembered Hank, he was the one who didn't get arrested.

"It's business, you know? Like those businessmen who get together to talk over a deal while shooting a round of golf."

"Except that this is the track and it will probably be over a few losing bets."

"Probably. You still hanging out with that guy, Tommy?"

I hesitated, finally nodding.

"Is he still floating those communal bets of his?"

"He won't take your money."

"You think he still remembers me?"

"You think you're easy to forget?"

He smiled and shook his head. "Tommy's a good guy. Tell him I'm sorry I pissed him off."

"My, you have changed."

"I mean it. I know what an asshole I was."

"You do?" I was trying, I really was, and I almost believed him.

"See this?" He held up his big left hand in front of my face.

"Yeah?" I wasn't sure what he was showing me.

"The ring. I'm married."

"You?" I was stunned. "Anyone I know?"

"No!" He laughed. "She's from Phoenix." Then he paused to look at me so oddly, like maybe he really was happy, quietly adding: "We have a little girl."

I didn't know what to say, but then I suppose anyone can get married and have a child. It's not all that difficult. But I'd never thought of Scully as a potential candidate. I did have to wonder if he was a good father and husband. But what sort of woman would marry Scully? That was the hard one. I couldn't imagine such a woman. "Well, congratulations," I finally said, trying not to sound as shocked as I felt. "That's fantastic. What's her name?"

"Grace."

"You named her after your mother?"

"It's a nice name."

Wow, I'd forgotten all about her. "How is your mom?"

"She's fine. I bought her a house over there so she could be close to her granddaughter."

"You bought her a house?" I took a step back and just stared, wondering how many more surprises he could spring.

"Yeah, in Apache Junction." He winked at me. "Mom always liked you. You should come over and play Turf Paradise some time."

"Well . . . maybe, but do say hi for me, and tell her I'm glad her son seems to have finally come to his senses."

Laughing, he patted me on the back. "You just won't let yourself believe it, will you?"

"No, I will. I just need a little time to get used to the idea."

I noticed him look over my shoulder and nod at someone, and when I turned to see who there was Hank walking our way with three men who did look like businessmen. Hank! His transformation was even more startling than Scully's.

"Nick!" he said when he recognized me. "I thought we might run into you today. How're the horses treating you?"

"I'm doing okay. Not as good as you, apparently. I mean, look at you."

He laughed and turned to the three men. "This dude's one sharp horseplayer. Nick used to give Tim and me some pretty good tips back in the day when we were just a couple of punks chasing a winning bet." He smiled at me. "Man, was that a long time ago."

"You guys are business partners?" It just seemed so improbable.

"Yeah. We're part of the company." Hank gave me a sly smile. "We're always looking for new investors."

"No thanks," I said, smiling at his three businessmen. "I like to keep my money off the grid, if you know what I mean?"

"The IRS still after your ass? Then we probably don't want your money, do we?" he said, winking at his companions.

"What would I be investing in if you did?"

"We market stuff. Synthetic growth hormones, health products . . . from South Korea," he added, glancing at the three businessmen.

"There's a big market for these . . . legal drugs?" I turned to look at Scully, who smiled, nodding his head. "Well, no thanks, I think I'll just stick with horses, though God knows there's probably a few of your products out in the barns somewhere.

239

So," I said, taking a step backwards. "I better get going. Don't want to get shut out at the windows."

"You got anything for old time's sake?" Hank asked.

I looked at Scully. He shrugged. It was cool with him if I declined, but Hank was showing off, and, well, why not, it had been a long time.

"Okay," I said, fishing around in my bag for the right printout. "See these?" I pointed to Ace of Spades and they all stepped forward to see. "These are his pace figures for his last three best at this distance. If he runs like this today, at worst he's going to be second. Then I'd have a look at these two." I was pointing to Branded and Rawhide. Then I saw Hank turn to look at the monitor and grin. Turning to see for myself, there it was, Ace of Spades was holding at 7 to 1.

"What's the story here, Nick?" Scully said with a big grin. "I don't remember you being much of a figs guy. And who's this trainer?" He was looking at his program. "This Mullins? I don't remember him."

"You will. You never get a price like this on a Mullins horse. Not around here. But this one's recent form seems a bit, shall we say, cloudy." I smiled broadly at them. "I'm predicting that the proper order of the universe will be reestablished here in about ten minutes."

"Now, that's the Nick I remember," Hank said, slapping my back.

I held out my hand and Hank took it. "Good luck, with everything," I said. I turned to Scully. "Tell the Graces hello."

I was thinking about Grace as I made my way upstairs, an attractive woman a year or two younger, who, when Scully was arrested, showed up at my front door in the middle of the night asking for help. I'd referred her to my friend, Wendy, who'd told her who to talk to, and they'd been able to do some good for him, but he'd been guilty and stupid and there'd been a gun and they couldn't do much about that. Yeah, the underclass, interesting—at a distance.

The Bet

When I got back to the box Tommy was talking to one of the
many losers he choses to tolerate, this one a short sloppy guy with
a long ratty ponytail who always wore a black Raiders t-shirt. At
least once a day he came around and somehow always managed to
extract from Tommy a useful piece of information or two. I
refused to speak to him. When he left Tommy sat back down
with heartfelt sigh.

"I don't know why you talk to that guy everyday."

He turned to me and shrugged.

"How long has he been coming around here, anyway?"

Tommy smiled at me. "I don't remember when he didn't
come around here, do you?"

I thought about it and laughed. "Not really."

"I'll tell you what. Why don't you take a crack at him next
time."

"No thanks, I've got problems of my own. Remember Tim
Scully?"

He looked at me blankly.

"Mister pierced eyebrows?"

He still didn't remember.

"The kid you told never to come around here again?"

"Scully!"

I nodded. "Guess who I just ran into down in the paddock?"

"Here?" He was looking around like he expected to see Scully
appear at any moment.

"Don't worry, he's not coming up here. But he did ask me to
offer you his apologies. He said he knows what an asshole he
was."

"Was? He really said that?"

I nodded my head.

He grinned at me. "You gave him a tip, didn't you?"

"Mullin's horse. Hardly classified information."

"Scully?" I could see him remembering. "Wasn't he the kid
you helped when he got busted selling meth? I remember now,"
he said, smiling at me, "he had an attractive mother."

"I did what I could."

"Uh-huh."

"Anyway, he appears to have transformed himself into something resembling a respectable citizen. Yes, I know it's a bit hard to believe, and this you probably won't, but he says he's married and has a daughter."

"The kid I can believe, but not the rest. Come on, a guy like Scully, he's never going to do anything that's straight. And that kid . . . what chance does she have with a father like that?"

"I know, all these fucked kids have to come from somewhere, but there he was down in the paddock with these three guys he said were businessmen. Investors, partners, or something or other, in his company."

"What company?"

"Synthetic growth hormones. He said it was legit. Honestly," I said when he looked at me incredulously.

"It can't be."

"Well, I suppose I do have a few doubts."

"A few? We are talking about the same kid? Remember how he stood right over there and accused us of taking his money? You do you recall that little incident?"

"I know, but it would be nice to think he's changed. That he's really sorry."

"I'll bet you any amount at whatever odds you want that he's still a lying little prick."

"No thanks."

He grinned at me. "Nick, you're too much of a nice guy for your own good. That kid took advantage of you, and now you want to believe he's changed? Well, I hope he has. I also hope he doesn't abandon that little girl and her mother or do something that gets him fifteen years in prison. But you know what?"

"Probably."

"He's got no moral code. No sense of what's right and wrong. There's nothing there but a kid from a busted home in a trailer park down in Long Beach whose mom couldn't control him. He was a drug dealer and probably a whole lot worse. He'll never change any of that."

"Maybe not."

I watched him glance over his shoulder. "You're sure he's not coming up here?"

"Tommy, I'm sure."

"Good." He seemed to relax. Then he smiled. "By the way, doesn't he still owe you some money?"

"Oh, probably, but there are a lot of people around here who fit that bill."

"Want to guess how many people owe me?"

"I don't have to guess, you cheap bastard."

Leaning over, he playfully smacked the top of my head with his program. "Because I give them information, not money. I want my losers to be self-reliant, not crying on my shoulder like yours do. The way you baby them, you should've been a priest."

"I'm not a Catholic."

"No? Well you sure can act like one."

"Fine," I said, trying to ignore him as I leafed through my printouts.

"You better hope that Mullins horse wins or that punk will be up here demanding his money back."

As it turned out, Ace of Spades did win, and easily, but by the start of the race his odds had plunged to 2 to 1—so much for my exclusive insight.

51

I couldn't get Scully off my mind. Up to a point what Tommy said of me was true, I am a nice guy, but I'm not that nice, and I'm certainly not naïve. I know there are people out there like Scully. I also know there always will be. People who only grudgingly go along with the dictates of the social world we all must inhabit to be fully human. It's like this: to live a normal life we need to take our social world as a given, as natural, as unquestioned, unthinkingly assenting to its rules, norms, roles, structures, practices, customs, meanings, and prohibitions. It's this that defines our existence. But such natural assent is alien to people like Scully. In that they are totally unlike the social theorists whose critiques of modernity counsel a radical questioning and rejection of this reified "second nature." Seduced by the implicit eroticism of transgression, the implicit danger of their thought, they naïvely and romantically advocate a radical rejection they've never actually experienced nor dared to live. Scullys don't reject like that. In fact, it's not really accurate to say they reject at all, for to reject one has to first feel the domination of this reified naturalness within oneself. Scullys have no such feeling. They're the ideal type of those without human naturalness, those who have never felt the normative tug of our fragile human world upon their behavior.

So that's where the losing began, with the unease I was left with for the rest of that afternoon. Sure I tried to shrug it off, after all, it was just a feeling, right? But by the next day I knew what I was in for. Although there is one consolation to be found in this, laughably ironic as it may be, that the one thing a losing streak will do for you is relentlessly narrow your choices down to one exquisitely simple little fork in the road: do I sit it out or play on through? Hence the pain is focused, the reaction starkly simple, though so very difficult to live with. And it's not like there aren't warning signs that a losing streak is looming, it's just that we don't see them for what they truly are until it's too late. Of course, by then all hell's broken loose and we're too stunned by the implacable logic unfolding within our lives to do much more than bear silent witness to its remorselessness. It's always about then that I promise myself I will not act pathetically or scramble about trying to make personal sense out of what is quintessentially impersonal. What I'm left with are acts of courage. No? You think it's a trivial thing to try and predict the future and then bet money you're right? Hubris and courage, they do still go hand-in-hand? Or are we now so divorced from the classical understanding of life that such a notion seems absurd? Has our age become so simple-minded that we just can't see it, how these are acts bravely asserted in the face of indifference? What you have to remember is that a losing streak is not just one thing gone wrong, it's a series, a serial misfortune that will extend out over time until I just can't take any more. Yes, but if I stop how will I ever know when it's finally over? You do see the problem.

My days at the track almost always start well. It's rare that I show up with a bad attitude, without my personal reserves of optimism and great expectations recharged. I'm almost always revved up and ready to go. However, as a bad day progresses and as I'm repeatedly hammered by miscalculation and loss I inevitably find myself in the grips of this notion that my optimism has been hideously misplaced. I hate that feeling, of knowingly living within a falsehood, just about as much as I hate anything, but there it is and there's nothing much I can do but sit there with the bitter taste in my mouth of being a fool, a racetrack sucker whose money is going home with someone else, an idiot who fails to understand anything anymore except that the world sucks. But it's not just the monetary loss that gets me, it's this intuition I have that the world has, for reasons unknown, or at least for reasons unknown to me, gone off the rails and there's nothing I can do about it. I can't change my game, not really, because I'm not doing anything wrong. That is I'm not doing anything different from what I'd normally do. It's just that for some reason normal no longer seems to be in play and I don't know why.

Do you know what it's like to live through a long winter? One that seems like it will never end? Of course you never start out thinking it won't, but then as it drags on and on you do begin to wonder. And maybe by then your life has been reduced to nothing but this endless stretch of tedious, dreary days. Perhaps you can't even remember what nice weather was like. If so, then perhaps you can also remember what it felt like when, in mid-March, snow still on the ground, you spotted that first nodding bloom of a yellow daffodil on the south side of the house. Remember how that felt when you realized that no matter what else might happen, for you this winter was over? Remember that profound, deep sense of spiritual relaxation that came over you? Well, that's what it feels like when I suddenly realize the losing is behind me.

PART THREE

Let's just say there's nothing that's
a sure thing before it happens.

The Bet

52

"I once asked a woman that question and she spent the next ten minutes trying to decide if I was teasing her."

"Were you?"

"No more than I'm teasing you."

She glanced quickly in my direction, not wanting to take her eyes off the heavy traffic. "Who was she?" she asked.

"Just a woman I knew in Florida."

"Florida? When was this?"

"Years ago. We used to play tennis in the morning before it got too hot."

"I didn't know you played tennis?"

"Do you?"

"No, I swim. So what was her answer?"

"She talked about her two children."

She turned to smile at me. "I bet that made an impression."

"I like kids," I lied.

"But she didn't answer your question."

"No, but I didn't want to hurt her feelings so I let it go."

"So how was she, in this life you've been living?"

"She was fine, but why are you making my question sound so foolish?"

"Isn't it?"

I turned in my seat to look at her. "I take it that means you're not going to answer."

"How's it been for me?"

"Yes, how's it been, living this life?"

"Well, I'm not sure. I think you first need to tell me what *it* is?"

"Like all of us, you've been living a life, and by that I mean your particular life. So I'm just wondering how it's been going. How you've found it. This living a life business."

"Nick, that just sounds so odd. Like living a life is the equivalent of renting a room."

"Odd? Like we don't each have a life to live? So doesn't that make for some sort of comparable experience? One we should all have something to say about? But not about all those things you've done, just about how it's been, being a person living a life."

"Well," she said, smiling at me, "then I guess I'd have to say it's been interesting. Especially today."

We came to an intersection where we were forced to wait for a left turn, but impatient as always, she eased my car out into the intersection and when the traffic thinned, gunned it.

"You do know," she said, "that most people aren't all that happy with their *it*."

"Really? Because I think their answers might surprise you."

"I know what my colleagues would say, that they're just too ignorant to know any better. Or they'd be miserable if only they were better informed."

"I must say, you and your colleagues have certainly shouldered a heavy burden, being the official arbiters of false consciousness."

"Heavy? Maybe for them, for me it's as light as a feather."

"So you'd really tell someone their happiness was based on a lie?"

"I might."

"Tell them they weren't really happy? That they didn't even know what true happiness was?"

"If they were ignorant and happy I probably wouldn't say anything, but I'd certainly be tempted if they were ignorant and unhappy."

"But either way, aren't you really just expressing your contempt? Or are you going to argue that this is just some form of higher, or true, sympathy?"

"What about you, where do you fall in this delicate balance? You and your survey?"

"I don't. I'm just trying to get a handle on user satisfaction. Just trying to gather a little more data. Though I've already got more than enough to show there should have been a recall or two."

"Uh-huh. What was her name, by the way?"

"Whose?"

"The first person. She was the first you surveyed?"

"I'm not sure."

"You don't remember her name? No wonder you're worried that our lives consist of nothing but unimportant details."

"No," I laughed. "I'm not sure she was the first. Though she certainly should have been the last."

"So?"

"Cherry."

"Lovely name. Topless dancer?"

"Hardly, Southern woman just have interesting names, which is part of their considerable charm. And don't let that name fool you, not only was she very bright, she was one of the nicest persons I've ever known."

"And?"

"And what?"

"I don't know, but it sure feels like you've leaving out something important."

"Have you ever been to Florida?"

She turned to smile at me. "You're changing the subject. I wonder why."

"Because you only think you want to know about her."

"Which I take to mean you really liked her."

"What's wrong with that?"

"Would you like to know what I really think?"

"No."

"I'm jealous. That's right," she said, looking at me. "Surprises me too. Now what do you suppose that means?"

"Take the next right."

"What?"

"Sorry, I should have been paying more attention to where we going. Just take the next right and then the first left." I waited until she had. "Now, see that old black Corvette? The bungalow just past that is where I lived when I first moved out here."

"With the palm tree?"

"That's it. Pull in over there so we can take a look." I was pointing across the street.

It's still nothing special, just a modest bungalow from the 1920s that probably served as someone's weekend beach house. Most of the neighborhood still looks like that even as Venice gentrifies. Two blocks to the beach, still mostly rentals, most in need of significant repair, but it looked good with its new porch and brick chimney looking straighter than it had in years. There were even bright flowers by the walk. I was also pleased to see that someone had recently laid down a makeshift gravel driveway between the house and the neighbor's fence. That would have solved all my problems when I used to hunt for a place to park on the weekends.

"How long did you live here?"

"Off and on, three years." She turned to look at me. "I did some traveling. Phoenix, Seattle, New Orleans, New York . . . Miami."

"Racetracks?"

"Among other things."

"Like tennis partners?"

"I used to need a lot of exercise."

"Who'd you play tennis with when you lived here?"

"Would you like to meet them?"

"You're still friends?"

"We see each other occasionally."

"At the track?"

"And elsewhere. Her name's Wendy, she's a lawyer, her partner, Sarah, works for Fox. We've known each other ever since our bookstore days. You'd actually be quite a surprise. I'm one of Wendy's biggest disappointments. She's been trying to get me coupled up for years."

"I've wondered about that," she said, putting her hand on my shoulder. "Whether you ever found someone and settled down. No family, of course, but I was hoping you'd at least paired off. But you haven't, have you? It's just been one woman after another."

"There were a few I could've been happy with, one in particular, but things just didn't work out. But you make it sound so pitiful. It really hasn't been. Come on," I said, patting her leg. "Let's get out of here."

We drove to the beach, where I directed her to a parking lot. "It's quite a scene, isn't it?" I said once we were parked, nodding to the throngs of people streaming by on the wide sidewalk.

"What? Oh, yes," she said, turning to look at me. "You know, it's not the thought of you with other women that bothers me, it's the thought of you being with someone like you were with me."

"Well, just so you'll know, I've never been with anyone like I was with you. For the most part it's just been sex."

"Nick, I know you. With you it's never just sex."

"Wow, am I a jerk."

53

It was lovely when we finally got out of the car. The air had that briny smell of kelp at low tide, the sun low over a slate blue sea, and though it looked cold, an offshore breeze held the sea's chill at bay, pushing the visible horizon back many miles out across the Pacific.

"Still noting things, I see." She'd been watching me. "Come on," she said, taking my hand and pulling me across the sidewalk to the sand.

At first we struggled to make headway, but the going got easier when we reached wetter, compacted sand, then at the ocean we stopped, watching the waves rolling underneath themselves as they reached shallower water, their tops shearing off and blowing away in the wind, a fine spray of bright sparkling droplets in the sunlight as the surging waves carried on underneath.

Sheets of water hissed up the flat beach almost to our feet, pausing a beat before retreating back across the sand. When the next wave rolled in she took off her sandals to walk towards it, letting it lap up over her feet to dampen the bottoms of her slacks. Laughing, she bent down to roll them up, then hurried to catch the retreating surge as it slid back down the beach. When she stopped her feet were covered with wet sand. Wiggling her toes, she looked up at me and laughed.

"Look out," I said, pointing to a large wave about to break. "You're going to get wet."

"Oops," she said, running back up the beach to join me.

When it broke we were forced to retreat, walking backwards to stay ahead of the spreading sheet of water. Then letting me go on alone, she stopped to let the surge swirl around her ankles and feet. When it pulled back her feet were completely hidden by the sand.

"I'm amazed," she said. "Walking on the beach with Nick."

"It's certainly taken you long enough to get here."

"Yes," she said, watching me with surprising intensity. A look I hadn't seen in a long time.

The sun was getting very low in the sky. The sea was a series of fat swells, a broad sheen of water, large undulations slowly rolling towards the shore. Shiny, almost oily, their surface seemed elastic, just able to contain the surging gelatinous mass of water, a sack that had to break, freeing a jumble of peaks and sharp angles that were finally absorbed and calmed by the beach.

Out in the swells a lone surfer sat very low in the water on his board, its sharp nose sticking up in the air like a tombstone, bobbing up and down with each passing swell. Three gulls shrieked in the distance. I turned to see them wheeling in the air above something left in the parking lot. There too was the car, the small bungalows along the street, the shaggy palms sticking up above the rooftops, and what remained of our tracks across the sand.

"I don't believe I've ever walked on the beach like this before," she said. "What about you? You must have walked on the beach when you lived here."

"Not that I can recall."

"Why won't you tell me?"

"Because it's not that memorable."

"You know, it's a funny thing about us. When I left—you're surprised to hear me say that, aren't you?"

"Very. I've been expecting euphemisms."

"We're too old for euphemisms. So when I left you back in Boulder I always thought we'd see each other again."

"I didn't."

"I know you didn't, but I held on to that belief for a long time. Of course, now that we have I find it's dredged up all sorts of unfinished business."

"With us, or are you referring to your marriage?"

"I'm not necessarily referring to anything, but you can't blame me for wondering what it would've been like if you'd been taking those walks on the beach with me."

"So everything's all right with your marriage?"

"Of course it is, but I hardly need to tell a gambler that things don't always work out exactly as planned. In which case a little second-guessing hardly seems out of place."

"I view second guessing as a professional failing."

"Talking about this makes you uncomfortable, doesn't it?"

"I just don't see the point. You are who you are, presumably living the life you've always wanted. A life, I might add, that you not only carefully picked out for yourself, but that never had a place in it for me."

"I see. So now you're going to feel sorry for yourself."

"I'm working on it."

"Fine, I'm more than willing to accept my share of the blame, but *just* my share. So if you think you're going to spend the weekend fucking with a clear conscience you're mistaken."

"Spend the weekend fucking?"

"Well?" she said, grinning at me.

"Fine, just so you understand something first."

"And what's that?"

"How difficult this is for me, because unlike you I never entertained any comforting fantasies about seeing you again. Instead, I went off and made a life for myself. As for blame, if it makes for a happier weekend I'll gladly shoulder the whole thing."

"Wow. I'd better be worth it, huh?"

"Fuck all weekend?" I shook my head. "You make it sound so squalid."

"Oh?" she said, grinning at me.   "You're not going to disappoint me, are you?"

Yes, I did wonder about that.

54

Back at the car, she used my keys to unlock her door, then got in and leaned over to unlock mine. When I sat down beside her she was looking at herself in the rearview mirror as she removed a silver clasp from her hair. Then she shook her head, letting her hair cascade down around her face, but when she gathered it up with her left hand to put the clasp back in I stopped her. Surprised, she leaned back in her seat to watch me. That look, those mannerisms, it was all so familiar. This was how she used to look at me, when she meant to say *it's just you and me, isn't it?* Suddenly, she sat up and lightly kissed me on the lips, then moistened her lips to kiss me again, a kiss we lingered over, and though it was incredibly awkward I did manage to turn in my seat and sort of take her in my arms, slowly moving my hand up to cup her breast. Yes, I was intensely aroused, but it was just so ludicrous that when she pulled back we both began to laugh.

"Um, maybe it's time to think about getting you back to your hotel?"

"Yes," she said, slowly sliding her hand down to my lap. "Too bad I didn't know something like this was going to come up. I would have planned on a longer stay."

"Still, in the end nothing but a fading memory."

"More like a lingering obsession. One that seems," she said, pointedly glancing at my lap, "to have suddenly swollen in importance."

"I'm not so sure. These are just the sorts of rare events that always trouble my handicapping."

"When did they get rare?"

"Well, maybe rare isn't quite the right word. Let's just say there's nothing that's a sure thing before it happens."

"*Before* it happens? But I thought that was the whole point of making a bet? You're not saying otherwise, are you?"

"What I'm saying is we've got this horse—"

"This horse thing, this is sort of your narrative equivalent of *I once knew this guy*, isn't it?"

"Lee, it's *all* happening at the track."

"So it would seem."

"So . . . I want to bet this horse, but I first need to assess her chances. Okay, I do a bit of handicapping and conclude that all things being equal she should win this race about once ever five times its run. She's got, in other words, about a twenty per cent chance of winning. That's four to one odds. What I hope to see, of course, is that the betting public thinks her true odds are much worse. Say five, or even six to one. That's my edge."

"Does she win?"

"She does, but how she does suggests that my initial estimate of her chances was too conservative. Now I'd like to say that a more accurate assessment of her odds would have pegged her at three to one. But that can't be right. Don't we really want to say that if we'd known then what we know now we would have said her true chances of winning were actually one hundred percent?"

"I thought you said they were three to one?"

"Even after the race? After all, she did win. So given the same circumstances why should she ever lose?"

"But she will."

"Even when the conditions are identical? Because if they are won't she always win this race?"

"One hundred percent of the time?"

"It's a puzzle, isn't it?"

"It certainly is the way you've stated it."

"Need a minute?"

"How about a week," she said, laughing.

"Don't bother, I know what you'll say, that what we're really talking about here are similar, not identical circumstances. So it's under similar sets of circumstances that we can expect this nice filly to win once every three or four races. Sounds reasonable. But we aren't handicapping classes of races, we're handicapping individual races, each one of which has its own unique set of circumstances. So why, given these very particular circumstances, would we ever expect her not to do again exactly as she's done today?"

"But what about the other horses? They will always lose, forever? Is that what you're saying?"

"Hard to believe, isn't it?"

"Yes, and repugnantly Nietzschean. Manfully embracing the sobering truth, the test of our wills, that what happened will recur forever, over and over again just as always with no deviation."

"I'm not that manly."

"That race you lost or misunderstood? Bad enough you lost your bet, but now you see you'll always lose your bet."

"I'd rather not drag Nietzsche into this," I said, laughing. "I'm just saying that the true probability for any particular horse winning any particular race is really one hundred percent. That it is and will always be one hundred percent. We just don't know beforehand which horse it is that's one hundred percent."

"But isn't that the point, the knowing beforehand? Doesn't sound to me like this way of looking at things is very helpful."

"Not so far."

"Maybe you need to change how you handicap."

"There's not much to change. We have this race, one that fits within a particular class of similar races, ones in which the winner almost always matches a certain profile, so in our handicapping we look to see which horses in today's race do and then grade their chances accordingly. But I still don't see how this indeterminacy isn't fixed at some point, after which, as I've just said, the winner's probability is forever after one hundred percent."

"Though you don't know which one that will be until after the race has run?"

"That's right. No event ever occurs with less than a one hundred percent probability, whether we know about it beforehand or not. There is a cusp of indeterminacy, but that indeterminacy is only in us, not in what happens. After the fact, they are finally congruent. We know what happened and now we know why it had to be that way. It's really the only way it could have played out. If only we'd known beforehand."

"So everything that's happened had to be? There's no indeterminacy in the world only in our understanding of it?"

"Why do I feel like I don't want to agree with you?"

"Because you started out wondering about probabilities and now here you are a radical determinist. I hope you're happy, now that you've very neatly eliminated all chance and indeterminacy from our world."

"Happy? Well, if I'm correct then I suppose I should already know the answer to that."

"But since you don't we can only conclude you haven't the faintest idea what you're talking about."

"All right, let's just say there is a residual bit of radical indeterminacy that escapes my simple-minded logic. I hope there is. I hope that whatever happens to us isn't always fated by necessity to turn out just as it has. I'm sure we would all welcome the introduction of a refreshing note of change in our lives."

"We might even embrace such a change," she said, grinning at me.

"Yes," I said, grinning back, "but unfortunately we humans are so prone to errors in judgment that our world will always seem more haphazard and unpredictable than it really is. So in the end what's the difference?"

"There's a big difference."

"Fine, so let's just flip this around and see if you like it any better the other way."

"Seriously? Does the truth even mean anything to you at all?

"Not for some time. I've learned to settle for just being close."

"I see. Well, things are, as they say, getting clearer."

"Oh, come on, no one ever does better than close."

"Yes, but at least they try to be consistent in their closeness."

"Just let me get this out, will you."

"Go."

"So the world, that which is, is truly open to different outcomes."

"This is your flip? From only one is possible to many are?"

"The one and the many, still good after all these years."

"Amazing."

"So now I'll argue—"

"For amusement's sake only, of course."

"Of course. So now I'm saying the world *is* truly open to different possible outcomes, and that contrary to what our understanding leads us to believe, is deeply uncertain. This appears to contradict our common experience, that once an outcome is fixed, that is, once something has actually occurred, it looks to us as if it had to have happened in just that way and in no other. But this contradiction is only apparent because this is merely the product of our understanding, which is after the fact and after the race. So what comes into being may seem preordained, but this certitude is only the illusory byproduct of our acts of understanding. What is depends for its existence on an amorphous plenum of potentialities that only get actualized at the last possible moment, which gives us very little chance to accurately gauge their probability for existence beforehand. This movement from the possible to the actual is real, but the actual is just one realization of this potentiality, and there's just so much more potentiality than actuality that we just have no idea what's really going to be until it is. And perhaps it just happens. So maybe the best course of action for the handicapper is to attune herself to those subtle clues of potential being as it queues up, as it waits until the last possible and appropriate moment to pop into existence. Don't even worry about probabilities."

"Pops into existence! Did you even hear what you just said? And how is this supposed to help you at the track? It doesn't sound to me like it could."

"It might show a profit if I could ever figure out how to make it work."

"Exactly. So, Mr. Prognosticator, how about what happens next? Can you tell me anything about that?"

"Next, meaning here and now?"

"Yes."

"I haven't got a clue."

55

She started the car, then carefully backed out into the middle of the parking lot.

"Maybe I should just let you drive this back to Philadelphia."

"I'm ready."

"What do you drive at home?"

"Depends on which home."

"You have more than one?"

"One's a vacation home."

"Incredible. And you have different cars at each?"

"No, I was teasing about that."

"But one's a Volvo? Right? Academics always drive Volvos."

"What about a Prius?"

"Those too, but I see you more as a Volvo person."

"Could it be a station wagon?" she asked, laughing.

"Okay, that's one. So the other will be something good in the snow but it won't be American or an SUV. A Subaru?"

"No Subaru."

"Where is this vacation home, by the way? And please don't tell me it's on the Cape."

She turned to look at me. "What's wrong with the Cape?"

"Isn't that a little too bourgeois?"

"I wonder who you think we are."

"How about the Vineyard? Poor middle-class academics aping the rich people."

"Nope."

"The Hamptons?"

"Now you are joking."

I really wasn't. But maybe they didn't have a lot of money, though she certainly looked stylish. It was hard to imagine her roughing it. "Okay," I said, "I give up. People like you have always been a mystery to me."

"You're such a snob. What's wrong with owning a second home?"

"Nothing, though most people find one more than enough."

"I see. So now I'm supposed to feel all guilty about our little vacation home? You must own a home by now. Some nice little doublewide you put on your VISA card."

"Sorry, still a renter."

"It's just a cottage. On Block Island?" She was looking at me like I might not know where that was, which I didn't. "We share it with Charles's brother. It was their parent's. We'd never be able to afford such a place on our own. It's where we spent our honeymoon."

"How exciting."

"Oh?" she said, watching me. "That upsets you?"

"No, I realize it's hard for you to talk about yourself if we have an embargo on mentioning Charles. You are married to the guy, after all, a fairly significant fact it's rather hard to overlook."

"Though you'd like to try."

"What about you?"

"All right, let's have it," she said, glancing at me as she drove. "What's bothering you?"

"Nothing's bothering *me*, I was just wondering if there was anything bothering *you*."

"Would you rather I just drop myself off back at my hotel?"

"So you really aren't bothered?"

"Nick, it's just one weekend."

"But—"

"One," she insisted, holding up one finger.

"Yes, but doesn't that seem to suggest you're not as happy in your marriage as you say you are?"

"Which bothers you because?"

"I don't know, maybe because it reopens issues I thought were settled a long time ago."

"Uh-huh. That's just what I thought. Like you're agonizing over some moral or ethical dilemma. You're just worried this adulterous weekend might upset your emotional equilibrium."

"I'm not saying another word," I said, slumping back in my seat.

"Well, I'm sorry you seem to think I'm such a wanton woman. Just how guilty do I have to feel before you'll be happy?"

"You don't feel guilty at all," I said, laughing at her.

"That's right, I don't," she said, turning to look at me. "But stick around, maybe I will by the end of this weekend. And by the way, Charles drives an Audi TT."

"I should've known."

56

When we got to her hotel she gave the valet the keys to my car. As we walked through the lobby I told her I needed to stop off at the gift shop to get a few things.

"Then maybe I'll just go on up," she said. "I need to call Charles, anyway. Say in about ten minutes?"

"If you tell me your room number."

"1125."

I gave her those ten minutes, then rode the elevator up and knocked on her door. She was still on the phone when she opened it, holding up her hand in warning before I could say anything. "Five minutes?" she whispered. I nodded and dropped the little plastic bag I was carrying on a chair. "So what did you say?" I heard her ask as I shut the door.

I was annoyed. At the elevators I gave the button a sharp jab, and when the doors opened down in the lobby I kept on walking, not stopping until I was outside standing next to the gnarly old banyan tree looming over the circular drive in front of the hotel. I leaned back, palms flat against its massive trunk. The bark felt like stiff leather. I looked down. The earth was damp at my feet. I could smell it. Patches of lime-green moss grew on the bare earth between the tree's large knobby roots. The hotel watered too much.

My reaction surprised me. But it wasn't like she'd done that on purpose, though I knew a few women who'd love to put me in my place like that. Still, inadvertent or not, all I had to do was ask one of the valets to bring my car around. There was nothing stopping me. Just hop in and drive off like this day had never happened.

I took my time walking back across the lobby to the elevators.

"Nick, where were you?" she said when she opened the door. "That was a lot longer than five minutes."

"Sorry, I got hung up talking to a couple of guys down in the bar. By the way, they said to say hello."

"There probably are a few people here who shouldn't see us together."

"Oops. Can't have you becoming the topic du jour over at the faculty club."

"It wouldn't be the first time. I'm a notorious conference fuck."

"What?"

"Ah," she smiled. "Finally got you."

"You got me when you opened the door and you were still talking to Charles. I hope that wasn't intentional."

"No! I couldn't get him off the phone because he was so anxious to tell me about his meeting today with his department chair. I couldn't just cut him off. I'm sorry." She took my hand. "Were you really down in the bar? I looked for you out in the hallway."

"I took a walk."

"Because you were angry. You still are," she said, studying my face.

"I'm fine. So, are we finally through for the evening?"

"We are now," she said, reaching around me to lock the door. "Looks like you'll just have to spend the night."

"No problem. I'll just sneak out in the morning while you're still asleep and you'll never even know I was here."

"What are you smiling about?" She was exasperated with me. "Tell me the truth, I do look heavier, don't I?" She'd taken off her sandals and slacks. Now I could see her light blue panties peaking out from underneath her sweater.

"Stop pouting, you look fantastic."

"I'm sorry," she said, looking a bit glum, "it's not very romantic, is it?"

"I was just thinking we might as well be married."

"Like you'd know how married people behave."

"They don't behave like this?"

"Let's see." She walked across the room to pull me up out of my chair, then wrapped her arms around my neck as she stood unsteadily on her tiptoes to kiss me. As she pressed her breasts against my chest I ran my hands up under her sweater to feel her deliciously cool back.

"Are we in any sort of rush?" she asked, pulling back to see my face.

"Not really."

"Because I'd like to take a quick shower and then call room service."

"I told you to eat more at lunch."

"I thought I had, but now I'm starving."

"You're just nervous."

"It has been a long time."

"With me, you mean?"

"I mean I haven't made love to anyone but my husband in a long time."

"I should hope not."

"I knew you wouldn't understand," she said, giving my back a sharp pinch.

"I understand perfectly."

"What about you? How many women have you been with, assuming you can even remember them all?"

"You know what?" I said, trying to pull away from her. "I don't even want to be having this conversation."

"Yes. Jealously. It's surprising, isn't it? You're lucky I don't make up a bunch of stuff just to torment you, because I can see that it would."

"Which is exactly why I don't want to be having this conversation."

"Remember the first time we made love?"

"Vividly. Remember how assertive you were?"

"I know," she said, sounding amazed. "I really was. But you, my God, you were huge. Much bigger than that," she laughed, rubbing up against me.

"I may be a bit older but I'll get there."

"I just hope you haven't worn yourself out with all your tennis partners."

"Well, we'll see, won't we? Now," I said, smacking her butt, "go take your shower."

Off came the sweater and blouse, then she turned and I unfastened her bra, which she flipped on the bed. Then smiling shyly like this was the first time a man had seen her naked, she slowly slid her panties down and stepped out of them. As I watched she ran her hands up under her breasts and lifted them, turning her hips to the side as she stretched, clearly posing, inviting me to look at her body. She certainly watched my eyes when I did.

"How is it?" I asked.

"Good. How's your pasta?"

"Better than I'd expected. I don't usually have much luck with hotel food."

She leaned back in her chair and tugged at her bathrobe to get more comfortable, then tucked her feet up in the chair and picked up her wine glass. I thought it mildly erotic the casual way she sat with her damp hair looking almost black against her white bathrobe, leaning back with the glass in her hand as she watched me.

"I hope you don't mind if one of us actually eats their dinner," I said, reaching for her untouched dinner roll.

"You know, I've been watching you. You eat more than you used to."

"I hope I don't look heavier?"

Frowning at that, she playfully stuck out her tongue, which surprised me so much that I sat my fork down on my plate to stare at her. "I've never seen you do that before. Is this something new?"

"Maybe," she said, shrugging her shoulders.

"Do it again."

"No," she said, pressing her lips firmly together.

"Careful you don't wear yourself out with that." I picked up my fork and took a bite of pasta while watching her stare out the window. "You're looking awfully pensive over there. What's on your mind?"

"Us."

"Don't tell me you're finally having second thoughts?"

"No, just thinking about all the choices I've made. Thinking how nice it would be if we could start all over and just make the right ones."

I smiled at her, reaching for her hand. "I knew I'd never get to finish this dinner."

"Sorry."

"I may never have told you this before, though that seems unlikely since I seem to remember telling you everything."

"Whether I wanted to hear about it or not."

"Exactly. But I've never wanted anyone like I wanted you. So I'm very glad to see you back again for this encore performance in our adulterous weekend. As for choices, if the ones you've made today are any indication, then I hope you keep right on making them."

"You're so much more obedient than you used to be."

"Also more agreeable. All you need to do is tell me what you want."

"I want to remember how it was."

"Sorry, I don't believe in the redemptive power of memory."

"I do," she said, standing and pulling me towards the bed.

"And waste my one big adulterous weekend trying to recreate something we can barely remember? I'd rather take a shot at creating some new memories, however they may turn out."

"My, this is dangerous, isn't it?" she said, grinning at me.

57

In the morning we walked down the street to a Peet's for a quick breakfast, and while we were there I skimmed the abstracts of the papers for her conference. I was surprised, a few actually looked interesting, though I would never have told her so if she'd asked. Back at her hotel, I asked that my car be brought around. I was driving out to Santa Anita, stopping off at my place on the way to get some clothes and the few things I'd need for the weekend. The plan was to rendezvous back at her hotel later in the evening. So I kissed her goodbye when the kid brought the car up from the underground garage, then got in and drove away, leaving her standing there with several other people waiting for the campus shuttle.

My house felt uncomfortably cold and dark, so I hurried around raising all the blinds and opening the sliding door out to the patio. Then *L.A. Times* in hand from the driveway, I flopped down on the couch in the living room to sit in the sun. I turned to the sports section to see about Santa Anita. First up, the pick six. No, there'd be no carryover today. Then the payouts for all the straight bets and exotics, followed by which trainers and jockeys had been in the money, the winning times and running styles of the top finishers, and if any post position had won or lost more than its fair share. You might say I was looking to see if there were any signs that normal had not been in play. No, just another typical day at Santa Anita, everything once again inexplicably falling in line with those statistical norms that repeatedly emerge from that chaotic mix of variables constituting life at the track. Will I ever become so blasé as to stop wondering about this great mystery? I will not.

Setting the newspaper on the end table, I leaned back to enjoy the sun. Then feeling drowsy, I swung my feet up and stretched out on my back. I let my mind drift. Thinking about Lee. About how familiar she was. Her mannerisms. The way she spoke, how she stood, the way she looked at me and made love. All that and more I knew, though I could hardly have articulated it. It was like a forgotten song I was surprised to find I could still sing.

I guess I must have fallen asleep, or perhaps I was daydreaming. Maybe I was just remembering. It was early October. We were up in the mountains by Tolland. We'd driven up hoping we weren't too late to catch the aspens. It was sunny and dry, though standing in the shade at that elevation felt like stepping into a translucent pool of cold water. But we were warm enough sitting in the sun that we soon removed our jackets. I remember her smiling as she playfully rolled over on top of me in the dry grass while overhead the few remaining golden leaves rattled and danced stiffly in the breeze. Finally, we lay side by side looking up through the swaying branches at that intensely blue sky. At those ever-changing streamers of high thin clouds forming in the lee of the Divide as the jet stream rode up and over the high peaks. It was a nice day, a memorable day. By the time we got home we were both overcome by a sweet languor. Snuggled down under the covers in her bed between cool sheets, we slept for hours. When I awoke her hand was on my chest and her face next to my shoulder. I pulled her hair aside and watched her for some time. I sighed to myself on the couch; the heavy price of remembrance. Too distant, impossible to recreate, like so much else, perhaps like everything else, moments like that can't possibly happen twice. They're just gone. So gone they hurt to remember.

Groaning, I stood and stumbled off to the kitchen. I couldn't believe it when I looked at the clock. Was it really 12:20? She'd really worn me out.

I walked back to the living room, sat on the couch and reached for my laptop, then logged into my Twin Spires account and toggled Santa Anita. Three minutes before first post. Expanding the little window, I watched as they prepared to load, then based on nothing more than a whim I bet five dollars to win on the third favorite, which was going off at 5-2. Really? A spur of the moment bet based on nothing at all? I never made bets like that. Then I noticed who the trainer was. Okay. Roger Stein. Not so good. Not that Stein's all that bad, I actually like the guy, but he rarely gets a good horse, which means he rarely saddles a winner. But at least he doesn't lose because he's unlucky, which is an interesting fact to know about Stein, one that sets him apart from those whose losing ways can seemingly only be explained by persistently bad luck. Stein belongs in a different category. A solid member of that small but interesting handful of low percentage trainers who, when they do saddle a winner, can always be counted on to get a big price. The trick, of course, is to have the patience to wait, not to mention the timing to be along for the ride when the lightening finally strikes. Well, not this time, his horse finished well out of the money, which left me with the feeling that some one, or some thing, had let me down. Nevertheless, laptop in hand, I walked down the hall to print out the past performances, then checked the trainer index. Stein had entries in two other races. One of his big owners must be in town. I took a look. Yes, interesting, but hardly likely. But why was I even looking? Stupid enough to bet on a whim, but to play a hunch that a whim might still pay? A horseplayer can't sink any lower.

Still brooding, I left the printouts with the laptop on the coffee table and walked out the sliding door to my small flagstone patio. It's nice back there, the scruffy date palm next door, the noisy birds nesting up there in the dropping fronds. I pulled a lawn chair over into the shade and lay back with my hands behind my head. I thought: maybe I'll just stay where I am and play the races on the web. It was already too late to drive out to Santa Anita anyway. I smiled at the rationalization. I wasn't winning. It was that and nothing else that kept me there. Twenty minutes later I wandered back inside to check the results for the second race. Small prices. So far I hadn't missed anything, which is what so often drives me, that fear I'll miss out on my reward when all my hard work finally pays off.

I took another look at the past performances, paying special attention to the eighth, an allowance optional claiming turf route for fillies and mares four years old and up. Maybe Stein's horse would do well. He'd obviously convinced Solis's agent. But the probable pace sure didn't favor her, a front-runner who faded quickly under any sort of pressure. No such uncontested lead today. And who knew what Solis might do. No, don't even get me started on jockeys. But as always there were several obvious choices, horses with good turf records and high percentage trainers who'd garner most of the money in the betting pools. But what if one or more wasn't a legitimate in-the-money horse? Better still, what if one or more was a toss-out? Well? But I couldn't decide. It just wasn't coming together, the race stubbornly remaining an unsorted collection of disjointed facts and possibilities. Then, finally, and in my own defense this was mostly out of sheer frustration at my inability to craft a reasonable bet, I just went ahead and bet twenty dollars to win and forty dollars to place on Stein's horse. How humiliating. Ironically, it was at that very moment, as I was wallowing in self-deprecation, that the thought came to me. Yes. Now I knew what I wanted to do.

Getting up, I closed all the blinds and locked the sliding door, then went to the kitchen and made a soy cheese sandwich that I quickly ate with a handful of blue corn chips. Really hurrying now, I gathered up some clothes and the few things I'd need from the bedroom and put them in a plastic bag from Ralph's, not forgetting to grab my jacket and laptop on my way out the door.

I sat in the car with the engine idling. Which route to UCLA would be quickest? The 10 to the 405? Wilshire? At least I knew where they were holding the conference. Yes, and I also knew where on campus to park. So why was I still sitting there?

58

I looked at the clock in the dash: 3:08. I'd made good time. Stuffing my laptop in my bag, I got out. It took five minutes to walk over to Royce Hall from Parking Structure Five, and several more to find the right room, and although I'd been worried I might need some sort of identification, the doors were standing wide open when I arrived.

It was a large lecture hall with many rows of neatly arranged chairs facing a dais on which sat a lectern and a long table. With the exception of the large windows along one wall overlooking campus, it wasn't unlike other conference rooms I'd seen. Yes, there was Lee sitting with three others at the table on the dais, all looking to their right as they listened to the speaker who was leaning on the lectern. No, she hadn't seen me walk in and she wasn't likely to now, either, not sitting all the way at the back behind some graduate students. Maybe I'd try to catch her eye later after she'd read her paper.

Not having been around people like these in some time, I was curious about the audience, but what struck me most, once I'd had a good look, was how familiar they seemed, like I must have known them in graduate school. That, I found amusing. That here they were all these years later in mid-career not only still recognizable but still looking so very much like they belonged in this rarified little social world. And me? How did I look? Like I still belonged? Now there was a terrifying thought.

Forcing myself, I began listening to the speaker. It sounded familiar. I must have read the abstract over at Peet's. Something about globalization bringing to the surface the nascent social and economic contradictions of capitalism. Something about the Left needing to overcome its theoretical impotence with a return to political economy. Something about the dead-end in which critical theory now found itself and the concurrent academic inwardness of philosophy, its inability to comprehend its times. Whatever. I got my computer out, sat it on my lap and turned it on. Reading from a prepared text? Now there was impotence. And what's with this making a fetish of theory? I looked up. And that trim little goatee? I could already see this was going to be a waste of time. Then the computer chimed its merry jingle and one of the students sitting in front of me turned to see.

"Sorry," I said. "Just trying to get into the campus network to check on something."

"You'll need a password."

"Yeah, I thought I might."

"So you're not faculty here?"

"No, just here for this one presentation. What about you?"

"I'm a grad student. In the philosophy department here at UCLA."

"How's the conference?"

He shrugged. "One of my committee members gave a paper . . ."

"So here you are."

"Why don't you use mine," he said, leaning back so I could see the laptop sitting on the chair beside him.

"Thanks, but it's not that important."

"Are you sure? It's no big deal."

"Well . . ."

"Here," he said, picking it up to hand it to me.

"No, you keep it up there and I'll come around and sit next to you. I'm Nick, by the way," I said, holding out my hand. "It's nice to meet you."

"Yeah, likewise. I'm Jason."

When I sat down he gave me his computer, and as I logged on to Twin Spires I asked if we'd heard from Professor Powell yet.

"Who?"

"The one on the end."

"The attractive one?"

"That's her. Professor Powell, from Penn."

"No. Is she a friend of yours?" He was suddenly looking a bit apprehensive.

"Just an acquaintance. Here we go," I said, looking at the computer. "Now . . . I just need to get to Santa Anita . . . good." I was surprised, there were still five minutes to go before the eighth. "You ever do this? Go to a racetrack?"

"No. But that's what you're doing?" He tapped the computer screen.

"I bet a horse in the eighth. I was hoping to see how things turned out, but they seem to be running a little late today. These are the horses in the race and their odds. See?" I pointed to the list on the screen. "And this," I said as I expanded it, "is the streaming video from the track."

"So the horse you bet is in this race?"

"Right here." I brought up the box that showed the bets I'd made.

"How does he look?"

"She. A lot better than the crowd thinks." I put the cursor on the odds. "See?" She was going off at 11 to 1.

"So, at 11 to 1, how much will you make?" It was the question they always ask.

"Twenty to win should pay around two hundred and forty dollars. I'm not sure about place, maybe another seventy-five. That's my horse right there." I touched the screen with my finger as they got set to load into the starting gate.

"Oh, oh."

"What?"

"Run Chicken Run—that's my horse—she looks upset. See?" The gate attendant was wheeling her around and around in tight little circles trying to distract her as Solis calmly patted her neck.

"So how much would I get if I bet five dollars?

"To win?"

"Yeah. What would that pay?"

"Sixty dollars, give or take, though I hope you realize she's far more likely to lose."

"And if she doesn't . . ."

"Well then we'd better hurry because they're just about to load." I opened the wager box, keyed in five dollars to win on Run Chicken Run, then moved the cursor, hovering over the submit button. "So," I said, watching him, "what's it going to be? Jason?"

"Do it," he said, and I sent the bet on its way.

"Now, what we want to see is our gal up at the front with an easy lead. No pressure. That's important because when they get to the top of the stretch she's going to need all the energy she's got just to hang on." Then they finished loading the horses, the bell rang, and they were off.

As expected, Solis got her quickly out of the gate and let her run to the front where she preferred to be, and rounding the clubhouse turn she did look good, just loping along uncontested setting an easy pace. But they began to bunch up in the backstretch, and by the far turn she was coming under significant pressure. Then she swung wide at the top of the stretch and one of the other horses came up along side her on the rail. By the quarter pole the two were very close.

"Is that what you were worried about?" Jason asked.

"Unfortunately."

Down the stretch, the inside horse began lugging out, and though her jockey shifted his whip to his right hand she just kept on coming, eventually bumping Run Chicken Run hard enough that Solis had to momentarily take-up. That's what cost us the race. Poor Run Chicken Run was too tired to rally, and they ran like that, first and second, for the last half-furlong to the wire. She lost by a neck.

"Damn!" Jason said, sitting back sharply in his chair.

"Sorry, I really thought she was going to do it."

He looked so chagrined, but it wasn't just that he'd lost, he'd also been stripped of the solace of being a winner. Now all he had was remorse.

He turned to look at me. "But you still had her to place, right? So at least you'll get something."

"Not much, since that other horse was the favorite."

He pulled his wallet out to pay me and I put a hand on his arm to stop him. "That's okay, Jason, this one's on me. Let's just call it rent for the use of your computer."

"No, I made the bet so I owe you five dollars." He took out a five and handed it to me.

"Sorry."

"It's no big deal. You lost more."

"Yeah," I laughed, "thanks for reminding me. But I'll be fine. That place bet should cover it."

Suddenly *Inquiry* began flashing on the tote board in the infield. "See that?" I pointed to the tote board on the computer screen.

"Inquiry?"

"Uh-huh."

"What does that mean?"

"Did you notice how that other horse bumped Run Chicken Run in the stretch?"

"They can do that?"

"Well, that's what they're trying to determine. Maybe that bump cost us the race. If so, they just might decide to disqualify that other horse, or at least move her down a position or two. Both of which would make our horse—"

"The winner."

They showed us several replays of the stretch run while we waited. It was a pretty good bump. The head-on shot captured it best. Then we had a shot of Solis talking on the phone to the stewards as both horses were led around and around in circles by their grooms. The wait was agonizing. I'd been disappointed by the stewards before. Then the camera cut to the tote board. There was number seven now on top with number four second.

"That's it? We won?" Jason was staring at me, clearly unsure of what it meant.

"We won."

"Yes!" he said, sitting up straight in his chair to pump his fist in the air.

I smiled. I found his behavior charming. It brought back a lot of memories of my early days. Then I looked at the audience. Most had turned to see. Almost afraid to, I glanced at the panelists. Yes, with the exception of the speaker, who remained lost in a dense text of empire, multitude, and a conceptually resurgent class struggle. I held my breath, hoping she wouldn't recognize me. No, all the way across the room I could see her gently shaking her head.

"So," he said, staring at the tote board on his computer screen, "how much will that pay?"

"Hang on. We'll know in just a moment."

Then the prices came up. She paid $23.60 to win and $8.30 to place.

"So I made forty-six, forty-seven . . ." he was doing the math in his head.

"Fifty-nine dollars, but I have to be honest with you," I said, patting his shoulder, "they're rarely this tasty."

He didn't care. I'm not even sure he heard me. All he could think about was this amazing place he'd just discovered where a smart guy like himself could make some easy money. Or so he may have thought, but there were a lot of unexpected twists and turns in the road that led from where he was today to where I now found myself.

I pulled my wallet out and took out three twenties and his five. "These are yours."

"I still owe you a dollar."

"Keep it. I'm not going to need it today."

"That's right," he said, looking excited. "How much *did* you win?"

"To tell you the truth, Jason, I don't even care. I'm just happy to win."

"But it's got to be at least four hundred dollars."

"Shh," I said, laughing at his enthusiasm. "I think I'd better get back to my seat." I held out my hand. "Thanks, Jason."

I walked around to my row and sat down. I looked over at Lee. Yes, she was watching me, but when I tried to look apologetic she rolled her eyes and looked away.

So what about that losing streak? Hardly. That wasn't even a real bet.

59

I knew the speaker had finally finished when I heard the applause, so I looked up to watch him tidy up, then walk to the table where he sat with obvious relief in the empty chair. Then with hardly a pause a tall man with a goatee stood at the other end of the table and walked briskly to the podium. There he began telling us about Lee, talking about her latest work and that she'd been at Penn for ten years, and when she saw he was through she too stood and walked to the podium, smiling warmly and whispering something to him the audience couldn't hear, though it must have been amusing because he laughed and patted her on the back.

"I was just thanking Larry for inviting me. It's been a long time since I've been in California, and I must say," she said, looking directly at me, "this weekend has only whetted my appetite for more." At that, many heads in the audience nodded. Like her, they too were probably from back East or the upper Midwest. That winter I'd lived in the East had been a shock. After so many years in the Sunbelt I'd forgotten what it was like to live through a long one. How tedious they were, day-to-day. I was glad to get back to California.

"So here we are on this beautiful afternoon talking about the prospects of a critical social theory, though I suppose," and she paused to look out the window at the late afternoon sun, "we might all be happier at the beach." She smiled and took up some papers in her left hand. "Did you know that Southern California beach culture remains one of our least colonized social enclaves? That commodification, reification, the totally administered state, and instrumental reason have failed to make much of an impression?"

I could see any number of people in the audience smiling. The moderator was nodding his head. It was an amusing notion.

"But what if this isn't just a joke," she said, smiling. "How ironic if our most viable form of resistance was discovered hiding out somewhere we all regard as frivolous and insignificant. But then where else would it be hiding? "

Too flippant? I was beginning to feel nervous.

"But it's not just beach culture. If we tried, I'm sure we could all come up with any number of such areas. Little resistant pockets seemingly cut-off from the mainstream. Relics, outlaw cultures, quaint by-ways, anachronisms sustained by the actions of people whom we might also describe as out of place and time."

Again, she was looking at me.

"So, do these anachronisms survive merely because they've been overlooked, or because they harbor an undomesticated strain of resistance yet to be fully eradicated?"

"But let's talk about indigenous forms of resistance, and by that I mean those whose occurrence in our social world is natural and unplanned. Not mandated by the administrative state. Not the result of technological change or the instrumental actions of social planners or technocrats. They're indigenous. They've grown up where we find them for reasons of their own. They are, we might say, native to the soil."

She paused to look up at the audience and then out the windows.

"Of course there are any number of social theorists who claim to discern other forms of resistance, in particular those which are said to reside out there on the periphery of global capitalism. Such resistance, they say, if not just an artifact of theory—always a possibility—will emerge, or is even now emerging, among those peoples most directly and negatively affected by the massive economic inequalities that exist between global capitalism's center and periphery. The claim, the dream, of course, is that this resistance of the periphery will revitalize at the level of theory the radical critique of global capitalism theorists of the center have diluted or left behind as theory has drifted from socio-economic structures to postmodern concerns. But just how long are we to wait for the peoples of the periphery to take this next step? It's a pressing concern, since the center's theorists have already summoned its theoretical counterpart into existence as if by theoretical incantation. The next logical move awaits, but so far the periphery has been reticent. But theory always has an explanation. Well, it always does, doesn't it?" she said, looking up with a smile. "These newly emergent, truly authentic forms of resistance, the resistance of the periphery, are being occluded by a temporary exploitation, a self-serving appropriation of this nascent resistance to economic arrangements by nationalist movements and religious fundamentalisms. The next step has been hijacked."

"But is this really true? It's certainly theoretically true, that is to say it springs from a well-rehearsed move in a well-known style of theorizing. A move that *always* makes sense to us. After all, theory demands it. But how certain are we that we have a handle on what's determinate and determined out there on the periphery? Is it even true that only there are we free to act outside the system? Perhaps these notions—inside, outside, periphery, center—don't properly conceptualize a global system, capitalist or otherwise. And why should we wait for those on the periphery to come to their senses? For them to finally see the truth of that which we've already grasped? Indeed, we may be in for a long wait."

"But let's not be so quick to denigrate our own forms of resistance, or the utility of a critical social theory that cultivates such seedbeds. Yes, I know these are not the radical forms of resistance we've dreamt of, but neither are they the fetishized hopes of incantatory theory. I'm not proposing, by the way, that critical social theory hasn't become complacent or acquiescent in the face of global capitalism, and I'm certainly not recommending that we simply go on as before pointing to the implications of those always already conditions of human social life discovered through reconstructive labors or quasi-transcendental arguments. And I'm certainly not saying we ought to restrict ourselves to talk about civil society, multiculturalism, discourse ethics, identity, différance, the Other, victimhood, or cultural studies. We don't need to do any of that."

I was growing concerned. Repeatedly, as she spoke, she was looking at me. Sooner or later someone was bound to notice. The moderator was certainly staring out at the audience. I looked at those sitting around me. Perhaps I should try to model my behavior on theirs. Try to blend in and be invisible. I glanced at Jason. No, he was a thousand miles away.

But I couldn't take my eyes off her. After all, I'd never been exposed to her in a professional setting before. This was all so new. The captivating play of emotions across her face, how she stood, her graceful movements and gestures, her presence and the sense of self she projected. I have no idea what any one else thought, but she sure looked the part to me, so serious and responsible, so thoughtful, so professional, so much the person she'd wanted to be, the person she'd tried so hard to become. But then it was all suddenly right there in front of me, obvious, immediate, with nothing out of place. We'd never had a chance. Worse, nothing had changed. I shook my head. Why had I allowed myself to stumble down this road again? Then Lee stumbled in her presentation. She'd been watching me. Concerned, I forced myself to smile as I leaned back in my chair. *See, nothing's wrong, go on with your excellent performance.* And she did seem to relax, though it was several sentences before she regained her composure.

Well, thankfully, she soon finished, and to polite applause. But I could see how relieved she was. I hoped I hadn't upset her too much, but perhaps not since she quickly smiled my way when she sat down. So, was this it? Were we finally finished? I glanced at the moderator. He was staring at me. A moment later he glanced at Lee, then stood and walked to the podium to thank her and to say there would be a short break after which the panelists would each make a brief comment and then take questions from the audience.

60

Before going their separate ways Lee and the other panelists took a moment to huddle together. Yes, of course I was watching her, though trying not to be too obvious about it. Still, I was slowly drifting her way. Maybe we'd speak, maybe not. Then an attractive woman came up to her from the audience and there was a bit of hugging. Then she pointed to a man standing among the chairs who waved when Lee waved. But the cookies on the table by the door distracted me. Oatmeal raisin. I took a bite and turned to watch. She was no more than thirty feet away, though still showing no signs of acknowledgement. Fine, I'd just take my cookie back to my seat and behave, though two might be better, this time peanut butter. Then someone came up behind me and I turned around. It was the moderator. He smiled and held out his hand.

"I don't believe we've met. I'm Larry Gould."

I could see him searching my shirt for a nametag so I looked down to where one ought to be and smiled. "No, we haven't, though I feel as if we have, having read several of your articles on Foucault. Nick," I said, shifting my cookies to my left hand so we could shake hands. "I'm sorry I missed your paper this morning."

"I'll have a few things to say about Foucault here in just a few minutes when we start up again."

"Looks like a good turnout."

"For a conference like this."

"I wondered. I haven't been to one of these in a long time."

"Oh? You should get yourself a name tag so we know who you are." He gestured to a pile of plastic sleeves on the table next to several sheets of stapled paper with crossed-off names.

"That's okay, I'll only be here for a little while."

"Are you sure we haven't met? You do teach?"

"No. I'm not an academic. At one time I thought I might become one, but I was led astray."

I felt a gentle hand in the middle of my back and turned. It was Lee smiling at us.

"Larry, this is Nick. I thought I'd better introduce him since I'm sure he hasn't introduced himself."

"No, in fact he has, and he's been very politely putting up with all my prying questions."

"Did you get any answers?"

"Yes, but it was all rather mysterious."

"Like what's he doing here this afternoon?"

"Simple curiosity," I said. "Like a trip back in time to a previous life."

"Yes, he claims he was led astray. I was just about to ask by what."

"Well?" she said, turning to look at me.

"Lady luck, I guess."

"I thought you claimed there's no such thing as luck."

"I do claim that. That's just a layman's term for something that's actually quite different, but since you're laymen . . . "

"Larry, Nick and I were friends in graduate school."

"In Colorado," I added.

"The reason he's being so mysterious is because he's embarrassed to admit it was gambling that led him astray. Playing the horses, in fact, not that he would have made a very good philosopher if it hadn't. Even more amusing, if you should happen to ask, he'll deny he's a gambler, but of course that assertion rests on any number of dubious distinctions."

"Hardly dubious." I looked at Larry. "As I've tried to explain to her, even though the factors I deal with may at times be rather obscure they are predictable, which is quite different from the brute randomness that characterizes gambling. Not that I don't take note of that randomness, but it rarely factors into my calculations. But she's certainly right about one thing, I would have made a terrible philosopher."

"And how have you been as a gambler . . . err, horseplayer?"

"Not bad, if today's anything to go by." I was pointedly looking at Jason, who stood with his friends by the back door.

Turning to see, Lee said, "I was wondering what you two were doing back there."

"Jason?" Larry asked, surprise in his voice as he stared across the room.

"Sorry, is he yours?"

"Jason's one of my better students. I hope I can have him back."

"I don't see why not. It's no big deal. We had a nice chat, then he found himself with a little more money than when we began."

"How much more?" Lee asked.

"That's Jason's business, but I'd be happy to tell you how much more I have."

"No thanks," she said, patting me on the back. "That smug look on your face tells me all I need to know. You see what a bad influence he can be?" she said, turning to Larry. "This is just how he was in graduate school."

"Yes," he said, watching me very carefully. "I don't doubt it. So you're here for Lee's paper," he said, finally putting it all together. "What did you think?"

"Excellent. I've always been her biggest fan."

"Oh? We might have to argue about that."

Yes, looking at how happy she was around him I thought we might. Just how close were they? Clearly, they were very good friends. Just as clear were his suspicions.

"Larry's here at UCLA now. Maybe you two will run into each other out at the track."

"Hardly likely," Larry said. "And I'm far too old to be led astray."

"Don't be so sure," I teased.

"Yes," he said, pointedly looking at Lee, "I suppose it does happen."

"What?" She had no idea what he meant.

"Nothing, dear," he said, taking her arm. "We need to get this started." He turned to look at me, then held out his hand. "Nick, it was very nice to meet you. Someday I'd love to hear a few stories about Lee. She never tells me anything."

"Yes, we should do that."

I watched them slowly make their way to the dais. As she sat I saw him place his hand on her shoulder, then bend down to say something. Whatever it was she seemed to have a long response and he listened for some time before he finally straightened up. Then she reached out to touch his arm and he bent down to listen again before nodding and patting her shoulder.

Jason refused to make eye contact with me as I walked back to my seat, so when I sat down I leaned forward and tapped him on the shoulder. "Dr. Gould tells me you're one of his better students."

"I wondered what he was saying."

"I told him I talked you into making a bet."

"Seriously?"

"Don't worry, they found it amusing, though they seem to think I may have led you astray. But Professor Powell sure was pestering me to tell her how much you won. I told her she'd just have to ask you."

He gulped. Speechless. The look on his face was fascinating.

"Jason," I said, patting him on the back, "you worry too much even for a graduate student. Look, here's the deal. Jason?" He looked at me. "People who don't know anything about it will always think they do. They will always think they do even when you show them they really don't. You understand what I'm saying?"

He nodded.

"Professor Gould over there?" and we both looked up at him. "Even though I'd gladly take him, he'll never go. Not out to the track. That's too far outside his boundaries. Too much in conflict with how he assumes the world to be. Which is wonderfully ironic, since that sort of incomprehension seems most rooted in a refusal *of* the world. Yeah," I said when he looked at me, "interesting, isn't it?"

"But you don't refuse?" he asked, grinning at me.

"Do you wish you'd refused that bet?"

"That's what I'd be thinking if I'd lost."

"Yes, but you didn't, and that seems to make all the difference."

"Easier to embrace the world when we win?"

"Easier to refuse when we lose?"

"Okay," he said, laughing. "So this is the sort of thing you do when you're out at the track?"

"That's right," I joked, "always embracing." But I could see what he really wanted to ask. "Maybe you and your buddies would like to come out sometime. You're more than welcome. You can sit in the box I share with some of my dangerous gambler friends."

"Well . . ."

"Here," I said, writing my name, telephone number, and email address on the back of a sheet of paper.

"Thanks," he said when I handed it to him. "I just might take you up on this." I smiled. The way he said it, it was like he'd finally found himself. "So, Nick," he asked, suddenly confident enough to use my name, "just why *are* you here?"

"Jason," I said, laughing as I leaned back in my seat. "Like I said, it's a long story. Who knows, maybe someday I'll tell it to you."

61

When it was over Lee and I walked out of Royce Hall together, and once we were out of sight she took my hand and led me down a gravel path under several enormous old eucalyptus trees. The ground at our feet was littered with long strips of bark, twigs, and larger branches, the air thick with that distinctive medicinal odor. Then she leaned back against a bare trunk and smiled at me.

"You're not sorry I came, are you?"

"No, but I was certainly surprised to see you sitting back there."

"You did very well."

"Thanks."

"Who's Larry?"

"Another old acquaintance from graduate school. He helped me when I first got to Duke."

"Helped?"

"I was very unhappy for a long time."

"Sorry," I said, reaching out to stroke her hair.

"I know," she said, taking my hand and pulling me close.

"He knows about us, doesn't he?"

"It's not a problem."

"And Charles?"

"Yes, they know each other. Actually, Larry's never forgiven me for marrying Charles."

"Because you should have married him?"

"Hardly. They've never gotten on, even in graduate school."

"And now he's met me."

"He thinks you're a smartass."

"He really said that?"

"Care to hear what else he said?"

"Not if it's going to hurt my feelings."

"He wanted to know if you were the one I'd been pining for when he and I first met."

"Pining?" I laughed. "He really said that?"

She nodded.

"What did you say?"

"I said, yes, believe it or not, he's the one. He's invited us for drinks at the Faculty Club, by the way."

"Do you really think that's such a good idea?"

"If you don't mention Jason. Ask him about Foucault's views on the Enlightenment."

"I just might. There were a lot of very smart gamblers during the Enlightenment."

"So Larry probably doesn't know about that."

"You're sure this won't prove too awkward?"

"I'm sure, but thanks for asking."

"Because I'm a little concerned by your apparent lack of concern. After all, I'm one who's not supposed to care what other people think."

"Yes. I was just wondering about that. What do you suppose has happened to you?"

62

"Did you know Engels owned racehorses? I know, surprising, isn't it? Not that it ever amounted to much. Just a small stable, otherwise, he rarely got out to the track. But of course Marx always insisted on tagging along. And Engels was a big bettor, or at least he was on his own horses, though Marx never bet, not even on his friend's horses. In fact, he despised the bookies. He said they preyed upon the working class. The working man, he said, was no less exploited at the racetrack than when selling his labor power to the capitalists."

"You ran across this where?" Lee asked, smiling at me.

"I think it was in one of those long footnotes in Engels' complete works."

"What a scholar."

"But what I really wanted to tell you about was the time they went to the track and Engels lost a lot of money betting on one of his own horses. Now, admittedly I'm reading between the lines here, but it certainly sounds like Marx was livid. I mean he must have been if he went to see the bookie who'd taken the bet."

"What about?"

"To demand that he return all of Engels' money."

"Did he?" Larry asked, looking amused.

"Of course not, that's why it's called a bet. So Marx got very belligerent, then he lost his temper. You know how he could be." I paused to look at them.

"Absolutely," Larry said.

"But the bookie, to his credit, did try to reason with him. Pointing out that Engels would have been only too happy to collect his winnings if he'd won. But by then it sounds like Marx wasn't listening. I know," I said, smiling at them. "Did he ever? So yelling something about how games of chance were dialectically impossible, he shoved the bookie, who fell to the ground."

"Very foolish," Larry said.

"I'll say, because the bookie got right back up and landed a hard right to Marx's stomach."

"I've always wondered if Marx could take a punch."

"Well, apparently he could, because he somehow managed a big roundhouse right in return, one the bookie easily ducked, however. Then deftly counter-punching with a flurry of sharp left jabs that snapped Marx's head back, straightening him up for the coup de grace, the bookie let him have it with everything he had, a crushing haymaker right to the jaw that sent Marx to the ground in a heap. A blow so stunning that for one brief moment the progress of history actually stopped, the whole of social existence teetering on the edge of the precipice. Thesis, antithesis, and then Bam! Aufgehoben."

"Thus was the dialectic born," Larry said, nodding his head like it made perfect sense.

"And this was something you read in a footnote somewhere?" Lee asked, refusing to humor me.

"That's what I'm saying."

"You know, it's not that far-fetched," Larry said.

"That he owned racehorses?"

"Plus, I just love this image of Marx out mingling with the proles thinking about exploitation. Annoyed beyond measure by their hopeless addiction to this pornographic fetishization of money we call gambling."

"It's a pari-mutuel system over here, Larry, we only exploit each other."

"But it is an interesting notion. I certainly would never have thought of it."

"Then it's yours. But do let me know if you ever find out it's actually true. Especially if you run across the names of his horses."

"If it is true you just might see me out at the track. I've always wondered what it felt like to take other people's money in such an unmediated fashion."

"Unmediated? I wish it were, but for some reason the track stubbornly insists on holding it for me until I win."

"But it is still a form of exploitation, is it not? And you're certainly not making or creating anything, which is why I suppose it seems like such a useless activity."

"Useless?" I smiled as I shook my head. "Such a Puritan. As for exploitation, I'm not the one who's a speculator in the capitalist economy."

"Me?"

"No money in the stock market? Not even in your retirement plan?"

"I've already had this discussion with him," Lee said, patting Larry's arm. "He's hopeless."

"Yes, but gambling is so destructive. Problem gamblers?"

"Losers."

"Oh, now that's nice," Lee said.

"You know what I mean, though to a certain extent I do agree with you. But so what? People have problems with all sorts of things. We're finding new ones for them to worry about all the time. So far as I can tell, addiction seems to be the contemporary excuse for everything."

"Though not at the track?" Larry asked.

"No, it's there, but contrary to popular mythology most of us aren't compulsive gamblers. The truth is, some of us have even found a way to make a living at it. As for useful, just how useful is what you do?"

"But what you do isn't useful at all," Lee said. "That's just the point."

"The pleasure and enjoyment to be found in play, in risk taking, the intellectual challenge and financial reward, none of that is useful?"

"Not bad," she said, smiling at me. "But you know we're right."

"You know what your problem is, temptation. You see it only in a negative light. In fact, if it were up to you people wouldn't be allowed to indulge themselves in any of the things they really enjoy. It makes you so uncomfortable, all that unfettered Eros raging out there beyond your control."

"Unfettered Eros?" Larry asked, tugging on his goatee. "Now it's Freud at the racetrack?"

"Possibly."

"Or perhaps Batille or Deleuze?"

"Good, God," Lee said, shaking her head.

"But gambling is erotic, isn't it? Hence the allure."

"Ah." I said, smiling at him. "I guess that's something you'll just have to find out for yourself."

"Is this how Jason got into trouble?"

"Because he won a little money?"

"No, because you gave him a little taste, a taste of Eros. A brief glimpse of that instantaneous libidinal satisfaction we've been led to believe is more properly repressed or sublimated."

"He's a young man. It was good for him."

"Yes, how very profound," Lee said. "The silly pleasures of gambling."

"Silly? The ritualized expression of our most fundamental hopes and desires, our optimism, our existential flirtation with randomness and chance, the deep connection we feel to our natural desire for becoming? And I know where you're coming from with this, by the way, even if you don't. That any one of these is more than enough to make gambling appear dangerous and uncontrollable, a threat to the survival of a stable social order, something to malign, condemn, and repress. Worse, gambling is transgressive, particularly in a theological sense, where games of chance are an affront to divine providence. Dangerous loopholes in our blind obedience to God's mysterious will. And whether it's that or a repressive social order, both hate becoming, one because it denies the possibility of any such random act in God's universe, the other because," and I paused to smile at Larry, "it might lead us astray."

"My, my," Lee said, staring at me in open admiration. "Where on earth did that come from?"

"Pretty good?"

She laughed and looked at Larry. "What did you think?"

"Yes," Larry said, nodding his head. "I believe I heard the Sirens singing.

"Really? Because that's not what I heard."

"But I'm still unclear as to what it is you get from all this," he said.

"The analytical part. The handicapping. The betting, that's secondary, though practically speaking it's all measured by the bet."

"So you'd prefer just to do the handicapping?"

"If I could, but most of my time is actually spent trying to make profitable wagers. It's surprisingly difficult to turn all that handicapping expertise into profit. But it's not the money so much as it is my ability to predict the future. That's what really excites me. When things turn out as expected. But it's more than just being right, it's anticipatory, it's being there for the moment."

"Like being there to see a mystery?" Larry suggested.

"Several mysteries. I used to focus on causality. Well, why not? Horse races are awash in physical causalities. So you'd think with all that to play with they'd also be highly predictable. After all, it's hardly like the random fall of the ball in roulette where sheer chance prevails and all one can do is learn to respect the laws of probability. But then again, maybe handicapping encompasses too many causal variables for there to be any real certitude. As we all know, even probabilistic reasoning often fails to gain much traction with truly complex events. So that's one mystery."

"And the other?" Lee asked, greatly amused.

"Temporality, and by that I mean that moment of occurrence when anticipation is finally realized. That now is so distinctive, so appealing, that one can not not be in it. So overwhelmingly present that any reflection upon its nature or significance must wait until it's over. It's then we see the mystery of becoming, this mystery of things coming into existence and the here and now in which this always and can only occur. A mystery most vividly present in such moments, though I suspect it's actually present in all moments, it's just that we're so rarely paying attention."

"Probably just as well," she said. "A life lived like that could get pretty tedious."

"So maybe that's why it takes a really critical moment, one which forces us to witness this coming into existence of what is. So here it is right in front of us, this generation of something out of what is not. Free of the past. Not an anticipation of the future. It's a shock, and we're shocked that we've never noticed before. But it's just now. This quiet, silent witnessing, this reverent pause in our normal waste of time as we watch how it's really accomplished."

"As always, so poetic," she said, smiling at me.

"I've got the end of this string. I'm holding it between my thumb and index finger. It's taut, clearly connected to something, though what that is remains hidden. I wait. I'm patient. I don't try to grasp the string too tightly. I just hold it gently in my fingers feeling the slight tension and resistance it offers to my movements. Suddenly I feel a slight tremor or vibration. Not that I can see the string actually move or tighten, but still, I know something is happening elsewhere out of sight; that in that moment something is going on even though I can't tell you anything about it. I know this by the gentle vibrations I feel in my fingers. Yes, whatever it is it's subtle, discreet, fleeting, and ephemeral, but it's really happening as I hold the string.

That's the sort of thing I look for."

"At the track?" Larry asked, clearly astonished.

"There. Here. Why not?"

"What a fascinating way to look at gambling."

"More like what a fascinating performance," Lee said.

"Which is what you always say when you think I'm not rigorous enough."

"There was nothing rigorous about it."

"Maybe not, but it certainly wasn't irrational, as if a performance isn't subject to critical standards of some sort."

"You see?" she said, looking at Larry.

"What?" I said. "That's a perfectly reasonable point."

"You always have a perfectly reasonable point because you're never at a loss for words."

"Oh, like the one necessarily cancels out the other?"

"No, but it does mean you bear watching," Larry said, smiling at me.

"You watch him," she said, standing. "I'm going to find the restrooms."

"That way," Larry pointed. "Past the bar."

When she was gone he turned to me. "Have you met Charles?"

"No, Larry, and I'm not trying to break up their marriage, either."

"It is interesting to see how she acts around you."

"For the better, I hope."

"I think so. Of course, I've known about you for years."

"I'm surprised. When she ran off to Duke I thought I'd be the last thing on her mind."

"Well, I don't mean to mislead you, but I knew enough to know there was someone like you in her past."

"Yes, and that's where I'm likely to remain, since she's out of here on Monday."

"And you'd prefer to continue this in some fashion or other?"

"Like it's ever mattered what anyone else prefers."

"Except in this case I'm not so sure she knows what she prefers."

"You really don't like her husband, do you?"

"Charles? He's alright, but I've always adored Lee."

"The funny thing is, I could have gone with her, not that she ever asked me to, she wouldn't, but still, I knew. But why? We both knew I wasn't what she wanted. I didn't fit the mold. So she went on without me. Only now she's unhappy? I'm curious. Do you suppose that's because she really didn't get what she wanted, or because what she wanted turned out to be a mistake?"

"Well, as we both know only too well, she's not very forthcoming. But if I had to guess I'd say she's struggling with this notion that perhaps she needs to make a few painful adjustments."

"That's me. A painful adjustment."

"I hope you're not married."

"No, and let's not try to read too much into that, okay? It's just how things worked out."

"Sorry. People always say I'm too nosy."

"I have a friend like you. A lawyer. In fact, she used to be a student right here at UCLA. You don't happen to have a sister, do you?"

"Yes," he smiled, "but she lives in Cleveland."

"I've known her and her partner for years, longer even than I've know Lee. Wendy Wasserman? Come out to the track sometime and I'll introduce you. I led her astray years ago and she's never forgiven me."

"Wendy Wasserman? The gay rights activist?"

I nodded.

"Nick," he said, looking very amused, "you're not at all who you appear to be, are you?"

"Lee's always said I was."

I heard footsteps and turned.

"I hope he hasn't led you astray while I wasn't here to protect you?"

"No," Larry said, politely pulling her chair back, "but I'm beginning to suspect he could." Then he turned to me, smiling warmly, surprising me.

63

We left the Faculty Club with Larry and said goodnight on the sidewalk out in front. As we walked away I heard him talking on his cell phone with someone about dinner.

"What about you?" I asked. "Where would you like to go for dinner?"

"Actually, I was thinking about a drive-thru. They do still have drive-thrus in L.A.?"

"Just a few. But why a drive-thru?"

"I don't know. Maybe because you've never taken me to one."

"That's because you're not the drive-thru type. But I suppose I could take you to an In-N-Out. That's where most people in L.A. go for a drive-thru."

"Are they any good?"

"For what they are they're fine, but hardly up to your usual standards."

"So where else could we go?"

"Well, if you had to choose, which would you prefer, a hot dog smothered in chili, or a hamburger smothered in chili?"

"Can't we just skip the chili?"

"We could, but . . ."

"Then I guess I'd prefer the hot dog."

"All right."

"Are you sure? You look a little disappointed."

"No, it's just that Pink's is going to be really crowded, and, well, things seem a bit smug at Pink's these days."

"Smug hot dogs?" she laughed. "Is that even possible?"

"Yeah, give me one of them smug dogs with chili."

"So where else did you have in mind?"

"Tommy's, but that's more of a drive."

"Are we in any hurry?"

"No, but it's not really a drive-thru, at least not in the classic sense, though we can still eat in the car."

"I'll manage." She looked at me and grinned. "Does this mean you're going to eat red meat?"

"Looks like I'll have to."

"No tofu burgers at Tommy's?"

I laughed and shook my head.

"Who is this?" she asked. Headed down Wilshire, we were listening to the car radio.

"Your really don't know?"

She shook her head.

"It's Link Wray?" I looked at her. "*Rumble?*"

"Still haven't heard it. So who are they?"

"They?"

"You mean Link Wray's a person? I thought you were going to tell that was the name of some obscure punk group."

"Hardly, though I'm sure they're all well aware of him."

"Unlike me, you mean."

"It's even his real name. Dude's got to be in his seventies by now, but he's still out there on the road performing. Crummy little bars. Blues clubs. Loudest fucker I ever heard."

"I know," she said, rolling her eyes, "and now known to only a few, but what a select and discriminating few you are."

"It's always been like that, even back in the 1950s when he was at the height of his popularity."

"But if he's still performing how does he meet your 1965 cutoff date?"

I laughed. "You remembered."

"I do now."

"Let's just say I've relaxed my standards a bit. These days I might even listen to something contemporary if it's obscure enough. But I still won't listen to any of that commercial junk you consume."

"That sounds like a much broader condemnation than just music."

"Probably."

"And now I really do remember," she said, laughing. "It's all those baby boomers. You've still got it in for them, don't you?"

"Shouldn't I?"

"Even though you're one yourself?"

"As are you."

"Barely, unlike you, mister malcontent, who's stuck right in the middle of his cohort."

"Yes, a miserable cohort that's been nothing but a pain in the ass my whole life. It's been very hard not doing what they do."

"I'm sure it has, especially now that you've finally run out of options for sustaining your nonconformity."

"You have no idea," I said with a laugh.

64

"This is it?" We were sitting in the car at Tommy's waiting for a parking spot.

"Trust me, it's better than it looks. Just think of this as one of those resistant by-ways of the lifeworld you were talking about."

Once we were parked I led her across the parking lot to the original Tommy's tiny burger shack. The line moved quickly—it never takes very long at Tommy's—and soon we were able to order. Five minutes later we were standing at the long outdoor counter on the other side of the parking lot trying not to make a mess of ourselves as we ate burgers smothered in greasy chili.

"What do you think?" I asked after she'd had a few bites.

"You're right, this is much too messy for the car." She pulled a paper towel from the dispenser fastened to the wall. "And it is good, though it can't be very good for you," she said as she wiped her hands.

"Like this weekend. Sometimes one just has to set common sense aside."

I watched her turn to look across the parking lot at the cars as they came and went, the people waiting in line for their orders, an interesting mix of Angelenos, everyone getting along as they focused on the immediate task.

"What do you think Habermas would make of this?"

She stopped sipping her Diet Coke to smile at me. "I think he'd see pathologies galore."

"He wouldn't want to engage anyone in some sort of communicative action?"

"No, like me he'd just stand here quietly eating his fries."

"You don't suppose Larry comes here?"

"Hardly," she laughed. "But I know what he'd say if he did. Where's the wine?"

"He could always bring his own. The brown bag beverage is hardly unknown around here."

"Or just go over there." She was pointing across the street to The Grog Shop's garish purple neon sign.

"Only if he likes malt liquor."

She smiled and took another sip of her Diet Coke, then sat the cup on the counter. "That's enough for me," she said, stacking everything on her plastic tray.

I watched her walk over to the trash barrel at the end of the counter and let it all slide off.

"I'm sorry you didn't like it."

"It was fine, but that was way too much for me to eat." She looked at what was left of my burger and shook her head. "I'm surprised a tofu eater like you ate so much. I hope this isn't like an alcoholic having that one drink and now we'll have to spend the rest of evening hitting every burger joint in town."

"You know," I said, using a paper towel to wipe my greasy fingers, "this is a timely reminder of why I don't eat red meat. Yes, it's tastes good, but it doesn't really feel all that good once you have."

"Well, I'm sure Larry will be fascinated. Of course he'll have to ponder it a bit first, but he'll eventually come up with something suitably theoretical. He always does."

"Doesn't that strike you as odd? This compulsion to make theoretically laden comments about whatever might happen to come along."

"Never underestimate the power of a theoretical position. Once you've taken the trouble to cobble one together there's just no stopping. It's just one ponderous observation after another."

"Like Žižek."

"Exactly."

"Still, I suppose you've got to love the profundity."

"Not me. All that profundity takes up too much room. Then what are the rest of us supposed to do?"

"I guess you're supposed to follow."

"That's right. Just filling in where we can. Manning the border posts. Fighting off the other tribes."

"Except that now you're thinking some of those other tribes might be more interesting."

"Only for a little clandestine fraternization."

I walked over to the barrel and threw in what was left of my order, then looked at my Diet Coke for a moment before tossing it in as well. To be honest, I felt a little queasy. I tore off a piece of paper towel and began wiping my hands. "Well," I said, "do be careful what you bring back to your tribe."

"You mean like an illiterate primitive?"

"If you're referring to me, and I'm pretty sure you are, I'm hardly illiterate. Not that we primitives care what you think."

"You should."

"Not from where I stand."

"Oh, and where is that?"

"In the gap between what I mean as the public me and the private me."

"Gap?" She shook her head. "Where do you come up with this stuff?"

"It's no small thing," I teased. "Or at least it better not be, since that's what ensures I'll always be able to escape myself."

"Of course, no final reconciliation or congruence here. Unattached. Just serenely drifting along oblivious to life's messy entanglements and complications. Gender, for example. Where's your gap there? We are all still social beings, are we not? Which means it's mostly unavoidable, even for you. It's not like you can just wave that all away by an act of will."

"But don't you see, just by saying that you've already opened it up. Already shown you have the ability to step back from whatever identity's been imposed upon you." I paused to look at her. "Can't you people ever just say *no*?"

"I'm certainly tempted to say no to this."

"Good, your very first act of refusal. Wresting a bit of autonomy from the iron grip of existence."

"*Wresting*?" She was grinning at me.

"Wresting. Because it's not what we do, it's what we *don't* do, that clears out a place in the heavy timber for our little meadow. Each act of refusal is like felling a tree, pulling a stump, cutting some brush. We need to maintain our clearing. We need to make sure the sun can reach the ground. So turn your back and walk away, say no, don't take the offer, turn it off, put it away, throw it away, don't pick it up, don't satisfy your curiosity, don't eat it, don't drink it, don't buy it, don't say it, don't think it, don't believe it—just don't do it.

"But maybe you say no too often. What if there's nothing left?"

"There's plenty left, and much of it just as I found it. I can't be worried about everything. Even I have to stop at some point."

She put her hand on my shoulder to smile at me. "What about aggregate behavior? Because I don't think you've left yourself much room to aggregate."

"Meaning?"

"No collective life? That this isn't just your personal liberation?"

"Well, I'm certainly not running around proselytizing, if that's what you mean."

"No, but haven't you now made every action, every thought or feeling, a burdensome choice, a judgment to be weighed and pondered? I'm just wondering if we're allowed to refuse *that*?"

"You think I've really boxed myself in, don't you?"

"No," she said, smiling at me. "I'm sure you'll think of something. You always do."

"It might take a few minutes."

"I have to say, you really are the most natural sophist I've ever known. If you were a student in one of my seminars I'd have to talk to my Dean about you."

"To get me tossed out of your class?"

"Yes, and quickly, before you infected everyone. *Can't you just say no?*" she said, laughing as she shook her head.

"Maybe you should give it a try."

"Maybe I already have."

Before we got back in the car she paused to look around.

"What?" I asked.

"I was just thinking what an amazing scene this is. Like those guys over there." She nodded in the direction of a bunch of dangerous looking vatos. Pochos no doubt deeply socialized by gangs and prison calmly standing in line with everyone else.

"The underclass of the capitalist economy. Stupefied by the endless consumption of what only appear to be chiliburgers. Mere simulacra. Socially constituted stand-ins for chiliburgers. The irreality of dinner at Tommy's where your stomach's never really full you just think it is."

"Now who are we imitating?"

"Baudrillard?"

"At least it's not Adorno."

"Adorno?"

"*Non-identical? Just say no?*"

"That reminds me, did you notice the Schoenberg building today? Next to the Faculty Club?"

"Arnold Schoenberg?"

"Lots of émigrés were out here."

"Adorno, of course."

"Mann, Horkheimer, Brecht—"

"Peter Lorre."

"That's right! And Fritz Lang."

"You're not going to tell me you've developed a taste for atonal music?"

"Atonal music has no taste. Anyway, Link Wray is about as sophisticated as my musical tastes are ever going to get."

"Hardly what Adorno had in mind when he tutored Thomas Mann."

"Get in," I said. "I want to show you something."

"I hope it's not too far. I'm finally getting a little tired."

"It's not. Actually, it's pretty close to UCLA."

Leaving Tommy's, I made a right onto Beverly and then a quick left into the parking at The Grog Shop. "I'll be right back," I told her. "I just need to get a copy of tomorrow's *Racing Form*. Can I get you something?"

"A mineral water would be nice, but don't take too long."

"Just lock the doors and I'll be right back."

I walked straight to the large cooler along the back wall, rescued two bottles of Calistoga lost in a sea of beer, then walked back to the front where I asked the clerk for a copy of *The Daily Racing Form*. Like cigarettes and lottery tickets, I knew they'd be there, and they were, stacked on the counter next to a smaller stack of *Today's Racing Digest*.

When Lee unlocked my door I got in and dropped the *Form* behind the seat, handed her a bottle, then had a long drink from mine. The Calistoga was wonderful after the sickening artificial sweetness of the Diet Coke. Then it was back out onto Beverly, which we followed all the way to Santa Monica Boulevard before taking Beverly Glen up to Sunset.

65

I thought she'd fallen asleep, but then she asked me why we were driving past UCLA. I told her I was taking her over to Kenter, which was on the other side of the 405. Why Kenter? I told her she'd just have to wait and see.

I turned left when we got there. No traffic, unlike during the day when it's jammed with commuters making their way between San Vicente and Sunset. But I like that street. Fairly narrow, meandering gently through a comfortable residential neighborhood that left its middle class roots behind long ago.

"So this is it," I announced, pulling over against the curb on the opposite side of the street. "Where Adorno and his wife lived back in the 1940s."

She leaned forward in her seat to see. "It's nice."

It's a handsome looking house. A two-story duplex with two separate garages underneath, where a short sidewalk to the right of the driveway leads to stairs up to the front porch where there are two front doors and two addresses and hints of the French Quarter in the black shutters, tall chimneys, railings, and large second floor balcony.

"Do you know which half was theirs?"

"I've been told the one on the right, but I really have no idea."

"I see they have a satellite dish for Directv. Do you think the Adornos would have?

"Don't you?"

"Where's this again?"

"Brentwood."

"So this is where he lived when wrote all those derogatory things about America."

"This is the place."

She smiled at me. "This is a nice surprise."

"You'll have to tell Larry."

"You don't think he knows?"

"Not a chance."

"For some reason this reminds me of Lukács' remark about the *Grand Hotel Abgrund*."

"Hotel Abyss?"

"It's a nasty crack Lukács made about the Frankfurt School. Actually, Adorno and Horkheimer. Saying they were riding things out up at the Grand Hotel Abgrund. Contemplating the abyss of absurdity and nothingness while partaking of its many comforts, its plush facilities, fine food, and entertainment, which was hardly fair, especially coming from Lukács."

"One can't live well and be authentic? Or did he mean they weren't good apparatchiks?"

"More of the latter, I imagine. Or maybe he thought they should have left for East Germany, like Brecht."

"Would you like to see his house?"

"Whose?"

"Brecht's. It's only about a mile from here."

"You know," she said, looking at me, "you're beginning to sound like a tour guide. But I've been wondering about that. Whether you brought me here for some reason other than just to show it to me."

"Not really, I just thought you might enjoy the irony. It's also interesting to learn a little bit more about the person who speaks."

"The person who speaks? Is that your way of suggesting this presents a problem for you? That Adorno once lived in Brentwood?"

"No, I just find it interesting that this is where he wrote *Minima Moralia* and *Dialectic of Enlightenment* with Horkheimer."

"*The shame of still having air to breathe, in hell.* Stuff like that?"

"Exactly. That he wrote stuff like that *here* is an important fact to know about Adorno."

"Because he shouldn't have lived here?"

"No, but where one lives does make a difference."

She laughed. "Then I'm glad you haven't seen where we live. You'd probably stop talking to me."

"Look, all I'm saying is that he had a life to live and this is where he lived it, or at least he did for a while. One that wasn't all that bad, either, at least from a material standpoint. Yes, I know, a damaged life, the homeless exile, the émigré, but he and his wife lived here in a community of sympathetic émigrés, and they participated fully in that life. So he was hardly holed-up here thinking and writing until he could get back to Europe."

"Yes, but they did go back."

"I know. You should see Thomas Mann's place over in Pacific Palisades."

"Not tonight."

"So that *here* is significant. That's what I'm trying to say. That here is the house, the street, the things they saw and encountered on a daily basis, all of which had an impact. We might even want to say that there were certain demands that came with living here."

"I guess his biographers must have missed those."

"You think that makes them trivial? That we can just ignore them because they can't be found in a text?"

"Ignore what?" she said, pointing across the street. "That they lived in a nice house?"

"But living here meant something to them. There was the sense of it. The experience of it."

"Which would have been different if they'd lived somewhere else?"

"Hasn't that been your experience? That where you lived felt like something?"

"I suppose."

"You don't find that telling? That here we can see for ourselves all those innumerable sensuous physical objects and their concrete aspects that made living a life here what it was? What it still is? So knowing that, seeing all that, humanizes him. Makes him much more the real person he was, living his life in the way this here demanded."

"Well—"

"He wrote something. He worked on it all morning. Then at lunch his wife drove them down to Santa Monica to their favorite lunch-counter where they had a nice meal. On their way home they stopped over on 26th Street to do a little shopping. Then in the evening they went to a party out in Malibu where he had an interesting interaction with Charlie Chaplin. Well, this is where that all took place. This is the real context, not some words on a piece of paper. Here was the real person, the one who walked down those stairs to their car and lived in this physical space. That other person, the one in the texts, is no more than a persona, a mask, a creation for others or for a certain manner of performance. That shadow person didn't matter nearly as much as the real person who came out here every morning for the newspaper."

"And then rushed inside to read his horoscope."

"So . . . "

"Yes?" she asked, grinning at me.

"Uh, I seem to have forgotten what I was going to say."

"I think you were about to claim this as hallowed ground."

"Yes!" I said, sitting up straight in my seat. "There should be a shrine."

"Poet."

"Just because I get a little carried away?"

"A little! I can barely see you anymore. I hope you're tethered to the car so I can reel you back in."

"It must be something I ate."

"At least that would be a rational explanation."

"Well, something seems to be in open rebellion," I said, holding my stomach. "That's what I get for trying to impress you."

"By eating meat? Maybe you shouldn't try so hard to show off."

"What choice do I have? For men, it's always already about access to women."

"I don't think that was Adorno's view."

"Then you don't know as much about Adorno as you think you do."

"Really?"

"Oh, yeah. Though he'd say it was all about dominance, class, social rank, and hierarchy. Where do I stand? Can I get any higher?"

"And you'd say?"

"That even if we grant that evolutionary pressures have significantly shaped our social behavior with the aim of furthering our species' chances for reproductive success, that doesn't change the fact that reproductive success comes one couple at a time. There's your domination."

"Don't you mean one *coupling* at a time?"

"Yes, and the less dominance the less coupling, and vice versa."

"God, I hate evolutionary psychology. Are you sure this isn't just a metaphor for something else?"

"No, everything's a metaphor for coupling."

"Only for men."

"Which is why access to women is a pretty good measure for dominance and hierarchical placement. A lot more fundamental in shaping how we live than economic structures, reification, instrumental reason, or the principle of universal exchange. And it's personal. Look at bonobos and chimpanzees—"

"Bonobos!"

"They're very closely related, but separated into two very different societies by the Congo River. So in one the males dominate, those are the chimpanzees, and over there they experience a lot of violence and competition. While bonobo society functions more like a matriarchy, which apparently makes for a far more harmonious social world. But in both, and here's the lesson, unless you happen to believe in human exceptionalism—"

"Which I don't."

"They're just as obsessed with social rank, hierarchy, and dominance as we are. If not more so."

"And access?"

"So I've been led to believe."

"Just who have you been reading?"

"I assume you've noticed how often powerful men stumble over this issue?"

"Of access to women?"

"Which commonly happens when they find themselves in a position with more access than they've ever dreamt was possible."

"Why are you so resentful? Don't you have enough women of your own?"

"It's not that, it's—"

"Or are you just trying to gain access to me? Is that what today's performance has been about? Because you've been on since I saw you sitting back there."

"You mean," I said, trying not to laugh, "I don't need to dominate all the men in your world to gain access to you?"

"What do you think?"

"I think we should probably head back to your hotel."

"Why? Need to count your women?"

"That won't take very long."

66

Sunday morning and it was a room service breakfast, Lee with her omelet and hash browns, toast and iced tea for me. No, I still didn't feel good. Then we went back to bed. When we got up the second time she began working her way through a stack of honors papers she'd brought with her while I tried to decode *The Daily Racing Form*. Several times she groaned as she wrote comments in the margins in red ink. Once or twice she shared a sentence with me.

"You don't flunk all of your students, do you?"

"No, they usually opt for an incomplete or withdraw before things get out of hand."

"I wonder if you would have flunked me."

Leaning over to pat my leg, she said, "No, I'm sure we could have worked something out."

"Ah, yes, tenure must be a wonderful thing."

"Oh? I'd be in serious trouble if I slept with one of my students, but sleeping with you is fine, that's just adultery."

"For some reason this conversation reminds me of an old episode of *Perry Mason. The Case of the Adulterous Professor*, or at least that's what I'm calling it."

"Just this once," she said, sitting very still as she stared at me.

"I wasn't saying otherwise."

"No? You men are always so concerned about the sexual history of your women."

"Lee, it never even crossed my mind. Okay? So stop pouting while I tell you about *Perry Mason*."

"I like to pout."

"So—and no you don't—there's this sleazy lit professor, and what he does, he seduces this beautiful young graduate student. "

"And she gets pregnant."

"You've seen it?"

"I didn't have to see it."

"Okay, so what happens next?"

"She kills him."

"Well, someone does, but—"

"What sort of literature?"

"I don't know. Poetry?"

"That works."

"So he teaches poetry, and he seduces this very young and very beautiful graduate student. Then her boyfriend finds out about it and confronts him in his office. They struggle. Then the boyfriend bops him on the head with a bust of Shakespeare and flees, mistakenly believing he's killed him."

"Mistakenly, because we don't really want him to be the murderer since he's already suffered enough."

"Absolutely. So, as it turns out, one of the professor's colleagues, a female lit professor, just happens to stop by, and when she finds him lying unconscious on the floor . . . because he once seduced her with his poetry and refused to divorce his wife, and she's very bitter about how he treated her and because she never got tenure, she . . . so how does she kill him? He's not really dead, right?"

"Just unconscious."

"So what happens next?"

"It's winter, it's freezing cold outside—"

"She opens the window!"

"And in a couple of hours she calls in an anonymous tip to the police and tells them she knows where there's a stiff."

"Exactly," I said, nodding approvingly.

"But they do catch her?"

"Of course they do, because Perry defends the boyfriend. He gets the poor woman up on the stand, and of course by now we all feel very sorry for her, but he gets her up there anyway and makes her read the dead professor's bad poetry until she breaks down and confesses."

"When we were in graduate school did you ever hear the story about Messina's wife?"

"Speaking of stiffs."

"About what happened when his wife found out he was screwing a grad student?"

"Did he use poetry?"

"Messina?"

"And that broke up their marriage?"

"Yes, though everyone knew he was like that."

"So she knew?"

"Maybe it was the last straw."

"Did he ever hit on you?"

"No, but he was very friendly. One of those guys who's always touching you." She shrugged. "I guess I wasn't his type."

"Had to be a blonde."

"Oh?"

"I took one of his classes when I was an undergrad, as did a friend of mine,"

"A blonde?"

"Yes, and very pretty. Later, when I was applying to graduate school, I went to his office to see if he'd write me a letter of recommendation. Turns out, he was happy to, but then he spent the next fifteen minutes pumping me for information about her. I must have said I don't know fifty times."

"But he did write your letter?"

"Eventually.

"So what you're really telling me," she said, laughing at me, "is that it was your woman who got you into graduate school."

"She wasn't my woman."

"Yes, but you wished she were."

"Yes, but she still wasn't."

"Same old story, huh?"

"I had other letters."

She laughed.

"Really. They wanted me. I did good work."

"Well, of course you did."

"So . . . about his wife? If you've finally run through all your mean innuendos."

"Oh! Right. At the time, what I heard was that his ex-wife wooed his new girlfriend away from him."

"So which did she really want, payback, or the other woman?"

"I have no idea, but since she got both she must have been very happy."

"I've always known there were guys whose behavior drove their women into the arms of other men, but into the arms of another woman is a new one."

"Is that what you think? That Charles drove me into your arms?"

"More like leapt."

"I'm serious."

"So what do you want me to say? I don't know a thing about your life with Charles. I'm just thankful we have a history together that precedes the one you have with him."

"Yes, but shouldn't I be finding this more difficult?"

"Probably," I said, rolling over on my side to slide my hand up under the sheet.

"But apparently not," she said, laughing when she reached for me.

When she came back from the shower I was already dressed and sitting in a chair at the table marking up *The Daily Racing Form*. I was determined to get out to Santa Anita.

"You should stay and have another nap," I said, glancing her way. "You still look sleepy."

"I'm fine. Can I ask you something?"

"What?"

"Are you surprised by this?"

"By us?"

"Yes. I know we've always been like this when we're together, but right now seems so unconnected to the rest of my life. I wonder if that's a good thing."

"You mean how easily you move from one man to another?"

"Yes," she said, smiling at me without a hint of embarrassment. "I suppose that is what I mean."

"Shocking."

"Yes, well I'm sure I'm not the first woman to find that a liberating experience. Maybe that's why I don't feel guilty about it."

"Maybe that's the liberating part."

"Only now I'm wondering what you'd say if I said I wanted us to keep in touch. That I'd like for us to be together as often as possible. Would you do that for me?"

"You mean would I do that for you *this* time."

"Would you?"

"*Met bid; held gamely.*"

"Which means?"

"Which means yes. Definitely. Sorry. I'm reading the *Racing Form*. See?" I held it up to show her. "I was looking at the past performances for this filly, Chilled Martini, and right here in the trip notes for one of her races it says *met bid; held gamely.*"

"And that's what you're doing?"

"Better than *willingly; not enough.* Isn't that sad? You can just imagine how that felt."

"Truly tragic."

"So many sad little stories; so many small tragedies. *Ducked out; lost rider. No speed. Two wide trip; empty.* Empty!" I laughed and shook my head. "I love that. Such sad brevity, so definitive, so bleak and hopeless."

"Can you find one that answers my question?"

"*Found best stride late?*"

Laughing, she reached for the *Form*. I watched her slowly turning the pages as she read the comments.

"*Bobbled start; rallied?*"

"Close."

"Ah, here we go!" She was grinning at me. "*Drew off; kept to task.*"

"You would like that one."

She sat the *Form* on the table and stood, then came around behind me and wrapped her arms around my neck, cradling my head against her breasts. She was still damp and smelled of soap. I felt her right nipple rubbing against my check through her bathrobe.

"*Passed tiring rivals,*" I read.

"Have a good day at the track," she said, patting the top of my head.

67

I couldn't stop thinking about her surprising proposal on the drive out to Arcadia. Frankly, the more I thought about it the less comfortable I felt. Wouldn't living like that just be a string of melancholy goodbyes?

I parked the car and began walking across the parking lot towards the grandstand. It's a pleasant sensation, being nearly alone like that in a large public space. Just as pleasing, they'd recently used tar to seal the thousands of cracks in the asphalt, now the bright sunlight reflecting off the cracks made an infinite number of shiny patterns.

I made my way upstairs to where I share a box with Tommy and several other handicappers. As I drew near I could see them, coffee cups, papers, *Racing Forms* strewn about, already engaged in that racetrack ritual of who looks good and whether they should pool their money in the pick six or perhaps in the superfecta in the seventh where the favorite looked vulnerable. I gave them a wide berth and kept walking. I was anxious about Lee. Amazed to find I still didn't know how to deal with her. Annoyed to see how the passage of time had let me down. It made me wonder what I'd done with all those years.

Trying to calm myself, I took a deep breath and then slowly exhaled. Better. Now I was noticing things: the San Gabriels; the people walking through the grandstand as others sat in their seats chatting; the horses warming up out on the backstretch before the first race; the rich, woody scent of mulch and the ubiquitous racetrack odor of cigarettes; the rolled-up *Racing Form* I held tightly in my right hand and my comfortably warm jacket;

the smooth concrete under my feet and the pleasing open expanse of the grandstand extending from where I stood all the way down to the Turf Club; the rows of perfectly aligned green seats, their bottoms neatly folded up awaiting bettors; the late scratches being read over the PA system as tractors droned in the distance, pulling the starting gate out onto the track. It struck me that if there was such a place then this was it, my perfect world. How lucky I was to have it.

When I got to our box I took my usual seat, the first of five in the top row from where it's a quick three steps up to the main concourse. Draping the *Racing Form* over my legs like a blanket to ward off a chill, I wondered if I dared to make a bet, a *real* bet, I mean, then I felt a hand grasp my shoulder.

"Where have you been? I left you three messages."

I twisted around in my seat. It was Wendy, accompanied by two very attractive younger women. "Sorry," I said, laying the *Form* over the arm of the seat next to me to stand. "I guess I must have missed them."

"I wanted to let you know we were coming today. I thought you might like to sit with us." She paused and seemed to relax, so I stepped up to the concourse for her customary hug and a kiss. When I smiled at her two companions, she said, "Nick, this is Karen," and she gestured to an attractive woman in her late thirties with short dark hair, "and this is Jean," smiling at a woman who was tall and thin and had a stunningly beautiful face.

"Let me guess," I said as we all shook hands. "Somehow Wendy's coerced you into coming out here today, and now you're suffering through her special introduction to horse racing."

"She only had to coerce us to skip work," the thin one said. "We've been wanting to check this out for a long time."

"And to win some money," the dark-haired one added.

"Yes," Wendy said. "We were hoping you might be willing to lend a hand."

"I'd love to. Why don't I come around after this race and see if I can make amends."

"It's a tough card today," Wendy said. "We could really use your help."

"I know. I'll be there."

When they left I picked up the *Form*. Not good, a maiden sprint for two year olds. Still, it might be playable, after all, these were all expensive horses with good connections and good trainers, horses *well meant*, as they say at the track. Yes, but other than a prior race or two and a handful of workouts there wasn't much to work with, which was why they weren't a normal part of my game. One really needed to be a specialist, an aficionado of sire statistics and trainer patterns, to see any consistent success. Tracking the data just as obsessively and meticulously as any stock analyst. Patiently waiting for spring when the two year olds first run. Patiently waiting for an opportune moment to plug that special expertise into one of the legs of a pick four or pick six. But I did give it a quick look, checking the entrants, noting their trainers, sires, dams, workout patterns, and jockeys. No, it wasn't hard to see who ought to win, but I wasn't foolish enough to think I had any special insight. But then the favorite did win, which made me glad I hadn't bothered to bet. So Karen and Jean, huh? Grabbing my bag, I stuffed the *Racing Form* inside and set off. Obviously clients, but what sort of business did they run?

I worked my way through the lines of people using the touch-screen betting machines by the stairwell, then made my way upstairs to the next level past the guy whose name I can never remember manning the entrance to the Turf Club. Please, no riff-raff, but he let me pass with a smile and a nod and I made a mental note to myself to drop off a little tidbit of useful information later in the day. That's how it's done at the track, where the social order is built on favors and obligations, in this case what someone knows and what someone else would like to know. I like that about track life.

I was surprised to see how many people sat with Wendy, though Karen and Jean were nowhere in sight. "Where are the ladies?" I asked as I sat down beside her.

"Oh? I didn't think you were interested." She sat her program in her lap to look at me. "You look worn out."

"Just a little sleepy."

"Un-huh. Where were you last night?"

"Nowhere. Just out kind of late."

"Until when, this morning? No wonder you weren't interested when I introduced you to Jean. Did you even notice how gorgeous she is?"

"Not my type."

"Really? I thought you liked intelligent women."

"I do, though they're certainly a challenge. Jean qualifies?"

"Well, let's see, she and Karen and their friends," and she nodded to the other people in her box, "own a pretty successful restaurant over in Pasadena, if that counts."

"A restaurant? They're so stylish, I was thinking they were artists who ran a gallery."

"So maybe you are interested?"

"Maybe. I don't know."

She watched me a moment before smiling. "Who is she?"

"She?"

"The woman who kept you out all night. The woman who must really be something if your reaction to Jean is anything to go by."

"I noticed her," I insisted.

"Not much. Well?

I sighed. It was difficult.

"Nick," she said, slapping my arm as she laughed, "you're embarrassed! Don't tell me you're mixed up with another little Goth chick?"

"Yeah, well I don't think embarrassed quiet captures the mix of emotions I'm feeling today. Now if we're talking about shock, surprise, disbelief, amazement, foreboding . . ."

"Are we?"

"You tell me. I've just spent the last two days with Lee. That's where I was last night, at her hotel."

"Lee?" She was puzzled, but in a moment it came to her. "Oh, my God. Are you serious? I remember you talking about her. But that was years ago."

I nodded my head, smiling rather forlornly.

"*The woman*," she intoned ominously.

"Ah," I said, sitting up straight to look at her. "So you and Barb have been talking."

"Yes," she said, patting my arm, "and sometimes I think she knows you even better than I do. But why complain about it now? If, as you say, you prefer intelligent women, then Barb's about as smart as they come."

"You haven't met Lee."

"So what happened?"

"Believe it or not, I was over at Midnight Special in the philosophy section, just minding my own business, when boom, there she was."

"And?"

"And she's here for a conference at UCLA. Philosophy. Social theory. Like what she did in graduate school. And if that wasn't enough of a surprise, we just seemed to pick up right where we'd left off back in Boulder. Like it was just the other day. But then it's always been like that when we're together. I guess I'd just forgotten."

"How'd she look?"

"Pretty good."

"So what went wrong?"

"Nothing went wrong."

"Nick," she said, smiling at me. "Where it concerns you and women something always goes wrong."

"Well, she is married and leaving tomorrow. If those count."

"Married?"

"Doesn't seem to bother her."

"What about you?"

"Not as much as it should. But it gets worse. This morning she proposed that we try to get together as often as possible."

"So what bothers you about that, if not for the fact that she's married?"

"I'm guess I'm just not in to bathos."

"Did you tell her that?"

"She never gave me a chance."

"We're not talking about love, are we? Surely, you haven't gone there."

"Of course not, though I do still enjoy being with her."

"So what's the problem? That there's just no way this can work?"

"That, and I'm not so sure I even want her anymore."

She watched me a moment. "So what do you want?" she asked.

I shrugged.

"Do you want some advice from an old friend?"

"Don't I always?" I said, putting my arm around her shoulders.

"You need someone. You always have. So here she is again, and yes, maybe it's not such a great idea, but we don't know that for sure, and if she's as smart as you say she is then maybe you ought to listen."

"It's never going to last for more than a few months."

"How about Jean?"

"She is very pretty."

"Yes she is. So what will you have with her?"

"What do you mean?"

"A few weekends? A little of the old this and that? Because with you they always end."

"It's not much, is it?"

"Nope," she said, patting my arm, "but that's my boy."

"Did you and Barb really talk about me?"

"She's worried about you. Of course, this new wrinkle isn't going to make her feel any better."

"What do you suppose she'd tell me to do?"

"Gee, I don't know, leave married women alone?"

"So now I suppose you're going to call and tell her all about it?"

"Won't need to."

"She's here?"

"Didn't you see who owns the Canani horse in this race?"

I got *The Daily Racing Form* from my bag and looked. There it was, Swag, owners, Caduceus Thoroughbreds.

"Jack's here too?"

"That's where Karen and Jean are, down in the paddock with the owner's party. Jack was gracious enough to invite them. By the way," she said, grinning at me, "Barb thinks Jean is gorgeous, too."

I groaned, not even wanting to try and imagine how that conversation had gone.

"Oh, come on, don't be such a baby. We understand how you are, for the most part we even like how you are."

I picked up the *Form* and forced myself to look. Swag was untried; another maiden race. I had no idea what he'd do. Did anyone? I wondered what Barb would have to say about how he looked down in the paddock.

"So, who do you like?" Wendy teased.

"I wish I knew."

She turned to look at me, then burst out laughing. "Yes, but how about in this race?"

"Ask Barb, she's usually got a pretty good handle on these sorts of races."

"When did you two talk last?"

"We text, or send e-mail."

"So you haven't met Chet?"

"Don't tell me he's here too?"

"Boy, you really ought to check your voicemail once in a while."

"You've met him?"

"Several times. Nice guy."

I stared at the infield, thinking about Barb and how she lived her life; so unlike Lee.

"Nick, stop brooding. She's happy. You did the right thing."

"What? No. I wasn't thinking about that," I said, looking at her. "I'm happy for Barb, but today might not be the best day for me to meet her cardiologist."

"Then why don't you just take off? I won't even mention I saw you. Go do something else today."

"No thanks, that's just how I got into this mess in the first place. When I should have been here and not in that damn bookstore. God only knows what might happen if I left today."

"So why weren't you here?"

"I thought a day off might help me shake this stubborn losing streak."

"That sure worked!"

68

I put the *Form* down and turned to Wendy. "Okay, it's Swag."

"You think so? It doesn't look like his sire's all that great with first time starters."

"Well, maybe today will be different."

"Maybe? Now that's reassuring. You're not going to be of any help today at all, are you?"

"Sure I will. After this race."

"You know, you really should go say hi to Barb and Chet when they get back from the paddock."

"I should."

But it seemed like I'd just opened the *Form* when I heard a familiar laugh. Then I looked up. It was Barb chatting with Karen and Jean as they walked towards us. Then I felt a sharp poke in my ribs. "Yes, Wendy," I said.

I stood to watch them approach. Jean really was attractive. How had I managed to miss that? Then I looked at Barb. She'd been watching me, and when I shrugged my shoulders she rolled her eyes. Had I really been that obvious?

She came to me and put her arms around me waist to hold me tight, then pulled back first to kiss me and then to whisper in ear. "I thought you might not come today after Wendy told you we'd be here."

"Not at all, I'm glad you're here," I whispered back. "Are you happy?"

"Very." She stepped back to smile at me. "How have you been?"

"Fine. Not so well today, but otherwise no complaints."

"Oh?" she said, exchanging a meaningful look with Wendy.

"Barb, really, I'm fine. I just need to hit a few winners."

"What do you think of Jack's colt?"

"On paper, he looks great. How'd he look in the flesh?"

"Good," she said, nodding to the horses in the post parade. He did look good, too, up on his toes, wheeling around a bit, very alert, almost playful. "Yes," she said, watching a moment. "A lot of nice horses."

"So where's Chet?"

"Sitting up there with Jack and Frank." She pointed behind us to the upper tier of the Turf Club.

"Wendy, think you can lose your money on your own for a while?"

"It's never been a problem before."

"You know, Wendy tends to exaggerate," I said as we walked up the steps together.

"I know." She stopped to look at me. "Are you sure you're all right. You look terrible."

"Thanks," I said, managing a half-hearted laugh.

"Are you angry with me?"

"With you? Hardly. I'm just a little tired and cranky, that's all."

"We are still friends?"

"Of course we are."

"And the news about Chet? You're really okay with that?"

"Yes. For once I'm actually being an adult."

"But there is something you're not telling me, isn't there?"

"Uh, not really."

"No? Because you know Wendy will."

"Barb, honestly, it's nothing."

We rode the escalator up to the next floor and made our way to the tables overlooking the track. Yes, they were all there, sitting on either side of a large table cluttered with dishes and glasses, watching the horses on a small television monitor. Jack was the first to notice.

"Nick, I haven't seen you in weeks. How're you doing?" he asked, coming around the table to shake my hand.

"Not bad. I like your colt."

"That was Frank's idea. It's been expensive, but . . . we'll see."

Frank leaned over and shook my hand. "I saw Tommy down by the paddock. He said he like's Swag's chances."

"He did? I bet he's talked to Canani." I turned and held out my hand. "Hi, you must be Chet. I'm Nick. I've been hearing a lot of nice things about you from Barb and Wendy. Thought I'd better get up here and tell you what a lucky guy you are."

"Thanks, Nick. I've heard nothing but nice things about you, too."

"Nick's sitting with Wendy," Barb told him, smiling affectionately.

"What do you think of Canani?" Frank asked me.

"Shrewd trainer. Pretty good handicapper."

"I was wondering, because even though he's trying to keep us realistic he still thinks Swag might fire first time out of the gate."

"Well, I hope you guys won't be too disappointed if he doesn't. But you know what they say about two year olds. Even though they may look terrible today there's no reason why they can't come back and win the next time. Of course, then you'll have some really tough choices to make."

"That's just what Julio said. Win today, and we'll have to think really hard about where to run him next."

"Which is why I'm glad I only have to bet them."

"Did you?" Jack asked.

"You know, I've been so busy trying to make sense of this race that I actually forgot. When was the last time that happened?"

"I'd say never," Barb said.

"At the very least, I need to put something on him to win."

"I'll go with you," Jack said,

"Tommy said he hasn't seen much of you lately," he said as we walked to the concourse. "You're not going into some other line of work, are you?"

"No, it's just this stubborn losing streak. But I've been here before. I just need to remind myself to be patient. Sooner or later the winning always returns."

"Still, if there's anything Frank and I can do," he said, stopping to put his hand on my arm. "Don't hesitate to ask."

"Thanks, Jack, but everything's fine. Now, if I ever really do tap-out or get cancer or something . . ."

"So," he said as we started walking again, "what do you think of Barb's new friend?"

"He's seems nice enough. What do you guys think?"

"He's certainly well regarded, though neither of us knew him. I don't know. I'm sure he'll be fine." Then he laughed and patted me on the shoulder. "But we sure do miss your handicapping."

We stood in the shortest line when we reached the tellers, and when it was my turn I said, "Twenty dollars to win and place on six."

Jack went next. "Five hundred to win on six."

"Did I hear you correctly?" I asked as we turned to walk away. "Five hundred to win?"

"I know. First time starter out of a sire who hasn't done much with first timers."

"Who's only going to pay $3.60 at best even if he does win? I hope you've covered yourself with a few exactas."

"A few."

"So you'll be all right if he loses?"

"He's not going to lose."

"I'm glad Tommy isn't here to hear you say that. We might need Chet to revive him."

"I know, never fall in love with a horse or a bet. But it doesn't seem right to bet against him."

"Come on," I said, turning him around. "Give me some money."

He took his wallet out to hand me. "Don't tell Frank," he said.

"Why? Is he nuts too?"

"It's just that he's not much of a bettor, it's the owning part he enjoys. He'd never understand betting against our horse. It would seem like a betrayal."

"Swag may be your horse, Jack, but he's still just a horse. And we're not really betting against him, we're just making sure that whatever he does today, win or lose, works to our advantage. Surely, Frank can understand that."

"Forty dollar exactas," I told the teller, laying the money on the counter. "One and three with six. Sixty dollar exactas. Two and ten with six."

"Thanks, Nick," he said as I handed him the tickets. Then he smiled. "But what if I want to do more than just cover my ass?"

"So do it."

Stepping to the counter, he said, "Ten dollar trifecta, part-wheel, six with one, three, two, ten, with all. Six dollar part-wheel, one, two, three, ten, five, with six, with all."

"Thank God there isn't a superfecta in this race." I said as he gathered up his tickets. "You don't bet like this all the time, do you?"

"Would that worry you?"

"Only if you lose."

The race went off and Swag was content to track the leaders down the backstretch, then on the far turn he edged closer and with a strong move had the lead by the quarter pole. But in the stretch he began to lug out, which allowed the two horses at his heels to close. Then he started to gawk, pricking his ears and cocking his head towards the grandstand. Yes, he'd heard the crowd yelling and now he was curious. You could just see him wondering what all the fuss was about. A bright guy, attentive and not overly concerned with the herd instinct, whether it was to lead or follow, I'd seen that sort of behavior before and it's easily remedied. More importantly, you could see that he wasn't just another one-dimensional racehorse who needed everything just so to win. That it was far more likely he'd turn out to be one of those rare sorts with good tactical speed. A horse that could more easily adapt to the changing circumstances that frequently crop up during the course of a race. But he wasn't going to win today. At the finish, though he was still full of run, he lost by a neck, one of the pressers nailing him shortly before the wire. Other than that it was an excellent first start. Next time he might not be so curious about his surroundings. Next time they might try blinkers. I thought he looked like an excellent purchase.

Frank and Jack looked stunned. "Next time," I told them. "His problem is he's too damn smart. Did you see how he was looking around in the stretch? Don't worry," I said to Frank. "You can see he's got good tactical speed. Most of them don't. You're going to win a lot of races with this guy once he learns to focus."

"He did look good, didn't he?" Frank said.

"I'll certainly be betting on him next time, though his price will be even worse than it was today."

"Next time he'll be the favorite," Barb said.

"Which means it won't matter much where you run him, not from a bettor's standpoint."

"Yes, but you still made a little," Jack said.

"Yes, so little," I said, holding up my ticket and smiling, "I'd better go cash this before I forget."

When I returned Wendy was there with Jean and Karen.

"Did you bet on Swag," Jean asked excitedly.

"Win and place, though now I'm kicking myself for not putting him on the bottom in a couple of exactas."

"Karen did. Wendy told her to bet Swag second with all the horses she liked on top."

"Good for her. So what do you think of all this?"

"I think I should've bet that exacta with Karen."

"Well, don't give up, beginner's luck may still strike. I've seen it happen before."

"I thought you hated beginner's luck," Wendy said.

"I hate all forms of luck, but then I might feel differently if I ever had any."

"There's not enough luck to go around?" Karen joked.

"There's not enough *anything* to go around," Jean said.

"Yes, well around here it's typically luck people run out of most, whatever else they may run out of usually flows from that."

"But Wendy said this is where you make your living. Is that really possible?"

"Occasionally. Lucky for me it's always fun."

"Same with us," Karen said.

"That's right, Wendy said you two have a restaurant over in Pasadena. Which one? Maybe I've been there."

"Cholla?" Jean said.

I shook my head. "How long have you been open?"

"Three years, though it certainly seems longer than that to me."

"I guess we're just fated to be workaholics," Karen said. "Wendy really had to keep after us to get us here."

"I know what you mean," Barb said. "Then who should I happen to meet? Why, the old handicapper himself," she said, patting my shoulder.

"Any beginners' luck?" Karen asked.

Barb smiled at me. "I think so."

"Yes," I said, glancing over at Chet. "And it seems your luck still holds."

"More than my fair share, I'm sure."

"Ah, hah!" Jean exclaimed. "So you're the one."

I noticed Jack slowly walking back to the table counting a large roll of bills. "Watch this," I said, nodding towards Jack as he spoke to Frank.

"How much?" we heard Frank ask, the amazement in his voice unmistakable. Then he looked at us. "Can you believe it, he bet against Swag."

"And to win," Jack said, correcting him.

"So now he's over here bragging about how much he won. Well . . ." he said as they both began to laugh.

"Yes," I asked, "and just how much did you win betting *against* your horse?"

"Enough that dinner's on me."

"No, on us, right?" Karen said, looking at Jean. "At our restaurant."

"That's right," Jean said. "We'll toast Swag's near victory and how much money we almost won."

"Don't worry," Barb said. "I'm sure Nick will fix you up with a winner before the day's over."

"I'll certainly try," I said, looking at Jean. "But unlike Dr. Danton's, so far my handicapping hasn't been all that reliable."

When we got back to Wendy's box I began a careful assessment of the past performances of the horses in the next race. Then I surprised myself, coming up with several choices that did well, as did the ones I picked for the next race, and the one after that. Of course, Karen, Jean, and friends were by then eagerly shuttling back and forth to the betting windows with my picks. Not that I was paying much attention to anything but my handicapping, though perhaps I should have been since Wendy later told me some paid quite well. It was when another one crossed the finish line first in the eighth that it suddenly dawned on me that something had changed. Relaxed, at peace, once again comfortable in my world—now how had that happened? For no discernable reason, or for no reason discernable to me, I'd wandered from home and gotten lost. Now, somehow, miraculously, I was back home. I hardly dared believe it, but then it always works like that when it finally ends: behind your back while you're not even looking.

I stood and stretched. "Well, that's it for me," I announced, speaking to Wendy. "Looks like everyone's happy."

"Happy? You've got to be kidding. What happened to that losing streak?"

I took deep breath. "I'm almost afraid to say."

"I'm sure glad you're not superstitious," she said, shaking her head.

"It's not that, it just makes me uncomfortable putting all my trust in something that practically begs to become another ironic disappointment."

"Nice. It's a wonder you can even get out of bed in the morning."

"Just because I refuse to live in a fool's paradise with the rest of you?"

"Right. Must be getting awfully lonely over there by now. Maybe you should stick around for the last race and go over to Cholla with the rest of us." She watched me shake my head. "You could always bring her along."

"I know, but she's going to be tired, and she doesn't know anyone—"

"It might help you think more clearly about your situation. If the two of you aren't alone all evening."

"Now how am I going to think more clearly with you and Barb around?"

"I'll bet you one hundred bucks she says she wants to come."

"Not if she knows who's going to be there."

"Nick, I saw that look on your face when I told you Barb was here with Chet. No," she said, not letting me deny it. "Now, we both know that should have been you, but of course it's not. So now along comes this other woman, and she's doing everything she can to get you back into her life. I wonder," she said, pausing to stare at me, "just how many chances like this you expect to get?"

"I know, but she's not really offering all that much."

"So you're so happy these days you can just walk away?"

"There's always Jean."

"Yes, there will always be a Jean." She rested her hand on my arm. "How long have I known you?"

"Too long."

"Yes, and in all that time I don't believe I've ever seen you this unhappy. So come with us tonight. See how she looks to you when she's around your friends. I think you'll be surprised by how that makes you feel."

"What if she doesn't want to come?"

"Good lord, can't you get this woman to do anything?"

"When has any woman?"

"So maybe Lee will take pity on you and be your first."

"That's not something she's got a lot of."

"Seriously? Now I really do want to met this lady." Then she looked at me and grinned. "So, that works for you?"

69

On my way out I stopped in the concourse to take another look at the nightcap, plopping my bag on the countertop of an empty concession stand and spreading the *Form* out in front of me. It was a tough one to sort out. One seemingly designed to torment the pick-six players still alive with second thoughts about the horses they'd left out to make their bets more affordable. Then it jumped out at me: Carla Gaines was the trainer of one of the entrants. I love long-shot trainers like Gaines because their wins—when they do win—come in clusters. It's one of my favorite plays. Better yet, it's a rarely noted and thus highly profitable pattern to bet. But don't ask me why it works like that because I really have no idea. On the surface it just makes no sense at all, but then that's true of so many things in life, as is the fact that it's often possible to turn them to our advantage if we're paying attention. So I wasn't about to waste my time worrying about why there was such a pattern, let alone what might explain it—if anything actually did—I was just hoping to make use of this little scrap of esoteric information in this one race.

Viewed within the context of mainstream handicapping factors there were four obvious horses to consider, plus several others that might tempt the betting public, being trained by high-percentage trainers or ridden by some of the meet's leading riders. Gaines's horse, I was glad to see, fell into none of these categories. It was very tempting.

"Nick, I thought you'd gone home?" It was Jean.

"Yeah," I laughed, "so did I, but then I decided to take one more look at this last race. Then this caught my eye." I pointed with my pen to the Gaines entry.

She bent over to look. "Old Stoner? He doesn't win very often, does he?"

"No, but his trainer's having a pretty good day. Did you notice that she won the first race? And that another of her horses placed in the sixth?"

She straightened up to smile at me. "Sounds like a bet's about to happen."

"I wouldn't be surprised," I said, pointing to the television monitor hanging from the wall on the other side of the concourse. Old Stoner was holding steady at 14-1.

"Wow! Maybe I should too. At least to win."

"Yes, and it wouldn't hurt to put him in with some of these other boys in an exacta or two."

"Well . . ." and she grinned at me. "Don't you think I should go tell Karen first?"

"That's up to you," I said, smiling at the hint of conspiracy in her voice. "But he's quite a long shot. Certainly not the sort of bet one can expect to win every day. Though that just means opportunities like this are rare. I'm only aware of it because I like to track a couple of crazy factors most people overlook."

"Such as?"

"Well, this, for instance." I turned and pointed to the Gaines entry again. "I've seen this pattern with her before. Week after week, nothing's happening, then she suddenly hits a series of winners, and all this over a very brief span of time. What's really inexplicable is how this one pattern seems to trump everything else. How what would normally be, at best, a marginal horse suddenly becomes a viable long shot play."

"And that's what you think's happening today?"

"I think it's likely enough to bet on. So," I said, watching her glance over her shoulder at the stairwell, "our little secret?"

"Will you show me what to bet?"

"Here's what you do." I reached for her program. "Take Old Stoner here and bet him to win. Whatever amount you're comfortable with. Then put him on top for six dollars in exactas with the one, four, and six, then on the bottom with the same horses in two dollar exactas. Okay?" I said as I wrote the combinations in her program.

"But why am I betting less if he's second?"

"Because if he is second—and I really don't think he will be— you'll at least cover your bets."

"Is that what you're going to do?"

"Nope. No insurance."

"But—"

"Jean, I don't know about you, but I've had it with hedging my bets. Beginning today . . . right here . . . right now . . . it's go for broke."

She smiled. "Does that include tonight?"

"Tonight?"

"You have no idea how informative Wendy can be."

"No, actually I do."

"And Barb. They both seem to know you pretty well."

"Jean, can I just say how embarrassing this is?"

"Nick, don't be silly. We've all been there. So," and she gave me a friendly pat on the shoulder, "this time we're going for broke? No more insurance?"

"That's right. This is *our* moment. For once we're the ones going home winners."

I escorted her to the shortest line at the Autototes and stood behind her watching as she carefully punched in her bets. A little hesitant, but she got the job done. Then it was my turn, but unlike Jean there was no hesitation at all as I bet a series of exactas spread out over a large number of tickets for a total of one hundred dollars, all with Old Stoner on top of two moderately priced longshots. Then it was two hundred dollars spread across multiple tickets with Old Stoner on top of two of the shorter priced favorites. Finally, I dropped forty dollars to win on each of five separate tickets. Yes, I was tempted to key Old Stoner in a few trifectas and superfectas, but I resisted. I was orthodox, conservative, wanting no loose ends to distract from the pleasure of knowing.

I turned to Jean and handed her my tickets. "After the race, can you cash these for me? I need to get going and it's a long drive. You won't need to sign anything, just scoop up the money."

"What if you don't come tonight?"

"Give it to Wendy." I grinned at her. "Just think how much fun you're going to have cashing all those tickets."

"You're certainly putting a lot of faith in your luck."

"Not me. For once luck's got nothing to do with it."

70

I called Lee once I was out on the 210. I had no idea what I was going to say. Then it rang a few times and there she was.

"Hi there."

"Hi. Where are you?"

"Walking across campus to my hotel."

"Walking?"

"It's not that far. Are you still at the track?"

"No. I should be there in about forty-five minutes."

"How'd it go?"

"It was interesting. How about you?"

"Fine. Interesting? What does that mean? Good, or not so good?"

"It means I did well for a change."

"And that was interesting?"

"No, I was referring to Wendy, who was there with some of her friends."

"Oh? What did you tell her?"

"Not much, just that I was in the middle of an interesting weekend. She's dying to meet you."

"You told her, didn't you? That I'm married."

"It came up."

"I can't believe it."

"I didn't tell anyone else."

"Oh? Who else was there?"

"Like I said, some of her friends. Doctors, two clients who own a restaurant in Pasadena, which reminds me, they've invited us over to their place this evening to celebrate."

"What are we celebrating?"

"A couple of these doctors own a horse. Today was its first race. It didn't win, but it still did very well, so they're going to have a little celebration in its honor."

"And you're sure I'm included in this invitation?"

"Yes, if you'd like to go."

"I might, if you fill me in."

"There's nothing to fill in. Just a pleasant evening with old friends."

"Who are these doctors?"

"Well, there's Frank and Jack. They own the horse."

"And?"

"Barb. She'll be there with her fiancé, Chet."

"What's she like?"

"Uh, nice, I guess."

"You guess?" I heard her snort over the phone. "Am I going to have to ask your old pal Wendy?"

"It's no big deal. Wendy introduced us a few years ago and we were together for a bit. So now we're friends and she's engaged to Chet."

"I've been expecting something like this."

"Like what?"

"That you'd be involved with someone. It would have been nice if you'd told me."

"Lee, there's nothing to tell. It's been over for some time."

"Then why are you being so evasive?"

"I'm not."

"I know I don't have to ask if you loved her."

"Lee, it never got anywhere near that serious."

"So she's going to be there tonight along with everyone else?"

"Yes, she and Chet. Her fiancé."

"I presume she knows about our weekend as well?"

"Probably. She and Wendy are pretty close."

"Did you ever talk to her about us?"

"No, but she guessed I had someone like you in my past."

"Guessed?"

"I don't know, she just picked up on something."

"Well, you must have told her something."

"Honestly, I never said a word. Why would I?"

"Because you love to talk, especially in bed."

"Lee, I've never told anyone about you, or our life together."

"Truly?"

"Have you?"

"Never. Would you tell me? About her, and your relationship?"

"If you asked, but like I said, there's not much to tell."

"And this Barb, she'll really be there tonight?"

"Uh . . . that's what I said."

"I'm ready," was all she said when I came in.

"Yes, so I see." She was dressed for combat, wearing a silky looking teal blue top and tightly tailored black slacks that accentuated her trim figure. She'd also pulled her hair back and wore a necklace, a thin silver strand with a large iridescent bead that was lodged down there between her breasts. Sandals too, ones I hadn't seen, and she'd done her toenails in some dark reddish brown color. I could still smell the faint odor of nail polish in the room.

I slipped my arm around her waist. "You look very pretty. Are you sure you wouldn't rather go to some nice restaurant close by?"

"I thought you wanted to go," she said, pulling away from me.

"It's a long drive, and I just had a long drive."

"You'll manage."

"I'm not so sure. I'm suddenly feeling a bit nervous."

"Oh?" she said, staring at me with big empty eyes. "Is there something you should feel nervous about?"

"No."

"What was it you said, something about this being a pleasant evening with old friends?"

"You're an old friend."

"So there you go," she said with a grim smile. "I'm sure it will be lovely."

71

I took the Arroyo Parkway—a stretch of highway I usually enjoy—marveling the whole way at my blundering stupidity. Any man even half my age knows what folly it is to mix current and former girlfriends. Elemental particles of immense energy crashing together, ripping my universe apart, swallowing everything up in a swirling vortex of ill will. But then in the middle of the Parkway it occurred to me how I had it all wrong. There'd be no struggle. Not over me. These were women I'd *known*. Past tense. If any contention did spring up it would be over bragging rights only.

I glanced at Lee. As usual, I had no idea what she was thinking, and not for the first time did I wonder why it proves so difficult to love intelligent women. Maybe it's due to their awe-inspiring cognitive equipment. They just work more reliably than we do, and a hell of a lot faster, too. That's factory, by the way, not after-market. Then there's this: a smart woman is always smarter than a smart man. Trust me, you can hang a lot of deductive reasoning on that axiom.

I guess the reason I'm raising this now is because I've often been perplexed by why these women choose the men they do. It's rarely much of a mystery why a normal sort of man and woman couple up. The reasons are usually fairly obvious, if not to them then at least to us. But intelligent women are different. There's something opaque in their decision-making that makes their actions hard for those of us who aren't to comprehend. Nevertheless, I'd still like to argue that they are more apt to pick for their mates men who entertain them. That's what my limited experience suggests, anyway. Unfortunately, entertain in this context is ambiguous, meaning stupid antics just as easily as wit and cleverness. Of course, I like to think I fall within the latter grouping, but the intelligent women I've known have been far too smart to tip their hand. So, yes, I'm just guessing. But this is not a guess: even the most intelligent woman is still going to choose this man or that man. So why shouldn't she choose the one she at least finds entertaining? Yes, but what about love?

I once knew this very intelligent woman who was getting married. We were good friends and I thought I knew her pretty well, but I couldn't have been more surprised when she told me. She was so casual about it. It just happened to come up during the course of one of our conversations. I hadn't even known she was serious about anyone. I even had to ask her who he was. So to me it all seemed rather odd and out of the blue. Anyway, I fumbled around a bit trying to articulate my confusion and she, being more intelligent than me, knew immediately what it was that was bothering me. Then not only did she articulate it for me, she even explained, which is the only time this has ever happened to me with an intelligent woman.

What she told me was that she'd finally decided the time had come to get married and start a family. That now was the time to move on to that other sort of life. Then she told me that the guy she'd picked was chosen solely because he happened to be the guy who was in her life at that particular point in time. She really laughed when she saw how surprised I was. What about romance? What about love? What about finding the right guy? She smiled and patted me on the shoulder. She said that from her point of view any man of a certain type was fine; that there wasn't any reason to be any pickier about it than that. So the man she chose to marry just happened to be latest iteration of the type of guy she liked—so he's the one who got tagged. At the time I didn't know what to say, but I'd like to think that if I'd had my wits about me I might have said that even men of a particular type aren't completely interchangeable. Surely, there are good choices and bad choices. Surely, even an intelligent woman can make a mistake.

72

As always, I easily found a place to park. Also, as always, it was a really good place to park. That's no small thing, and it bothers me to squander all that good luck on something so trivial. I'd rather spread it around a bit. I'd use valet parking.

We had no more than stuck our heads in the door when Jean appeared. "Nick, you came!" she said.

"Lee, this is Jean. She and Karen own this restaurant. They were with Wendy out at Santa Anita today."

Lee smiled as they shook hands. "It's lovely," she said, glancing around the restaurant.

"Thank you." Jean pointed to the rear of the restaurant. "It's back this way. Everyone's here. By the way," she said, touching my arm. "I almost forgot, you left something at the track today. I'll have to get it for you later."

As we followed her Lee turned to me and raised her eyebrows. "Yes, lovely," I said, making a point of not noticing Jean's graceful gait.

She took us to an alcove where a large table sat in front of a retro looking semi-circular padded banquette. Yes, they were all there, all watching us with the same look of surprise and curiosity. When I glanced at Lee to see her reaction I actually jumped. She was glowing like radioactive metals.

Wendy was the first to stand. She came over and tilted her head for a kiss on the check, then turned to Lee and smiled, not an unfriendly smile, but not a smile of unambiguous welcome and friendship, either, and whatever it meant Lee returned it in kind. I felt a bit like a witness to a series of signals in an overly expressive nonverbal language, one I didn't fully comprehend, one with roots in some sort of primal communication dating back at least to the Pleistocene when it might have served to smooth the way as small bands of hunters and their families came warily together at a mammoth kill. Has much really changed for us since those days? Aren't we still the same desperate animal? Maybe a little patina of civilization, but that's about it.

"Lee, let me introduce you to Wendy," I said, taking her hand. "Wendy, this is Lee."

"It's so nice to finally meet you," Wendy said.

"Thank you. It's so nice to finally meet you, too."

"Yes. So," I stammered as they both turned to stare at me. "Let's introduce you to everyone else. You've met Jean. This is Karen."

Lee smiled and shook her hand.

"And these two handsome gentlemen are Frank and Jack." I pointed across the table. "They own Swag. The horse I told you about? The one who almost won his first race today?"

She smiled and nodded her head.

Then Barb, not waiting for my introduction, stood and held out her hand. "Hi Lee, I'm Barb, and this is my finance, Chet."

"Barb," Lee said as she took her hand.

"Glad you could make it for the celebration," Chet said as he stood.

"Oh," she said, glancing my way, "I wouldn't have missed this for the world." And then turning to Jack and Frank: "And congratulations on Swag's first race, by the way."

"Thanks," Jack said. "Though he could have done better. But maybe next time, right Nick?"

"Uh—"

"Yes," she said, cutting me off, dangerous mischief in her eyes. "That's just what Nick said, didn't you?"

They all waited, staring at me. I don't know, for some reason I'd gone mute. Maybe I was too busy counting the millions upon millions of dust motes settling down upon us.

"Canani called us on his cell phone," Frank said. "Guess what he said?" He looked at me for a moment. "Nick?"

"Uh . . . not to worry? That he came back from the race in great shape? That next time he'll get Espinosa to ride?"

"Solis," Frank corrected.

"That's really what he said?" Barb asked.

"Just about. Julio thinks we should wait at least three weeks before we run him again."

"Lee," Wendy asked, breaking into the conversation, "did Nick ever drag you out to the track?"

"No, he'd stopped doing that sort of thing by the time I knew him, but of course I still found out about it. You know how he is," she said, turning to stare at me. "Can't keep a secret. So I did know, but apart from a few odd things about his behavior there wasn't much to suggest he'd actually become a gambler. But I'm not that surprised. Did you know he claims he was led astray? Correct me if I've misquoted you," she said, turning to me with a malicious grin.

"You haven't."

"I'd like to ask you something," she said to Wendy. "Nick and I had this protracted discussion about whether or not it's proper to call him a gambler. He claims it's not. That what he does isn't like what we commonly refer to as gambling, though that's how it looks to me. I mean," she said, turning to stare at me, "he even looks like a gambler."

"Well," Wendy said, "I suppose I'd have to side with you. That it's a form of gambling, but we know what he means. Compared to people who clearly are gamblers, Nick's not much of one."

"I guess I just don't understand the difference."

"The most important difference," I said, once again in full command of my voice, "is the one I've already explained to you, that we have radically differing personal psychologies. I don't need what your so-called real gamblers need when they play the horses. I don't even enjoy risky behavior."

"No, poor baby," she said, patting my back, "you really don't."

"You know what he reminded me of this afternoon?" Jack said. "That old cliché about never falling in love with a horse or a bet. That's hardly the talk of a big risk taker."

"I was talking about life at the track, Jack, not about *life*. Even I know there's a difference."

"Of course you do," Lee said.

"Lee," Barb said, smiling at her, "why don't you come over here and sit with me. Nick, you can sit over there with Wendy."

After we were settled Karen asked if we'd like something to drink and I said I'd love a Coors. Lee asked for a martini.

Soon, I began to relax. The talk at the table was mostly about the race and what Frank and Jack should do next or about what Canani was likely to suggest and how much that was going to cost them, though Lee and Barb weren't paying much attention, apparently having a conversation of their own, one that appeared friendly, though I couldn't actually hear much of what was being said.

"They seem to be getting along," I said, leaning over to whisper to Wendy.

"You never told me she was this pretty."

"No? Well, she hasn't changed much."

"I can see what you mean, by the way. She's definitely not the type who's going to do something she doesn't want to. If you really want to see her again I think you'd better do what she says."

"Yes," I said, staring at the two of them. "But I've been wondering, do you think it's possible for a man to have too many ex-girlfriends?"

"Now that worries you?" she said, shifting in her chair to look at me.

"You mean now that I'm sitting here across the table from them?"

"Yes, how *does* that feel, looking at these two women who've moved on without you? Two women who would've been perfectly happy with you if you hadn't felt compelled to go off and do something else."

"Well—"

"Barb? It wasn't because you thought she could do better."

"Yeah? What about what I need?"

"Can you even tell me what that is?"

"Uh . . ."

"Now, I will admit that Lee's a bit of a surprise. That she's not exactly what I was expecting. But I can certainly see how she might be what you need."

"Aren't you overlooking something rather important?"

"What? That she's married? Because she doesn't seem very married to me."

"Uh-huh. Well, she's certainly not going to break up her marriage over me, that I can tell you for sure. She just wants me around for a little fun when the opportunity presents itself."

"Nick, trust me, no one's ever going to put up with you just for a little fun."

"Then I have no idea what she really wants."

"So why not ask her?"

"Because she'll just say what she's said already, that she's surprised to find how much she enjoys having more than one man at the same time."

"What?"

"Not like that," I said, laughing at the startled look on her face. "That she doesn't feel any guilt when we're together. That she finds that surprising, which has got her wondering why she shouldn't have more than one man at the same time."

"Don't you think that lack of guilt says something about her marriage? Or do you believe she'd be capable of doing something like this with just anyone?"

"Of course not."

"Which means it's far more likely this has everything to do with how she feels about you."

"Possibly."

"Possibly?" She shook her head at me. "Let me tell you what I saw when she first walked in here."

"You don't like her, do you?"

"What I saw, and don't change the subject," she said, smacking my hand, "was jealously. Now why, I wondered, should she be jealous?"

"We've talked about that, and it's not jealousy, she's just competitive and wants everything her own way. If you knew her better you'd understand. Look," I said, sighing deeply, "even if it is all about me that still doesn't tell me what I should do about it. Not that I've ever known how to deal with her."

"Barb is so right about you."

"Oh?"

"It's always been about Lee."

"Whatever," I said, standing. "I'm going to the bar for another Coors."

The bartender sat the glass down on the bar in front of me and poured enough to fill it two thirds of the way to the rim. I took a sip. It was painfully cold and crisp when I swallowed.

Leaning on the bar, I turned to watch Jean and Karen scurrying about out in the restaurant's main room. They worked hard. Then Jean looked my way and smiled.

"Nick," she said, walking over to speak to me. "Stay right here and I'll be right back."

I looked at the bartender. He was pretending like he wasn't there.

When she returned she was holding a thick envelope. "I believe you left this," she said.

I hefted it in my hand. It was heavy. "Thanks. I can't believe I went off and forgot this."

"No, thank you," she said, casting a guilty look Karen's way.

I laid the envelop on the bar and peered inside. "Good lord. How much is this?"

"$3,786 dollars," she said, tapping the envelope.

The Bet

I poured the rest of the beer in my glass and looked up at the bartender. He raised his eyebrows and stared at me. I shrugged.

"Just how often do you do this sort of thing?" she asked.

"I've won more any number of times, but I've rarely won any this easily." I took a drink. "Jean, you'd have no way of knowing this, of course, but for the last three weeks it's been nothing but losing. Worse, I haven't been able to do anything about it. But this," and I tapped the envelope, "means I'm no longer standing in the shadows."

"Yes, and you even got Lee to come," she said, looking past me towards the other room. "Things really do seem to be looking up."

"At the moment, but you never know."

"No, you never do," she said, reaching out to touch my hand.

"Well," I said, a bit startled, "thanks for taking care of this."

"My pleasure."

73

We were walking back to the car. Lee was being very quiet. I, of course, was wondering why.

"So what were you and Barb talking about? It looked like you two really hit it off."

"Okay," she laughed, "what is it you want to know?"

"Nothing. I was just wondering what you two were talking about."

"Were we talking about you?"

"Well?"

"Your name came up, but we talked about a lot of things. It was fun comparing notes on what it's like to be a woman in a professional career. We've got a lot more in common than you might imagine. Did you know she's interested in bioethics?"

"Is she?"

"She's still very fond of you, by the way."

"Yes, well I've had a lot of practice being the loveable ex-boyfriend."

"She told me it was all her fault. I told her I felt the same way."

I stopped walking to stare at her. "Sounds like the two of you were having a contest to see who'd upset me the most."

"If so, I'd be the winner."

"You know, it was really something sitting across the table from you two tonight. It was like looking at an exhibit of Nick's failures."

"I know," she said, taking my hand, "but we're working on that."

"I guess."

"You haven't changed your mind, have you?"

"No, but it does seem rather pathetic. And what happens if I get greedy and want more?"

"Do you?"

"Actually, I do, and that really is your fault."

"Like I said. So what about Wendy? Since she seems to know everything."

"Tonight, you mean?"

"Yes. I could tell she doesn't approve of me."

"I wouldn't say that."

"No? So what were you two whispering about?"

"She said you're very attractive, and not quite what she was expecting."

"Whatever that means."

"She's just frustrated by my failure rate with women."

"Meaning Barb."

"Mostly. So now she believes she's found the missing piece to the puzzle."

"Me?" She shook her head. "Well, I guess that explains her hostility."

"She's not hostile."

"My goodness, all those poor women you've disappointed, and all because of me."

"Yes, because you're *the woman*. And now, oh my God, she's back!"

"The woman?"

"I know," I said, laughing with her. "I hope that doesn't annoy you."

"It's too silly to annoy me."

"Good, because I've been known to make it through an entire relationship without even once thinking of you."

"Oh?"

"Okay. Maybe once or twice in a comparative sense, but that was it."

"And how'd I measure up?" she asked, putting her hands on her hips.

"*The woman.*"

74

When we got back to her hotel I flopped on the bed and grabbed the remote while she walked into the bathroom. It was hard finding anything worth watching. Finally, I settled for ESPN where they were deep into a discussion of the NFL playoffs.

"Bedtime," she said when she came back, tugging on the covers to get me to move over. "I've got a long day tomorrow and I need to be up early to make a few calls."

"Charles?"

"No, we talked this afternoon. It's just some work stuff."

"Okay." Work stuff? I sat very still. Had she just lied? I turned to look at her. I couldn't tell, but then why would she? I finished taking my clothes off and left the room. When I came back the room was almost completely dark, illuminated only by her small reading light.

"I'm cold," she whined, flipping the covers back for me to join her.

"I'm not surprised. What happened to your t-shirt?"

"I'll get it later."

"I thought you were worried about your long day tomorrow?"

"Just how long do you think this is going to take, old man?"

"Old man?"

"You used to have more stamina."

"So did you."

She took my hand and placed it on her lower stomach. "So now you're giving me directions?"

"If I didn't you'd just roll over and go to sleep."

Later, just when I was sure she'd fallen asleep, she startled me. "Nick, what's in the envelope?"

"What envelope?"

"The one you tried to hide from me at the restaurant."

"It's nothing, just something I got from my accountant."

"You're such a shameless liar," she said, smiling at me.

"No I'm not. Why don't you just tell me what you saw, and—"

"You'll make up another story to keep me from finding out the truth?"

"The truth? Is that still a valid concept?"

"I'm still hanging in there with it, though it's certainly never slowed you down."

"It's money. Jean gave it to me when I went to get a beer."

"Jean?" she asked, her eyes wide with surprise. "How much?"

"$3,786. Turns out, Jean's my new lucky charm."

"I wish you'd stop using Jean to tease me. She makes me feel very middle-aged."

"Me too."

"So, are you going to tell me?"

"Because I couldn't hang around, I asked her to cash a few wining tickets for me after the last race. That would have been at about the time you and I were talking on our cell phones. She was to keep the money for me, or give it to Wendy if we didn't show."

"But why were you being so secretive about it?"

"Because she didn't want her friends to know she'd made a lot of money betting with me on the last race."

"Betting with you?"

"There was a longshot I liked in the nightcap, so when I told her about it she just sort of forgot to share that information. So she had to be sneaky so her friends wouldn't think she'd been sneaky."

"As were you."

"Not enough, apparently."

"What you're really telling me is that everyone knew I might not come, which is why they all looked so surprised to see me."

"No, I said *we* might not come. I never said the decision was yours."

"You didn't need to."

"Well, so what? There really aren't any secrets any more, or haven't you noticed?"

"Is that so?"

"Oh? And what's that supposed to mean?"

"It means I'm very sleepy, and it's been quite a day," she said, yawning.

"And that's it?"

"It is until tomorrow," she said, rolling over on her side with her back to me.

"Lee?" I leaned over her shoulder to see her face.

"In the morning," she said with her eyes closed.

75

Not only did Monday morning arrive, we were up early to greet it. Lee showered first and left the water running for me, but when I stepped in I had a surprise. Why do they all take such hot showers? Or is that some sort of universal joke they play on us?

We'd planned on a room service breakfast to save time, and in a few minutes she came wandering in to get my order. I told her I wanted a smoothie and a bagel with low-fat cream cheese. In another minute or so she came back, laughing.

"They want to know if mango will do."

"For a smoothie?"

"It's that, or nothing."

When I got out of the shower I heard her talking and laughing with someone on the phone. I couldn't make out much over the drone of the exhaust fan but at least she sounded cheerful. Yes, of course I wondered who she was talking to. No, of course I didn't ask.

I dried off and got dressed. When I came out she was sitting at the table by the window reading the *L.A. Times.* Sitting down across from her, I picked up the sports section. Then the kid showed up with breakfast. Lee had him spread everything out on the table in front of us. He was wide-awake and enthusiastic, bubbling over with good cheer. I felt guilty resisting his well-meaning attempts at conversation.

"How's that smoothie?" she asked when he left.

"Mango," I said, making a face.

"After you drop me off why don't you get yourself something good for lunch."

"I should. Maybe I'll go over to Hugo's and get some Mexican food."

"So," she asked between dainty bites of her omelet, "any other plans for the day?"

"Not really. There's no racing. I'll probably just run a few errands. Whole Foods, primarily. Maybe I'll have another chat with that interesting young woman in the deli when I get my stir-fry tofu."

She looked up, watching me. "How young?"

"I don't know. Somewhere under thirty."

"Somewhere?"

"Haven't you noticed how hard it's getting to guess someone's age? There's older, and there's younger. She's younger. I only noticed her because she's got all these amazing tattoos. Sort of Japanese looking, all very colorful, running up and down her arms and across her neck. There's this marvelous flock of crows in flight, not that you can see very much, which makes me wonder how those tattoos might look hidden away like that under her clothing. Do they continue on across the lost continents of her body, merging somewhere like mighty rivers making their way to the sea? Or just wander off on their own across trackless wilderness? And what about pins and rings? She must have a few of those marking off her more interesting destinations. A woman like that doesn't need a lover, she needs an explorer."

"I never knew Whole Foods was such a wellspring of eroticism, but maybe that's only for men of a certain age. You'd better be careful, all that energetic sexuality might prove to be more than you can handle."

"Or my body's lack of textuality might make me feel too self-conscious. What I should probably do is get a tattoo of my own somewhere she'd enjoy finding."

"I'm not so sure. One look at that needle . . ."

"Right, which pretty much dooms me to older women. Is that what you're saying? Because it's a lot harder than you might think, finding one not only with assets but no problematic ex-husbands or psychologically dependent children."

"I'm sure, but they've got to be out there somewhere. Maybe they just don't realize how unusual you are."

"No, that part I think they get."

"Not unusual like that," she said, laughing. "Just that you're not the sort of man one typically runs across every day."

"Finally realized that, have you?"

"Oh, I think I've always known that."

"Well," I said, smiling at her. "We've certainly been here before, haven't we?"

"I felt sick to my stomach."

"You did?"

"Didn't you?"

"I do now."

"That's the smoothie."

"Yes, and don't change the subject because I want to get this on the record while I still can."

"I'm not."

"So, when you left you felt ill? Is that what you're saying? Because if you are then I'll admit to a certain mopiness."

"You're mopey right now!"

"So?"

"Yes, I felt terrible. Full of self-doubts and regret."

"But very determined."

"Yes, and now very sorry."

"So you have changed."

"Quite a bit, unlike you."

"Because I didn't need to."

"You know what, I'm just going to let that one pass, but only because I'd like you to answer a question for me."

"A question? No thanks," I said, looking like I might bolt from the room.

"Calm down," she said, taking my hand. "Just one simple little question. What harm can there be in that?"

"Plenty, if I know you."

"I'm just curious to know if you think we made a mistake. Going our separate ways like we did. Yes," she said, preempting me by holding up her hand. "I know, I left you, but however we choose to characterize it, I'd just like to know if you think it was a mistake."

"Jesus, Lee, what difference does it make now?"

"Can't you just tell me?"

"Yes, at the time that's just how it seemed, but if it got you what you really wanted then probably not."

"Forget about me."

"Then I guess it all depends."

"On?"

"On whether or not I would've been allowed to play the horses. Forced into involuntary servitude."

"A job, you mean?"

"Yeah, one of those. In which case it would have been a monumental mistake if you hadn't left."

"I let you play the horses yesterday, didn't I?"

"Let, as in you could have stopped me but you didn't?"

"Uh-huh."

"Well, bearing that in mind, and with the benefit of hindsight and all, and stipulating that there would have been no job, then, yes, *ceteris paribus*, it was a huge mistake."

"Good. Then I have something to tell you."

"Uh, this isn't going to be one of those awful things I need to know for my own good, is it? Because this is not such a great day for knowing stuff like that."

"Well, I'm not sure. I guess you'll just have to risk it." Then she stood and pulled me up out of my chair. "I've done a lot of talking this weekend, both to friends and colleagues, and it looks like I should be able to come out here permanently—if I wanted to."

"Permanently?"

"Oh, don't look so worried," she said with a laugh. "I've thought it all out and you'll be just fine. Now, I can't make this happen overnight, but it shouldn't take too long. Certainly by the end of this summer."

"Summer?"

"Now, I know this is terribly unfair, putting you on the spot like this, but I really need to know what you think. Not that you'd ever tell me not to, I know that, but I would like to hear you tell me how much you think I should."

"So start with that?"

"Yes," she said, grinning at me. "That would be an excellent place for you to start."

"You do realize how annoying this is, only now getting the opportunity to say anything about it."

"I know."

"So . . . since you've already put the words in my mouth. Yes, I'd be thrilled if you moved out here. In fact, I wish you'd done this years ago."

"I should have."

"But there is just one little thing."

"Oh? And what's that?"

"I won't share. Yes, I know, but now I'm changing my mind."

"Wow, a first demand already."

"I'm not joking, Lee."

"So that's what it will take, no sharing?"

"Yes."

"Then no sharing," and she nodded her head like that sealed the deal.

"But—"

"Charles? He'll be fine. Our comfortable little marriage has been winding down for some time. I don't imagine either one of us will be all that upset when it finally ends."

"And that's it?"

"I'm sorry. Does that sound too cold-blooded?"

"Just a bit."

"Well, that's just the way it is, and please don't start feeling sorry for him."

"I'm wasn't."

"No, but you were working up to it. Trust me, he'll find someone. He's pretty cute, you know.

"I thought it was all about his intellect."

"And smart."

"Thanks, I feel so much better. But you do realize you haven't really explained anything? You know, like normal people do?"

"What is it you don't understand?"

"What is it I *do* understand?" I sighed and shook my head. "Look, I know you don't like to talk about your feelings—"

"You do enough of that for the both of us."

"I know, and I don't mean to imply that your lack of self-absorption isn't often quite refreshing, but even for you there are moments that demand at least a modicum of self-revelation."

"I see. So just this once you'd like for me to indulge you?"

"If you wouldn't mind."

"So when I look back from where I am today what I see is that I was happiest with you. Now, I really have no idea why that's the case, but there it is and I'm no longer going to try and pretend otherwise. Not that Charles isn't a nice guy or hasn't been a good husband. But, now . . . well, I suppose that's about it."

"So being with me—"

"You know what I'd really like? No questions."

"None at all?"

"Not even that one."

"I was just going to point out how none of this would've happened if you hadn't come out here for your conference."

"Yes, but you have been on my mind."

"But it still came down to nothing but luck, and ironic luck at that."

"Which I'm sure you must hate."

"No, I'll take it, just like I do at the track."

"Good," she said, dropping her arms around my waist to pull me snug against her body. "Now, be still," she commanded, smiling up at me.

"But . . ." I managed to say before I felt a sharp squeeze in the middle of my back.

"Understand?" she asked, watching me be quiet.

I said nothing.

76

"Nick," Jason asked, "how about a beer?"

"Well . . ." I paused to consider it. Normally, I don't drink during the races, but it had been a pretty good day. "Thanks. Maybe a Coors?"

"Anyone else?"

Yes, everyone else.

"Come on," I said. "I'll give you a hand."

As we walked up the concourse he said to me, "Tommy and the guys still seem pretty amused."

"Just a little."

"*If I know one thing*," he said, imitating Tommy. Then when I smiled: "See, even you think it's funny."

"It was certainly funny when you said it. Of course, now I'm going to be reminded of it every time one of your inexplicable longshots comes in."

"It's not that impressive, Nick. You're all much better handicappers than I am."

"That's not true. When it comes to a horse race no one has exclusive access to the truth. If your way works then it's just as good as anyone else's. And the guys already knew you were a pretty good handicapper, though none of them can understand how you make it work."

"It works because of my data."

"Yes, I know," I said, rolling my eyes, "you and your data."

"I wish you could've seen the look on your face when I showed up with all those printouts. You were surprised to see me again, weren't you?"

"I knew you were interested. What I didn't expect was that you'd start coming out here all the time. Have I mentioned how much trouble you've gotten me into?"

He smiled at me. "Once or twice."

"Why is it all my fault, since you clearly have a mind of your own?"

"You did get me started."

"As they've reminded me."

"Well, it can't be as bad as all that if Larry's still speaking to me. In fact, he has so many questions I'm beginning to think he's jealous."

"What I hear is how Jason needs to focus on his dissertation. That he can't if he's wasting his time hanging around with a bunch of losers like us."

"So she does include you in that?"

"What do you think?"

He laughed. "I wouldn't worry about it. The common assumption seems to be that I'm temporarily obsessed with a foolish little diversion. Given enough time I'm sure to get bored, if I don't run out of money first."

"Have you?"

"Not yet."

"Well, my official position, just in case anyone should happen to ask, is that you'd be wise to think of your future."

"She still won't come back?"

"Not after that pretty little filly broke down right in front of us."

"How awful."

"It was awful. But you," I said, smiling at him, "seem to have tapped into this inexhaustible supply of young women. It seems like you bring a new one out here every weekend."

"It is kind of amazing, isn't it? But when the word got around about what I was doing they were all suddenly lining up to tag along. I hope Tommy doesn't mind."

"Tommy? He likes having them around. Like grandkids."

"Tommy's got grandkids?"

"Is that surprising?"

"Well, it's just that none of you guys seem very . . . uh . . . ordinary?" He laughed at what he'd just said. "Is that the word?"

"How should I know? Ask Lee."

"It's just that I have a hard time picturing any of you guys living what might be described as normal lives."

"I certainly hope you don't think that graduate student lifestyle of yours is normal."

"Nothing at the university is normal."

"Or anywhere else. Normal is a myth."

"Yeah, you would say that, given all this," he said, sweeping his arm out in front of us.

"This? Trust me, Jason, it's never going to feel more normal for you than this. Ever."

"Yeah," he said, looking around at the swirling sea of bettors. "I do worry about that."

"But it's not impossible to do this and still have a life. Like Tommy, who's got two married daughters and really is a grandfather. Actually, with the exception of me, all the guys are fathers."

"They sure don't act like it."

"No?" I stopped walking to look at him. "You know, I just realized something rather odd."

"What's that?"

"That even though I've heard them all mention their families any number of times, I don't believe I've actually ever met any of their families." I stared at him. "I guess they really exist."

"Now that does create an interesting problem."

"Oh, no," I said, taking him by the arm. "Let's not have any more of your interesting problems. Okay? Let's just stipulate, right here, right now, that they all have real wives and real children and leave it at that."

"But can we? Just unilaterally stipulate they exist like that? Because I'd hate to think our decision determines their existence."

"It certainly doesn't in my universe, but then I can't speak for yours now, can I? Wherever the hell that is."

"I don't know, Nick—"

"Good, one more thing you *don't* know. Maybe that balances out all those singular things you apparently *do* know."

"You're not still annoyed because I got that race, are you?"

"No, but I'll never understand how you can claim to have known that was going to happen. Poor old Tommy's about ready to declare you the luckiest handicapper he's ever met, and he hates to fall back on luck as an explanation even more than I do."

"As I tried to explain to you . . . and I even showed you guys right where it was in my spreadsheet."

"That's true, you did, and for a moment or two it actually seemed to make sense. But Tommy's right, what's so puzzling isn't that so much as why you picked that to focus on in the first place. It's very contrarian, but I don't suppose you realize that."

"I do now."

No he didn't.

The Bet

EPILOGUE

. . . the interpretation of chance.

"You know, I've been hesitant to bring this up, but since you already have . . ."

"I've brought something up?"

"That everyone thinks I'm a gambler."

"Yes, but not a stereotypical one."

"Some distinction."

"Well?"

"It's something I read in Benjamin, about what he calls the gambler's natural state of mind." I smiled. "I know, me reading Benjamin."

"Why not? Everyone else is."

"Of course it's all very melodramatic, but the point he wants to make is that this state of mind partakes of a debased, though still divinatory, presence of mind."

"Divinatory?" she laughed. "You gamblers certainly hold yourselves in high regard. Did he actually know anything about gambling, or was this just something he read?"

"He quotes a few writers who seem to know what they're talking about, though it's strictly limited to games of chance. It's all very Dostoevsky. Bottom line? There's no handicapping in Benjamin."

"But I thought they raced horses in Europe."

"They do, but for some reason he wasn't interested, or maybe he just never ran across anything in his reading he found useful."

"How'd you find this?"

"Poking around in *The Arcades Project*. He's got a little section in there on gambling and prostitution."

"They're connected?"

"In his mind they are. So even though I found it annoying, I was interested enough to see what else he'd written."

"Were you in a debased, but divinatory state? Whatever that means."

"What he says is that gambling consists of a series of repetitive acts, each a reflexive response to a new constellation of factors. Each timed down to the last possible moment when this reflexive response or act is most in tune with divination. The building tension, then the instantaneous response to cues too subtle to be brought consciously to mind. And because this sequence is repetitive, because it happens over and over again, it results in a form of mental intoxication. It's in this debased state that the gambler trades upon an emergent presence of mind, a rare but natural state of mind never meant for the gambler."

"Who is it meant for?"

"For humanity. To elevate, or direct us beyond ourselves to the highest objects."

"But because the gambler's highest object is a bet, or money, it's a debasement."

"That's the argument. The gambler debases humanity's gift, this rare and natural state of mind, though even the gambler is somewhat attuned to its higher aim, the divinatory reading, though the objects divined are random acts of chance in the service of winning money. Again, hardly the highest objects."

"So where does capitalism enter into this? It always does with these guys."

"The gambler's intoxicated state of mind is like that state of mind we find in capitalist economies. Life is phantasmagorical. It's disjointed. No one has any substantive identity in or across time. Every experience is new and unconnected with anything else. Our actions lack any significant cognitive content or intentionality, being merely reflex actions made without calculation. Made repeatedly. We're just the chips we've bet lying on the gaming table."

"Though you're claiming this description doesn't fit what you do."

"Not when it fails to leave room for human intervention, ingenuity, or calculation. Or, as he himself puts it, the interpretation of chance."

"I bet it fits most people."

"It fits if they gamble like that, when gambling doesn't amount to anything more than a spontaneous reflex action. You know the cliché, the heroic but intoxicated gambler anxiously waiting until the last possible moment to throw it all down on the outcome of a single random event. I don't do aberrant behavior."

She smiled. "Oh? What do you do?"

"Prognostication, which is a state of mind that, unlike divination, is firmly rooted temporally, spatially, and historically. One that makes critical use of historical data as its basis for making predictions expressed as probabilities. I'm not betting on sheer chance working in my favor. I'm not in some mysterious state of mind. I'm not cut-off, standing alone and alienated with reference to nothing but random constellations of factors without historical precedent, free of all considerations of context or genesis."

"Who said you were?"

"You, if you insist gambling is just guessing. But if it is then there's no place for calculation, which means I'm not a gambler."

"The interpretation of chance. I like that."

"I prefer calculation."

"Perhaps, though I still don't think there's much calculating going on out at the track."

"There's a lot more than you might think. Don't forget, even in the face of sheer randomness it's always possible to intervene in our favor. Look at the roulette players who've been banned from the casinos. But the key move here is calculation, because calculation is what frees up that necessary space within which I *can* intervene. More importantly for me, it's only this intervention that allows betting to be turned into a way of life."

"And you've never been intoxicated?"

"Would it please you if I said I had?"

"It would, actually, because then it might sound like fun. The way you talk, you make it sound like it's nothing but hard work."

"It is hard work."

"Whittling away at randomness?"

"Why not? Even the most cursory glance at the variables in a race is enough to give me a sizeable edge over those who just guess or are too lazy to do the work. Better still, the more I work at it the more sophisticated my approach becomes. Then I really do start to whittle away at randomness."

"And you're sure there's none of this presence of mind stuff lurking in there somewhere?"

"If I had to rely on divination I'd quit, if I didn't tap out first, which is essentially the same thing. Although there is definitely something unique and distinctive about the moment of truth, when the bet is revealed for what it truly is. Like I told Larry, it's a moment that seems to inhabit an unusual form of temporality. But the connection here I see is to the mystery of becoming, which is hardly what Benjamin is referring to. He really does mean divinatory. I just have no idea what that could ever mean to a horseplayer like me. I've certainly never experienced such a state of mind."

"Maybe if you won more often."

"Yeah, that must be it."